ALSO BY LIA HABEL

Dearly, Departed

DEARLY, BELOVED

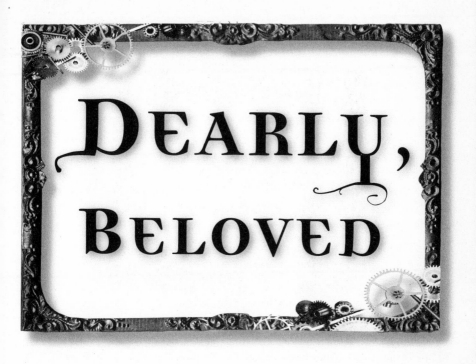

DEARLY, BELOVED

A Novel

Lia Habel

BALLANTINE BOOKS [DEL REY] NEW YORK

Published in the United States by Del Rey Books,
an imprint of The Random House Publishing Group,
a division of Random House, Inc., New York.

DEL REY is a registered trademark
and the Del Rey colophon is a
trademark of Random House, Inc.

Grateful acknowledgment is made to Paul Roland for permission to reprint an
excerpt from "The Ratcatcher's Daughter" by Paul Roland from the album *Masque*,
copyright © 1990 Lithon Music. Reprinted by permission of Paul Roland.

ISBN 978-0-345-52334-1
eBook ISBN 978-0-345-52336-5

Printed in the United States of America
on acid-free paper

www.delreybooks.com

2 4 6 8 9 7 5 3 1

First Edition

Book design by Elizabeth A. D. Eno

For my father, who still remains convinced that horror movies will rot my brain, despite the fact that I have now built a legitimate career on my many critical viewings of Fulci's zombie vs. shark showdown.

We are going to die, and that makes us the lucky ones. [. . .] We privileged few, who won the lottery of birth against all odds, how dare we whine at our inevitable return to that prior state from which the vast majority have never stirred?

—RICHARD DAWKINS, *Unweaving the Rainbow*

The modest virgin, the prudent wife, and the careful matron are much more serviceable in life than petticoated philosophers, blustering heroines, or virago queens. She who makes her husband and her children happy [. . .] is a much greater character than ladies described in romances, whose whole occupation is to murder mankind with shafts from their quiver, or their eyes.

—OLIVER GOLDSMITH, *The Vicar of Wakefield*

Dearly, Beloved

1 • Nora

When I got to the top of the hill, the zombie caught me. I dropped my parasol and leather-bound digital diary in shock. He pulled me to his body from behind, imprisoned my tiny hands in his so I couldn't fight back, and parted his cold lips at the nape of my neck.

I squealed with delight, even as I drummed my boot heel on his shin. "Bram, let go!"

"Never," he growled against my skin following the kiss, his voice causing me to flush. Before I could protest further he actually picked me up, starting to spin. Laughing despite the ridiculousness of it, I kept my eyes open, watching the scenery fly by—especially the hilly area to the east that eventually rose into the city of New London, Nicaragua. The capital of New Victoria. The heart of all the world I'd ever known, now transformed, somehow shattered—half dead and half alive.

Dawn was just beginning to cup the earth in her pale hands. To the west, miles off, the mansions of the rich and titled lay mostly abandoned; only the odd light dared to advertise the presence of people. A few lights shone from the city, the shimmering of holographic building facades and electrified advertisements, but for the most part New London still slumbered on, dimmer than I ever remembered it being. There was only the red-tinted lantern on the top of my fallen electric gas-lamp parasol to light our way upon the low hump of earth that marked the location of the Elysian Fields, the underground housing complex my family called home. I might've chosen one of the colors meant to advertise the romantic availability of young ladies—pink for dating, etc.—but I wasn't romantically available.

I was spoken for by the zombie, and the leaders of feminine teenage trends had decided red should be the color for that. The color of sympathy for the dead. I normally didn't care about such things, but in this I was willing to be trendy.

Bram freed me, and I staggered away from him, eventually falling to the ground amidst my skirts. "That's the only way to make you be still sometimes."

"So . . . unfair," I panted as he limped over to join me. As he did, he glanced at the city himself. The view was spectacular, and the area landscaped to invite enjoyment of it, with circular pathways and benches crafted of the same marble used for the gated entrance located at the base of the hill. Although it was exposed, it was also isolated—and thus the perfect place to sneak away to every morning. "You're bigger than me."

"I enjoy the walk up here as much as *being* here, you know. When you run ahead—that's unfair. Besides . . ." He sat and fixed me with his cloudy blue eyes. "You think you'd know by now that when you run from me, every instinct I have wants to chase you."

As I caught my breath to reply, I found myself staring at him. Bram Griswold was two years dead and still so handsome and full of life, his ghost-white features expressive, his body tall and strong. The light atop my parasol didn't chase the shadows off his face fully, didn't highlight his brown hair, and I was reminded of the first time I'd seen him, cloaked and lit by streetlamps.

Then, I'd thought him a monster. Now, I loved him so much I didn't know what to do with myself.

"The zombies came from here," I reminded him. "We should probably walk yards and yards apart. If anyone *was* watching us, they could get nervous."

"I should be the one in front, if we're going that route." Picking up my digidiary, he handed it to me. "And I'd rather not think about that."

Chastened, accepting the book, I felt the warm April breeze stirring my black curls, playing with the hem of my long pink dress and the bit of red ribbon Chastity had cheekily tied to the hip holster for my pistol. The fact that my beau was dead didn't disgust me, didn't scare me. Not after all I'd seen. Everything was still so fresh, and I wasn't sure if this was ultimately a sign of madness or compassion.

I truly was my father's daughter.

"We're here, at any rate," I said. "Assume the position."

Laughing, Bram moved back. "I didn't die just so I could be your pillow, you know."

"Then why are you always the perfect temperature?"

We sat on the grass as a New Victorian sometime-schoolgirl of middling social rank and a Punk miner, member of a tribe my people had long ago exiled to the southernmost reaches of our Territories, should never sit—Bram lying on his back, watching the sky slowly banish the stars, me on my stomach with my chin and my backlit digidiary propped up on his lifeless chest. Alone. It was horribly scandalous, naughty behavior—and to us, commonplace. We'd been in the thick of it during the Siege almost four months ago, the attack by hordes of mindless, ravenous, "evil" zombies upon the city. We'd spent months afterward holed up in the jungle on an archaic airship with a heteromortal crew of scientists and soldiers, returning to the city only when it seemed like the vaccine my father had created against the reanimating illness known as the Lazarus might work. Our courtship had taken place on secret army bases, aboard airships, and finally in Eden. Altogether, it had been a marvelous success. But now we were back in civilization, and we had to be more circumspect. At least according to Papa.

I pushed him out of my mind, even as I tried to do the fabulously stupid, petty, useless thing he wanted me to, using my fingertips to access my school-issued digital copy of *Deportment and You: A Text for Young Ladies of Refinement.*

"Oh, look. Handily enough, this chapter talks about Punk manners, or lack thereof," I said teasingly as the book loaded. "Want to do the end-of-chapter quiz with me? I'll try to find the least insulting questions."

"As if the answers won't also be insulting?" Bram said, his lips quirking. "I know how your people work. They're polite to your face, and get you the second your back is turned. No offense."

"None taken. You speak God's truth." I flicked through the pages. "Okay, then. How about courtship etiquette? That's extremely relevant to our interests."

"Is this chapter going to club me over the head with yet more ways I can't touch you or talk to you?"

"Pretty much."

"Skip that one, too."

I paged through and laughed, turning the digidiary around to show him a section about wedding etiquette. "Look. This part is seriously about forty pages long. This is *curriculum* at St. Cyprian's, a school that costs my father a small fortune every year. That he's insisting I try to keep up with, even though, you know, Apocalypse."

Bram tilted his head to the side, as if regarding a puzzle. "Forty pages about weddings? Don't you usually just go to a judge or a preacher for something like that?"

"Girls are supposed to obsess over them. Aunt Gene wanted me to."

"Is this a hint, Miss Dearly?" As he asked this question he drew a serpentine pattern on the small of my back with his fingers, just above my bustle, and I shivered a little. And not just because his hand was freezing.

"No!" I flushed and shut the digidiary, sitting up and hurling it halfway across the hill. As I did, I released a primal scream— well, as much as I could. I still looked and sounded immature, even though I was now seventeen. Bram laughed and pulled me back down, and my cheek found his shoulder. "I give up for another day. I tried, but studying how to be a lady is *still* too mind-blowingly stupid to focus on, given all that's going on in the world. Tell me a story?"

Bram thought for a moment, and then started in on a story he knew I'd like—about the big Punk cities I'd never even heard about before I met him. About how they were founded where the Punks had fought battles against the southern tribes to maintain the borders of their settlement area, and how they were populated by a mixture of Punks and mysterious southern tribesmen, peaceful accords having been reached after years of struggle. The actual stone and metal buildings, and how they were vastly superior to holograms in every way; the automaton shows; the Punk fashions. His voice was rough and low, a sound I adored. A sound I could lose myself in.

As he spoke, I watched the sky brighten. I wanted to see the rest of the remaining world—from the glacier-locked Wastelands of the far North to the deserts of the South. All of it. I couldn't drive, but that didn't stop me from occasionally imagining myself stealing the keys to Aunt Gene's electric horseless carriage and flooring it. I knew the world was changing, reacting to the revealed existence of the undead. Reacting to the fact that two weeks ago a few vaccinated people had been bitten during a riot and still contracted the Lazarus. Reacting with fear, with anger, with . . .

I stomped on that thought before my imagination could run with it. Since learning of the postvaccine infections, fear about what the living might do if they lost their feelings of security around the "civilized" dead had been threatening to consume me, and I was growing sick of it. It kept robbing me of sleep, forcing me to forge guesses about a future I couldn't possibly know. It was changing my father, too, making him both demanding and distant, taking him away from me again. It kept ruining moments like this. And it had no *right* to.

Bram finished his story. His lips found my brow, the sensation instantly identifiable due to the bit of thread that stitched his broken lower lip together. I loved his every scar. They would never heal, and he bore them all so patiently. "Have you heard a word I've said, little one?"

"Sixty percent," I admitted, looking to the city again. "Sorry."

"No blame here. What do you need?"

"Nothing." I pushed my nose into his soft blue shirt, enjoying the pleasured sound he made in response. "Just wondering if I'm ever going to be allowed to leave this hill again."

"I think it's honorable that you're trying to do what your dad wants." Bram's cool hands moved about my waist, and before I knew it he'd drawn me up and seated me atop his chest so he could meet my eyes. I smiled despite myself, my fingers curling around his leather suspenders. I loved that he refused to dress like a New Victorian fop. "That biter kind of threw a wrench in the works. Once Dr. Dearly and the other researchers know more, we might be able to get back on track."

"I hope so." I glowered at my far-off book. "We were on the same page before the riot. The turn he's taken these last few weeks, insisting I stay close to the EF, focus on schoolwork—it's infuriating. And he hasn't been home in days. I could've walked to Morristown and back without his ever having known."

Bram reached up to play with my ringlets. I wasn't wearing a hat or gloves—more sins to stack up. "Chin up. It's because of him that the living and the dead even have the chance to try and co-exist. He's naturally going to feel responsible for every set-back. There'll be more issues before all is said and done . . . more violence. I don't accept that, but at the same time, I know it's bound to happen. If we can just get more of the living vaccinated, educated, maybe things will calm down all around." He frowned. "Maybe the violence against the undead will stop."

Nodding, I thought of the high-functioning zombies still hounded in the streets, still in hiding. They had it far worse than we did. "That's why I hate being kept here. I want to be out in the city, helping them."

"Believe me, I'm with you on that. But the last thing the city needs is a bunch of undead vigilantes skulking about. Or pro-undead, in your case, seeing as I know you'd want to be at the head of the charge."

This idea appealed to me. "Explain exactly *why* we're not doing this, again?"

Bram chuckled, and leaned up to press his forehead to mine. "The sun's rising."

"Please don't tell me you're also a vampire. *That* would break my heart." It was a stupid joke—vampires weren't real—but I didn't want to go back.

"Nope, just a guy biting his thumb at all the New Victorian 'don't touch the girl' rules. Darkness helps with that."

I sighed. "I know."

Bram moved me, stood, and offered his hand. I took it and let him pull me to my feet. We made our way across the breadth of the hill to fetch my digidiary, then started the trek back.

Arm in arm.

*   *   *

Coming home just wasn't the same anymore.

The Elysian Fields had been, at one time, a wonder of modern engineering. An underground neighborhood with multiple levels, each capped by a liquid crystal screen that mirrored conditions outside and surrounded by walls that projected virtual trees, clouds—everything designed to look as real as possible, with none of it real at all.

Given that it had served as a giant crucible of infection for the zombies that invaded New London, it hadn't fared very well. The fake sky was no more, the screen dark. Strings of electric lights now dangled from the streetlamp poles, the city's attempt to provide the few residents of the Elysian Fields enough light to live by until it was repaired. Half the grand Victorian houses were unoccupied. Only the most basic services had returned to the central commercial area—the grocery, the clinic. The hat shop was gone, the confectioner's boarded up like something out of a five-year-old's worst nightmare. Broadsides were pasted on every suitable surface: THE ELYSIAN FIELDS WILL RESUME FULL OPERATIONS BY FALL 2196. THE CITY OF NEW LONDON THANKS YOU FOR YOUR PATIENCE AND SUPPORT. Signs announced stops for the new trackless EF trolley service: A SAFE, DEPENDABLE WAY TO REACH THE SURFACE AND NEW LONDON.

My Aunt Gene had once called the EF a "hole in the ground." It actually seemed like one now. Too bad she was still missing; she would've loved to rub that in.

And yet, I loved it more than ever. I loved my neighborhood of Violet Hill, even though the streets were now stained—with what, I didn't like to imagine—and many of the mansions beyond repair. I loved my brick house most of all, especially because it had managed to weather the undead storm so miraculously. Within its walls I'd kissed my mother for the last time, before the disease my father then knew so little about both took her away and cruelly brought her back. I'd watched my father die there, little knowing he was bound to carry on after his heart stopped. In that house, I'd been attacked by Averne's undead minions, and on the roof, I'd fought back and ended up in Bram's arms. Not that I was initially thrilled to find myself there.

That thought made me smile. By the time I reached the front door and unlocked it, I was ready to stiff-upper-lip-it for another day, soldier on.

"Quiet," I turned and reminded Bram, putting a finger in front of my mouth. "When we pass through this door, we become well-behaved young people again. Whether we want to or not."

Bram hooked his index finger around mine and drew it away from my lips. Meanwhile he laid his other hand on the door, effectively trapping me, his eyes unapologetically focused on my face. "That presumes we were doing something wrong up there. Now, if you *want* me to do something worthy of blame, I can give it the old Punk try. Dr. Dearly might not like it, though."

Blushing at the idea, I covered for myself by finding the knob and opening the door, forcing him to stumble in after me. He laughed and tightened his hold on my hand, pulling me closer— but then we both saw something that made us go stock-still.

Dr. Beryl Chase was waiting for us in the foyer, in front of the huge sweeping staircase.

"Dr. Chase?" I said, my girlish voice surprisingly large in the empty hall. She turned to look at me, and at once appeared relieved—and yet, not. I figured I must look much the same.

"Oh, um . . ." Bram shut the door and locked it. "I promise, we weren't—"

"Miss Dearly, Bram . . ." Dr. Chase was still in her dressing gown, and she held something in her hands. It looked like a box of playing cards. She twirled it over and over, the motion fussy and unlike her. It pinged my suspicions, caught me and pulled me back from my embarrassment. "No. It's not that."

"Did I wake you when I got out of bed?" I let go of Bram's hand and hugged my digidiary and parasol to my chest. "I swear, we never go far. We just like to be alone." Dr. Chase and I had been sharing my bed ever since our return from Colombia. We'd tried to cram everyone we could inside the house—Dr. Chase and her zombified fellow engineer, Dr. Baldwin Samedi, the younger members of the former Company Z, and my father's top medical researchers.

"No. I know you've been getting up," she said. "As long as you come back quickly, I never worry or say anything. You're young. You deserve every moment you can find together." Dr. Chase looked at the cards, and slipped them into her pocket.

Something was wrong, and my thoughts went in one immediate direction. "Is it Papa?"

Dr. Chase smiled. It didn't reach her apple green eyes. "I was going to try to distract you while I got my thoughts together, but I might as well just say it."

Bram moved forward and grabbed a painted chair from its place by the stairs, carrying it over for Dr. Chase. He urged her to sit, and she did so gratefully. Behind him, a pair of Father Isley's cats trotted down the staircase. "What's the matter?"

I moved closer, my hands going cold. "What's wrong with Papa?"

"Nothing. But Dr. Salvez just called." Disheveled as she was, her reddish hair poufy and her skin free of makeup, the middle-aged Dr. Chase was still lovely—though at the moment very pale. She looked at her lap. "You know that during the riot that took place after Captain Wolfe's execution, several people were bitten by zombies. Two of those people died and reanimated, even though they had been vaccinated."

I nodded. My neck felt stiff. I couldn't forget that night—

especially the way the news had crushed my father. That was why I'd chosen to try and obey him until this latest storm cloud passed, even though I resented it with every fiber of my being. But as frustrated as I was, I was also growing increasingly worried about him.

"The biters they arrested are still in police custody." Her hands started to shake slightly, and my heart started to pound in sympathy. "Which is good. Because, as Dr. Salvez let me know . . . they have evidence that the problem isn't with the vaccine, or any living response to the vaccine."

I had no idea what to say to this. Because that left only one terrifying option—one I didn't want to contemplate. "Then what's the issue?" Bram asked. He sounded grim.

Dr. Chase gripped her robe to still her hands. "They've confirmed that one of the zombies is carrying a different strain of the Laz. Something new. Something the vaccine isn't designed to deal with."

And just like that, everything I'd dreaded seemed to be coming true. Bram swore. "We're back to square one, then," I whispered. "There'll be another Siege. They'll hunt down the dead."

"No." Dr. Chase sounded as if she wanted to will her denial into existence. "*No*. The biter with the new strain is still isolated. He can't infect anyone else. The two who contracted that strain lost their faculties upon awakening. They tried to attack the people attending them, and they were shot in the head. So far, it's contained."

"No, it's not that easy," I said. "The whole reason we came up here, all of us—the zombies, everybody—is because we thought it would be safe. That because they were vaccinated, the living felt *safe* enough to let the nonviolent dead survive!" I looked at Bram. "Should we leave? Get away from the city?"

"No," he assured me, though his eyes were serious. "Not right now. Not without knowing more."

"But we have to do some—"

"What do you expect us to do?" The rebuff was delivered so sharply that I flinched and Bram blinked. Realizing from my look how she must have sounded, Dr. Chase covered her face with her hands. "I'm sorry. That was uncalled for."

"It's all right," I tried.

"No, it's not. I just keep thinking about having to run—we thought it was just protestors clashing at the riot, but think about it. A zombie with a new strain of the Laz was standing not fifty feet away from us! What little footage they've shown of him on the news is murky, and the researchers who've been allowed to take samples from him say he seems perfectly ordinary, but I've heard he was like a demon. That he was everything we've worked so hard to prove that sane zombies *aren't*. And he could have gotten any one of us!" She took a breath and held it for a second, attempting to calm herself. It didn't work; she babbled on. "And I still have to wake Baldwin up and tell him. He sleeps so soundly, it always terrifies me to wake him up . . ."

When I heard Dr. Samedi's name, I understood. Although their relationship existed in a state of limbo, Chase and Samedi had history. I wasn't the only person with beloved dead people in her life; I wasn't the only person who was scared. She was right. I had to stay focused.

But so did she.

I moved to sit on the floor, at her knee, so I could look up at her and hopefully keep her attention. "Are we the only people who know?"

"No. Dr. Salvez said the press has been alerted. We can't keep secrets any longer. It would hurt us more in the long run."

Great. I set my things aside. "Then what *are* we going to do, Dr. Chase?"

She didn't respond right away. When she did, her voice was still halting, but ultimately controlled. "All we *can* do is work through it. Dr. Salvez said the vaccine still seems to be effective against the original strain." She looked uneasily at me. "We can't meditate on the two people who were infected. We have to try to think, instead, of the thousands of people out there who are safe because of your father's work."

"But we don't know if they're safe," I said. "That's the thing. There haven't been any large-scale zombie attacks. We don't really *know* if the vaccine works—they had to rush it out so quickly. And if the living don't feel safe . . ." I trailed off. I didn't want to think about it.

"But there are thousands of families out there with dead relatives, Nora," Bram said. "And I haven't heard of a single casual infection, so that's promising. Dr. Chase is right. We need to try and keep things like that in mind."

"What if there are others, though?" Dr. Chase asked. "Other strains? Other zombies with this new strain, wandering around?" Her questions seemed to ring out like gongs. Neither Bram nor I answered.

I couldn't think of any answers. I didn't want to.

"Let's not worry about that now," Bram reiterated. "Let's deal with what we do know. Let me get the boys together—you worry about Doc Sam."

I rose. "Are you leaving, then?"

"For the ships, yeah." The ships, the NVS *Erika* and the NVS *Christine,* were where the majority of Company Z's doctors still worked—either on zombie-related research or on caring medically for the undead. "Once this news gets around, the city is going to explode. We'll need manpower there. I'd take you with me, but . . ."

"Papa," I said, irritated. He was on the *Erika.*

Bram nodded. "And in case something goes wrong, we'll need people here at the house to execute DHE. I'll leave Chas and Ren behind, too."

"I know." The Dearly House Exit was his new contingency plan. Still, I was disappointed—and worried. "Go."

Bram touched my chin, then ran up the stairs to fetch the boys. I helped Dr. Chase up and saw her into the kitchen, where I put on the kettle for tea. She sagged against the wall, and I knew that even in this small thing, I was doing my bit.

Still, after everything I'd done in December, it wasn't the same.

2 • Bram

I hated New London, but I tried to deal with it. That's what everyone needed to do right now—just *deal*.

Of course, that was easier said than done.

I'd told Nora the truth—I wasn't completely pessimistic. At one time I had been in total agreement with my superiors that the majority of living society couldn't handle knowing about the existence of zombies, so the fact that so many living people rushed to the defense of their dead was both humbling and heartening. Now that everything was out in the open, I truly hoped some sort of living–dead compromise could be reached. We wouldn't be around very long, after all. Even with preservation and medical care, all zombies were doomed to rot. If we could keep anyone else from being infected, the living wouldn't have to put up with us forever.

But I was born of a poor, hardworking family and put through my paces as an army captain, and the "okay, but" instinct was genetically embedded in me. And seeing things as they actually stood in the city—that always made me question my judgment.

Aside from the EF, the west end of New London had suffered the most from the Siege, and cleanup was still under way. There were few people on the streets as yet, and we traveled past boarded-up shops and smoke-stained houses, basket-bearing servants and municipal trucks loaded with construction supplies. Eventually we took a detour to avoid a bit of road reconstruction, and neared the center of the city. Flat screen advertising boards mounted on the sides of buildings and the zeppelins floating overhead reminded people not to expose themselves to zombie bodily fluids; notices about new vaccine shipments were mixed in with the usual digital ads for fabrics, teas, and "health corsets." There were a few military men and cops on patrol, but not half as many as there should have been. As usual.

"We're going to have to go past the Morgue," I announced. We had to drive through the city to get to the port on the eastern side.

"Great," John Gates grumbled from the passenger seat of Nora's aunt's Model V. "Coalhouse," as he preferred to be called, was a tall, muscular black guy, the right side of his face skeletal, the rotting eye loose in its bony socket. He compulsively fingered it and its piece of supportive foam, as well as his hearing aid, making sure everything was still there. "This morning is awesome. Not only do I get to work with the people who tried to kill us, I get to tour the zombie ghetto."

"Don't even start. We're not helping the army, we're helping Dearly," Tom Todd said from the backseat. The partition between the front and back parts of the carriage was lowered, and I could see him fiddling with the flat screen in-cab computer. "How do I adjust the volume on this thing? God, why does everything in the Territories have to be so *complicated*?"

"Hell if I know." We were all Punk-born, all similarly wary of anything too high-tech, even if we'd gotten used to using such devices in the NV army. Computerized equipment never felt . . . authentic, though. Honest. Even if it was occasionally helpful.

"There it goes." Tom was a short, broad, bald young man

with strong arms and a patch of smooth gray skin sewn over the hole where his nose should have been. He wore a metal leg brace around his left knee, atop his pin-striped pants. It squeaked as he settled back to watch video clips.

"This is bad," Coalhouse said, looking at me with his good eye. "What are we going to do?"

"Help out where we're needed, first of all. See what happens."

"It's on the news," Tom said. "And these clips are preloaded, right? This isn't live. So word's gone out."

My back tensed. "Hooray."

Tom's head waved back and forth as the news announcer nattered on. At one point the gent on the screen sniffed and referred to zombies as "overgrown leeches," to which Tom countered, "So says the *mummy*? Better cold than old, pal."

"Leave it be," I counseled. "There it is."

The "Morgue" was actually the southern end of Dahlia Park, a large, gated plot of grass and trees in the middle of New London. Two weeks ago Captain James Wolfe, my former company commander, had been executed there for high treason—selling out tribal secrets to a Punk, Major Dorian Averne, and working with him to kidnap both Dearlys in a twisted bid for redemption. Convinced that Dr. Dearly had engineered the Laz as a form of biological warfare against the Punks, Averne had gone along with Wolfe, all the while plotting Nora's death as "punishment" for the imagined sins of her father. Him, I'd taken care of. In a way. He was dead and gone, at any rate.

I didn't like to think about it. Even though everything traced back to them, I still felt partially responsible for the Siege. If we'd caught and killed all of the Grays—the mindless dead pawns Averne and Wolfe had managed to smuggle into New London to do their bidding—the illness wouldn't have spread. None of this would've happened.

The Morgue wouldn't have happened.

Over the last month or so, the place had slowly become occupied by hundreds of zombies. The pro-zombie minority was,
although vocal, still a minority. The streets weren't safe for a dead
man at night, and quite a few had become homeless—either because they were ostracized by their living families, or because
they'd drawn the short reanimation straw and forgotten who
they were or where they were supposed to be. In addition, zombies had trickled into the heart of the city from its outlying suburbs and from small towns to the near north and south, where
the flight of individuals from New London before the threat was
fully understood led to minor outbreaks. After months of disor-
ganization, they finally started to band together and form a sort
of unofficial camp—one that citizens decried and politicians
railed against. But they had nowhere else to go.

The Morgue was one of the reasons I kept hanging around the
ships, doing my part, even though Company Z was no more.
Months ago the army had honorably discharged us, breaking up
their secret zombie-only Lazarus eradication unit as a publicity
move—their last insult. I should've walked away then, like I
meant to, but . . . in the end, I couldn't. And I wasn't alone. Tom
and Coalhouse and a few other former members of Z-Comp also
routinely swallowed their pride and showed up to help out the
doctors and soldiers. None of us was getting money or govern-
mental brownie points for it. We wouldn't have taken them. We
did it because helping Dr. Dearly was still the best way we knew
to serve the zombie community.

Didn't mean we had to like how close it put us to the feds,
though.

The camp looked uneasy. It was overwhelmingly gray—the
color of the stained canvas tents and rough wooden lean-tos, the
worn protest signs propped up against tarp-draped generators,
the trampled grass. The zombies gathered within. I wondered if
they knew about the new strain yet. I wondered if I ought to say

something to someone, spread word that they should lie low. There were so many of them—more than I could ever hope to help. Hundreds of intelligent zombies, the result of thousands of infections. Only a few of us made it to the other side mentally intact. The rest became flesh-hungry killers.

Killers it'd been my job to take care of.

"It's not your fault," Tom said suddenly. "It's not any of our faults. We were on that mission, too." His voice stiffened—but not with accusation. For emphasis. "You blame us?"

Did I look that obvious? Clearing my throat, I tamped down the accelerator. "No. Never."

I did blame myself, though.

When we arrived at the port it was to find that although news about the new strain had just gotten out, it was already shoveling proverbial coal into a raging fire. The *Erika* and the *Christine* were each moored at a long stone dock, and the wooden barricade spanning both appeared shockingly undermanned. The area in front of it was thick with press and protestors, most of them attempting to get access to the *Erika*. The government researchers there were the natural target for torches and pitchforks. It was exactly as I'd feared.

So, having already armed ourselves back at the house, we threw ourselves into the fray—same as always. Shoving my way through the crowd, I prepared to deal with Commander Norton, the living soldier who'd been assigned dock security. He was a jowly, hangdog man we'd nicknamed the Barricade Beast. He didn't like letting us through, he didn't like us pitching in—we were no longer officially soldiers, and we had no clearance. He didn't like us in *general*.

Today, though, upon catching sight of us, the man nodded and pointed to a portion of the barricade. I saw a few other

Z-Compers there. "Thanks for showing up, boys. Could use you there. This is gonna get worse before it gets better."

"Right," I said. Exchanging greetings with the red-coated living troops and our old friends, we settled in for the long haul.

Which ended up being hours. Hours during which the crowd multiplied, my stress level crept steadily up, and I wondered what I might've gotten us into.

"You need to get *back*," Tom told one of the roughly five billion reporters swarming on the docks a short time later, his teeth clenched.

"And *you* need to talk to me!" The reporter was a young man with spiky black hair, probably close to our age. Somehow he kept popping up at the front of the crowd, no matter how many times we physically chased him off. "Why are they trying to keep us away from the doctors? I want to interview a doctor!"

"The only good zombie is a zombie dead for good!" screamed a sign-laden living protestor located behind him.

"Oh, I'll give you an interview. How're you with four-letter words?"

"Give it up," I told Tom, before turning my rifle around and using the butt of it to once more prod Mr. Curious into the pen with his fellow media people. "No comment! We're dead, remember? Dumb as a box of rocks?"

"Yeah right!" Before the young reporter could get anything else out, he was swallowed up by the crowd. Those who found themselves newly at the front started badgering us instead.

"We're running out of room down here!" Coalhouse yelled from farther down the line. I turned to look at him and saw him pause, shoving his wobbling eyeball in yet again.

"Dude, take out your bloody eye!" Tom shouted. "You're going to lose it!"

"We're not in a battle!" Coalhouse countered.

Tom gestured widely. "Does this not look like action to you?"

"Tom," I said. "Bigger fish."

"*Exactly*. God, he is such a child. I told him to leave it behind in the carriage."

"Commander Norton says T-30 to additional men!" Ben Maza, Cheshire-faced and ashen, told me from my left. "His unit should've been relieved by now, but the troops were diverted to Dahlia for some reason. Must be more protestors there."

"At least we know they went somewhere useful," Tom griped. "I swear the Morgue makes up half the entries in the *New London Times* crime column."

Another zombie, Franco Neale, laughed. "The army made an intelligent decision. What next? Airborne pigs as t'e heroes o' romance chapbooks?"

Flashes went off, the reporters' voices rising in a cacophony of new questions. Fighting the tension that was building inside me, I took a breath I couldn't use. The Company Z guys weren't technically my men any longer, but I still hated the fact that I had so few of them to call on. I'd lost so many over the last few months. And if today's news proved to *be* the tipping point, the zero hour event that made living–dead relations impossible—I knew it was my responsibility to get them out. All of them.

"In your own words, what makes you different from a host?" Mr. Curious was back. I turned my head, and almost smacked my cheek into the digital voice recorder he was stretching out over the barricade. "What can you tell us about the apparent resurgence of the plague?"

"Host" was what the media had taken to calling mindless or evil zombies of the sort who'd invaded New London, the sort Company Z used to clean up after. There were many things that made myself and my friends different from them. The fact that on average we'd "awoken" far more quickly than they had, before our brains were completely starved of oxygen, our personalities and memories thus better preserved. Our ability to understand what our condition entailed, to accept what had happened to us, and to handle our new cannibalistic urges and heightened senses. The choices we'd made. In the case of Company Z, the postmortem medical care we'd been lucky to receive.

Our self-control, although mine was starting to wear very thin.

"Look, you need to get back," I reminded the reporter, taking a step forward. He didn't give up ground. There was a sort of crazed light in his brown eyes; he struck me as a human-shaped mass of energy with a roaring metabolism. "For your own safety. Don't make this harder than it has to be."

It was as if I hadn't said a word. "Tell us about Miss Nora Dearly! Rumor has it her immunity is due to her father's experimentation with different forms of the vaccine. Why hasn't *that* vaccine made it out to the population at large?"

The reporter next to him leaned in and added, "Is it true Dr. Victor Dearly created the Lazarus, and that this fact is being covered up by the government? He knows the most about the illness, his daughter is the only immune individual to be discovered to date—even his government-issued underground house has gone strangely undisturbed!"

It seemed I stared at the reporters for an eternity. I could feel something dropping out under my stomach—like the dock had given way beneath me.

They were parroting Averne's arguments. His men had created the Siege, the Morgue—*this*. This mass of scrabbling, loud, angry humanity . . .

It all came crashing in on me. Something snapped.

I was on them before I knew what I was doing.

The second reporter abandoned his line of questioning pretty damn quick when I punched him in the sternum, the air in his lungs escaping his throat with a strangled cough. The younger reporter, Mr. Curious, soon had a busted lip and a potential black eye, and I was dragging him over the barricade to make him a matching set, the smell of his blood only compounding my anger, when Tom finally pulled me off. "Bram, stop it!"

"That's a load of lies!" I roared, my throat rattling, the "scary zombie" voice taking over. "Lies that got thousands of good people killed! If either one of you repeats it to *anyone*, I will *find you* and make you regret the day you ever learned to put pen to paper!"

"I want him arrested!" the older reporter was screaming. "Now!"

"You want the cops to fight your battles for you? Don't think you can take me?"

"Bram! Shut up and look!"

Energized by anger though I was, I did my best to listen to Tom, to stop struggling and do as he said. He yanked me around by my shirt, and I looked in the direction he guided me.

One of the living soldiers had his rifle pointed at me—trained on the only area that mattered when it came to the reanimated. My head. His voice quavered as he told me, "I don't want to do it. I know you're not crazy, Griswold. Calm down."

Slowly, still shaken, I lifted my hands and tried to conquer the flood of emotions surging through me. They were right. I'd rushed out of the house to help, and here I was doing the exact opposite by giving in to my anger, acting like a lunatic. "I'm good."

The soldier lowered his gun gratefully, and opened his mouth to say something—but then we were all driven forward, the crowd of reporters and protestors suddenly and violently surging into the barricade. The wood creaked, and the first few rows of people cried out in fear and pain as they were crushed from behind.

"What the hell?" Tom asked.

The living soldier had fallen, and I offered him my hand. He accepted it and recovered, and all three of us took two steps toward the *Erika*—only to witness the same thing again. It was as if the crowd had spontaneously become a lurching monster, a blob attempting to shove its way forward. Before we could even swear, a nearby portion started to part, people practically climbing over one another like ants escaping a hill of sand. They were clearly attempting to get away from something—I couldn't see what. As we stood there in confusion, the end of the barricade nearest the *Christine* broke apart with such a massive crack that I heard it over the cries of the crowd, relieving the pressure. Reporters and protestors started to flee en masse down the dock, away from the ships, trampling over the injured.

A beat later an old man with an anti-zombie sign in his hand staggered into the widening gap. He was nearly missing one of his cheeks, the flesh torn down to the bone and flapping loosely over his jaw, his upper teeth exposed. All of us stared at him in silent horror, almost in denial, as the shrieking crowd flowed around him.

"Zombies attacking!" Commander Norton yelled. *"Prepare to engage!"*

Fear solidified my riled emotions, separated them like fat on water. I had no idea what this was, but I knew it wasn't good. "Coalhouse, Tom, assist at the evacuation point. Franco, Ben, we need a fallback line closer to the *Christine*." I wasn't their captain any longer, but apparently that fact meant little when it came down to it—the others hurried off, none of them questioning me. Facing the living soldier, I told him, "Find Norton. Tell him to concentrate on the *Erika*. Protect the researchers." Shaky as he appeared, he too raced away.

With them taken care of, I tried to think in terms of priorities. That's all I could do. Whatever was happening, I had to stop it from turning into a complete train wreck.

"You have to move!" I bellowed at the crowd. Nearby reporters screamed and tried to scatter, but couldn't get far. Although the area was emptying out, it was starting to slow due to confusion and the sheer number of bodies involved. A few people didn't even attempt to run, rooted to the spot by fear.

Knowing how little time we had, I literally took matters into my own hands. Catching a couple of catatonic reporters by their jackets, I dragged them under the barricade and pushed them toward the water. "Go! Get off the dock and move farther downshore! Swim if you have to!"

Realizing that I'd just handed them a map out of this mess, the reporters finally listened to *something* I said, slipping around the barricade and leaping into the ocean like a herd of lemmings. Cameras, recorders, and digital diaries were abandoned. As the crowd thinned I was finally able to see past it, to make out the source of the threat. What I saw made my dead stomach attempt to twist.

A huge, disorganized column of dead people appeared to be fighting its way toward us. Men, women—children. They hadn't yet reached the barricade, but a few of them were savaging the living reporters and protestors still blocking their path. I saw teeth sinking into skin, nails tearing through clothing. Blood foaming, spurting. Flesh stretching like hot rubber. A thousand memories flooded my brain, and yet I couldn't have grasped on to a single one of them if I tried. It was the riot, all over again. It was the horrors of war, of the Siege, all over again.

But that wasn't the only thing that hit me.

Hot on their tail was a mob of murderous-looking living people—armed living people. As I watched, one of them caught a dead lady by her hair and pulled her to the ground, cracking a steel pipe across her skull.

The zombies were being chased. Hunted.

The soldiers saw it, too. Norton's voice rose above the screams of pain and fear. "Living civilians mixed in with the dead! Keep steady, gentlemen!"

I started to move, only to find Mr. Curious was still standing next to me, his hand over his bloody mouth. "I can't swim," he said, before I could order him into the water. He took a trembling breath, slung his camera cord over his neck, and unhooked a cane from his belt. "But I . . . I know bartitsu!"

"That's nice," I told him. "They know biting."

Mr. Curious looked up at me helplessly, his face white. Shoving him in the direction of the *Christine,* I said, "Make yourself useful! Get belowdecks and start yelling at anyone who'll listen—we need to lift the gangplank once everyone's on board!"

To his credit, the young man immediately did as I said, leaving me to run in the opposite direction. My body felt heavy and hollow at the same time, and I was convinced that I would have no choice but to start shooting, myself—to count the biters as hosts. That idea didn't sit well. In theory, with the vaccine, the dead were no longer infectious. If I shot these particular zombies, I might as well shoot the people chasing them. Hell, the zombie who'd indirectly caused all this—the newfangled biter—had been arrested, not blown away. Besides, the crowd was thick with the living. I could hear the army men relaying the same warning about collateral damage, accompanied by an order to hold fire.

That gave me hope. I ran faster.

As I got closer to the back of the crowd, Tom soon joining me, it became apparent that the great majority of the invading zombies were terrified, and weren't lashing out save to clear a path or escape their attackers. For their sakes, I knew what we had to do. If bullets started flying, it'd put us right in the thick of it, but it was the only way. "Norton!" I yelled.

I found him near the *Erika*'s dock. He turned to look at me, unmistakable fear in his eyes. "You do *not* give my men orders, Griswold!" Turning to a subordinate, he said, "Get a line going. Prepare to target the zombies and shoot to kill. All of them."

"No! There are living people chasing those zombies. They're trapped, that's why they're fighting back!"

"As a living man, let me make it abundantly clear to you how little of a *crap* I give about zombie motivations!" Norton was swiftly turning red. "Who knows what they did in the city that started this!"

No. I couldn't let this happen. Leaning into his face, I said, "You do this, zombies citywide might retaliate. We haven't forgotten that the army turned on us at the last minute in December. Decided all zombies, good and bad, were going to die. Remember that?"

Commander Norton said nothing. I had my in.

"We can handle this. Get your men, get the living to this dock. Leave the dead to us. There are *kids* out there!"

"Griswold—"

"With all due respect, sir, this is what we were *trained* to do!"

It took him a second, but in the end he nodded. "My men! Aid the living!"

That left us to our half. "Time to punch some skulls," I yelled at Tom. "We need them down, not dead!"

The squat tank of a zombie cracked his knuckles. "I love this part."

Pulling my gun's strap over my shoulder, I threw myself into the crowd, seeking out the violent dead. It was easy enough to home in on them—I just let myself give in again. Let the rage wash over me. Soon the tang of fresh blood was all I could smell, growls and screams all I could hear—and it was those signs I followed to their source. One by one Tom and I pulled the attacking zombies off their targets and punched or kicked them to unconsciousness before tossing their bodies to the dock. At one point Tom used his rifle like a cricket bat, swinging the stock viciously upward to connect with the base of a zombie's skull. The injured living and the frightened dead we directed to the *Christine,* where I could see Franco, Ben, and Coalhouse working to receive them, helping them to dodge the attacks and ushering them on board the ship.

Distantly I heard Commander Norton ordering his men to prepare to intercept the living mob. As I grabbed my last biter, a wild-eyed young woman in a ragged dress, out of the corner of my eye I saw the red-coats moving to secure the barricade. The girl fought me tooth and nail, screaming like a rabbit in a snare, forcing me to risk my own hide by head-butting her into submission. She went quiet, knocked out, and fell with a strange sort of grace to the dock when I dropped her.

In one of those weird, slow-motion moments that seems to attend times of disaster, I found myself thinking that the people we were fighting were almost boring to behold. Not enemy soldiers. Not monsters. It hadn't been hunger that'd driven the woman I just incapacitated, like the ones we'd always taken down in the wild, in the tiny villages—cleaning up after the Laz so the living didn't have to come into contact with it. Instead, she'd been the prey.

She had every reason to get mad, to strike back.

Threat dispatched, I slowly returned to myself and looked up. The living mob was nearly upon us, and they weren't slowing. I knew we couldn't take them on. We couldn't let the situation escalate to that level. Let their fellow living deal with them.

The last zombie cleared the barricade. "Finish getting everyone through, then come back me up," I ordered my friends, who raced off. Until they returned, I *was* the fallback line on the *Christine*'s dock. I pulled off my rifle and raised it so it was easily seen. "Only zombies and authorized personnel allowed through," I cried, lending my voice to the calls of the soldiers.

The living mob didn't slow. I could hear them shouting, yelling foul things about the dead. What few soldiers there were didn't stand a chance. The mob was out for blood. Within another few seconds they'd breeched the barricade; I could hear Norton screaming at his men to continue to hold their fire. I lowered my weapon and pointed it in the direction of the living, though I didn't touch the trigger. I didn't want to have to do this.

Thankfully, I wasn't alone much longer. Soon Coalhouse was at my side, then Tom. "They're raising the gangplank!"

As a unit, we backed up—rather quickly, all things considered. Halfway down the dock we turned and ran, the living fast closing the gap. It was by the skin of my teeth that I managed to leap up and grab the plank as it rose, and I hauled myself up before turning around and helping my friends. Tom came quickly, but just before I could give Coalhouse my hand, his right eye slipped out. His left eye widened in panic and he ducked down to collect it as Tom screamed, *"You have got to be kidding me!"*

Anger shooting through me again, I leaned far over and caught Coalhouse by the collar the moment he straightened. Tom held me by my trousers as I pulled Coalhouse up as far as his own arms, allowing him to help himself. A few of the living attempted to jump for us, and ended up hitting the water. Bullets pinged off the ship's metal hull. Someone down there had a gun, and was willing to use it.

I thought how one of those bullets might've ended up in my head, and pulled my gun's strap over my shoulder again. "We'll talk about this later, Coalhouse."

"Everyone belowdecks." It was Dr. Charles Evola, one of the younger medical technicians. His golden hair was in disarray, his monocle out and swinging from his waistcoat on a length of cord. Behind him, members of the crew dashed out of the ship with weapons in hand, preparing to take up guard. "Come on, Bram. I need you."

I turned around, just in time to get a flash in the face. He'd nearly died, and Mr. Curious was still story-happy. "This report is going to be amazing."

"What's your name?" I managed to grind out.

"Havelock Moncure," he said grandly. "Editor and sole reporter for *Pheme,* the Aethernet's top rumor rag. You are going to be *famous.*"

Wait. This kid wasn't even a real reporter?

The boy gasped when I snatched his device away. Opening it, I pulled out its storage card, dropped it on the deck, and crushed it underfoot. I then thrust the thing back into his hands and grabbed his cravat, dragging him close. "I want to know your name because I owe you a card. You stay up here. If I hear about you hounding anyone, I will throw you overboard."

That threat worked. The beaten young man nodded furiously.

I let him go, and followed Evola inside the ship.

As Evola and the other doctors worked on making room for the newcomers in the med bay, I went to get a head count and see how many needed attention. When I had the chance to continue with the medical training I started back at base, it'd been aboard the *Christine,* so I knew the ropes.

Ben and Franco'd already managed to isolate the injured living on A Level; several techs raced past me, headed there. I found the zombies gathered on B Level, most of them shouting or crying hysterically. Inside the metal ship, the noise was incredible. Tom and the others were busy trying to calm them down and keep them together—for the safety of the living staff, if nothing else. They were a ragtag lot—an equal mix of men and women, of all ages, maybe fifty in total. Some were dressed in worn but colorful finery, diaphanous shawls and candy-striped skirts and shiny top hats decked out with feathers and glass jewels. Others wore ratty street clothes. One man was seated in a wooden cart. For some reason, I could smell flowers.

The ones contributing the most to the din were two women. They stood in the middle of the crowd, part of it and yet seemingly blind and deaf to it. One of them—tall, with tangled rust-colored hair and a face that could be best described as "mushy"—was taking the other to task. Her back was to me; all I could make out was long hair the color of red wine, part of it twisted up with a silver comb.

"I told you this would happen! They're turning against us again. We have to move, we have to protect our own!"

"This is a misunderstanding," the other woman replied.

"What's going on?" I asked.

The red-haired woman turned, and I found myself staring at her perhaps longer than I should've. Her skin was as pale as marble, her eyes inky and almost unearthly. Her black dress set both off. "Who are you, sir?"

"Name's Bram Griswold. I'm here to help."

The rusty-haired woman seemed not to notice me. "We weren't even *doing* anything for once. No big show, not stealing anything, not running any scams. Just carrying out your little utopian idea. Free clinics. How nice. Until one of them gets freaking *ambushed*!"

The woman I'd spoken to lifted a hand. "Claudia, hush." She returned her eyes to mine. "I'm Mártira Cicatriz. Leader of the Changed. This is my sister."

"The Changed?" Tom asked from the edge of the crowd, narrowing his eyes.

"We're a group of zombies interested in peace," Mártira said. "We raise funds, sometimes we picket against anti-zombie injustice. We were providing medicine for the poverty-stricken undead in the Morgue when those people came."

"Why were they chasing you?"

Claudia cut her way in front of Mártira, glaring at me. She wore trousers and a shirtwaist. "Because they were the *living*. What more explanation do you need?"

"*Claudia.*" Mártira shook her head, and tried to engage with me again. "We'd been there not an hour. Suddenly, those *people*," she stressed, looking at Claudia, "started gathering, yelling. Eventually they attacked. So we ran for the port. And thank God we did. Thank you—all of you." She did her best to take in my men with her hands—before they faltered and she ended up pressing them to her chest. "I didn't know some of us would attack. Those poor living souls."

"Those living people *targeted us* for no reason! There are more of us out there, still!" Claudia argued. "Groups that broke off. If the whole city is like this, we can't just stay here. In a *government* boat, no less. We have to go help them!"

Tom pointed out, "You can't leave the ship yet. For your own safety."

"You guys haven't heard the news?" Coalhouse's eye was back in. He sounded sulky.

"News?" Mártira's innocent expression told me they hadn't. "What news?"

Before I could launch into an explanation, Evola came up behind me. "What're we looking at?"

"Look, any of you need medical attention?" I directed my question to Mártira.

"Yes," said a voice I hadn't heard before.

"Laura!" Mártira cried, looking around frantically at the sound of it.

Another zombie girl materialized from within the crowd, her arm curled about the shoulders of a young dead boy. At first I thought she was wearing some sort of fanciful circus costume, something from a play or show. It wasn't until she reached Mártira's side, the smell of flowers intensifying, that I realized what it was.

The girl was a walking garden. Flowers and vines had sprouted from within her very flesh, and were looped through hundreds of buttonholes and slits made in her shabby maroon gown for their passage. Once outside they were wrapped around her limbs and waist. The otherwise baggy dress was thus almost grafted to her, stems and thorns pinning the excess material to her body. A kerchief partially covered her apricot-hued hair, but her gentle, blood-bronzed features were readily visible. She might've been extremely pretty when she was alive. She looked about fourteen or so.

"Whoa," I heard Coalhouse breathe, sulkiness gone.

"Dog was hurt." The boy huddled closer to her at the sound of his name, refusing to look at any of us. "He won't show me."

"Bring him." Even Evola seemed to be transfixed by her.

"You see?" Mártira said to Claudia. "Our sister knows what's important."

Claudia opened her mouth to continue arguing, but then just shook her head and stormed away.

"Brief them," I told Tom and Coalhouse. "And stay with them."

We took Laura and Dog to one of the cloth-partitioned makeshift hospital rooms, walking by a few other repairs in process—a dead man's leg being laced shut, a woman having a pump installed in her wrist for medication. She'd probably get a matching valve in her thigh for drainage. It took a lot of work to keep us going, work that Dr. Dearly had largely pioneered.

"I need a better address than 'by the fire hydrant in the Morgue,'" one tech said to her patient, pulling a curtain in front of us as we passed.

Once we were alone we sat the boy, soon to be the latest recipient of Dr. Dearly's work, on a stainless steel table. There we discovered his hand dangling from his wrist, useless, the bones crushed.

"Oh God, Dog." Laura turned her troubled eyes on us. "He never says anything. I didn't know he got his hand under it. We were separated by a carriage for a minute. When I got to him he'd fallen down . . ."

"It's all right." Evola started digging about in a nearby crash cart. "We could stabilize it with pins, or a splint. It won't work, but it won't do him any harm. Or . . ." He looked at the boy. "We could cut it off. Might be cleaner."

Dog appeared around ten years of age. He was dressed in a patchwork silk jacket and faded blue trousers, with a turban of dirty cloth wrapped about his head. At Evola's suggestion he pulled the turban down over his eyes and tried to grasp onto Laura's skirt again.

"Dog." Laura moved to hug him. "They're trying to help."

It was a horrible decision, but one that had to be made. "Dog, I know you don't know us, and I know it's hard to think about. But a hand that doesn't work is just going to get in your way. Doesn't matter if it's floppy or stiff. I think if we just set it, a couple weeks from now you'll be so annoyed by it you'll try to cut it off yourself. Might make it worse."

The boy shook his head violently.

"Mr. Griswold is probably right," Evola said. "Besides, maybe we could make you a replacement. We've done that before. Why, the young lady my friend here is courting? Her father's got a whole fake leg made of metal. It is a thing of beauty, let me tell you."

The boy peeped out with one eye.

"I bet Doc Sam would love to make a hand for you." Probably

not, but maybe Dr. Chase could persuade him. I smiled at Dog. "C'mon. You're a big guy. What's it going to be?"

It took him a few minutes, but in the end he nodded before burrowing his face into Laura's shoulder. She shut her eyes and held him.

To Evola, I whispered, "Do it fast."

He nodded and withdrew a circular saw from the cart, before removing his monocle and replacing it with a pair of goggles. Then, with all the speed of a highly skilled nurse delivering a shot to a child, he darted in, grabbed the boy's useless hand, and flicked the saw on.

The second the saw started whirring, Dog rebelled. He started thrashing against Laura, who gasped and struggled to hold him closer. He bit her in retaliation, swift, scared strikes born of blind panic, managing only to earn himself a couple of mouthfuls of what was essentially salad.

Quickly, before he could do any real damage, I pulled Laura away and took him into my own arms. His silent fit continued, but I was stronger. I managed to get a grip on his forearm and hold it out, steadying it so Evola could get to work.

As the saw dug into the boy's flesh, I encouraged him. "Go ahead. Bite me. I know you're scared, and that's okay. But you can't bite the living, so bite me."

He did. He didn't get through my clothes, but every nip brought back memories of being cornered and bitten in the mines down south—of the day I died, and got up again, and kept walking. Normally these were not memories I liked to dwell on, but today they offered me a strange sort of comfort. A sense of grounding. A reminder of what I was.

I needed to remember what I was. What I was capable of if I forgot.

When it was done, Evola wrapped up the stump. The boy

eventually calmed down. The procedure couldn't have hurt him badly—we could feel many things, but not a lot of pain, thankfully. All the ways it changed our bodies for the worse, the Laz at least extended us that one kindness.

Laura looked at me. "Thank you."

I released Dog and stepped back. "No problem."

"Let's get some meds in him before he goes," Evola said, going for his faithful syringes. "He doesn't have a wrist valve, and I don't want to bother with one before the hand situation is resolved, so it's going to have to be through the neck."

"I have some." Laura reached into her pocket and drew out a vial of some purplish stuff. "At least we won't use up yours."

Evola took the vial from her and squinted at it, studying its contents, before popping the rubber cork off with his thumb. He touched a finger to the liquid, then to his tongue.

"What are you *doing?*" The sort of stuff that routinely went into all of us—preservatives, hydrating solutions, antibacterial fluid, the things Dr. Dearly had developed to keep us fresher, longer, as well as socially acceptable in terms of smell and texture—could *not* be good for living consumption.

"It's water, a little alcohol," Evola declared, smacking his lips. "We've never used anything this color. Where did you get it?"

The girl looked afraid, almost abashed, as if the situation was her fault. "A living person sold it to us. A lot of it—all he had. Mártira used almost all of the money we'd saved up to buy it. We've been going to the Morgue and giving it away."

The back of my neck tingled in anger. "Snake oil. Someone's selling the undead fake drugs."

Evola took a cleansing breath. "Apparently." He tossed the vial into a biohazard bin and told the dejected Laura, "Never you mind. We have plenty. And for the record, people pay what they can here. I've used my own money to get zombies their meds."

Laura appeared confused. "But Claudia said the living and the feds wouldn't help us . . ."

"Miss Claudia was wrong. Bram, hand me the usual cocktail?"

Laura looked at the floor and lapsed into silence as I went to work. After a few minutes she asked, almost as if she couldn't believe it, "You're really a living doctor for the dead?"

Evola finished Dog's injections and grabbed a needle, threading it as he spoke. "Mmm. Only recently earned the title, but yes. Around here they call the surgeons and doctors who work directly on the dead 'techs,' as opposed to all the doctors who work behind the scenes on zombie research." He started stitching up the tiny hole in Dog's neck. "Few years ago I was studying to become a plastic surgeon, and putting myself through school by working for a funeral home. Sounds morbid, but my area of expertise was reconstructing corpses of people who'd had nasty deaths. Helps the family. Company Z recruited me before I was finished with my education. I was *that* good at mashing flesh together into something resembling a human being. A regular prodigy."

"So you weren't scared when you saw the dead moving?"

"Oh, first time I screamed like a girl." Evola grinned at Dog. "But then I saw people I could help. Also, a way out of my mortuary insurance payments. Anyway, Mr. Dog, let me wrap up the hand so you can take it. Maybe later on we can mount your own skin on the prosthesis. You'll look good as new. You'll be Cyborg Dog! Stalwart defender of the playground!"

Dog actually smiled.

When we rejoined the rest of the "Changed," it was to find the group newly somber and uncommunicative. Tom and Coalhouse must've broken the news. By noon they were anxious to get off the boat, and insisted that we allow them to gather abovedecks. We'd cleaned up and medicated as many as would let us, and an inspection of the group reassured us of the fact that no biters had gotten on board, so we let them.

The biters were still being cleaned up down on the dock, put in irons and led away. There were a few the army didn't bother with right away, and I knew they had to be dead. The sight of their prone bodies occasioned whispers and sobs among those remaining. I hoped they were all victims of the living, as horrible as that idea was—I didn't want to think that Tom or I had killed any.

Once the army finally fortified the barricade, the *Christine* lowered her gangplank. The undead disembarked as soon as it was safe for them to do so.

Mártira came to thank me before departing. "Laura told us Dog should expect to hear from you. Ours is the large house on Ramee Street. You are always welcome."

"Come *on*. We need to *go*," Claudia called to her. She was waiting with Laura and Dog by the gangplank. Laura had her arms wrapped self-consciously through the vines growing around her waist. Coalhouse was standing a short distance from her, practically drinking her in with his eye.

"Same here," I told Mártira. "I'll be in touch. And if you could tell us where you found that grifter . . ."

"It's in the past. We'll just be wiser next time." She shook her head. "The medicine hawker scammed us, yes, but perhaps he had a family to feed. A sick mother. I'll never know. He was a traveling man, and I dealt with him weeks ago. He must be far from here by now."

"That's . . . generous," was all I could think to say.

The red-haired zombie shrugged. "Ever since dying, I find it very easy to forgive. Which is why I can't believe my brothers would . . ." It seemed she wanted to say something more, but in the end stuck with, "I'm so sorry."

"Wish I could say the same." Still, she struck me as idealistic to the point of foolishness. "But I don't want that guy stealing from anyone else."

"Very true. But my main concern right now is getting my brothers and sisters home. Protecting them." Mártira looked into my eyes for a moment longer before curtsying. "Take care, Mr. Griswold." She joined her sisters, and all three swept away.

Havelock appeared seconds after she left. His face was puffy and starting to bruise. "I should report you to the authorities," he huffed.

"Are you going to?" I was too tired to argue with him. I just wanted to know. "The army's right down there. I'm sure a guy named Norton would love to talk to you."

The boy glanced out over the ocean, and decided, "No. Because you did save my hide. I guess." He sniffed. "I do want a new chip, though."

"You got it." I pointed to the ramp. "Now get lost."

He did so. Evola came over to stand with me near the barbette and watch him go. "I heard that kid talking. Is it true you punched him?"

"Yeah." I was calmer now—calm enough to regret my actions, to recognize how depressingly similar they were to the actions of the zombies I'd just had to take care of. "I know I shouldn't have. Ever since we came to New London, I . . . it's harder. There's something about this place that makes the Laz flare. It's too crowded. Too big." Yet another reason I liked to keep the boats at my back.

"You're, what, eighteen now?" he asked, and I nodded. "Christ, I'm only six years older than you. I feel about forty." Evola sighed. "So I'm telling you this as a friend, not someone in charge. You need to be careful for the very simple reason that up here, jail is not what you have to worry about. You're a Punk. You served in the New Victorian army, yes, which is why they're letting you stay here, but the two tribes are still enemies. If you get caught up in something, they'll deport you."

He wasn't telling me anything I didn't know. He was right. The royals would jump at the chance to get rid of me. And where would I go? The Punks destroyed zombies on sight—and I *couldn't* go home. My mother and my little sisters probably thought I was truly dead, and thank God if they did. It was healthier for them. Healthier for me. A clean break.

And I couldn't lose Nora. I loved her. I'd yet to say the words, because I didn't want to freak her out—it'd only been a few months, after all. But I knew I loved her. Needed her. I didn't need food, or water, or even oxygen, but I *needed* her. I'd never met a more spirited, intelligent, accepting, drop-dead-again *beautiful* girl in my life. She was my first, my everything, the thing that made me actually pray in church and try to tolerate the city and put up with her tribe's insane courtship rules—which all seemed to boil down to "if you like a girl, you basically can't do anything in public to show her how you feel." Lord, I was getting sick of having to tiptoe around them. Especially when the Apocalyptic ride we were all currently on was showing no signs of slowing down anytime soon. My time was short. I didn't want to waste it.

"Right," I said, recalling myself. "I'll be smart. But I think we've got more important things to worry about than my small-town transplant angst."

Evola ran his fingers through his hair. "I know. That little boy. What a mess." He returned his eyes to the zombies marching down the dock. "I hope they make it through this."

"Yeah." I turned my own attention to the *Erika*. "And speaking of that mess, I'm going to go get an update."

3 • Nora

"Okay," I said, thunking a blank leather journal on the edge of Ren's cluttered computer desk. "The Dearly House Exit plans."

Renfield Merriweather peered at the tome. Skinny in life, he'd become a scarecrow in death, all elegant half-revealed bones and long limbs. He wasn't nearly as hardy as the other dead boys, which was why he almost always stayed behind as base support, wherever that base happened to be. He found his spectacles on the desk, somewhere amidst all his mixed-tribe gadgets and computer equipment. "Why hasn't Griswold had me digitize this? I could cross-reference maps, databases . . ."

"He prefers to work it out on paper."

"Benighted fool." Ren, NV that he was, loved his tech. Although he shared the guest room with the other lads, his computers and toys had come to dominate one side of our attic—the other side belonged to the dead priest, Jacob Isley. Surrounded by stacks of papers and books, Isley was still solidly asleep on his cot, stretched out like a body on a mortuary slab. Cats lounged everywhere. Isley had a thing for them, and took in as many strays as he could.

"No time for names. We need to double-check the carriage

situation, the weapons situation. We follow this, we can all get out of here in under ten minutes if it comes to that." I'd decided that I couldn't spend my time moping. I needed to work, to contribute.

"Has everyone else been informed? From a logistics standpoint, that should be our first concern."

"Everyone except the sleeping wonder there. Chas should be up soon. She wanted to tell her mom." Looking to his computer array, I found myself staring unfeelingly at the steam-holographic projector I'd once seen him use to play Aethernet chess with Vespertine Mink. "The others went to the boats. Which is precisely where I want to be. If things go wrong—" I pressed my lips tightly together before anything else could slip out.

"I don't think that would be very wise, Miss Dearly. We don't know if our assistance is even required."

Tearing my eyes from the desk, I said, "I hate sitting around and *waiting*, though. I don't know about you, but it makes me go insane."

"Yes, I figure I'm already more insane than not." Ren's posh northern accent only augmented his sarcastic delivery.

"I am not in the mood for jokes! Remember the last time this happened? When I was at Z Beta Base and no one would tell me anything, no one would let me go anywhere or help . . ." That was a big part of it. Logically I knew I had no reason to leave the EF, but I *loathed* being kept on the sidelines.

"We'd probably create more problems if we *did* go." Ren brushed a few curly auburn locks out of his face. "Look. Are you afraid this development will make the living want to round up the dead again?"

Ren was incredibly observant for a dead guy who needed glasses. I nodded once.

"Well, keep in mind that some of our people fought for their dead. They didn't hunt them down and kill them indiscriminately, like the Punks. No one's called for the new pro-zombie Prime Minister to step down, have they?"

"No. Not yet." I had to keep reminding myself of that. "I just don't like this. Only a few months ago the government tried to kill every dead person. Permanently."

"I know. Zombies have every reason to be distrustful of the authorities. But those of us who have a firm grasp on reality know that we need to keep our wits about us."

Opting not to say anything, I opened the book, my stomach still in knots. I could only pray that Renfield and Dr. Chase were right—that cool heads would actually prevail. They had, for a while. There was hope, just . . . no certainty.

Not like we hadn't played with those odds before.

Before I could do anything else, Chastity Sweet appeared in the doorway. She was a tall dead girl with bleached-blond hair, blue-tinged skin, and a silvery metal jaw covered with hand-carved designs, a prosthesis designed for her after she lost hers during a mission for Z-Comp. Uttering a strangled sound to get our attention, she unhooked a digidiary from her leather belt and opened it, holding it up so we could read the screen. Her throat had been crushed during the battle with Averne back in December, and her spelling hadn't improved much since then: *Mom wok up n turned on the news n there are fites going on in the city.* Beside the note, she'd drawn a little mushroom cloud with a frowny face.

Its eyes were X's.

So much for cooler heads.

Once the news broke about the new riot taking place on the docks, everyone in the house knew they would have to work together to keep me corralled. It was the only way.

As soon as Aunt Gene's former butler, Matilda, woke up,

Dr. Chase stationed her at the front door. Matilda didn't seem to mind. The poised, ebony-skinned woman was content to sit on the floor in front of the door with a lap desk and a toffee bar, going through the household bills.

"Have you *seen* the letters your aunt's creditors have been sending?" she asked me absently one of the times I edged into the foyer to glare at her.

"No, and I don't want to." Aunt Gene had gotten us into massive debt before her disappearance. I supposed I should count it as unfinished business, but the fact that she was most likely dead sort of wiped the slate clean.

Alencar, the chauffeur, manned the back door. He bowed whenever I walked past. Dr. Chase and Renfield insisted on shadowing me, so I kept moving, pacing. As I did, I turned my cell phone over in my hands. Bram had bought both of us phones back in February for my birthday—a gift that was extremely practical, and thus extremely Bram. His was plain and grudgingly used; mine was a minisculpt, black, shaped like a mermaid hugging her tail against her head. Bram wasn't currently responding. My father hadn't answered any of my emails in days, and every time I tried to call him, I got a busy signal.

For hours I remained in a state of infuriating helplessness, practically a prisoner in my own home. I knew the others weren't trying to be cruel, that they only meant to protect me. But in moments like this, I understood what Bram and I were up against. The riot two weeks ago had been the turning point for me, when I finally got that the real enemies we were going to have to face weren't Wolfe and Averne, but Time and Fear. How little time I would have with him, and how fear could cut that even shorter. More than just being with him—I wanted to stand beside him on the front lines. I'd gotten a taste of freedom last winter, and it almost physically hurt to have to return to my old life of manners and rules.

I wanted my new life back.

Eventually Dr. Chase and Dr. Samedi sought me out, and found me walking in circles in one of the long back hallways, underneath one of my father's favorite mythological murals. "There you are, Miss Dearly. Baldwin and I are going to install Miss Chastity's voice box."

This was enough to get me to look up from my phone. "I thought it wasn't finished yet?" Sam had been toiling over her artificial voice box for months now.

"Funny thing. I mentioned how much better it'd make me feel if Miss Chastity could talk, given all that's going on." Dr. Chase glared at Dr. Samedi. "That's when he chose to inform me it's actually been completed for almost a month. He was enjoying the quiet. I've already boxed his remaining ear."

Samedi slipped a hand into his chestnut hair and adjusted his stitched-up head slightly, tweaking it to the side. The zombie's skull was full of hardware that allowed his brain to communicate with a thick metal collar installed around his neck, permitting his body to move even when his head was severed from it. A tremor zipped down his spine, and he narrowed his gray-lidded, feminine eyes. "Thank you. You just admitted that if I do go deaf, it's only because external forces are constantly assaulting me."

Dr. Chase shook her head and looked at me. "Would you like to help?"

In spite of everything, I found myself asking excitedly, "Really?"

Just then my phone rang. I looked down to find that it was Pamela Roe, my best friend. "Is it Dr. Dearly?" Samedi asked.

"No. Pam." I didn't have to say anything else; the two adults nodded and saw themselves out. "You okay?" I asked upon opening the phone.

"Yes." Still, Pamela sounded nervous. "You've heard about

the new strain? I'm just calling to let you know I probably can't get down there today."

"Yeah. Sorry I didn't call sooner, myself."

"Dr. Evola hasn't been home."

"He's probably working overtime." He'd been rooming with the Roes ever since the Siege, preferring to stay closer to the hospital ships. "Look, why don't I come over there?"

"Not to put too fine a point on it, but no way in hell, Nora. The city needs time to calm down. Dad won't let us leave the house."

"That's why I'll come to you."

"Not a good idea. And your father wouldn't like it."

"Who said I'd tell him?" She made a disapproving noise in response. "Besides, Pamma, not even the ravenous dead can stand between you and me."

"Don't remind me. And don't you dare. *Please* give me one less thing to worry about."

Rolling my eyes heavenward, I said, "Fine. Anything I can do for you from here? Otherwise, I'm going to help the docs with something."

"No, there's nothing you can do. I'll call you if there is. I'll text you later anyway."

Frustrated anew, I hung up and considered just leaping out a nearby window and running for the surface. My imagination extended this little adventure to include clobbering an army man, donning his uniform, and marching toward the nearest disaster.

In the end, for Pam and Papa, I went in search of Dr. Chase.

It turned out that "helping" didn't add up to much more than handing the engineers tools. It was hard to be contented with that, but I tried.

Chas was set up on the desk in my father's dark, masculine

study. Every lamp in the place was positioned about her, since the windows were still boarded up. The initial phases of the "operation" involved cutting into her throat and scraping and snipping all the ruined flesh away. Samedi let her keep her digidiary, and she occasionally wrote things like, *Dont u think I need that?* or *Tckls!* in response to his actions. After perhaps forty minutes, the device itself—a curious golf-ball-sized construct of metal and wire—was popped into her neck.

Admittedly, watching Baldwin and Beryl at work was absorbing. The first time I met them I'd been told they were an amazingly inventive team, and they truly did seem to function like two bodies sharing a single mind. He could make a suggestion and she'd already be halfway done with it, reaching for a spot welder or twisting a plastic cap into place. Occasionally they would murmur together like two soothsayers puzzling over a goat's entrails, completing each other's sentences.

"Stitch or staple the remains of her trachea . . ."

". . . bottom should replicate a ring of cartilage, I thought. Stability. No more smoking for you, young lady." Sam leaned back, tucking his scalpel between his lips. Sterility wasn't a concern when operating on the undead, obviously. "All right. Speak."

"I'm no-ot a do-og, you kno-ow," Chas responded, her first words since the battle in Bolivia. Aside from sounding somewhat computery, it was definitely her own voice, only healthier than I remembered it. She seemed to speak somewhat laboriously, though, her neck and chest rolling noticeably as she fought to get the words out. She moved to sit up, and Beryl aided her.

"Chas!" I hopped up and wrapped my arms about her shoulders from behind. "It's so good to hear your voice."

"Tell . . . me ab-out . . . it." I could see the muscles of her throat flexing as she remembered how to use them.

Samedi shooed me out of the way so he could study his handiwork. "There. Let's get the wires in, and then I think the best way to close this up would be to install some small D-rings along either side of the incision and have her lace it up until the skin stretches to accommodate the new hardware. Then we can put in a permanent suture."

"I think you're right," Dr. Chase said. "Miss Dearly, can you hand me the pliers?"

Chas turned excited eyes on Sam. "Like a . . . neck corset? No, I'm keep-ing the . . . lacing! I can use different . . . colooored . . . rib-bons!"

As Samedi reached past me for an additional bit of wire, I heard the sound of the front door opening, followed by the un-mistakable voices of the undead boys. Without waiting to see if anyone else had heard, I raced for the door and down the hall. It seemed like it took an hour to reach the foyer, when in fact it took only seconds. "Guys!"

Bram was at my side before I could say another word. I wrapped my arms around him and squeezed as hard as I could. He curled his huge hand around my head, guiding it to his chest, and I took advantage of the opportunity to rest my eyes and lean against him, if only for a brief moment—had we been alone, I would have happily remained there. "Everyone good here?" he asked.

"Yes. What's going on?"

"The usual." He urged me back, his hands on my shoulders. "City's in an uproar again, troops and cops are spread thin. Never enough of them."

"Great." I stepped away a few beats later, a proper young lady once more, and turned my attention to Coalhouse and Tom. "Are you guys okay?"

"Oh yeah," Tom said, his peeved tone belying his words. "Just disappointed that alcohol doesn't work the way it's supposed to anymore, that's all."

"Your girlfriend's in surgery," I told him. "Sam's done with her voice."

Tom's bald eye ridges jumped in surprise, his lips splitting into a sharklike grin. Coalhouse chuckled. "Really? This I gotta see."

Something in his sentence set the other two off, because their expressions transformed from "there's no place like home" to "oh, hell no" in the space of two blinks. "You know, you only see with *one* of those lumps in your head," Tom said. "Maybe you should give the other to me for safekeeping." He extended a hand, frowning.

"That was not acceptable, what happened back at the docks," Bram said to Coalhouse.

"Can we talk about this later?" Coalhouse asked, glancing uneasily at me.

"No. We talk about it now." Bram pointed at his useless eye. "I don't care if you wear it when things are quiet, but you've got to take it out whenever there's the chance of action. You knew this back at base."

"But this isn't Z Beta. There are people on the streets, they'll see me . . ."

"You're a *zombie*. If you're not missing body parts, you're doing it wrong!" Tom yelled. "You put us in danger today. And it's because you care what you *look* like?"

"Danger?" I asked, only to be ignored.

"Oh, and he didn't?" Coalhouse pointed angrily at Bram. "Like he didn't flip out?"

"What?"

My tone of voice was enough to arrest them, to stall their dispute. Still, they all had that funny, stiff "zombie pack" posture—like their bodies were ready to throw down if dominance needed to be physically established, even if their minds had yet to consciously go there. I'd seen it before.

Bram cleared his throat. "We'll get into it later. Go see Chas."

"Guess I'm not the only immature one, huh?" Coalhouse said, before stomping in the direction of the hall. Tom shook his head, then followed.

"Immature?" I asked once they were gone. "What's the matter?"

"Let's just say that I'm more pessimistic now than I was this morning." Bram reached for me again. "I'm glad you didn't come. I would have been worried sick."

I pushed his scarred hand away in annoyance. "Talk."

With a rumble, he said, "We had to take on some zombies, okay? Back up the army. Thankfully, it didn't turn into a bloodbath."

"Oh God." Cue me immediately feeling like a jerk. "I'm so sorry."

Bram shrugged, though I could tell he was still troubled. "Let's get everyone settled and then we'll talk. We're safe, that's what matters."

Respecting this, I gave up. Even though I still had questions, suddenly I wasn't half as worried as I had been. The Punks could take over the world with giant mechanical dinosaur clowns and I wouldn't bat an eyelash. No matter what might be happening, no matter how many fires might be burning, being with Bram always seemed to make things at least *feel* better.

He was okay. He was here. He was home.

Now I just needed my father.

"We can't do anything right now. I went over to the *Erika* and spoke to Salvez already."

"I *swear*, if I hear that phrase *one more time* . . ." I kneeled on my chair. "Anyway, what did Salvez say?"

"Like Dr. Chase told us—the Laz has mutated."

"There's more to it than that."

"I wish I knew, Nora."

It was dinnertime, and Bram was trying to get some food in him—the usual. Tofu. Protein used to trick his body into thinking it was getting the flesh it wanted, mixed with a digestive enzyme since his stomach no longer worked. Between statements, I gave him five chews. Under the kitchen table Dad's Doberman pinscher, Fido, begged.

"You didn't see Papa at all?"

"No. I asked for him, but got the runaround. Like usual. Every time I go over there lately, he's busy. I feel kind of shut out of the research side of things."

"Is it dangerous there? Should we *be* worried about him?"

"I told you about the living mob and the zombie attacks. We left once it got calmer and more army reserves arrived. See? I'm not holding anything back this time."

"I want to see him, Bram." I leaned my elbows on the table and fixed my gaze on one of the household signs Dr. Chase had used her talent with calligraphy to create: ZOMBIE-ONLY SILVER-WARE GOES IN THE CANISTER. "I just want to know that he's safe."

Bram chewed five times. "Give him more time. The news just broke earlier today."

"I know. And I know that he has the world on his shoulders. That's why I've tried to be respectful. But Bram . . . I can't *do* this anymore."

Looking into Bram's eyes, I could see that he understood. "I'm getting to that point myself. Somehow I've ended up a grunt on the ground again. Still fighting people. But I am *not* army anymore. Don't want to be. Problem is, now is not the time to pitch a fit about it. We've got to stick together. Do what needs to be done."

Putting my head in my hands, I tried to think. Bram patted my

back, wiped his mouth, and said, "Look, I did get some info."
Lifting my head, I saw that he was cleaning off the fork and knife
he'd used to eat with. "Here—I get to do the medical briefing
this time."

"Go for it." It was better than nothing. I pillowed my cheek
on my folded arms, turning my head to watch.

"So, you know the illness that makes zombies is fluid-borne,
and caused by prions."

"Yes." I knew that prions were proteins, technically the same
as other proteins already located in the human body—simply
shaped differently, and thus diseased. They were wont to bend
healthy proteins to look just like them, causing a deadly chain
reaction that, in the case of the Lazarus, reanimated the dead.

Bram held up his knife and fork. "So imagine these are prions.
They're made of the same stuff—both metal, in this case—but
they're different shapes." He stuck the tip of the knife through
two of the fork tines. "Let's say the knife is the 'bad' one. So
the knife sticks to the fork, and reshapes it. The fork turns
into the knife." He spirited the fork under the table, leaving the
"new" knife. "And it goes on to stick itself into another fork and
change it, etcetera, etcetera. Eventually the infected person hits
the ground—and in the case of the Laz, sits up again."

"And we're all terribly grateful for that."

Bram chuckled, and brought the fork back out. "Now, proteins are made of amino acids. The way the antibodies created by
your father's vaccine are supposed to work is . . ." He used the
fork to spear a leftover glob of tofu—just on two tines. "They
stop up the gap by sticking to a specific amino acid chain. They
plug up the hole." He mimed the tip of the knife trying to connect to the fork and encountering the blasted tofu. "The bad one
can't bond with the good one, so infection can't take place."

"So what makes the new form able to bypass that?"

He slid the base of the knife between two other, unprotected tines. "The connection is made between a different set of unprotected amino acids."

"How?"

"Prions *are* capable of evolution, even though they have no DNA of their own. The question is, when did this mutation come about? Why haven't we seen it before? Is Patient One the only one with it, or is it present in other zombies? Did he get it from someone else?"

"Patient One?"

Bram lowered his educational cutlery. "That's what the researchers are calling the biter. They haven't managed to identify him yet, and word is he won't talk. Both infections trace back to him. The zombie who bit your dad all those years ago is the first zombie on record, and they call him Patient Zero. They never found the 'first ever' zombie, the one who *made* Patient Zero—he has to be dead by now."

"Have you seen him?"

"No." Bram frowned. "Salvez did say they've already put your samples under the microscope, though."

"And?"

"You're still immune."

"Goody. Let's hold a parade." I knew my nigh-miraculous immunity stemmed from my own stubborn genetic makeup, not antibodies. Still, I asked, "So what happens if there are other strains out there?"

Bram didn't respond immediately, studying his plate. "I don't know right now," he decided. "We have plenty of options, but none of them are good."

That wasn't what I wanted to hear. "What if we have t—"

"You stupid, rotting fool!"

Jerking my head up, I looked over at the kitchen door just in time to see Dr. Richard Elpinoy, my father's top geneticist, stalk past. A door slammed and my father hobbled up behind him, supporting himself with a mahogany cane. The dark-skinned, white-haired Dr. Elpinoy's trench coat gaped in front, the buttons barely connecting over his stocky frame.

"Come back here!" my father bellowed. "Come back here and look me in the eye when you say that!"

"I've said enough!" Elpinoy turned and glared at my father. "You've spent the entire day moping about, practically praying for death, as if you suddenly agree with Wolfe! That traitor! I'm half inclined to give you what you want!"

I'd never heard my father *or* Elpinoy speak like that. I was so shocked that I momentarily forgot to exclaim over the simple fact that Papa was home, or even leave my seat. Bram appeared absolutely dumbfounded.

"Are you threatening me, you pompous piece of—"

"Threatening you? Hardly! I'm telling you that your behavior's unacceptable! And I think you know it, too!" Elpinoy dared to put a finger in my father's face. "I've been with you since almost the beginning on this—you asked for me by name. We were colleagues at school. You trusted me once, and I've been telling you for *years* that the final cure to this whole hellish mess lies in genetic engineering! In substituting a new protein for the original Zr-068 protein, thus rendering the diseased prion impotent. You have one last chance to turn your research in the right direction!"

"And I told you," my father roared, swinging his cane at nothing in particular, "that solution would be too difficult and expensive—oh, not to mention *stupid as hell*! What are you going to do, change the genetic makeup of everyone on *earth* because of *one* illness?"

"When that illness causes the dead to come back to life and hunger after the flesh of the living? *Yes!*"

"Vaccination is the easiest and most robust method of combating the Laz!"

"It took us *years* to come up with a vaccine! We do not have *years* to come up with another! And what happens if a new strain arises? And another, and another? What do we do then, Dearly? Tell me!"

I started to stand up, and Bram followed suit. "Why is Dick challenging him all of a sudden?"

Elpinoy heard Bram, and finally turned to look at us. "I'll tell you why!" He stormed into the kitchen and got right up in Bram's face, forcing him back. "That bastard is going to get us all killed, that's why!" Fido slipped from under the table, slicking his ears back and growling at Elpinoy. Bram caught him by the collar.

For the last few minutes I'd been numb. Now my entire body went hot. "Don't you dare call him that!"

"I'll call him whatever I like, missy!" Elpinoy rounded on me. "I'm leaving. I'm not about to march to that man's insane drumbeat anymore. Unless drastic measures are taken, the Laz is just going to keep mutating until it's turned the entire world into a graveyard. I'm not about to let that happen!" He turned to my father, who was entering after him. "I quit."

Bram's mouth dropped open. "Dr. Elpinoy, you can't do this!"

"Oh, I can. I quit. Do you hear me, you stubborn rotter? I quit!" With that, Elpinoy started to stomp away. "I'm clearing out my room! I'm leaving this accursed house!"

"Go!" my father thundered a few steps closer, almost getting my foot with his cane. "I never want to see your face around here again, you hear me?"

"Papa!" I reached out to capture the sleeve of his coat. "Calm down. Please, just calm down and talk to us?"

"Nora?" My zombified father looked at me with his dark, milky eyes, his entire body going still.

"I've been trying to call you for days." I traded his sleeve for his wrist, and felt how tense he was. Consciously or not, he was prepared for the hunt, for the fight. "What's wrong?"

"Nothing." I could tell he was trying to disguise his anger, but he wasn't fully successful. "Go to your room, NoNo. I'll be there soon."

I shook my head. "Come with me. You need to rest."

My father tossed off my hand. "I'm fine. And you don't need to worry about me. You have Mr. Griswold to look after you." He looked at Bram and uttered a short, phlegmy laugh. "I won't be here forever, after all."

Bram let go of the dog and stepped forward. "Sir, she's right. You need—"

"I will tell you what I need if and when I need it!" Papa shouted. We were both taken aback, and said nothing in response. For a moment I saw despair wash over my father's aristocratic features, before they hardened once more. He marched out without another word.

Bram took my hand again. I didn't even feel it.

Bram didn't ask questions. He knew that I needed to get away. He went upstairs and got a gun for himself and a hat for me, and took me outside. There he tucked me into Aunt Gene's carriage, and together we headed for the surface.

The drive was slow and quiet, apprehension thickening the air between us. I was still trying to decide if I couldn't believe what I'd just seen, or if I was only frightened by how easily I *could* believe it. Papa's anger reminded me of Samedi's fight with Wolfe. During that final encounter Samedi'd gone about his violent business so easily, so passionately—his reanimated mind and body aligning, like a series of dark stars, to the task of beating and biting Wolfe. The idea that my father might be capable of the same thing made my skin crawl.

Compared to what I'd seen on the news the city had quieted down significantly, though parts of it still appeared on edge. Even through the closed windows I could hear sirens in the distance. Bram chose a route that took us off the main streets but kept us close to the EF, and we ended up driving through an upper-class neighborhood—nothing like the dominions of the very rich in the countryside surrounding New London, but nice enough—where several houses stood with their front entrances thrown open to reveal lavishly lit interiors, the fences surrounding them bedecked with flowers and strings of electric bulbs. Competing parties—maybe debuts. Well-heeled ladies and gentlemen walked past, laughing, seemingly ignorant of the current state of the world. The Season was on.

Seeing them actually gave me some hope, though it was impossible for me to enjoy the sensation. More smothering mourning crepe had been sold in the last few months than snowy debutante satin, and yet some people were still celebrating, carousing, *living*. The entire city should look like this.

After allowing me a few silent minutes to marvel, Bram started back, turning onto West Herbert Avenue. The lights were on in the police station there, and people were still tramping in and out—most of them clad in black. Everybody was in mourning for somebody. Shops were closing down for the day, peddlers packing up their street carts, and the few people abroad seemed to hurry from one pool of lamplight to the next, wary of the shadows. Living people either tried to stay close to the zombies accompanying them or attempted to avoid the zombies they passed entirely.

I finally rubbed at my eyes, and Bram reached over and touched my shoulder. "Are you okay?"

I nodded. I felt like I should cry, but I was too confused. "He's never spoken to me like that. I mean, I half think I deserve it for some of the things I've done, but still . . ."

Bram pulled the carriage over to the side of the road and took my hand once more. I gave in and let myself tear up. He leaned over and kissed my clothed right shoulder, where he'd once bitten me, and my cheek.

Shutting my eyes, I tried to concentrate on the sensation of his touch. "He'll come home to scream at Elpinoy, but he won't answer my emails."

"He's scared," Bram said, his deep voice right in my ear. I could almost feel it in my bones, more nourishing than my own blood. "Like you said, he has everything riding on him. But he loves you."

"I know. He's done this before—thrown himself into his work. After my mother died, he did the same thing. I know I have to think of it that way. It just hurts."

Bram looked down at my hand at the mention of my mom. "Yeah."

Releasing a shaky breath, I said, "I still keep wishing things would just go smoothly. For everyone."

"Chances of that happening?"

"Slim to none." Doing my best to convert a hiccup into a sigh, I wondered how much I ought to rant—for I knew half the things I wanted to complain about were petty. I wasn't so consumed by my own drama that I couldn't see it. "He didn't even see me. He didn't want to deal with me. And he thinks he gets to tell me what to do? That he knows what's best for me?"

"If it's worth anything, I need you." Bram wrapped me up again, and tangled his fingers in my hair. "You guys aren't the only ones feeling the pressure. I lost it, for a few seconds. Beat up some guys spouting conspiracy theories that sounded an awful lot like Averne's. They said your name, like they had any *right* to, and I went off. That's what Coalhouse was talking about."

This statement didn't offer me any comfort. It caused me to hook my chin worriedly over his shoulder and loop my arms around him, eyes on the carriage window. He'd told me he had maybe three years left before he gave in to his illness, lost his self-control, and so *three* had become a mantra of mine, my lucky number.

I didn't want to think about the fact that he'd quoted that figure four months ago. So two and two-thirds left. Or less than that?

"You're the only thing around here that makes sense sometimes," he whispered against my temple. "You remind me of what's important. What I have to lose. I feel safest when I'm protecting you, caring for you—I feel at peace. So whatever you need me to do, tell me. I'd put a bullet in my own head for you."

I clutched him with renewed intensity, another tear escaping my eye. This was never going to end. Even if we did leave New London.

Behind Bram the window of the carriage exploded with a suddenness that threatened to stop my heart. A pistol—though to my panicked mind it resembled a cannon—was thrust through it, and for a moment I thought I'd been shot, my cheek stinging. As Bram turned, roaring, I saw the air glittering and realized I'd been hit by broken glass. The gun hadn't been fired.

"Bram!" I screamed.

Behind the gun—seemingly miles behind it—stood a figure wearing a mask crafted of some sleek black material. It looked as if it'd been modeled after a crow or raven, with an enormous downward-curving beak and eyeholes filled with smoked glass. It would have been comical if whoever wore it hadn't had a weapon trained on me.

"Careful, Brother!" I heard someone else shout, the voice electronic and ghostly. "They're insane!"

Terrified, caught off guard, it took my brain a moment to make sense out of what the gunman yelled. His voice seemed to come from everywhere at once, warped, distorted—like Chas's. "Get out of the carriage, necroslut! Do it now! Take your dead man and get out of the goddamn carriage!"

4 • pamela

Watching the Delgados from my bedroom window had become something of a bad habit of mine.

Emanuel Delgado was no longer a fishmonger. No living person would willingly buy food from a zombie—truthfully, you couldn't blame them. I don't think even Mr. Delgado blamed them. But to make ends meet his wife had been forced to resume her job as a charwoman, and he had to take whatever work he could get, at whatever hour it happened to come. My brother, Isambard, helped his fellow zombies deal with their unpredictable schedules by looking after their dead five-year-old daughter, Jenny.

He was picking her up now. I watched him speaking with her father in the shadowy courtyard between our buildings, the little girl clinging to his pants leg, ecstatic to be reunited with her babysitter. As I worked on braiding half of my straight brown hair into a bun, I wondered what they were saying. Someone in a nearby building was listening to the wireless, and I couldn't hear over the sound of it.

> *"Come to me, or my dream of love is ov'r!*
> *I love you, as I lov'd you when you were sweet,*
> *When you were sweet sixteen."*

Now that my little brother was undead, I treasured him in a way I hadn't been fully capable of before. I wanted to know what he was up to every moment of the day—and when I didn't know, I started to imagine the worst. I longed to protect him, to shield him.

Until the bitter end. Until he finally—

Stop it, I told myself. *You can't change anything. Stop it. You're safe. You're safe.*

Hurriedly, I turned back to my schoolwork. St. Cyprian's was still closed, but our teachers had been doing their best to keep after us via email and Aethernet conferences. To hear them gripe, I was one of the few students who routinely responded. A lot of the girls were apparently blowing their studies off, but I was a scholarship student; I couldn't afford to slack, even in the face of the Apocalypse. So I'd spent the afternoon studying geography, doing my best to distract myself from news of the emergent Laz strain. I willed myself not to worry about it too deeply, especially after talking with Nora.

Worry was something I needed to avoid.

After the Siege was over and my family had returned home, I'd been fine. For weeks I'd existed in a calm, capable state of super-heroineishness—a help to my parents, a guardian for Isambard, a shoulder for Nora to cry on via telephone. Every time I tried to reflect on what I'd been through, it was like I couldn't even re-member it.

Then the nightmares started.

It all came back to me in dreams—the flight through the city, the monsters hunting us, being unable to save my brother. The horrible things I'd had to do to survive—killing people, chop-ping up body parts. The nightmares always woke me, surges of irrational terror putting my body and senses on high alert, even though there was nothing around to be afraid of. Sometimes it felt as if I was having a heart attack at only sixteen years of age—my chest on fire, my breath short, my limbs tingling.

I knew it was anxiety. I'd been anxious and prone to worry my entire life—about Nora's math homework, about my mother's plans for me, all things great and small. And so I hid it. I told no one. Because my brother was dead, and my parents were traumatized enough, and Nora had been through the wringer, too. There were a thousand reasons. But now all it seemed I *did* was remember. The memories and the fear were constantly with me, constantly intruding, turning my every thought into a heart-twisting regret or a terrible prophecy. I found that the only way to stop the worry, the only way to pop the bubble of building, nameless anxiety, was to force myself to pay attention to something else. Like schoolwork.

Now I was on chapter thirty of this semester's text; Nora was still on chapter two.

Turning the pages of the digital book somewhat frantically, I started perusing a section detailing the science behind the new ice age, the many cataclysmic events that had led humanity to crowd around the Equator and form new tribes. Just holding a book, learning mundane facts, seemed oddly distant from my new reality. To think it had formed such an enormous part of my world before. Now, for all the time I put into my studies, they seemed so . . . pointless.

Issy's punctilious knock sounded on the door. I jerked in my seat before realizing what it was. "Come in."

My brother opened the door just wide enough to step inside, and bowed. I bobbed my head. Even now he insisted we genuflect to each other—though since dying he'd loosened up quite a bit. "You can't come in unless you can curtsy like a big girl, Jenny," he said, ducking his head around the door again. He was now frozen at fourteen, his brown hair forever short. His skin had taken on a purplish hue that almost hid the mole on his cheek. We were both of Indian descent, mostly through our mother's side.

"I can curtsy!" she insisted.

"May she come in, Pam?"

"Of course."

And thus in toddled the littlest zombie I'd yet met. Jenny Delgado had lost some grace and some words since the night I found her wandering the streets, but still had quite the personality. After making sure Isambard was watching her, she carefully spread out the skirt of her pink pinafore and curtsied. I couldn't help but smile, and stood up to return the gesture, which made her wiggle with glee. She came running for me, and hugged me around the legs.

"Very good! What's up, Issy?" I carefully combed my fingers through Jenny's baby-fine, dirty blond hair. She'd shed some of it already; I didn't want to pull any more out. It wouldn't grow back.

"Mom's starting dinner. She asked me to come get you."

"Great." So much for avoiding worry. I plucked a ribbon out of the display of them on my vanity and waggled it at Jenny to get her attention. It drew her white-speckled eyes like a lodestone, and her chapped lips parted. "Look after Issy-monster for me, okay, Jenny-bear?"

She let go of me and captured the ribbon, placing it over her head, as if it might stay there of its own volition. "Jenny-bear!" She turned on Issy and flexed her fingers like claws, laughing giddily. I left Issy to deal with her and made my way downstairs to the kitchen.

Mom was busy shaping scraps of leftover dough from my father's bakery into dinner rolls. The sleeves of her cotton dress were pushed up, revealing her plump arms. She spotted my distorted reflection in the copper pans hanging from the ceiling as I entered, and glanced at me over her shoulder. "Ah, there you are! I could use your help."

"Of course." Without interrupting her, I slowly removed my apron from its hook by the door and took a look around.

Inwardly, I sighed at what I found.

She'd taken three chickens from the freezer and laid them out on the counter like headstones, one after another. She was doing it again.

"The potatoes are in the basket," she said as she opened the oven door. "Lately it seems like pickings are growing slim at the market. Perhaps people are afraid to bring their wares to town? It worries me."

I took a breath. "You know what worries me, Mother?"

She slid the rolls in. "What, pumpkin?"

There was no good way to put it. "Mom, you're not going to cook all of these chickens, are you? There're only three of us eating."

Mom shut the oven door and turned to look at me, her eyes wounded. "Four. There are four of us eating. Five, if you count Jenny."

"Mom . . ." I decided to just come out with it. "You have to stop cooking for Issy. He can't eat it. His stomach doesn't work anymore." A few months ago when she'd done this, it was understandable—almost cute. Motherly overachievement. But now it was getting scary. She wouldn't *stop*.

My mother stood up straight, marshalling her bulk around her. It was a posture I knew well from childhood, and it instinctively made me shrink down a bit. "Pamela Roe, Isambard is your brother. It would be heartless not to include him at the table."

"He *is* included, Mom. Dad makes him his tofu every day—"

"That stuff?" Mom tossed her head. "No. I won't hear of that being the only thing he's given. They feed prisoners better."

During the Siege, I'd been incredible. I rescued Vespertine Mink, got my parents to safety, and slew the evil dead. I even hit Michael Allister when it came out that he wasn't interested in me, that he'd been using me, even after I put myself in danger to help him. I'd lashed out at someone out of anger. And I never wanted to have to do any of those things ever again. I just wanted everything to return to normal.

An even more selfish part of my brain wanted my mother to return to a place where she could take care of *me*, not the other way around.

"Mom . . ." I didn't know what to do, but I was willing to try anything. "Why don't you let me cook dinner tonight?"

Her eyes widened. "For all of us?"

"Yes." My mind raced, hitching its wagon to this idea. Maybe I could just put one bird in, carve it up so it looked like more, and hide the others in the back of the freezer. "I mean, I should have more practice cooking, shouldn't I? For whenever I . . . if I . . . do get married?" I iced the cake. "You can spend the time with Isambard."

That got her. Mom immediately started picking at the knot in her apron strings. "Yes! That will be . . ." She shook her fingers free, apparently willing to forget about her apron, and moved to hug me. "What a good girl you are, Pamela. Always helping others."

"My pleasure."

Mom released me and almost flew to the door. She stopped in the hall, though, and turned back. "Oh, I meant to ask you—did you finish your studies?"

I turned my back to her, put on my apron, and began selecting potatoes from the basket on the counter. "Almost."

"No problems?"

I lied. "No, Mom."

"Really?" She started wiping her floury hands off against each other. As usual I couldn't tell if she was relieved, unconvinced, or somewhat disappointed. "That's good to hear."

I had no real reply for this, so I found the peeler in the drawer and started removing the potato skins in long, thick strips. Anything to stay busy. My mother observed me for a few more pensive moments, taking her daily parental inventory, before moving down the hall. As I heard her call for Isambard, I berated myself for feeling any resentment toward her. I wondered what she was thinking, what she expected of me.

The more things change, the more things stay the same.

Despite my efforts and my good intentions, the chicken came out of the oven half burnt and half raw. Apparently, cooking ability was not genetic. I chopped the edible part of the chicken up and threw the pieces over a thick bed of vegetables in the biggest dish I could find. It would have to do.

When everything was finished and on the table, I sat with Isambard and Jenny in the parlor while we waited for Dad to close up the bakery. I was drained. The screen on the wall was tuned to a children's show where a puppet was being made to sing a song about treating others as one wished to be treated, but an unending ticker ran across the bottom: *We would like to remind our loyal viewers that the source of the new strain of infection IS STILL ISOLATED. If you are vaccinated, there is no need to fear any particular zombie. NORMAL PRECAUTIONS APPLY.*

I messaged Nora on my cell phone but got no response. I wondered if she was busy with Mr. Griswold, and did my best to ignore the feeling of jealousy this idea stirred up. In theory, I liked Mr. Griswold—he'd saved our lives, and appeared to be quite honorable—but my last brush with romance hadn't gone well, and I still wasn't over it. Neither was I used to sharing my best friend.

A few minutes later my father came up from the bakery to join us, bearing with him two servings of jiggly, enzyme-laden tofu within the thinnest of braided crusts, a recipe he'd perfected for his undead son and now sold in the shop. My mother bustled through with a plate of butter. "Dinner, children! Turn off the screen!"

Once everyone was seated, my father led us in a prayer of thanks. Upon its conclusion Mom said, "Everyone should know that Pamela cooked dinner tonight."

My father looked at my mother in bewilderment, before peering at the dish before him. "Really? Well, thank you, dear."

"You're welcome," I said. I looked into his eyes, trying to telepathically tell him—if such a thing was even possible—why I had. I couldn't tell if he understood. His face seemed almost devoid of emotion. He looked tired all the time now, his dusky, freckled skin rough.

"Did you get the mixer working again?" Mom said. "Oh, Isambard, mind your shirt."

"Yes, dear. It was just the cord." Dad took a bite of his meal and chewed it slowly. "This is actually very . . . good," he offered, a cough mangling the final word. His eyes darted to mine and away again guiltily.

Review accepted. Glancing at my own food, I wondered if I even wanted to try it.

"Yet another reason to be proud of her. Here, Isambard, try a bite."

"Mom, you know the rules," Issy said, his nose wrinkling. "No meat."

"Well, I honestly think those are more like *guidelines,* dear."

My mind wandered as everyone engaged in the usual chatter, my fork twirling in my food.

It was only the sudden explosion outside that recalled my attention.

All conversation ceased. Even Jenny went silent and turned her face up to the ceiling. I wasn't sure what we'd just heard—it sounded like muted cannon fire. My heart started picking up, and

I laid my hand over it, as if it were a distressed baby animal I could comfort with my touch.

"What was that?" Issy asked.

"Nothing," Dad said. He helped himself to the tiniest second helping of casserole. "Had quite a few party orders this week. Likely some fair assembly is enjoying fireworks. I can't believe people are trying to carry on with the Season as if nothing's happened."

Yes. Yes, I could accept that. I'd *make* myself accept that.

"I want to see fireworks!" Jenny demanded.

Recovering, I rose and placed my napkin beside my plate. "May I take her?"

My father nodded. "Of course. You should be able to see from the front window. Don't go outside."

I released Jenny from her chair and picked her up. She weighed so close to nothing, it was heartbreaking. Isambard accompanied me as I carried her to the parlor and opened the window. "They'll be up in the sky, Jenny-bear. Like stars come to visit us."

We watched the sky expectantly. I didn't see any fireworks, though, nor did I hear any further explosions. "Maybe they just sent up one," Isambard said. I could hear the disappointment in his voice. "That'd be weird, though."

"Noooo, want to see fireworks!" Jenny started pounding her fist on my shoulder, and I captured her hand in mine to prevent her from continuing.

My phone started to ring in my pocket, and I curved my hip out slightly. "Isambard, can you get that?"

He reached into the deep pocket of my dress as I struggled with Jenny, drawing out my pink cat-shaped cell phone and opening it. "It's Nora. Hello, Miss Dearly," he said as he lifted the phone to his ear. He suddenly pulled it back and made a face, and I could hear her shouting on the other end.

Letting go of Jenny, who curled her freed hand into my hair, I took the phone. "Nora?"

"Pamma! Did you hear that explosion?" She was out of breath.

"Yes, just now. What was it?"

"I have no idea! But someone just stole our bloody carriage! *From us.* As in, we were *in it*!"

I pulled the phone away from my ear and stared at it. Isambard gave me an inquisitive look.

"Go get Dad and tell him we need money for a cab," I said, trying my best to sound authoritative and in control, like a big sister should. I moved to set Jenny on her feet before I dropped her. My arms were starting to shake uncontrollably.

Oh, God, not again.

5 • Nora

I was grounded.

This shouldn't have fazed me, after all the running for my life and shooting at things I'd been known to engage in, but still—*grounded!*

At first I was almost pleased that my most recent brush with death had been enough to get my father to talk to me like a civilized human being. We called the house once we were on our way there. When the Roes dropped us off, Papa was waiting in the foyer with Dr. Chase, and they both came forward at once. As Papa took me in his arms I could feel how hard he was fighting to keep his own dead weight upright, and I instantly forgave him for his earlier outburst.

While my father directed my head so he could look at my cheek, I trained my eyes on Pamela's. "It's okay," I said, for about the twentieth time.

Pam gave me a reproachful look. She wasn't buying what I was selling. She always could pick up on my lies, white or black. "I told you not to wander off without telling anybody," she said. She sent Bram a frigid glance. "I thought you would *listen.*"

Before I could say anything, Papa took over. "I feel that I ought to be the one addressing that issue." His voice reminded me of the few times in my childhood I'd managed to get myself into serious trouble—or what seemed like serious trouble at the time. The time I'd "run away," getting as far as the train station with my doll and a pocketknife before being caught. The time I'd put a handprint in every lemon tart in Mr. Roe's bakery after taking the "if you touch it, you must take it" rule of party food too far.

"I'm sorry," I said, taking the Voice seriously. "I really am."

Bram spoke up, moving to stand behind me. "I took her. It's my fault. I'm sorry—for the carriage, everything. This guy in a mask broke the window, and I figured I could take him . . . but then his buddies showed up. There were four of them. I had a gun, but at that point I just didn't want to get taken out and leave Nora to handle them. It all happened so fast." I could hear the regret in his voice, and I knew it wasn't just for the loss of the carriage. The hijackers had won without firing a shot. That didn't just anger him, it angered me. Made me feel even more powerless.

My father shook his head. "No. You did the right thing in giving it up. A carriage is not worth shooting people over."

Pamela's gloves were fast becoming wrinkled rags, the way she kept tugging them back and forth. "Dr. Dearly, the horrid man who did it called Nora a nec—" I shot her the very best "I love you, but shut up" look I could muster. Pam got it and complied with a heavy sigh.

"Dr. Dearly, if I may," Mr. Roe said. "From what the police told Mr. Griswold, it seems there's a new wave of living people attempting to flee the city. The constables said it was likely the culprits wanted the carriage for that reason."

"You've already reported it to the police?"

"We were a block away from a police station when it happened," I said. "I only called the Roes because we were closer to them than the EF."

Papa took off his glasses, his right hand shaking ever so slightly. His left remained gripped on my shoulder. "I assume this latest exodus is related to the news about Patient One?"

"Probably," Bram said. "And the wireless news in the cab said someone set off a pipe bomb, too. Just left it in an empty alley. No one was hurt, thankfully."

"Only a few doors down from us," Mr. Roe added. "We heard it shortly before Miss Dearly called."

"I see." Papa's hand tightened on my shoulder. "Mr. Roe, thank you for coming to my daughter's aid. If you would send me a note telling me how much the cab cost, I'll happily pay you back for it. Dr. Chase, if you could see Mr. Roe and his daughter out, I'd be much obliged."

Mr. Roe offered a hand to Pamela. "Of course. My pleasure. Good evening, everyone."

Pamela bit her lower lip and came forward to hug me. "Call me tomorrow, okay?"

I hugged her back tightly. "Promise."

Once they were gone, my father turned me around where I stood. "We need to have a chat. Let's go to my room, shall we?"

This was Not Good.

"Sir," Bram interjected, "maybe before you do that we should get the whole house together, talk about what we're going to do. What all of this means. At the very least, with Elpinoy gone, we're down two carriages. We've only got two left for the household to use. Three, if Evola will let us keep his here."

Papa leveled a look at Bram. "Yes. I'll deal with that and *you* later. But right now, I need to speak to my daughter."

I cast a beseeching look at Bram, but didn't have time to say anything. Papa marched me in front of him, up the stairs and down the hall. He opened the door to his bedchamber for me, and I entered reluctantly, as if I could delay what was to come. Only a few times in my life had my father been truly angry with me—more often he had humored me in everything.

He shut the door and leaned on it. "I don't know where to begin."

"Papa, we didn't *mean* to find trouble. It sort of just . . . happened."

He fumbled for the light switch on the wall beside the door. As he stood there before me, slightly bent over, his arm stabbing uselessly into the air behind him, I found myself seeing him for what he truly was—not a weary, scarred man, but a member of the living dead, reborn and different. So often I dealt with him as someone I'd never expected to have a few extra years with, all the while ignoring the fact that those years were going to be so short.

In the end I was going to lose him, too. Again.

This, along with the fact that I'd just had a gun pointed at my face, muted my usual temper. As he turned the lights on, I folded my hands together behind my back, ready to listen. I had no idea what was coming, but I'd listen.

"What did the thief call you?" my father inquired. "Miss Roe began to tell us—what was it?"

Recollection of the term filled me with an oozing, disgusting sense of shame. "A . . . necroslut." I'd never heard the term before, but I could guess what was being implied.

Dad gripped his hands tightly about the handle of his cane. "What else?"

"We got out. We told them we didn't want any trouble." I hated even thinking about it. "One of them told me I should be ashamed for siding with the dead. That's why they were taking our carriage. They were using something to change their voices, it was weird. Then they drove away."

Papa didn't say anything. I didn't like how cold he was—far

better he should treat me as he had before. "We weren't *doing* anything," I stressed. "We were just sitting there."

He held up a hand to shush me. "I'm not blaming you—and when the police find that man, I will punch his teeth back into his throat for what he said. But Bram shouldn't have driven you out alone at night. I trust him with my life, I admire him, but he is still courting my undebuted, *underage* daughter. Heavens, compared to other parents, I let you both get away with murder—but the line must be drawn somewhere."

"It's not his fault. You upset me." My voice threatened to tighten, to rise, and I fought to keep my tone somewhat reasonable. "We weren't going out to neck somewhere. He knew I needed room to breathe. To think. I've been cooped up—"

"I realize that. And I realize etiquette is not the real issue here." Papa moved past me, and I stepped aside to make room for him and his cane. He sat on the edge of his bed. "The real issue is your safety. Which is why I intend to send you to Belize. To your relatives."

This statement sent my train of thought careening off the rails. If he'd just said he planned to sequester me in a diving bell until I came of age at twenty-one, it would have made more sense. "What?"

All at once my father's control disappeared. He slumped, his voice weakening. "It's the only way."

I stepped forward, my cheeks heating. It was Cyprian's all over again. He'd rushed me off to boarding school, never giving me a choice, never explaining why—because he'd unintentionally infected my mother, turning her into a host. "No. I don't even know anything about them. I've never met them in my life."

"Nora—"

"Because they *disowned* you for marrying Mama!" That was the only bit of ammo I had, literally the only thing I knew about my father's family, so I tried to deliver it with all the frustration and anger currently in me. "I won't go. And that's the thing. I know how upset you are, how serious all of this is, so I've tried to be a dutiful daughter of late—but I can't hide forever! And you need to stop avoiding me, keeping things from me!"

"'Keeping things'?" Papa's eyes glinted, and he dug into his waistcoat, drawing out his plain black cell phone. "I know you've been trying to call me. Do you know why your calls keep getting bounced?" He raised the volume, and I blinked. The thing was ringing. Had it been ringing all this time?

Papa punched a series of buttons angrily with his thumb, and hurled the phone to the bed. It was his voice mailbox.

"I know you created this plague. I know where you live, Dearly. It's easy enough to find things on the Aethernet."

"You should burn in hell. You should be forced to watch every part of your body go through a meat grinder while you look at a photograph of my son. My son didn't deserve to die, you rotting son of a bitch!"

There were dozens of such messages, each one vile. At the end I barely found it in me to say, "Where did they get all of these ideas?"

"Pundits? Misinformation on the news? Who knows. Someone found my number, published it on the Aethernet." Papa collected his phone. "Do you see why I worry?"

"I'm sorry." Things made more sense now. Still, I said, "But Papa—if anything, this means you should leave."

"I can't. I can't leave my work. My teams."

"*Exactly.* If we all go together, that's one thing, but I can't leave everyone. *You.* If things get bad again, I have to help. Don't you see? I don't want to be a soldier, but I still want to *do* something with my life. I'm not a little girl anymore."

"And you're far from a woman." My father shook his head. "I just want you to see that there's a difference between being able to defend yourself and actually inviting tragedy into your life by

acting recklessly. The carriage thieves were obviously opportun-
ists, but people have used you to get to me before. I won't let
that happen again."

"Papa . . ." I pushed my hair back in aggravation. "Papa, it's
not like I'm normal, okay? I live in a house with a bunch of walking dead people. I'm wrapped up in the whole thing. You can't
expect me to live as if nothing out of the ordinary has happened
to me. When I was a child you always let me be myself, let me do
my own thing."

"It was safe to do so then. And I thought you were no longer
a child." My father flexed his hands angrily around his cane. "The
world has changed forever, Nora—changed, and not changed at
all. Even if the dead *weren't* walking the streets, do you think I'd
let you run about like some parentless foundling? At your age?"

"Are you even listening to yourself? I'm not going to say the
H-word, but I'm going to imply it by staring at you *reeeeally* hard
right now."

"I *am* being hypocritical, it's true. I know I'm the last person
who should lecture anyone about being impulsive. But you are
my daughter." He slowly relaxed his hands. "And you're the only
real family I have left."

Had he given up on finding Aunt Gene alive, then? Sobering,
I walked over and sat beside him. He pulled me to his side and I
leaned against him and shut my eyes, relief flooding into me at
this simple display of affection. Sometimes my feelings about my
father confused me. When I'd thought him truly dead, I wanted
him back more than anything. Now I needed him, and I didn't
need him. I wanted his attention, and didn't want it.

"I'm sorry if I frightened you earlier, or hurt you." He set his
cane aside. "I'm so exhausted I'm almost unfeeling now."

"Frightened" wasn't the right word for it, but I decided not to
make a scene. In the moment, he'd been hotheaded and unthink-

ing; now he seemed in control. "What Elpinoy said—do you really think you're to blame for the plague?"

Papa stroked my hair. "It's a hard thought to shake, yes."

"But it isn't your fault." I looked at him. "If you'd killed the zombies that showed up all those years ago, instead of helping them, studying them . . . then I wouldn't have this little bit of time with you. I wouldn't have Bram—I never would have *met* him."

"I know. It's just . . . scary. Scary, the idea that this illness might continue. Might change, and change, until it's conquered the globe."

"Papa, I'm scared, too. But I can't live like this either. Everything's different."

Papa was quiet for a moment. "I know it's difficult."

"I was happy to help organize the house when we arrived here, get everyone settled, but I don't want that to be the only thing I do. And studying? Seriously? I should be helping you. Or doing something to help the zombies in the Morgue, or—"

"No. I forbid you to visit that place. It's dangerous. You should see some of the injuries that come from there." He sighed. "Nora, I just don't want you to become so obsessed with the present that you can't see the future. That is my great sin. It shouldn't be yours."

Looking down at the carpet, I took a breath. Because I knew what he meant. A future without most of the people I currently loved.

"Our situation is very tenuous. As you've now heard." He removed his glasses. "We need to try to fit back into society. We have the right to exist, to carry on with our lives, but we are also blessed with the wisdom to know when to lay low. That doesn't mean I don't trust you. That doesn't mean I don't respect your need to fight. I just want you to think more than I do." He pointed at the sagging skin of his face, and then knocked his metal leg. "Look at what my mistakes have cost me."

Instead of saying anything, I nodded. I could see the truth behind half his arguments, and with the other half I wasn't getting anywhere.

"Now, I'm going to take your advice and get some rest. Then I'll head back to the lab and get to work."

"Without Dr. Elpinoy?"

"Oh . . ." Dad let off an annoyed tongue-pop, and rose to see me to the door. "By the way," he said as I entered the hall, "you're grounded for a week."

I spun around and glared at him. *"What?"*

He lifted his cane, touching the end of it to my chin. I batted it away. "You won't move elsewhere, so you're grounded. I don't even want you out in the EF. I want you to remain here in the house where you're safe, until some sort of order is restored in the streets. Then we'll talk about how you can help."

"But we don't have that long. What about those masked freaks? We should go after them!"

"You're a smart and independent young lady, Nora, and I would have it no other way. But it is *not* your duty to save the world. And if you won't opt to remain safe, I'm not above *forcing* you to remain safe."

That did it. "I think you lost your right to ground me when you faked your own death. Just saying."

He lifted an eyebrow. "Do you want to make it two weeks?"

I could have broken him down. I could have reminded him how his secrecy about the undead had taken my mother from me and almost gotten me killed. I could have reminded him how he'd abandoned me instead of telling me the truth, and how this translated into his having—in theory—about zero authority over me.

But I also knew he already blamed himself for all of those

things. I couldn't be that cruel. I'd already taken him to task; I didn't need to do it again.

"Besides, I have a project you can work on." He stepped back, so I could better see into his room. Rows of brown cardboard boxes were arranged along the far wall. "Do you know what's contained in those boxes?"

"Information about Aunt Gene." He'd been making various inquiries for months. As a show of goodwill I added, "Sir."

"Exactly. Go through them again and see if I've missed something. That top one contains information for my lawyer. If we ever find out what happened to her, and it turns out the Allisters lied . . . I want to string them high." His eyes narrowed. "I don't trust Lord Allister."

I didn't understand this, but I knew I didn't trust his son. According to him, my aunt had been with his parents when the Siege struck. "That makes two of us."

"Good. You can start in the morning. You can actually do some homework, too. You *will* complete your education. Now, go get someone to stitch up your cheek. Good night, NoNo."

Instead of doing so, I curtsied and marched to my bedroom. Once there I proceeded to terrify a few cats by digging out my collapsible scythe, the morbid entrenchment tool Samedi had built, from under the bed to practice with. I meant to tire myself out so I could sleep. I wasn't worried about the cut on my cheek; it wasn't that bad. I had bigger things to worry about. The city, my father, Bram . . .

A second later the tingle of apprehension these ideas caused blew up, fanning out into an anger so profound it was almost comforting. It wasn't the last straw—it was the last gallon of kerosene. I started swinging the double-ended scythe at nothing in particular, in time with my furious thoughts. Then, panting, I hurled my weapon against the wall and sat down. I drew my knees up under my skirt and wrapped my arms about them, be-

fore hiding my face in the cool folds of fabric. Even if I was immune to the new strain, that didn't mean I was special. All things
considered, I was just as vulnerable as the next person. The same
as anyone else. No better. No safer.

And grounded. *Pfft.* I thought I'd left things like that behind
with knee-length skirts and pigtails.

I fervently wished I were back in the jungle, with Bram at my
side—a messed-up version of Tarzan and Jane. Innocent, in a
way. Primed for adventure. Free.

My version of safe.

6 • Laura

"Once upon a time, there was a pretty little girl named Calendula," I whispered as I drilled my fingernails into my own flesh.

It didn't hurt.

I'd been picking for hours at the tips of my shoulders and finally managed to scrape out enough skin to create little divots. Slowly, carefully, I began to worm my index fingers inside— deeper, deeper. I looked to my right and watched my nail cutting the flesh, my cuticle disappearing, the wormlike wiggling of my fingertip beneath my skin. Beside me in the living room loft, Dog laid his head on my pile of water-stained fairy-tale books and princess novels, sadly stroking his new wrist stump.

Below us, people were shouting.

"Fourteen!" Claudia yelled. "Fourteen zombies killed or arrested today! Arrested . . . *pah*. We all know the living will execute them in the end. The only reason they're still alive is because of those zombies on the docks!"

"Who were working with the *living* to aid us." Mártira's voice was full of pain. "There was no reason for what happened today. None."

"None? They attacked because they were in danger. They used the weapons they had. They did what zombies *do*!"

"You say that as if it's a *good thing*, Claudia. The dead can make the choice not to attack the living, if they're still capable of making choices. We can *help* them make that choice."

"Hagens is still out there," someone else said; a safecracker named Joe. "Other people are still out there. And all of this was caused by Smoke? That slimy pyromaniac? What if they do trace him back to us, come lookin' for more info about him? Or think the rest of us have that new strain, too? Wipe us out?"

"Exactly!" Claudia said.

"All because you'll take in any stray zombie what comes." Joe sounded exasperated. "Like they're hungry kittens."

In the loft, Dog moved closer to me. I wasn't sure if it was in response to the mention of Hagens or Smoke—we both feared the former, but only Dog disliked the latter. About a month ago Smoke, mostly silent and horribly rotted, had followed Mártira back to the den after one of her first free clinic attempts in the Morgue, along with a handful of other homeless zombies. Hagens found us soon after. I'd thought him frightening only in appearance until hearing about how he lashed out during the riot, and still found it difficult to conceive of the poor man as evil. True, now we knew that a different sort of sickness had made him, but he never *seemed* different. He'd been quiet. Maybe a little secretive. And there was nothing wrong with that.

We all had our secrets.

Sliding my fingers back out—my flesh suckled at them—and patting Dog's side, I reached for the packet of seeds sitting on my bedroll. A *whole* packet—a gift from Abuelo, who found it in the trash. Amazing what people threw away.

"Forget Smoke," Claudia said. "Mártira, because of you, the core of our gang has survived. You talked about us being an all-zombie gang before, a force to be reckoned with." Her voice cut through the air. "We can't continue to take in orphans and raise money to throw away on water. If we're going to make a difference, we have to step it up. They're attacking our people! We should strike back, like we used to!"

"They don't mean you," I assured Dog as I tore open the packet with my teeth, then shook out a few of the precious little seeds. Carefully, I placed four seeds each in the shallow furrows I'd created in my shoulders.

"We're not talking about this now," Mártira said. "Not until everyone has been found and settled. And to think, discussing things like this where Laura and the other children can hear . . ."

"Those *children* used to steal for you. Laura is fifteen," Claudia argued. "I was robbing houses at fifteen. You always shield her from everything!"

With that, I heard steps on the ladder that led to the loft. Claudia was coming, and that meant I had to work quickly. Willing myself into the shadows, I shoved the seed packet beneath my pillow and caressed my shoulders, urging my skin to resume clinging to my flesh. I'd water the holes later.

"Laura? Are you up here?" She sounded cross. And closer.

Drawing the shoulders of my gown up and pushing my hair forward, I answered, "Yes?"

My sister climbed into the loft and wrenched aside the black netting I'd draped between her side and mine. Death had made Claudia hideous, her face strangely softened and filled with decaying blood. She looked like an old woman rather than the eighteen-year-old she was. "What are you doing?" she asked, her voice hoarse. Dog edged away from her.

"Dressing," I told her as my hands went instinctively, protectively across my chest. Claudia always destroyed whatever I grew, and so now I kept my plants close to me, let them root themselves in my very body. Myrtle at my wrists, ivy at my hips, roses at my waist, and soon, calendula on my shoulders.

I was no longer alive, but I might help something else to live.

Claudia's eyes moved over my body, her upper lip curling. They then darted up to the little wooden shelf above my bedroll where I kept my few belongings. Inwardly I cringed, knowing what was to come.

I'd forgotten to hide them.

She reached over me, grabbing two chipped terra-cotta pots from my shelf. Each held a handful of sandy earth swept from the street and a struggling seedling. Before I could plead for their lives, down they went. One smashed apart on the floor below, the other hit someone. "Hey!"

"I've told you ten thousand times—if you're going to sell flowers, you steal them from toffs' gardens. You don't *grow* them! You're a flower girl, not a farmer!"

Dog hid behind me, and I sent back a hand to comfort him. "But stealing is wrong, Claudia."

"Not for people like us. It's how we survive. It's only because Mártira coddles you that you get away with such pathetic work." She smacked the wall. "If our parents'd thought about how 'wrong' it was to steal, you'd've been a corpse years ago. You'd've starved in infancy!"

I'd heard this argument before. My father had been a road agent, preying on travelers outside New London. He and my mother were in prison—had been since I was ten. He was the reason Mártira set up shop in the city. He'd told her to be smarter than him. Get other people to steal for her.

I took a different tack. "If they'd done right, they wouldn't be away from us now."

"Oh, shut up! I'd yank out the things growing *in* you if I didn't think your intestines would come with them." Claudia rolled back onto her blankets, glaring at the ceiling. "Get out of here!"

I obeyed, shimmying my way onto the ladder and helping Dog

mount it above me, doing my best to support him as he learned how to climb down with one hand. The Grave House on Ramee Street was large, a dilapidated and abandoned old place, its dirty rooms smoky and mostly devoid of furniture, but nonetheless overly crowded with people. It was located in the run-down northwest section of New London, the part most New Victorians liked to forget about—the slums where children begged and charity workers cringed and aristocrats never ventured. Once, it had only been our center of operations, our main den. Now it was all we had, even if it couldn't fit everybody.

Taking Dog by the hand, I wove my way over the warped wooden floor, past tables crammed with card sharps and beggars and pickpockets and frightened ordinary folks, most of them gambling to pass the time. In the corner, one of the street performers was sawing away on his fiddle, the tune horribly cheery in the face of all that had happened. A few people laughed; a few people cried. Everyone appeared ill at ease. A group of streetwalkers, now forever out of work, were gathered about the filthy front windows smoking cheroots, ashes raining on their colorful skirts.

Near the fireplace where Smoke had often sat, burning small objects on the hearth for his own quiet amusement, I found my eldest sister. When confronted with her, my first instinct was to stare, as always. Mártira's skin was smooth, the color of new parchment. Not a single wound marred her flesh, and her only blemishes were the many black veins that seemed to crawl through her skin like cracks in a piece of fine pottery. Her hair hung to her waist; her black eyes were clear, like chips of obsidian, her lashes so long and dense that the whites were often shaded. She moved with a spectacularly disturbing grace, like a mermaid dancing in the oily River Styx.

To think, I'd created such a thing.

"Mártira?"

She looked at me and smiled. "Laura. Dog." She spread her arms. She didn't have to say anything more; I flew to them. Wrapping me up, she kissed me and told me, "It'll be all right, dove."

"Are you all right, though?"

"Yes. We'll recover from this. It's just been a day of disappointment and pain . . ." She let go of me, and Dog moved to my side. Looking at him, Mártira said, "I'm so sorry about your hand."

Dog shrugged. It might've been from fatigue, but I decided to say, "He's taking it like a man."

"Good." Mártira sighed. "I confess, I'm at a loss for what to do. But we'll figure out a way. We always have."

"If you need money . . . I don't think Claudia's found the last coin you gave me to hide for the gnomes." Leaving a penny for the gnomes that lived in Grave House was a bit of mummery from my childhood, one I still enjoyed. I'd grown up on Mártira's stories. The Rat King in the sewer who ate bad children, the gnomes that could be bribed to protect a thieves' den.

"No, dove. Leave it."

"She'll find it anyway. She always does."

Mártira smiled softly at me. "But perhaps she won't. Nothing is guaranteed. Anything, anyone, can change."

For the first time since that morning, I smiled. Mártira was my only protector, and the only one I needed. She'd opted to join me in my condition back in December; she wouldn't even abandon me to the jaws of death. She was going to turn her life around, my life around. I had to believe in her.

I heard the door opening, a new wave of voices. "Hagens!" Claudia shouted.

My belly tightened and I quickly ushered Dog behind Mártira. We moved just in time. Soon the crowd was parting to let Maria Hagens and a few other zombies through. They looked like they'd been through hell, and they moved toward the fireplace without hesitation.

Hagens terrified me. Everything about her was sharp—her eyes, her voice, her short hair. She'd served in a zombie-only army company before joining up with us, and looking at her, you could believe she might have a pile of human skulls saved up somewhere, horrible war trophies. Her features were angular, her eyes hard. Her exposed cheekbones glowed in the firelight like ossified war paint.

"You made it!" Mártira cried. "Thank God!"

"God, maybe. You, no." Hagens cut her eyes at me momentarily. Claudia soon appeared at her side, gazing up at her almost adoringly. "But maybe I shouldn't snap at you right off the bat. Maybe today was the object lesson it should have been."

"I don't know what you're talking about. I'm just glad you're safe."

"I *told* her," Claudia said. "I told her we should have gone out to find you."

Hagens moved closer to Mártira, her expression growing even more furious. "Let me put it this way, in words that'll be real easy to understand. You're out of chances. We have to show the humans that we are not to be trifled with, or they will *keep doing this.* You—"

"Cicatriz! Your gang better reach for the sky!"

At the sound of the voice calling from outside, the newcomers started to panic and the old-timers did their best to hush them up. Several men lifted sections of the floor and tossed their bottles and weapons within, while others moved closer to the half-boarded front windows, on alert. One looked at my eldest sister and nodded.

Mártira took a moment to compose herself, then brushed past Hagens. "We'll discuss this later." She made her way to the door and stepped out onto the front porch. I followed, Dog at my heels.

Outside in the darkness stood twenty living constables, guns at the ready. Heading up the group was a dark-haired man with the intense blue eyes of a husky dog. I'd hoped I'd never see him again.

"Inspector Ramirez," Mártira said, moving forward. "It's been a while. I expected you before now."

"Yeah, well. End of the world and all that." He looked Mártira up and down. "Death's been good to you, Márta."

"You're too kind." For once, my sister didn't sound hopeful or wistful. She was all business. "I'll save you some words. If you're looking for your protection money, we don't have it."

"Because you spent it on swill," Claudia muttered, moving to join us.

"And we likely won't again," Mártira said, eyeing Claudia. "We're turning over a new leaf."

Ramirez glanced past us into the house, sizing up the situation. His fingers tightened uneasily around his gun, while the men behind him remained labile and anxious, ready to bolt at a moment's notice. "Honestly, I heard your entire gang was killed. I'm surprised to see so many of you."

"You probably heard that the Grave House Gang is no more, which is true. Maybe a quarter of the old group reanimated, and a quarter of that number well. We're about fifty original members, forty newcomers. Some from other gangs, some not."

"Well, that's a shame." Ramirez looked at me as I lowered my arms to hold Dog, and then back to my sister. "Especially after today, when it'd be right easy to tell my boss you're harboring more crazies. Saw some of your people in the cage. Realized a visit was long overdue." As he spoke, several members of his crew backed up, as if expecting us to attack.

"Even if I wanted to give you your money, I couldn't," Mártira said. "The beggars are making less because the living don't think they need money for food. The whores are out of work, naturally. The street performers have had to start wearing masks and gloves when they can, even the ones that don't normally dress up. And they've been going out without the pickpockets, because I will no longer accept money from illegal act—"

"So your people are still going out?" Ramirez tipped his hat back a bit, his smile slow. "You know they can't work on the streets for free. That's not the deal."

"The deal changed the minute you died," I heard Hagens hiss. I didn't dare turn around to look at her. "We can take them."

Mártira ignored her. "Fine," she said to Ramirez. "Give us a few weeks."

"They want to question you guys about today. That's why I rushed over here."

"Give us a few weeks, keep the coppers off our backs—I'll pay you double."

"No!" Hagens protested—all for naught. After a moment's contemplation, Ramirez nodded his agreement. He and his men retreated into their LED-festooned police carriages, and we retreated into our den. It was over in seconds. Like usual.

"Double?" whined Joe. "We're gonna have to get back to hittin' businesses."

"This is what I'm talking about," Hagens shouted once the door was shut. "You have no reason to submit to that slimeball, none! He's a human, he's weak. We have sharper senses than the humans, we have the ability to infect them if they're not vaccinated or the vaccine doesn't work . . . He should be groveling on the ground, begging you to spare his life."

"Miss Hagens, hush."

Mártira moved through the crowd, back to the fireplace. As she passed a few of the older gang members, they mumbled things to her. I caught one saying, "For a moment, you sounded like the old you."

"Like hell will I *hush*!" Hagens pushed her way after us. "Twice now—*twice*—humans have hunted me through the streets like an animal! I'm not standing for it anymore. I've been telling you for *weeks* that we have to leave! Regroup somewhere safe, make some plans!"

"Suit yourself, Miss Hagens. I am not having my people attack a group of living coppers. All that would do is get every single one of us killed." Mártira frowned. "Remember, for all your blustering, you're clean. We're not. Even now, we need to avoid undue attention. Same reason I knew we couldn't tell the people we met today everything we know, even though we should've."

Hagens didn't even pretend to listen to her. "Oh, I'm leaving. And I'll take anyone who wants to go with me. I know not everyone here is content to pay to play humanitarian. Some of us want to do *more*. And if that involves violence, so be it."

Mártira spun around and snapped, "Do *none* of you hate your past lives the way I do? Has death filled *none* of you with regret? A desire to change?"

Her questions hung unanswered in the air. In time, a few of the older gang members shook their heads to indicate that no, death had had no such effect on them. Then a few more. Mártira's expression stiffened. Claudia glared at me, as if I'd somehow infected my eldest sister with my ideas of right and wrong.

Perhaps I had.

"They have the right of it," Hagens said. "There's no shame in doing what you have to do to survive. *Thrive.* From everything I hear, you knew that once—and you were damn good at it."

She was right. I knew there were people out there who still feared my sister because of the things she'd done before she died. That was half the reason she was still our leader now. I was grateful to be ignorant of the details.

And yet, I wasn't so ignorant that I didn't feel the cold crush of fear. If Mártira was cast down as leader, what would happen to us?

After a time, Mártira asked, "Who would go with Hagens? Leave the city?"

Claudia said, "If we're calling a vote, the leaders have to—"

"Enough! Who would leave?" Mártira shouted. "Tell me now!"

About half the gang raised their hands. One of the street-walkers came forth and said, "They chased us, ma'am. They meant to kill us. You ask me, it's crazy you want to stay! What if they pin Smoke on us, like Joe said?" A hum of approval punctuated the end of her sentence.

"Smoke?" Hagens said. For a split second I couldn't tell if it was fear or fury I saw in her eyes. "What about Smoke? Has something happened to him? Where is he?"

Mártira looked to the crackling fire, her movements slow. She ignored Hagens's questions. "Very well. Then *I* will take you. We'll leave tonight." She lifted her head, turning her black eyes on Hagens. "But we will not act out of anger. Not anymore."

Hagens stared hard at Mártira before rolling her shoulders and catching Claudia by the arm. "You will soon, if you're smart." Hagens turned her back on us, dragging Claudia along. "Soon enough, you will."

7 • michael

"Lord Allishter?" my father's mistress asked as she stumbled into the pool of pale morning sunlight designed to fall—through the magic of custom architecture—directly on my faux ivory desk. I took my breakfast on a silver tray there every morning. "Oops, wrong Allishter!" She giggled. "Wrong bedchamber!"

"Miss Perdido," I said, squinting up at her. Catherine "Coco" Perdido was highly beautiful—and at the moment, apparently highly intoxicated. The young woman's fat honey-brown curls, which had no doubt been arranged becomingly around her heart-shaped face the night before, were drooping, and her kohl-smudged eyes were narrowed against the light. "Do come in. Wouldn't do to have the servants see you."

"Oh! Kind opf you. Very dutiful son, you are. Sh'know, while I'm here, I wanted to ashk you . . ." The woman shut the door, turned the lock, and instantly sobered up. "You left a note behind the loose wainscoting again?"

"I did." I paused, because I was honestly too exhausted to elaborate yet. I'd gotten my mask off and hidden mere moments before her arrival. I was dirty and my muscles ached and my thoughts were consumed by just how much time had been wasted

last night, just how much money pissed away—and all for nothing.

I was taking too many risks. More than I'd planned on. This
couldn't be all for nothing.

Coco didn't prod me. She tossed her valise upon the Turkish
carpet and collapsed into one of the overstuffed green velvet arm-
chairs flanking the whitewashed fireplace, fussing with her hair.
She'd thrown a tan duster over her sparkling black evening gown,
but the garment still clashed against the forest-and-cream décor
of my suite.

"Question." I leaned forward. "When you deliver my notes,
do you make *sure* they go precisely where I tell you? The Silver
Bridle pub in La Rosa, yes?"

"I follow your instructions to the letter. If you actually put
names on them instead of numbers, I could try to get them into
someone's hands, but . . ." Coco shrugged. "I'm not usually
invited into the best houses, now, am I?"

"You can get into any house you like, Miss Perdido," I informed her, doing my best to keep my temper in check.

"How?" she snorted.

"The same way you got into this one. I believe, to put it in-
delicately, that the keys to the castle are kept between your legs."

Coco's eyes opened fully. "I won't be talked to like that! I
might be a—a—"

"Prostitute?" I tried, helpfully. "Former two-penny actress?"

Twisted with rage though her features became, she was still
sublimely beautiful. My father never employed less than the best.
He'd kept a mistress as long as I could remember, and I'd never
had cause to dislike any of them. They'd played with me when I
was a child, told me how handsome I was as a youngster, and
now treated me to kind and deferential conversation. Although
their continued youth was beginning to disturb me, somewhat.
Coco looked young enough to be my sister.

"*Lord Allister's* mistress! I'm an honest woman." She stood and picked up her valise. "You know what? Deliver your own damn letters. I don't even see why you bother with paper notes, you obsessive little freak. Write your friends emails like a normal boy, and never speak to me again. Or I'll tell your father everything!"

All at once, the fear I'd tried so hard to ignore all night burned through me. My father aside—without Coco I'd have to deliver the notes myself. *No.* That wasn't an option. I'd be spotted, or my carriage recognized. Everything would unravel. God damn it, I'd not spent the night riding around New London, watching ten thousand things go wrong, just to be talked back to and possibly unmasked by an overglorified whore!

I would not be humiliated again. Ever again.

As Coco started to storm out I gained my feet and caught her by the arm, twisting her around to face me. Boy though I might be, I was still taller than her, and able to squeeze her flesh till she released a cry of pain.

"Stupid," I told her. "What is it with mouthy, stupid women ruining my life lately?"

"Let go of me!"

"Not until we get a few things straight." I gripped her arm even tighter, and she dropped her bag. "First of all, you work for my father, you work for me. Or I'll tell him a pair of cuff links came up short, a silver knife—oh, the things you could be accused of taking. And a slut who steals is a slut who never works again." She opened her mouth, but I spoke first. "You think he'd side with you? You're nothing more than a plaything for him. Don't act like you're some king's pet, the balm for his loveless marriage. He makes you sneak in and out like a streetwalker. You are not his first pillow-warmer, and you certainly will not be his last. If I were you, I wouldn't jeopardize my chance to save up while my flesh is firm and the work is steady."

Coco's eyes rounded. Finally, she was listening.

"For your information, my parents have access to my email and Aethernet history now, and digital ghosts are hard to exorcise. Ashes tell no tales. Which is why I need you to shut your trap and continue to do what I pay you for, before I'm forced to . . . well. Have I made myself clear?"

It took a moment, but she nodded. "Please . . . don't. I have a little boy . . ."

"As long as he's not my illegitimate brother, I do not care." Releasing her and returning to my desk, I removed the day's mail from a bottom drawer. Five letters on honest-to-God parchment paper sealed with black wax stamped with a generic image of a raven, each bearing a series of random numbers in the top left corner. I slid them into a large envelope. "Your money is inside. Leave my mail behind the wainscoting when you come back tonight."

Coco regarded me suspiciously, but took the letters, sliding them into her bag as she retrieved it from the floor. "Anything else?" Her defeated voice cheered my mood considerably. When women just did what they were *told,* oh, how easy life became.

"That will be all, Miss Perdido. You may go." The woman did so, swiftly. You'd think I'd savaged her.

Once she was gone I realized I had no choice but to involve my father in some aspect of this after all.

My family was currently staying at Bestia del Oro, our country home in northeastern Honduras—close to the Talgua, or the Cave of the Glowing Skulls, an ancient pre-Colombian ossuary full of bones coated in light-reflecting calcite deposits. It was a territorial landmark, and nothing I wished to think about now that I'd seen the dead up and walking.

My father's library was located squarely in the middle of the building. The hallway leading there was lined with enormous windows on the eastern side, and long, horizontal flat screens in fanciful silver frames on the western. The screens were already on and tuned to the news, the sound muted. I could see the headlines reflected in the glass as I glanced outside, making out the shapes of other mansions in the morning mist.

ORIGINATOR OF MUTANT STRAIN OF LAZARUS MOVED TO DRIKE'S ISLAND

ARE MILITANT ZOMBIE GROUPS INEVITABLE?

PRIME MINISTER TO ADDRESS PARLIAMENT TODAY RE: UNDEAD

The sprawling white house at two o'clock was Éclatverre, the Minks' country retreat—oh, the conversations Vespertine Mink and I had had along her garden fence since our flight from New London. I spent a while contemplating them, before moving on. I wasn't looking forward to what I had to do.

When I came to my father's door, I knocked.

"Enter."

I did so, bowing the instant the door was closed. "Good morning, sir."

"Ah, my idiot son. Help yourself to a cup of tea." My father, Lord Leslie Allister, waved toward the large brass samovar in the center of the oval room. Not once did he divert his eyes from the thirty or forty floating displays surrounding him, a sectioned globe of light created by scores of tiny high-def holographic projectors located throughout the gilded library. Then, to the air he said, "Virtual rat batch 23-3.41, terminate testing, destroy file." One of the screens went black.

I tried to swallow the insult so casually tossed my way—like every morning since the Siege. "Experiment not going well?"

Dad shrugged. "Unassigned screen, access virtual rat batch 23-3.42. Rez and run at twenty-times speed." My father always appeared to take everything in stride, to calmly accept situations rather than emotionally oppose them. Despite the fact that he made everything look effortless, his face was creased, his sandy hair edging toward colorlessness, his eyes careworn.

I joined him in the middle of the sphere once I had a cup of tea. Along with NVIC and the usual financial channels, he was also keeping an eye on T-SPAN and footage from security cameras located within the Maria Bosawas-Allister Memorial Animal Preserve and Gene Bank, home of Allister Genetics, the source of the vast majority of our family fortune. Usually if one was both a lord and involved in business or industry, any professional titles were mere formalities, indicators of either inheritance or more than average investment—but my father actually worked for his paycheck, refusing to delegate, often micromanaging.

One of the cameras was following a group of hunters in the brush—new aristocracy, naturally. "People are still trying to squeeze more hunting in, even though the Season's supposedly under way." He frowned. "Computer, email relevant employees— ten more tigers in the vat by Tuesday. They always want to bag a bloody tiger. And after all that's happened."

"There were parties going on in New London last night," I told him. "Dregs presenting their girls to other dregs, most likely. Not even the walking dead could get the true blue-blooded deb- utantes to come out before May." The Season—when the rich and titled moved closer to New London and Parliament was in full swing—usually ran from March to August. Of course, the Siege had changed that. My family was not the only one reluctant to return to its house near the city, and Parliament had been in emergency session since December. Like my father, I was forced to conclude that those trying to engage in Seasonal activities were either stupid or suicidal. Or in denial.

"Hmm. Just behave yourself in town. I don't need a repeat

of that bit of stupidity with Miss Roe and Miss Dearly." His lip actually curled as he spoke the latter name. "I've told you for years that she's too much like her father. That she'd lead you to ruin."

"Yes, sir," I got out.

"Don't make me regret giving you a certain amount of latitude again. You will not get another chance."

His words cut, and for not the first time I wished I hadn't spilled my guts upon my return so many months ago. But I'd had so much to atone for. I didn't want to think about Roe, latitude, or sowing anything. Hell, my "friends" couldn't even get their orders straight so I could *sow* the freaking bomb where it was supposed to go. "Yes, well—"

"Quiet." Dad held up a hand. "Cue sound from screen showing T-SPAN."

Parliament was engaged in a new round of dead-related talks—and, as usual, those "talks" seemed to involve a lot of screaming, finger-pointing, and outright mockery. On the screen the PM, Lord Esteban Alba, stood at a podium. Since becoming Prime Minister back in December he'd started shedding his silvery hair, leading to the creation of an ever-increasing bald spot. "No. The suggestion by Lord Ashburn is not up for consideration—nor do I hope it will *ever* be. There is to be absolutely no talk of sending the undead to camps, receiving areas, or anything of the sort. Quarantine has *ended*."

Lord Cecil Khan, an earnest middle-aged man with skin like flawless brown book leather, jumped to his feet and declared, "With all due respect, Prime Minister—this is not an issue of civil rights. This is about keeping track of the diseased who walk among us!" Many on the floor cheered at this outburst.

One of the northern country MPs, Alejandro Meral, stood up and countered, "You're exactly right—and I urge you to think on that! What would you have us do, Lord Khan? Punish the *sick*?

The majority of the infected out there pose absolutely no danger to anyone. These are ill people, not monsters! Their families have spoken for them, even threatened to take up arms to defend them, and we ought to respect that."

Lord Khan stood up again and gestured with his digidiary at Meral. "They're destined to *become* monsters—don't lie!" He turned his attention back to the PM. "Point is, we ran the Punks off for doing little more than these dead scoundrels have done. We made a swift, forceful decision that undoubtedly saved us years of violence and heartbreak. We need to do the same thing here!"

"You're exaggerating!" cried Meral. "The Punks burned computerized factories, attacked the aristocracy, acted like mad neo-Luddites. People were murdered in cold blood. The dead who attacked the city were mindless, and a living man was responsible for them being there in the first place."

"What about the attacks at the port yesterday? Were those zombies 'sane' until they started biting?" yet another lord argued.

Lord John Ashburn rose. "We should quarantine them all in the Elysian Fields. The EF is mostly empty at this point—it's the safest place for them. At the very least, those gathered at Dahlia Park should be forced to move down there."

"Oh, yes!" yelled Meral. "Stick them underground. *Bury them alive!*"

Talk of the dead just made me angry now, but I did my best to listen rather than tune it all out. I hated to think about the fact that New London was swelling with zombies. I hated to think about the fact that the government, under Alba, was *protecting* them.

I hated to dwell on the idea of Miss Dearly still living in New London with a bunch of maggot men. With one maggot man in particular.

It didn't matter. She would soon learn the error of her ways. And Dad would never have to know about it.

"I want a job," I said. "Since school is still out."

Dad seemed genuinely surprised by this, and ordered the screen to mute before turning his piercing eyes on me. While I've always known my lot in life was to follow in my father's footsteps as owner, chairman, and CEO of his beloved company, I'd never before displayed real interest in anything having to do with Allister Genetics. I needed something to do with my days, though. An alibi. Especially if Coco decided to turn against me.

I needed something to deflect attention away from my nights.

Clearing my mind, I did my best to render my face as unreadable as possible. It's a skill of mine. When I was but a child I discovered the intense joy of hiding my true self and emotions from my parents, and then from my schoolmates at St. Arcadian's—learned about the freedom that comes from suppression. If no one knows your motives, if no one suspects you or even truly understands you, you can get away with anything.

"Is this about money?" he asked.

"No." I could get all the money I liked from my mother—a fact I decided not to remind my father of. Things were going so well. "I just want to continue to prove myself to you, my lord. To make up for sneaking away to help Miss Roe. I know now that it was not only stupid, but selfish of me. That my first concern should have been my family."

My father thought about this for quite a while, leaving me in suspense. "I think we can do that, then." He looked into my eyes. "Success takes effort, son. A willingness to work. I'm glad to see that trait in you. I know we've treated you harshly these last months, but as I said—you have one more chance. That alone should show you how much we love you."

"Yes, sir."

One of the screens in his globe flashed—an incoming call from my maternal uncle, and my father's closest friend, Lord Robert Cross. Turning away from me, Dad said, "Come back around eleven. We'll find something for you to do."

"Thank you," I said, bowing, and favoring him with a slight smile. I then returned to my room, my heart going a mile a minute. My father'd been surprisingly easy to deal with. Coco was good.

Now I just had to figure out how I was going to deal with everyone else.

8 • pamela

Isambard was dying, and I couldn't help him.

At the bottom of a coal bunker encrusted so thickly with soot that it felt like a forest floor, I held my little brother and wept because I couldn't help him. He was curled up in pain, and the most horrible thing was how tightly he tried to cling to me even as his body began to weaken—how hard he fought not to leave me. I wanted to scream at God and Evola and Coalhouse, wanted to rage and hurt and kill—*anything* to convince *someone* of the sheer unrelenting unfairness of it all, that a boy so willing to fight for his life stood absolutely no chance of winning.

But I couldn't help him.

Then we were in a lifeboat, one so flimsy that I felt certain we would sink like a stone into the choppy black sea if God forgot to hold us up. I covered Isambard with my body, praying without ceasing that the New Victorian troops wouldn't spot him, wouldn't shoot him, all because of what he had become.

Isambard begged for his mother. But I was not his mother, and I couldn't tell him what would become of her—not only because I was still crying so hard I couldn't speak, but because I didn't *know*.

"Mom! Mom!"

Suddenly I rocketed awake, gasping for air. My heart was racing, aching, my senses overwhelmingly sharp—the weight of my clammy nightgown like a thousand pinpricks, the air so heavy I felt like an artifact buried in clay. Even the darkness seemed to have color, my vision was so vivid.

"I'm safe," I chanted. It came out like a puppy's midnight cry for its mother. "I'm safe. I'm home. I'm safe." I tried to ignore the sound of my own heart, the sting in my chest, the tingling numbness running up and down my left arm. I knew it would go away eventually. I had to keep telling myself that.

As usual, I sought a distraction. I strained my hearing into the darkness, hoping I hadn't woken anyone up. I was always afraid the screams I heard in my dreams were my own—my imagination cannibalizing the very terror it created. I didn't want to frighten my parents. A small and selfish part of my soul craved their concern, but in the end I had to acknowledge that they'd been through hell, too. It was only right to try and make life as easy as I could for them. Even if I suffered for it.

Sometimes I felt stretched so thin that I wondered if there was anything left of me.

I didn't hear anything. Once I thought I could manage, I slowly climbed out of bed and stood there in the dark with goose bumps rising on my skin, balancing on my heels to keep my toes off the floor. How did Nora deal with this? She'd been through just as much as I had. How did she handle it?

Even though she'd been grounded a few days ago—not to mention the fact that my clock said it was 3:12 A.M.—I dug my phone out from under the pile of books on my vanity and sent her a message. I needed to talk to *someone.*

Is everything okay?

Yes. Are *you* okay? When I am definitely not?

Telling myself she wouldn't respond, I got to work changing my nightgown. The thought entered my head that I could go downstairs and have a taste of wine, but I dismissed it. I still felt guilty for using alcohol to get to sleep back in December.

My phone beeped. I jumped, before calming myself down and picking it up.

> Yeah. Are you? Trouble sleeping?

She was awake. I sat down on my bed and smiled a little. It meant a lot to me that she'd understood, even if she didn't know the whole story.

> Yes.

Her response was almost instantaneous.

> TELL ME ABOUT IT. ;P

I covered my mouth with my wrist to hide my laughter. I didn't have to respond; she kept texting. She was probably going insane in the house.

> Really, email me and tell me about it. Hid phone and di-
> gidiary under my mattress. Papa clueless.
> Dr. Chase snores. This is her: -_- o O (ZZZ)
> Can you come over and help me with the Gene thing this
> week? Papa might let you.
> 4 days and 20 hours. ;P Gotta hide phone again. <3

I put my own phone away and took a cleansing breath. "I'm safe. It's okay."

The squeaking of a hinge in the night argued against my mantra.

Gathering my nightgown off the floor, my heart ticking like an old clock, I tiptoed to the door to listen. Someone was walking the hallway outside, their footsteps scraping slowly in the direction of Isambard's room. Had I awoken Issy? Had he come to check on me and then retreated? He'd told me his hearing was much sharper now—that the Lazarus wanted him to stalk his prey by sight and sound and smell. Maybe he'd heard me talking to myself.

I knew exactly how to open my door so it wouldn't make any noise. Poking my head into the hall, I listened. If he was awake, I could talk to him.

But instead of Isambard's footfalls, I heard a voice. Mother's.

My beleaguered heart sinking, I walked toward Issy's room, keeping to the wall. Aside from Mom's voice the house was so still that I could hear the sticky sound made whenever one of my bare feet left the wooden floor.

Issy's door was open. I peered around the corner, holding my breath. Mom was standing over him as he slept, dead to the world. Her hands were held before her body, and her torso rocked back and forth on her hips like part of a hinged Punch and Judy doll.

"Heavenly Father, be merciful," I heard her whisper. "Heavenly Father, please, cure Isambard, I know You can cure him. I know You can bring him back to life, as You did Your son, Jesus. As You did the real Lazarus."

Cupping my hand around my mouth, I leaned away from the door and let my shoulder blades hug the wall. I willed myself not to cry.

"Death is nothing to You, Lord. I trust, I have faith. You are all powerful, all merciful." She was starting to sob, her words tangling in her mouth. "Please, cure my son, *please.*"

I couldn't take any more. I ran back to my room, my heels never touching the ground. Shutting my bedroom door, I backed up to my bed and allowed gravity to take over, ending up supine atop the blankets.

Only then did I let myself weep for my poor mother, my brother, and all we had known.

The next morning I *felt* like a zombie.

Midway through a morose breakfast, during which Mom kept cutting up a slice of apple into smaller and smaller pieces for Isambard, Dr. Evola opened the front door. "Just me. Headed upstairs to die now," I heard him say as he shut and locked it behind him.

Mom and Dad left the table and moved to the foyer. The minute they were gone I stood up. Isambard made furious, whooshing arm movements at me, bidding me to go eavesdrop. I did, moving as close as I could to the dining room door without being spotted.

"Are you well, Dr. Evola?" I heard Mom ask.

"Not truly at death's door, not yet," he responded. The cherub-haired, monocled Charles Evola normally spoke in such young, chipper tones—but not today. "It's a madhouse over there."

"You've been gone so long!"

"I couldn't leave." I heard him put down his bag. "Most of our living volunteers quit, as well as some of the living staff. They're afraid of the new strain. We've been scrambling since."

"Is there any news?"

"Not that I've heard. Dr. Dearly's never available when I go over—only a man named Dr. Salvez. Plus I'm a tech, not an epidemiologist. I don't understand half the stuff they deal with anyway."

"We're glad you made it back safely, at any rate," Dad said.

"Thanks. It means a lot to me—especially the fact that you let me stay here. If you'll pardon me, though, I would love to get a shower. Then I'll collapse. If I take up your couch for the next twenty hours? I apologize in advance."

"I'll leave your plate in the oven, Dr. Evola."

"Mrs. Roe, I love you. I'd duel your husband for you, but I'm pretty sure he'd annihilate me. There wouldn't even be enough left to reanimate."

The sound of feet on the stairs told me that Dr. Evola was headed up. I took my seat just before Mom and Dad walked back in. *Good or bad?* Isambard mouthed at me, as he scraped the apple bits off of the table and onto the floor.

I waggled my hand at him to indicate, *So-so.*

Isambard used his ignorance to advantage, asking about Dr. Evola as my parents sat down. Dad answered his questions, and I let my mind wander again. That the very people who'd been so eager to help the dead before were now turning tail was deplorable. I almost thought of volunteering, but I wasn't that ambitious, or that willing to leave the safety of my house. My conscience called this cowardice, and I agreed with it. But fear won out.

"Pamela?" my mother said, calling me back to reality.

"Yes?"

"Would you mind going to the market for me today? I didn't get the chance this morning. And can you manage alone?"

My heart stopped. My father gave up speaking to Isambard and looked at Mom curiously. "Alone, dear?"

"Things are calmer today. It's not far." Mom's voice softened, and she didn't meet our eyes. "I don't want to risk . . . with the anti-zombie . . . Issy . . ."

"Yes," I told her, before her unfinished sentences could linger long in the air, unacknowledged. "I'll go."

"No. I can do it," Dad said. "Or keep an eye on things so you can, Malati."

My nerves started buzzing at the thought of going outside, but I had to shake my head. "No. You have work. Mother has things to do. I can go. I've gone hundreds of times." After what I'd seen a few hours ago, I had no choice but to do whatever my mother wanted. Even if it terrified me.

I had to be strong for her. For all of them. There was no point in pretending I could ever do otherwise. I now knew that in keeping my mouth shut, I'd made the right choice.

The market near our house was busier than I was used to. I kept my head down, concentrating on remaining calm as I stood in line at each of the usual stalls, which were almost exclusively staffed and patronized by living people. Soon my basket was heavy with fruit and vegetables, the smell of hot straw filling my nose as the sun rose higher in the sky and beat down on my bonnet. I'd done well. I'd gotten through without incident.

But I lost it just as I was getting ready to go.

In order to exit the market area, I had to walk through a narrow brick archway. Standing to one side of it, newly arrived since I'd passed under it on my way in, was a zombified busker with a dancing parrot on a leather lead, playing a fiddle and singing an ancient song, his voice sad and low.

> *"If she'd been a colonel's lady,*
> *I could not have loved her more.*
> *But she was the ratcatcher's daughter,*
> *And I not long for shore."*

It wasn't the song. It wasn't the fact that his dirty hat was upturned, awaiting the generosity of passing strangers. It wasn't the sight of the bird's dull, tattered feathers as it shuffled back and forth.

It was the fact that I'd never seen the man before in my life, and he was standing in what my mind still viewed as Ebeneezer Coughlin's spot. And he was dead. His skin was melting away from his muscles, discolored and sickly-looking. His teeth were stained, his eyes turning to pools of jelly in his sockets, like solidified tears. And I loved my brother, I loved my friends, but in that second all I could see was the decaying busker and his spiritless parrot, and on the street beyond him, more dead people. And in the city beyond them, in the New Victorian Territories, in the world, more dead people, some that would hunt and claw and bite, and I could do nothing to stop it . . . and it was *Mr. Coughlin's spot,* where he'd played his instrument with a single arm and amazing skill. Mr. Coughlin, who'd died even though I tried to help him, and killed the zombie that had bitten him, and gone to jail for it, and oh . . . *God.* It wasn't fair, it wasn't *fair* . . .

The basket slipped from my fingers, landing beside my feet with a squeaky, uneven bounce. I knew I was hyperventilating. I tried to breathe slowly, shutting my eyes, my nose burning as tears fought for escape. I had to breathe. I had to get home. I was turning into a mess, right where everyone could see.

"Miss? Miss!"

I forced my eyes open. A man stood before me, his face vaguely familiar—but I couldn't place him. Panic gripped me anew. I was having a meltdown, and now a strange *man* was speaking to me, when I had no chaperone, no one to defend me.

The man looked about and then offered me a gloved hand. "I know this is highly irregular, but perhaps you'd do me the favor of accompanying me off to the side?" His voice was deep and warm, his accent aristocratic.

It took me only a second to decide that I would do as he asked—it was easier than fighting, easier than running. People were staring. One more brick in the foundation of my little life was crumbling into dust, and I was almost ready to give up caring.

I didn't take the man's hand, but backed up to where he indicated. He picked up my basket—he carried one as well—and moved to join me. "I'm so sorry," I managed to get out as he set both baskets beside me.

"No need for that." He opened his coat, revealing a gold-tooled pistol in a holster at his hip, and reached into an interior pocket, pulling out a handkerchief. The sight of it caused me to recall Allister and all his apparent kindnesses, twisting the knife. "Here. Don't speak. Breathe."

I took the hankie and put all my effort into doing so, pinching my fingers around my nose and breathing through my mouth. My left hand, I laid over my chest. Seeing this, he said, "Are you in pain? Should I call for an ambulance?"

"No. Please. It'll stop."

Nodding uncertainly, the man maintained a respectful distance. After a few minutes the episode passed and I began to feel more embarrassed than scared.

"The last time I saw you," he ventured, "you were dealing with things by screaming bloody murder. This can't be an improvement."

"What?" Confusion chased away some of my misery. I looked into his face again, and it hit me—his eyes. Those hazel eyes had once looked upon me with sympathy, even as he told me that I had to accept that my brother might be killed if he took us to the ships. "Colonel Lopez!"

The gentleman dropped into one of the smoothest genuflections I'd ever seen. "No longer Colonel, but yes. Keep breathing."

The last time I'd seen Edmund Lopez, I hadn't paid much attention to what he looked like. I'd been more concerned with my dying brother and thinking up suitable punishments for Michael Allister. Now I saw that he was a man of average height and strong build, perhaps in his early thirties, with chiseled features and skin the color of dark burnished burl wood. He wore a thin black moustache as well as fashionable sideburns, and was dressed impeccably in a dark suit and top hat, a beautiful black great coat, and shoes so shiny they reflected the hem of my skirt.

Suddenly I felt ashamed of my two-year-old dress, my shabby gloves, my plainly braided hair. "I'm sorry, I didn't . . ." I cleared my throat. "You remember me?"

"How could I forget?" Lopez smiled gently. "You know, if anything good can be said to have come out of the Siege, I'd say it was the number of brave young people who rose to the occasion. Er . . . it strikes me that this could be taken as an awful pun. Dead rising and all that."

I couldn't think of a response to this. I felt my cheeks heating. "Thank you," I almost whispered. Someone outside of my family really thought that about me? Someone who'd been in the *army* thought that about me?

"I hate to be so familiar, but it's Miss Roe, isn't it? I believe that's what that boy called you."

"Yes, Mr. Lopez," I tried.

Lopez's eyes darkened a tad. "Ah, not 'Mister' either." Before I could question this, he gestured to the archway. "If you are certain you don't require medical attention, may I at least escort you out to the street? See you safely home, perhaps? How may I be of service to you—if you would like help at all?"

Again I decided to accede to his offer. "I'd like that. Home, that is."

"My distinct pleasure. If anyone asks, I am an extremely doting cousin three times removed."

He picked up the baskets and waited for me to fall in beside him, and we walked in silence past the offending busker and out onto the street. When I told him I lived only a few blocks up, he looked relieved. I couldn't blame him. It felt odd to be walking with someone I'd never been properly introduced to, even though I owed him so much.

Eventually he said, "If I may, how is your brother?"

"Zombified," I informed him as I tried to clean up my tear-streaked face. "But well. Very well." I settled on the idea even as I spoke of it. "You should come in and see him. He owes you his gratitude. We all do."

"I would hate to impose." His gait was measured and swift, positively martial.

"No, no." It seemed like the best idea in the universe. "I'll tell my mother who you are. My father works just next door. I'm sure they'd both like to thank you." It occurred to me, "And I should apologize . . . for anything I might have said the night of the Siege."

"I do hope you're referring to the fact that you bellowed an order directly into my ear at one point?" Amusement glittered in his eyes, though distantly. "I'm lucky I'm not deaf on that side."

Twisting his handkerchief around my left index finger, I admitted, "Yes . . . that. Please forgive me."

Lopez chuckled softly. "You are a hundred times forgiven. Honestly, if I hadn't helped myself to a solid swig of port before I left base, after hearing the orders we'd been given? I might have been screaming right back at you."

After a few more steps we were at my front stoop, and I wondered at how quickly we had gotten there. "This is it. Won't you come in, sir?"

"If the invitation is extended, it would be an honor—but I'm certain your parents will be far more concerned about your recent fit than the strange man you met in the marketplace. I'd just like to see you safely inside." He climbed one of the steps.

Oh, no.

He stopped on a dime when I darted in front of him, peering curiously at me. "Oh. Um . . ." Looking into his startlingly bright eyes, I just came out with it. "Please don't tell them."

Lopez frowned. "Miss Roe, you're not well."

"It's . . . it's nothing. Please. My mother and father have it worse . . ." I shouldn't go blabbing about my family to a stranger. I knew that. I tried hard to swallow the words, never breaking eye contact with him.

Lopez was silent. He pressed his lips together and ultimately said, "I'm not keen on the idea of helping you keep secrets from your family, Miss Roe. They should know you just had an attack. They've taken you to see a doctor, have they not?"

"Please." I put every ounce of fear, every shred of fatigue into the word that I could muster, my shoulders sinking. "I'm fine. I know we've not been introduced. That you don't owe me anything. That we shouldn't even be talking . . ."

"No, we shouldn't." Lopez passed me my basket and considered my proposition for a moment before shaking his head. "Very well. But then I would rather not come inside. *You* and your parents owe me nothing, not even thanks. I did nothing to earn it."

"That's not true."

"It is true in that I could have done much more." He reached into his coat again and drew out an embossed ivory calling card. "Here. I'll leave my card for your parents. I'll try to call on Sunday, that's probably the least inconvenient time. And if I'm not welcome, please, have them send me an email. There shall be no hard feelings."

Disappointed, I accepted the card. "If you prefer."

"I do." He tipped his hat. "Go inside and have a cup of tea. Rest. Please give my regards to your brother and your parents. Good afternoon."

I curtsied and watched as he set off in the direction of the market again. I felt guilty, realizing I'd made him go out of his way.

When my eyes fell upon his card, my guilt was immediately replaced by shock.

He was, indeed, neither *Colonel* or *Mister*.

He was *Lord* Edmund Lopez.

9 • Nora

The hold music I was being forced to listen to was atrocious. Something about a "gilded cage." Leaning my head back against Dad's gun cabinet, I did my best to tune it out. Kept in the house, sitting on the floor, surrounded by boxes and stacks of paper—I felt positively claustrophobic.

A voice finally cut through the music, but only to tell me, "Your wait time is forty-five minutes." There were so many people still missing that a special hotline had been set up for those trying to find them.

I hung up. For days I'd been following my father's orders—and getting nowhere. It was like Aunt Gene had dropped off the face of the earth. A few months ago I would have been ecstatic had that actually occurred, but not now. Not when my imagination couldn't help but continually review all the horrible things that might've happened to her.

I stretched my left leg out and hooked the toe of my boot around a pile of folders, pulling it closer. The top file contained information on the Allisters, and I paged through it for the fiftieth time, uncertain what I should be looking for. I knew the basic story—that Aunt Gene had stayed with the Allisters following my abduction-slash-rescue, that she fled the city with them, and that she went missing at some point. And there, it stopped.

The door opened and Bram stepped in. I didn't look up, but I pressed my knees together beneath my long aubergine dress. I'd been sitting with my legs splayed open, relaxed, uncaring. "What's up?"

"Went into town, took a look at the lost-and-found posters," he said as he edged himself into a narrow space of bare floor next to me and sat. "Only saw the ones we put up asking for info on your aunt."

The gate in front of City Hall was covered in flyers made by those still searching for loved ones, as well as those who'd taken in wanderers. Occasionally, bouquets of flowers, small plush animals, and tea candles would appear beneath the slurry of paper, offerings made in memory of the missing and deceased. "Thanks for looking, at any rate."

"Pleasure." He leaned over to glance at the file in my hands. "Went to the cops, too. Still no information on the carriage."

"What else is new? I'd still like to know why those guys were wearing those stupid masks."

"Probably bought them all at the same store. Maybe that'll come back to bite them."

I couldn't help it. "Is that a threat or a promise?"

"Nora, you're the only person I'll ever bite. And you know it." A smile ghosted across his lips. "You think I'd cheat on you with common criminals?"

"How messed up is it that I find that really romantic?"

Bram chuckled, and kissed my temple. It occurred to me that the last place we should be hanging out alone was a room that contained a bed—not that there was much danger of *that* with a dead guy. "Any luck on your end?"

"Not a thing." I handed him the folder. "But there's nothing in here about Michael." Bram made an adorable face when I said his name, and I took the opportunity to scoot closer, as if I wanted to comfort him. Noticing this, he slid his arm around my shoulders. "So I'm almost starting to think I should try to talk to him. As vomit-inducing as the concept is."

"Why?" Bram tossed the folder into a random pile. "He was with Miss Roe and us the whole time. Unfortunately."

"Yeah, but before that he was with Aunt Gene. He was the one who told Pam she was with his family. Besides, you heard what he said. That he likes me." I stuck my tongue out to show Bram exactly what I thought of that idea. "So maybe he'd talk to me. I don't know. I feel like it's the only direction left to go in."

Bram thought about this, his eyes lidding. I could almost identify, by the little emotions that flitted across his masculine features, what he was internally arguing with himself about. Even in death he was so alive. His skin was like purest white candle wax, his eyes like faded mercury glass baubles—inanimate objects— and still they conveyed so much.

"I know what it's like to hold out hope," he eventually said. "But you have to be prepared to accept . . . she's gone. And you'll never know what happened to her. That the Allisters are telling the truth. I think your dad has more problems with this than you do. I'm not saying it's time to give up, I'm just saying it's a possibility."

"I know. I feel bad, though. We didn't get along in the end, but I wouldn't have wished this on her." Leaning back against his arm, I decided to confess. "Things up here aren't like we imagined they would be, are they?"

"Not entirely." It was honestly a relief to hear him say it.

Drawing my knees up, I encompassed them with my arms. I'd been debating whether I should tell him, and in that moment, I decided it was the right thing to do. "Papa wants to send me away."

"What?" Bram turned to look at me fully. "Where?"

"Belize. To his relatives. I don't even know them. It's a long story . . . let's just say Mama was poor and they hated her for that. They cut him off. Aunt Gene eventually married a man from the South and came down here to join him. She was the only one who'd talk to him." I'd always considered that fact mere family history, a dry, boring dust mote of information—but this time, as I said it, it seemed suddenly so important. So human. Cold as she was, Aunt Gene had truly loved her brother.

We couldn't give up looking for her. We had no right to.

"Is he going to?" Bram's voice was tight.

"I think I managed to talk my way out of it." Steadying myself, I went on. "Obviously, he's terrified. And he has reason to be. But next time he comes home, we have to talk. I'll be honest with him. I'll tell him that he has to give me some freedom—or I'm going to *have* to get it behind his back. And I'm sorry if that makes me sound selfish. But I want to feel useful. Hanging around the house squinting at legalese doesn't cut it."

Bram leaned forward and brushed his cool cheek along the edge of my jaw, and my eyes seemed to shut of their own accord. "You don't sound selfish. I get it. I want to follow his rules because I respect him, but I think he's kind of confused right now. Not himself. I hate to say it, but it's the truth."

"After this week, then, no more." Lifting my hand to the edge of his vest, I pulled him closer to me. "Because neither of us has time for this. Alone or together. But if I end up having to go slightly underground . . . you don't need to sneak around or lie for me. That's all I'm saying."

"I sneak around and lie for you every morning. Well, did." Bram put his hand over mine. "We'll play it smart. And besides, I think I have a mission lined up that he'll agree to. Maybe we should look at it that way. Chance to prove we can go out, handle ourselves like adults, come back in one piece."

"Mission?"

"Got some zombies in the city who need help. Not in the Morgue. Been holding off till you can go. Sound like a good place to start?"

"Yes! Finally!" Pulling back, I bounced a little where I sat. "Between that and doing something about Michael—God, it sounds stupid, but I already feel better."

"Maybe it's my reptile brain talking, but I don't want to hear about the thought of Michael making you feel better."

Grinning, I said, "Sorry." I lowered my eyes to the tarnished watch chain draped atop Bram's brown vest, and reached out to follow its length to his pocket with my fingers. I slipped my hand inside, drew the watch out, and opened it to find the photograph it contained. Bram and his little sisters. "I have to try everything, though. I bet your family looked for you. Maybe they're still looking."

Bram reached out and gently extricated his watch from my hands before closing and repocketing it. "I honestly hope not," he said, before standing. He seemed genuinely troubled by the idea.

"What's wrong?"

"Nothing." He put on a smile. "Really. It's nothing."

I have a pretty good bull radar, and his statement made it go off. I didn't press it, though. Bram'd had a rough life, and the hard-won right to brood about it in private if he wanted to. "I'll look everything over again later. Lord knows there's nothing else to do besides this and arms training." Standing up, I brushed down my skirt and held up two fingers. "Two days and twelve hours. I think I'll celebrate by setting off fireworks on the front lawn. In my underwear. While I dance."

Bram laughed. "Promise?"

"Pinky swear." I curled my little finger and tried to grab his hand. "Come on!"

Bram twisted his pinky with mine. "I'm holding you to that, then. I can't court a girl who doesn't keep her word."

"Oh, I'll so do it. It's on."

Bram shook his head, but was having a hard time fighting his laughter. "Dr. Dearly will kill you."

"Around here, dead is normal." I held out my arms. The long sleeves of my dress were puffy at the shoulders, with inserts of close-fitting black lace beneath. The effect on my pale skin was appropriate. "I think I'd look awesome as a zombie, personally."

Bram's expression went from jovial to mortally serious in about one second flat. He turned fully toward me and captured my upper arms, pushing me gently up against Papa's gun cabinet. "Don't joke about that," he said, his voice focused and intense. He let go of me with one hand and gestured at his face. "You *can't* become like this. You physically can't. We've talked about this before."

Forcing a laugh, I said, "I have to joke about it, Bram. Just like the rest of you do. It's laugh or cry, live or die."

"I know. It's just . . . the hijacking reminded me of that. You have one shot at living." He slid his big hands up my arms, over my shoulders, and cupped the sides of my face. "You're perfect the way you are, Nora. Don't ever think I want you to change, to be something you're not."

Had Bram felt the fear, too? Just a few weeks ago, terrified and overwrought, I had watched him while he slept, convinced he'd be taken from me. I didn't want him to know. He was the strongest person I had ever met in my life. All my striving aside, as self-loathing as it might sound—I wanted to be worthy of him. I admired him *that* much.

"I won't do anything stupid," I promised, sneaking my hands up to lay them on his chest, marveling at the power I felt there— even as I failed, as always, to detect a heartbeat. "Believe me, I want to be safe. I want all of us to be safe."

Bram slid the thin pad of his thumb over my cheekbone and nodded slowly. My breath caught as he started to lean closer, the motion of his neck fluid. We hadn't kissed properly since Colombia, and I could still recall every second of the last one he'd given me. Sick as it was, I'd loved the sensation of his cold lips so much that I couldn't even comprehend the idea that warm ones might be better. I loved how firmly he had kissed me, just hard enough to hint at the sensation of a bruise. He was the only boy I'd ever kissed, and I knew he was perfect.

Thank goodness no one was around to see just how eager I was to disobey my father. Or possibly judge how disturbed I was. But if other people wanted to call me a "necroslut"—fine. That's what I'd be. And I would *never* feel ashamed about it again.

His lips were just about to touch mine when the door opened and I heard Pam say, "Nora? Matilda said you were . . . Oh."

Spoke too soon.

Bram grimaced and sort of whirled away from me, ending up at my side facing the door. I straightened, hoping disappointment wasn't evident on my face. Pamela's eyes whisked between us, and I thought I could read some disapproval there—but she clamped down on it a second later. "I'm sorry."

"Nothing to say sorry for, Pamma," I said, infusing my voice with cheer. "I just didn't know you were coming over. We're probably breaking all sorts of—" Bram cleared his throat, and I course-corrected. "What's up?"

"I just came over to help, like you asked." Pamela removed her bonnet, glancing up at Bram coolly. "Unless I'm no longer needed."

Bram bowed. "Miss Roe. Forgive me, I have something to . . . do. Elsewhere." I flashed him a grateful look as he started to see himself out.

Pam released a breath. "No . . . hold on, Mr. Griswold. This likely concerns you, too."

"What is it?"

She reached into her satin reticule and pulled out a calling card, which she handed to me. The name on it was unfamiliar. Lord Lopez? I wasn't up on the society lists. "I ran into him on the street. He never said anything about being a lord while I was with him."

"Wait, you spoke with this guy?"

Bram stepped back and took the card. Unlike me, he seemed to instantly recognize who it was. "Wow. How'd he get to be a lord? Or was he one when we met?"

"Who is it?" I asked, growing annoyed.

"The guy from the docks," Bram said. "The one who came out to meet us when we landed the airship there."

Pam pointed at her skull. "You know, aimed a gun at Mr. Griswold's head?"

"Oh!" I exclaimed. "Him! Well, in my defense, a lot of people have threatened to shoot Bram in the head."

Bram smirked. "Thing is, he's also the guy who gave part of Company Z a chance to get out of their death sentence. Got them off the docks. And I say that without understanding why. I definitely owe him."

"He might call on my parents on Sunday," Pam continued. "I thought you might like to be there. Maybe you could get some answers."

Altogether, about fifty members of Company Z had died between New London and Averne's base, almost half the force. I knew their names because I'd helped Bram write letters of condolence to their families, sealing the envelopes and addressing them so he could concentrate on the actual words. If any of the others still had their unlives due to this guy's intervention, we all owed him. "Absolutely," I said, smiling at her. "Thank you, Pamma."

She nodded and looked to the sea of paperwork, her dark eyes widening a tad. "Goodness. Where do we pick up?"

"Somewhere around . . . Shark Food." Pam pulled her mouth to the side, realizing whom I meant.

"Ladies," Bram said, saluting casually with two fingers as he went for the door.

Before I could tell him goodbye or pull Pam into my world of detective work, the sound of laughter floated up from the street outside, accompanied by the squeal of tires. Bram paused, his head turning. "What was that?"

Pulling my skirts up, I threaded my way through the papers and boxes, opening the doors that led out onto Papa's balcony when I got there. The noise grew louder—a lot of whooping and hollering.

"Quiet!" someone yelled—a woman. "We're out in public! There are security cameras everywhere!"

"The sky's dead, cameras might be, too! Ain't no way you're ruining this for me, Bel!" a man countered. "Today is a day for miracles!"

Glancing down, I saw that three dirty, dented carriages and a canvas-covered truck had stopped in front of the house. People started exiting the vehicles, many of them armed. My heart rate picked up. "This doesn't look good."

Bram was soon at my side, his hands wrapped around the balcony railing. "Agreed."

"What's going on?" Pamela asked, her voice tremulous.

"We don't know yet," I told her as I entered the room again. "Come on. Downstairs."

"But if they're downstairs . . ." Pam was practically contorting her hands around her purse. "We should stay here. Lock the door. We don't know what they want!"

As I took a breath to steady myself, Bram moved toward the gun cabinet. It was now regularly left unlocked, and it didn't take him long to find a rifle and ammo. He loaded up, and I wrestled with my instincts. I wanted to go with him. If we were being invaded again, I wanted to protect my home.

Pamela clearly saw how torn I was. Her eyes broadcast and

somehow amplified every argument her mouth could have made if she let it. It worked.

"Do you want me to stay here, too?" I asked her, feeling my shoulders rising.

Pam nodded, guilt creasing her features. "Yes," she said. She might have felt guilty, but she sounded relieved. "Stay here with me."

The doorbell rang, a massive gong that set my teeth on edge. Pamela'd become so skittish since December—I didn't know what to make of it yet. She never talked about it, even when I asked. Until she decided to open up all I could do was try to be a good friend, try to give her what she needed.

Slapping the side of the cabinet, Bram told me, "You've got weapons, then." He flicked his safety off, then on again, and looked at me. "Don't open the door unless you hear three knocks, then two."

This simple, genius detail reminded me why I fell in love with him in the first place. "Right."

He left the room and I shut the door and stationed myself before it—but didn't lock it. I could hear Bram's heavy, limping footsteps as he made his way down the hallway. He was on alert, slow and sure in his movements.

"Lock the door," Pam said as she backed up toward the balcony, home to the rose trellis I'd had to climb the last time something like this had happened. It struck me that my father's bedroom was an incredibly unlucky place.

"Not yet," I told her. I opened the door just a touch, to listen.

Downstairs, someone approached the front door, his or her—most likely her—heels clicking on the marble. Matilda, I figured, my anxiety rising. I should suit up and run out there with Bram. He needed backup. Pamela could handle herself.

Suddenly, Samedi shouted, "I'll get it! It's for me!" Blinking in surprise, I listened as his footsteps overtook the others and the door opened. "Password?" Samedi asked, voice infused with a sarcastic sternness.

"Your mother has never known the pinch of a corset," the woman I'd heard in the street replied.

"That is an *old* password."

"I figured it'd be the only one you'd recognize. Time flies when you're having fun, I see." The woman's voice was warming.

"Baldwin?" a male voice outside said. "Is that *you?*"

"No," Samedi drawled. "It's someone wearing my face. Remarkable what they can do with anti-rejection drugs these days."

"Oh my gosh, it's actually him! It's the Undertaker!" someone else shouted.

"Okay," I asked aloud. "What in blazes is going on?"

Pamela grabbed my arm, startling me. "They're unloading something outside. It's under a tarp. *Please* lock the door!"

Doing as she asked, I prepared to go take a look—but then five knocks rang out. Pam jumped a mile. By the time I opened the door, Bram was already halfway down the hall again, his gun on his back. He looked back and crooked his finger, beckoning us. I quickly followed, taking Pamela by the hand along the way. She squeezed mine fervently.

As we descended the stairs, Dr. Chase entered the foyer and caught sight of us. She looked at Sam once in panic, before apparently deciding to give up, her features softening. She came over to meet us as Renfield and Chas entered the room, the short train of her green velvet dress swishing behind her. "It's all right. There's no danger."

"What is it, then?" Bram asked her.

Chase glanced at Samedi again before telling us, "We're replacing the carriage."

Samedi opened the door, revealing a crowd of about fifteen people. For a moment I cursed the fact that we'd left all the

weapons upstairs. They were a rough-looking bunch, an assortment of men and women in various styles of plain, lower-class
dress, many with pieces of mechanical detritus or equipment
strapped to their bodies. One girl, young and with bay-colored
pigtails, was clad in pin-striped trousers and a newsboy's cap, and
apparently unself-conscious about it. None of them were dead.

"Jesus, man." A broad, muscular man with greasy brown hair
and a cleft palate scar, the one who'd spoken before, stepped
forward. "It *is* you."

"In the oh-so-transient flesh," Sam said, a smile sneaking onto
his lips. "Good to see you, Ronnie."

Ronnie rushed into the house and swept Samedi up, hugging
him like a rag doll. Sam hurriedly reached up to grab hold of his
head. "Oh my God! Baldwin! You're alive!"

"In a manner of speaking. Put me down! Don't you know I'm
a walking biohazard?"

"Ronnie, please," Dr. Chase said, stepping forward. She smiled
at the man, and I was struck by how young she looked. "You're
going to snap him in two, and he's already been through that
once."

"Beryl!" Ronnie did as she said, but only in order to capture
her instead. She laughed as he shook her up and down in his glee.

"What the hell's going on in here?" bellowed a deep voice
from outside. I peered around Bram just in time to see another
man approach the door. He was also broadly built, but taller, with
a long mane of tightly curled black hair and a goatee. "Samedi?
You there?"

Samedi brushed off his gray suit. "Rats. Glad to see you've still
got your cousin under control. He's only caused you, what,
about eight heart attacks?"

The curly-haired man roared with laughter and stepped inside,
grabbing for Sam's hand. "By God's thumbs! Samedi! When

your message came through I thought it was a joke! I was gonna come here and shoot the idiot who sent it in the freaking face!"

"Nice to know you look before shooting nowadays." Samedi grinned as he clapped the man's shaking arm. "Great to see you, Ratcatcher."

"Are you sure these people are safe?" Bram asked Dr. Chase.

She laughed, voice lilting. "I'd trust any of them with my life. It's okay."

"Not about to trust 'em with the house, though," Samedi said as he pointed outside. "Let's conduct our business on the street, eh? This place isn't mine. Don't need your apprentices gnawing the gilding off the walls like a bunch of termites. Might be hazardous to what passes for my health nowadays."

Rather than cause offense, this statement sent "Ratcatcher" into high hysterics. "Outside, outside!" he ordered.

The crowd backed up, instantly obedient. I stepped up to Bram's side as he moved to follow, and laid a hand on Pamela's shoulder, hoping it would reassure her. She went with us, though her face told me she was far from eager to do so.

Once outside, a few of the younger visitors ran back to the carriages, perching upon them or dangling from them as they saw fit. They watched Samedi closely, apparently quite enthralled. "What happened to you, man?" Ratcatcher asked Sam. "God, your skin's like ice. You get bit back in December?"

"Oh, no. I'm first generation, or close to it. Been dead for four years now."

What? I looked up at Bram for confirmation of this. His slow nod told me that he understood my concerns—four years was ancient, for a zombie.

How much longer did he have?

"Wow." Ratcatcher finally looked at all of us, and encompassed us with a wave of his arm. "Who're these guys?"

"My new crew." Samedi picked us out, rattling off introductions.

"I'm honored." Ratcatcher bowed, and then laughed again, his barrel chest shaking. "I'm just . . ." He lifted a fist to his cheek and exploded it, stretching his fingers out. "Mind. Blown. After a while I gave up on seeing you again. Even the usual suspects didn't know what'd happened to you . . . believe me, I asked around. I thought you were dead in a ditch somewhere. Or back in prison."

Renfield held up his hands, finally daring to speak. "Wait, wait. Dr. Samedi, you were actually in *prison?*"

"A long time ago," Sam snapped.

"Seriously?" I knew Samedi's work with Company Z had been rewarded with a pardon from the New Victorian government, but I wasn't told for what. I didn't know he'd done any actual time. "Okay, that's it. Papa hangs out with ex-cons. He is never going to lecture me about anything else, *ever*. If he tries, I will laugh in his face."

Ratcatcher couldn't stop laughing, himself. "Oh, yeah, he got locked up for smuggling New Victorian tech into the Punk territories. Huge black market for it down there. This was long before he met the ginger," he noted, pointing at Beryl. "But he escaped. It was brilliant. You see, he spent months collecting bits and pieces—a pen there, a paper clip here. A spare pipe when he was on laundry duty, a spatula when he was on KP. Slowly, he used his mechanical genius to convert his cell into the cab of a walking tank." Chas squished up one eye and dropped her jaw in disbelief, and Ratcatcher nodded. "It's true. And one day he threw the switch and stomped away with part of the bloody jail."

Silence greeted the end of this story, as everyone turned to stare at Sam—Dr. Chase included. He sighed and said, "Is that how it got spun? Christ. I *was* on laundry duty at Drike's—fixing the industrial washers. Didn't take long to figure out how to

break them, too. Messed one up so bad they had to order a replacement and ship it out. I got out inside it. Scurried back behind Punk lines fast as my two legs could carry me. Ask Fi—"

Ratcatcher lifted his arms, as if invoking the gods. "No. Don't
ruin it for me. I'll believe what I want to believe."

He was the only one on that page. The rest of us continued to
gawp at Sam, Beryl excluded—she just rolled her eyes. "You *escaped* from Drike's Island?" Pamela asked, voice practically a
whisper.

"Doesn't matter. I'm a free man now." Sam turned slightly
from us, mouth grim. "Anyway, if you thought I was dead, please
don't tell me you fenced my equipment."

"Oh, hell no, man. I got your back." Ratcatcher clicked his
tongue and pointed to the truck. "There she is. Meanwhile,
sounds like you owe your new crew a few bedtime stories. You're
depriving them of an education."

"Later," Sam muttered as he hurried over to the truck and the
mysterious object that had been unloaded from it. We weren't
kept in suspense much longer. He drew the tarp off with a flour-
ish.

The thing under the tarp wasn't a carriage.

It was an honest-to-God pre–ice age *car.*

The long, low, sensuously curved vehicle was painted a chilly
shade of silvery blue and trimmed with bug-eyed headlights and
a delicious amount of chrome. The only flaws I could see were
two odd attachment points mounted over the front wheel wells.
Then again, I didn't know anything about historical cars—maybe
they were meant to be there.

"I know I was just babysitting her, but it still hurts to let her
go. Ain't she a stunner?" Ronnie said, moving to join Sam. Renfield wordlessly trailed after him, expression filling with blatant
physical longing.

Sam slid a hand over her hood. "Oh, she is; 1956 Rolls-Royce

Silver Cloud. Tell me I was wrong to con all those innocent souls. Their money was turned into this through the magic of the black market."

"Nineteen fifty-six?" Renfield gasped. "She's older than the angels. Almost two hundred and fifty years. And she still works?"

"Oh, yeah. Had Belinda convert her to run on electricity," said Rats. The woman who'd spoken before nodded. She had a handsome, square-shaped face beneath a cloud of kinky hair. "Keys are in the ignition. Everything else is in the trunk."

"Perfect."

"Welp." Ratcatcher wound up the tarp and tucked it under his arm. "I'd love to stay and shoot the breeze, but this is a bit out in the open for us." He moved to hug Sam, and Sam returned the gesture, patting his back. "But it is great to see you."

"Likewise," Sam said. His voice sounded almost wistful. "Sorry to get you out here."

Ratcatcher held up a hand, indicating that Samedi should give up. "No, man. You saved Ronnie's life. I'd do much more than drop off a ride for you, and no one will know about it. I'm just . . ." The big man pondered for a moment, before laughing again. Taking a step back, he addressed the young people hanging on the vehicles. "Y'all tagged along with us 'cause you didn't believe you'd actually see Baldwin Samedi, the Undertaker, the *legend*. And here he is. Not even the grave can hold him back. That's what I like to see!"

The crowd cheered. Within a few whirling, busy seconds they were all on board and on their way, the vehicles circling back toward the Elysian Fields entrance. "You rock, Undertaker!" someone shouted from the back of the truck. We watched them go, silence reigning.

Bram started it. "The Undertaker?"

"Nickname," Samedi said, tone disdainful. "Cue the looks of disapproval."

"The legend?" Pamela asked, crossing her arms over her chest and bestowing upon him one of those very looks.

Beryl fielded that one. "He was very good at smuggling. Taking things *under* to the Punk side? Ha-ha?"

"And cons?" Renfield ventured. "Anything else? I feel like we ought to know everything you've done, so we know what *not* to tell the cops."

"I've been pardoned. Beryl has amnesty." Samedi reached through the car's open window, and next thing I knew I was doing my best to catch the set of keys he'd lobbed at me. "If any cops show up, they are not our problem."

"Wait," I said, looking at Dr. Chase. "Amnesty? For *what*?"

She colored slightly. Before she could say anything, Samedi took over, in a tone that would brook no backtalk. "We needed to replace one of our rides, I replaced one of our rides. I've done my good deed for the day. This conversation ends now."

"We could have bought a new one," Bram said. "This thing's going to attract tons of attention. And why didn't you go pick it up—"

"Because I'm trying to avoid being killed in my sleep, all right?" Samedi shot back. Bram went quiet, astounded. "I'm a bad man. There, I said it. And there are probably at least fifteen equally bad people in this town who'd make me dead for real if they knew I was back. Understand?" He backed up. "That part of my life is over. I just want to do my job, help my friends, and go to my grave with something approximating dignity."

Samedi turned and started off in the direction of the front door. Beryl met my eyes, an unspoken apology in hers, and walked after him.

"That was awe-some," Chas said, looking back down the street. "Did you see that one guy with the stubble? He was *cute*. Too bad he's not deeeead."

"Did you know all this, Bram?" I asked, looking at the keys.

"No," he said after a moment. "Well, I knew some of it, but . . . clearly, not everything. Let's just get this thing up to the house."

As I watched the boys back the Rolls into the driveway, its paint gleaming despite the lack of light, I decided my own potential secrets and sins were pretty innocent after all.

Samedi had us all beat.

10 • vespertine

Twenty pairs of unseeing eyes stared up at me, awaiting my verdict.

As I tapped my chin, trying to come to a decision, I said to the air, "Screen, on. Current game."

The large screen on the wall to my left instantly obliged, its glow suffusing the attic. I was engaged in a computer match on Aethernet Chess Live under my new username, NotHere1. "Bishop to E3," I decided. I knew it was a hopeless move, but I'd yet to work out another direction to take. "And volume up."

While my adoptive father's family was known for crafting exquisite string instruments, my adoptive mother's native family, the Turcios, was involved in the business of industrial diamonds and crystals. Grandfather Turcio was currently making use of our extensive summer property to host his company's biggest clients, and the string orchestra he'd hired was positioned not thirty feet from where I currently stood. Electric lamps conquered the darkness outside, highlighting the well-pedigreed "wild" trees in our fairy-tale garden from beneath, throwing branch-shaped shadows my way. Even though my bedroom was in the attic, low tinted windows were set along the walls, allowing me to watch everything from my own private crow's nest. Being but seventeen, I was unwelcome at the party. I'd yet to debut. If I were of age, of course, I'd have been parading down there like a cow at a cattleman's auction.

Carefully, I looked the twenty ball-jointed dolls over again. They'd just arrived that day, sent up from New London in well-padded wooden crates. Each doll was a work of art painted in soft, dreamy hues, their glass eyes clear, their lips luminous. Each wore a fanciful gown that, at my word, could be re-created in my size. Most upper-class girls preferred to use holographic design programs to create their custom gowns, swapping out virtual ribbons and cuffs while drinking tea and chatting with their friends. I didn't. It was too overwhelming, too easy to give up and pick out something, anything, rather than go through all fifteen thousand button options. I vastly preferred for my favorite seamstress to prepare a china doll fashion show for me, by the old custom. Call it conceit.

The door opened. I didn't look up. It had to be a servant putting clothes away—caring for my clothing was pretty much the only chore they were permitted to perform for me. Privileged though I appeared to be, I made my own bed, dusted my own furniture, served myself from the kitchen, and scrubbed my own toilet, because I knew that no one else would. I seldom paid attention to the servants for that reason, and they were strictly sworn not to pay more than the usual attention to me, not even to speak to me.

Thus my surprise upon hearing a quiet, "Ahem."

Tearing my eyes from the rose-colored walking dress I'd been contemplating, I found one of my mother's maids, a downright fat young woman named Suzanna, staring at me intently from a distance. Her hands were knotted up in her apron, her cheeks pale.

For a moment I actually felt a mild rush of . . . not fear. Excitement. It was she who was testing her luck; I was just along for the ride. It was like watching someone *else* put a leaning tower of chips down on a roulette table.

"Screen, off," I said. Once it was dark, I lifted my chin. "You realize what you're doing. If my mother comes to learn of this, you will be punished."

The maid didn't speak. She didn't dare take it that far. She took a few steps away from me, but didn't leave my room.

I stood up, abandoning my project. "This better be good. For both our sakes."

Suzanna's eyes betrayed her terror. She wasn't trying to be cheeky; she wasn't confident of her ability to flout the rules and get away with it. Something incredible had to be going on for her to come up to fetch me like this.

Once she knew I would follow, the maid led the way downstairs. Luckily I was still wearing my aquamarine gown and faceted jade jewelry from earlier in the day, and had yet to take down my blond hair from the beribboned style I'd worked it into, so I didn't look completely a fright. I moved after her, unsure where our little adventure was headed.

When we got to the first floor, Suzanna slid open a hidden door in the wall and entered one of the many back service hallways that connected the rooms in Éclatverre like a circulatory system. She shut the door on me, and for a second I grudgingly admired her cunning—she was splitting us up. *Nice*. I knew where the tunnel let out, though, and took the long way around to the butler's closet, which was directly across from the music room. The orchestra was right outside, their music mingling with laughter and conversation.

Suzanna didn't emerge. I waited for a minute or so, anger beginning to replace my excitement. If this was some sort of trick, oh, my mother was going to hear about it, and Suzanna was going to have read the whole of Thackeray's surviving canon to me . . .

Then, through the music room doorway, I glimpsed something odd.

There was a young man lying facedown on the carpet within.

My irritation only grew. *This?* That stupid woman had come up to my room, dared to communicate with me, to put her job in jeopardy, for *this?* Drunken partygoers were my mother's responsibility, not mine. Besides, I couldn't be alone in a room with a strange man. Was Suzanna insane?

Wait. Perhaps he was dead. That would be easier to deal with. Even if he reanimated, that would be easier to deal with.

"Sir?" I called from the hall. "You need to make your way outside again. This is most unseemly."

The man sent his arms out, responding to the sound of my voice. He was alive. He tilted his head to the side, and my stomach flip-flopped.

It was Michael Allister.

Michael Allister was facedown drunk on the floor of our music room.

I knew then he must have asked for me by name. Suzanna wasn't stupid, after all. I hurried into the music room and shut the door, hoping she'd hear the sound and leave. "Mr. Allister, you'd better be on your feet before I turn around."

"Miss Mink?" His speech was slurred. "Oh, good. You made it."

I turned. He was pushing himself up, but not as quickly as I'd have liked. In fact, after a moment of exertion Michael fell back onto his rear and stared incredulously about the room, as if he couldn't remember how he'd gotten there. His suit was rumpled and covered in mysterious stains, his sandy hair a mess.

"Nice room. Is that a holographic training piano?" He waved his hands in the air like a barmy wizard. "Piano, on!"

Sure enough, a handsome tuxedoed instructor flickered into being at the keyboard of the black baby grand. "Accessing program. Please wait . . ."

"No, piano! Off!" I yelled, striding across the floor. The hologram obeyed, and soon the piano stood alone, just like the harpsichord, the wall-mounted rows of violins and violas and cellos, and my polished harp in the corner. "Allister, get *up*."

Michael pointed at my feet. "You cannot tell me what to do, Miss Mink. Not tonight. Not ever. I'm in control, see?"

"Oh, yes. In control of your liquor, too."

"That!" He struggled upward and once more fell. "Is an unfortunate side effect. I think I'm going to need lessons from Coco." He started to giggle like a schoolgirl. "Coco. How on earth could you ever keep a straight face while making love to someone named *Coco*?"

I moved right up to his side. I had no idea who Coco was—a whore? Was Michael already following in his father's footsteps? Everyone knew about Lord Allister's revolving door of trollops. "A side effect of *what*? What are you doing here? Do you not realize that half of society is just beyond that wall? That if they see us, we are done for?"

"No, no. We're not." Michael managed to grab my hand after several attempts. Who knows how many hands he currently thought I had? "I would never hurt you. You're the only girl I can trust."

I took my hand back, distaste burning my throat. "Trust, yes. But nothing more. You shouldn't be here."

"Bah, you think I want *you*? What is it with girls thinking I want them?"

I struggled to maintain my cool. "That's not what I'm saying."

"It is, too." Michael started digging about in his coat pockets for something. I hoped it wasn't a flask. "You're all put out because I still want Miss Dearly. It's understandable. I don't judge you for it."

"*What?*" We'd met along the border between our country properties several times since the Siege, and our short conversations had always kept to the topic of that night—the things we had seen, the horrors we'd been through, and our mutual hatred of almost everyone else who was on that filthy airship, regardless of the fact that we owed them our lives. "You said she's a worthless, pro-zombie loser! Those were your exact words. I know, because I remember agreeing with you, and I'd never agree with anything else!"

"Well, she is, as long as she's got that deadmeat on her arm. But I think we can . . . I think *I* can . . . fix that. Fix her."

"Why did you even come here? You don't have permission to be here."

"If I don't need anything, it is permission. Er . . . you think of a prettier way to put that." Michael's eyes were far too bright. He continued to search through his pockets.

I tried one last time. "Allister, get up. Or I will kill you where you sit, and tell my mother that I came upon a body, rather than a boy, in our music room. Lord knows it'd be less scandalous."

Michael's response was to find what he was looking for and fling it at my feet.

It was a severed finger.

I screamed and danced back before the hem of my dress could touch it. He started laughing again. "Oh, the look on your face! Hot potato! Hot potato!"

"Wh-What . . ." I kept walking backward, unsure what else to do. "Where did you get that? Oh God, Allister, what did you *do*?"

"Calm down. Women!" Michael finally managed to climb to his feet. "I didn't cut it off. It was another Brother's turn to kill one, and he made me take it as a souvenir. You have to kill one in front of the others. Give your number and kill one. So they know you're serious." He held up a finger, and I noticed he was missing his glove. "I? I will not do that. It's vulgar. I need privacy for mine."

"They? Who's 'they'?"

"The Murder. Stupid name, right? I didn't pick it."

I didn't know what to say. I'd never heard of such a thing before. "Is it . . . it's some sort of anti-zombie club?"

"Not a *club*!" He reached out and caught the edge of the piano to keep from stumbling around. "You make it sound like we get together and build models or something!" He pointed at his trophy. "We get together and kill *them*. Make their supporters run like mice."

I looked at the finger, and fought the urge to vomit. Every lushly curved instrument in the room, every bit of filigree on the ceiling, every painted flower on the walls, seemed calculated to make that half-rotten finger look all the more horrific.

"Got an invitation about a month back. Don't know who sent it. They use an old-fashioned letter system. Masks. No one knows anyone else. The only thing I know is we're all upper-class." He knelt down to retrieve the finger, studying it. On it, something glinted. Gold.

A wedding ring.

"I don't understand," I tried. Oh God, what was Michael doing?

He looked at me as if I were an incurable idiot, then back at the ring. What he went on to explain was not what I wanted to hear. "Brothers who brought the corpse man tonight said he was walking with his wife. 'Till death do us part,' right? Said she screamed and cried till she puked. Then they knocked her out, took the zombie into the sewers. Kept him tied up, waiting, in an old underground livestock tunnel. Chopped him to pieces." Michael took off the ring and shined it with his bare thumb. "I'm going to wear this, I think. For good luck."

I'd never heard Michael speak so cruelly before. Everyone I knew flung knives made of words at each other, cut one another off at the social knees to remain on top of the metaphorical heap, and I happily played along with such games—but I'd never attacked someone. Ever. Not like he was talking about—had done.

Because he *had* done this. He wasn't just talking. He was holding the proof.

"Why, Mr. Allister? Why would you do this?"

Michael pocketed the finger again and slid the ring onto his right hand. "Because I have to. Because Miss Roe and Miss Dearly drove me to it. I don't care a fig about the Murder, but the way they're doing things, they're very useful. Somehow they've got underworld contacts like you wouldn't believe. They're my chance to do what I need to do. Then walk away, no one ever the wiser. Dad never the wiser."

I wasn't terribly close to Michael—he was a boy, after all, and went to a different school—but I'd met him often enough, before the Siege, to think of him as a very quiet, boring individual. He followed the rules, or at least appeared to. He never called attention to himself, and he was rarely the subject of gossip. The other boys I knew seldom talked about him, never seemed to go out of their way to include him in anything, but he had his friends. His father was so powerful, he had to have friends.

So I couldn't believe what I was hearing. This was entirely unlike him. It had to be the liquor talking, the liquor making him act bombastic and brash and bold. I'd never seen any evidence for the idea of *in vino veritas*. With boys it was more like *in vino bullitas*.

Some confidence restored, I said, "This is about Miss Dearly, then? Are you going to do something to her?"

"No!" Michael laughed, the sound off-kilter and eerie. "I

would never hurt her!" His voice hardened. "But she'll learn. And Roe. Someone has to pay for the plague."

"I agree with that, Mr. Allister." And I did, but right now I was prepared to tell him I owned property on the moon if it would get him out of my house. I tried to steady my face, my voice. "Look, there's a party going on outside. Is that what brought you here? Surely your driver isn't drunk."

Michael squinted at the curtain-shrouded windows, faded from without by the party lights. The silhouettes of the revelers outside were superimposed one over another, a congealed beast with many heads. "No. I thought of you after I got out of the city." He flung his arms out. "This morning I was down, but now I am *up*! Dad's got me pushing paper at his office, my bank account is full again—do you know how expensive drinking has become since December? Maggot-men pickling themselves, must be . . ."

"How did you get in here?"

Michael scoffed. "I knocked at the door. What do you take me for, a lout?"

I breathed a sigh of relief. My mother hadn't seen him, then. "You need to go before anyone sees you. Come on, I'll show you out."

Michael nodded, and allowed me to take his arm and lead him forward. He reached out his free hand as we neared the doorway, strumming the strings of the instruments on the wall, stirring up a set of notes that almost seemed frightened of one another.

When I got him to the foyer he turned to me and said, voice suddenly cold, "You won't tell anyone."

"No. But you have to stop giving me things to tell."

"I have to tell someone. I think that's it. I'm tired of not telling. Not acting." He tried to touch my cheek, and I thrust his arm away. He caught mine, pinning me. "I'm going to cut Griswold's heart out and show it to Miss Dearly. So she can see it's dead. That it never beat for her. And then I'm going to put a bullet in his head. And I need privacy for that. Can't do it in front of the others."

"Please." Disgust aside, my patience was wearing thin. "I don't want to hear about what you're doing, or what you *think* you're going to do. Once you sober up, you'll look upon all of this with regret. You're going to find that filthy thing in your pocket and—"

Michael gripped my cheek with a sudden passion, and I couldn't help but cry out. I felt my face flush with shame—he had no right to touch me. I should hit back. *Roe* had once hit him! More than that, I should tell him how utterly insane he sounded. I should threaten him with the police, the asylum.

"Listen," he said. *"Just listen."*

"Let go of me and I will," I whispered.

He did, slowly. His eyes were bright, his cheeks red. When he spoke, I could smell the whiskey on his breath. "They embarrassed you, too. Put you in danger." He leaned close to me—far too close. "So you want to hear. Don't you, Vesper?"

My chest tightened. "No, I don't. I don't want to know anything. And you're *drunk*. You won't re—"

At that, Michael actually slapped me. Shock froze my higher brain functions. I had no idea what to do, save to cup my cheek. I just wanted him *gone*.

"Drunk or not, I'm going to win. Like my father. My father's even got doctors from Dearly's side jumping ship, *begging* to work with him. One was at the office today, telling us how stupid Dr. Dearly is, how Dad can help. He always wins. I *always* win."

Michael let me go, bowed, and staggered out into the night. His blue carriage was parked outside, and no driver seemed to await him. For a minute I thought about calling him back, taking his keys from him—but then I recalled his hands on me, and I stopped caring. Instead I shut the door and sank to the gleaming marble floor, gripping my head in my hands. I desperately wanted to unsee what I'd just seen. Not just the finger. Michael.

I should tell someone what he'd done.

I also knew that to do so would be pointless.

He was right. He would win. I'd be labeled a slut for having a boy in my house, unchaperoned; my reputation would be sullied. His actions, on the other hand, would earn a collective shrug. Even I, had he submitted everything he'd just said more soberly, would have shrugged. I didn't care if a random dead man died or lost a finger or two. And no one would believe he was scheming, dreaming grand, violent dreams—because I certainly didn't. The Murder? Please. Most boys I knew could barely dress themselves, much less organize an anti-zombie conspiracy.

I forced myself to think logically. Liquor obviously made him act completely out of character. He and his fellows were just playing rough and drinking too much. Probably just beat up a passing dead man on the street. That's all. Such things had become commonplace since December.

Yes. That had to be it.

I returned to my room.

This time, I locked the door.

11 • Bram

Late Friday night, I approached Samedi about helping Dog.

He and Beryl were in the study, as usual. The opulent, wood-paneled space was now overrun by power cords, computers, crates, and stainless steel machinery. Beryl was seated on Dr. Dearly's desk, listlessly bobbing a tea bag in and out of a mug. Samedi stood beside her, his head off and positioned upside down on a spidery brass armature. He held up a bag of medicated saline cocktail with his left hand, which connected to a valve on his neck hardware via a long plastic tube. Talk about feeding your head.

When he heard me, Samedi's eyes opened. "To what do I owe the pleasure?"

"Charity." I sat down on one of the crates, resting my elbows on my knees. "Remember the zombies I told you about, the ones we had to take on the *Christine*?"

"Mmm?"

"One of them was a little boy. Mute. Evola had to amputate his hand."

Beryl stopped moving her tea bag, sympathy filling her eyes. "Poor thing."

"And we told him maybe you'd make a replacement for him."

Beryl held up a hand to preemptively hush Samedi, who'd started to pick up his head. "Of course *we* will." She peered at him over the top of her mug, wordlessly challenging him to disagree.

Sam put his head back down and tipped it so he could fix me with bleary eyes. "Fine. Schedule every second of my rapidly diminishing time on Earth. Lord knows I get into trouble if I'm left to my own devices too long." He extended his right arm, as if he expected me to pass him something. "Do you have the hand?"

My lips separated a second before I actually formed my reply. "No. The kid was, like, ten. What was I supposed to do, tell him I was going to borrow one of his body parts and get it back to him later?"

Samedi snorted. "Well, yes. What am *I* supposed to do, guess at his measurements? Guess where Evola aimed?"

I offered, "We could go see them in person. Find out."

"See who in person?"

I looked over and saw Nora standing in the doorway. "The zombies I told you about. The ones on the ship."

"Are you sure we can trust them?" Samedi asked. "Like I said, I can't exactly go skipping merrily through New London."

"Fairly sure, yeah. The woman leading them is kind of spacey, but she also seems understanding. A couple of them lost it on the docks, attacked the living. Living started it, though."

Nora made a contemplative sound. As she turned from the door, she noted, almost absently, "You've got Sam, then. Leave the other old codger to me."

"You kiss our young, pure Mr. Griswold with that disrespectful mouth?" upside-down Sam shot back.

"Baldwin, honestly," Dr. Chase admonished.

I held my tongue and tried hard not to smile.

*   *   *

When Dr. Dearly came home on Saturday night for a shower and a few spoonfuls of food, we circled the wagons. After managing to corner him in the kitchen, Nora started out by preparing his dinner for him while he put his remaining biological foot up. The moment he hefted his fork, she got to the point.

"If Dr. Chase and Dr. Samedi come along, can I go with Bram after church to help some zombies in need? I'm ungrounded tomorrow, and things have calmed down a little. It's not in the Morgue." She didn't resort to sweetness or cajoling—her tone was direct.

Dr. Dearly looked at her, then me. Having promised to let Nora see how far she could get on her own, I said nothing—but mentally I reviewed the various arguments I'd collected. *Sir, we both need direction. We want to be of use to you, we respect you, but we'll make our own way if we have to. And honestly? Sometimes, I need her with me.*

The doctor continued in heavy silence. Before Nora could bolster her argument by going into further detail, or I could open my mouth, he put down his silverware and said, "Yes."

Nora held still for a moment, surprised—but then moved to hug her father around the shoulders. He patted her elbow. "I promise, we don't want trouble."

"I believe you. The others will be with you. And the dead need all the help they can get." Looking at me, he added, "Give me an hour alone. Then, Bram, if you'd accompany me to the ships?"

I agreed, but something in his tone suggested he was going to rehash the conversation we'd had following the hijacking. That'd been a mess of safety and etiquette concerns—so half reasonable, half stupid—and it worried me to think that he might wander back there, maybe get bogged down in the mud of his own mind. He'd given in so easily.

So a little more than an hour later, when we got into his non-descript coffee-colored carriage, I decided to take the bull by the horns. "Dr. Dearly, about the trip. We're going to go help—"

"I trust you won't lead her to ruin. I'm just glad you're going with her."

Thrown slightly off guard, I said, "But a few days ago you went over all the rules again, sir. I'm just trying to do right by you. By her."

"I know I did. I know you are." He hushed, concentrating on his driving.

Confused, I tried to piece together a reason for this apparent waffling. As I did, I couldn't help but look at the man. Our differences hadn't seemed so stark back at base. Although he was a good friend, he was also my elder, my superior, and he looked it now. In the midst of a worldwide revolution, he was dressed in a full black suit and top hat. He comfortably piloted his electric carriage through city avenues, living monuments to both an era long past and the new one modeled on it. I sat beside him in my usual clothing—soft trousers, collarless shirt, suspenders, second-hand jacket, and practical wide-brimmed fedora—feeling somewhat out of place.

In time, he spoke. "I couldn't have created a better man for her. I want you to know that. But you must understand—I was a father before I was a zombie. An older man before I was a dead man. There is so much in my life I cannot control anymore that I find myself looking for areas I *can*. I worry even when there should be no cause for worry. I ascribe importance to things that, in theory, should matter about as much as the dreams of a fly. And I am sorry."

I understood perfectly. "Yes, sir."

"I just don't want either of you to get hurt. But I've been thinking about what she said for a few days—she's right. Before long, all of this—the good and the bad—will be past. She needs to see it. Know it. Remember it when we are gone." His voice grew soft. "Yet the world is a dangerous place, and the night has a thousand eyes that will outlive both of us. That's all I ask you to consider."

"Understood."

"I fell into the habit of spoiling her when I was so often absent from her life. When I had so much to hide." His cheek twitched slightly. "I still would, if I could."

"Even if you did," I assured him, "trust me—she's not the worse for it. In fact, I'm pretty sure she loves you for it."

Dr. Dearly chuckled. "I'm glad you think so." After another pause, he said, "I want you with me on the *Erika* tonight. I've been chasing help away when I need it most. Salvez told me you've been volunteering at the barricade, but you shouldn't be there. Leave that to the others."

The way he phrased this request dampened the relief it might have otherwise brought me. I didn't like the idea of leaving anyone behind, even if they were stationed only a hundred yards away from me. Still, I was ready to jump at the chance to do what I saw as more important work. To have a tool in my hands other than a gun. "Thank you."

"We're going to make it through this." He seemed to remember something. "Oh, and someone dropped this off at the boats for you."

He reached into his pocket, steering with one hand, and passed me a slip of yellow paper. It was covered with crabbed handwriting that appeared to have been done with something wide and rough, maybe a piece of charcoal.

The Changed

We are all dead, the living and dead alike.
It is no longer safe here among those who have not changed.

*Be with your brothers, admire in another what you cannot
have, dance and sing.
Look for the light along Country Road 6.*

The Changed had apparently moved—but at least I knew
where to find them. And it was out in the country. Definitely
safer than the city, all things considered.

Maybe things were starting to look up.

I spent the entire night on the boats—about half that time with
Dr. Dearly, and the other half helping to patch up zombies with
Evola. Charles looked tired, the bags under his eyes so pronounced that he could barely wear his monocle. When I asked
him if he'd taken a break recently, he shrugged and said, "Don't
like to impose on the Roes more than I have to. I've actually been
trying to sleep here or in my carriage when I can."

"Then why stay with them at all? There's always room for another cot at the house. And we could actually really use your carriage. You could carpool with the other doctors."

Evola shook his head uneasily. "I'm sorry, but no. I prefer to
be closer to the boats." After a second, clearly ashamed, he added,
"I don't like the idea of being underground. It makes me feel
trapped."

Him and Nora both. I texted her to let her know about her
father and the note, adding that if we were going to be looking
for a light, we'd better set off closer to sunset. She urged me to
meet her at church anyway, like we'd originally planned.

When morning arrived, I cleaned up and went directly to the
Cathedral of Our Mother, the pre-ice bank turned house of wor-
ship. Nora met me in the saffron-carpeted aisle beside our usual
pew, smile brilliant, dressed in what she knew full well was my
favorite gown—a pistachio green silk number with horizontal

strips of forest green velvet that emphasized what little shape she had. "Any bad news?"

I dared to take her hand and kiss it. A living lady in the pew behind ours glared at us, while the two young zombies sitting beside her bickered about whether accepting a communion wafer constituted cannibalism. "Not a bit."

"Good," she whispered, bouncing a little on her toes. "I put together a basket of medical supplies and things this morning. I barely slept last night. I feel like I can finally *breathe*."

"Good idea." As I slid into the dark wooden pew beside Dr. Chase and Father Isley, the only other members of the household I could see present, I caught sight of Pamela coming up the aisle. "There's Miss Roe."

Nora turned and waved at her friend. Pamela looked to her father, perhaps asking for permission, before braving the crowd of churchgoers and hugging Nora. "Morning, everyone. Where's Dr. Dearly?"

"Still at work." Nora scanned the pews to the left of us and appeared to be debating something with herself. "I hate to ask this, but have you seen Michael today? I still want to talk to him about Aunt Gene."

Pamela tensed a bit. "No. I don't exactly keep an eye out for him. He's probably up in the balcony with the lords, and you can't see into it from here." She looked anyway, her head turning toward the back balcony with its columned supports, where the aristocrats perched high above the hoi polloi.

"Sorry. Just wondering." Nora smiled apologetically. "Anyway, we're going to visit some people later on with Chase and Samedi. You're welcome to come if you want."

Pamela turned back, surprised. "Visit? Who? Where?"

"Bunch of zombies. As for where . . ." She pointed at me.

"Country Road Six."

"What? That's in the middle of nowhere." Pam looked from me to Nora. "Have you ever met these people before?"

"No, not yet. Bram has."

Gripping her little drawstring purse tightly, Pamela said, "Let me guess—you didn't tell your father where you're going. Nora, you're going to get in trouble again!"

Nora lifted a finger. "You're assuming things. Papa's fine with it. Yesterday he actually struck me as sane."

"Yeah," I agreed. "He was great last night—more like his old self."

Pam looked at me. "He's letting her do this?" she demanded. There was a strange, accusing sort of panic in her voice, and I stood up. "Did *you* convince him?"

"Miss Roe," I tried, glancing around at the crowd. The prerecorded organ music was picking up, a hint the service was due to start soon. The flexible flat screen tapestries displayed upon the walls shifted designs, showcasing the Stations of the Cross. "I didn't convince anyone of anything. She's not grounded anymore, and we're not going alone."

"I'm right here, guys," Nora said, annoyed. "Look, Bram promised to help this dead kid. He lost his hand."

"I'm sorry for that, I am. But let Mr. Griswold handle it. Besides, Lord Lopez might come today, and I don't know when. You have to be there."

"Blast, I forgot about that." Nora sighed. "Look, I can't hang out at your house all day. If I miss him, we'll just have to meet up other time. But I'll go with you after the service. We'll figure it out."

Thinking that was the end of it, I moved to escort Nora into the pew. Pamela stood in the aisle for a moment before turning on Nora again, lips pale. "I can't believe you're doing this."

Nora lowered her voice. "Pamma, doing what? What's the matter?"

"I gave you a chance to talk to Lopez, and now you act like it's an imposition. You'd abandon it to go do . . . what? Ride around the countryside? With *career criminals?*"

Nora was thrown. "It's a charity visit. It is the sort of thing the people in this very building have been encouraging us to do since we were *two.* And Samedi and Chase are good people."

"Last time it was just a *walk* through your neighborhood with lots of *workers* around, when you could have come with me. You said that's when Mr. Griswold first tried to grab you." I coughed and looked at the intricate plaster ceiling. "The next day, I lost you. You were taken into the night and I didn't know if you were alive or dead."

"What does that have to do with me going on a visit with at least three other people, Pamma? And you don't even know if this guy is definitely going to show up. I don't get what the problem is."

"You don't get . . ." Pamela stared at Nora as if the very idea was an impossibility. "You just don't care, do you?"

"What? That's not fair," Nora said, her voice growing chilly.

I finally decided to move forward, placing myself close to the middle of them without stepping between. "Come on. We can settle this later, all right?"

Pamela snapped, "It is *none* of your business! This is about *us.*"

Chastened, I shut up. Nora was looking at Pam as if she'd punched her in the chest. "I'm not blowing you off completely. But I have to do what I can to help. I'd help *you* if you'd tell me what's wrong."

Pam started to say something else—opened her mouth and sort of screwed up her torso, as if winding up for the shot. But instead of following through she turned sharply and stomped off, returning to her family. Nora stared after her, deflated.

Offering my hand, I began, "Nora—"

"No." She straightened her arms by her sides and moved to

join me in the pew. "Not now. Later." She sat down, and I followed suit, my eyes on her. I couldn't tell if it was anger I saw on her face or something else. All the heads I'd blown open over the years, all the missions I'd been on, and I still counted Girl Problems as something out of my league.

Pamela left after the service without saying a word. Nora turned off her phone.

As soon as we returned home, Nora drew inward. I gave her space until late afternoon. When the time finally came to strike out on our errand, she didn't seem half as eager to go.

"Are you sure you're okay?" I asked while we waited for the car at the front door. I took her hat from her hands, arranging it upon her bed of dark curls and tying the ribbons beneath her chin. Maybe it was weird, but I liked fussing over her from time to time—buckling her holster, helping her put her things on. It made me feel protective. Hell, it gave me an excuse to touch her.

"I will be," she said. "I just have to figure out what Pamma needs from me." She pulled some hair free of the knot I'd tied. "I don't know what her issue is. She was fine during the Siege. That pretty much set the bar for 'worst stuff we would ever encounter.' I'm used to her worrying, but I'm not used to her being . . . like this."

"She's been through a lot. We all have," I said, before a beep caught my attention. Samedi was ready to go. "C'mon. We can talk about it later."

Despite the fact that it was flashy, we were taking the Rolls because Sam wanted to put it through a test drive. It was a tight fit, but Renfield was able to share the front seat with Dr. Chase, while Chas and Nora were appointed laps. Nora recovered some of her good mood, joking about wanting to sit on Tom's lap *with* Chas. Eventually I just made a show of grabbing her and putting her on my knee, which caused Chas to fan herself furiously and sent Nora into gales of semiembarrassed laughter.

"I'm not seeing this," Beryl said, shielding the left side of her face with her hand.

"All right. Arms in, safeties on, let's do this," Sam said from the driver's seat.

"Oh," Beryl said. "We all have weapons, right, children?"

Coalhouse and Chas sang, "Yes, Mom."

As the car started up, Nora slid onto my lap proper, leaning her head against my shoulder. Good trip so far.

"How far away is this place?" Tom asked.

"More than an hour west of here," Sam said, eliciting a chorus of groans from those with long legs, myself included.

It was about four-thirty when we hit Highway 2. The drive was pretty enough, and interesting from an outsider's perspective. I'd been told that land was a limited resource in New Victoria, but each off-ramp we passed seemed to lead either to some small town or gathering of houses, all of them with names like "Sandthorn" and "Appleton"—never did I catch a glimpse of another city. Between these there were almost comically large, inexplicably empty tracts of green, terraformed wilderness, interposed by a few areas of marshland and farmland. Miles and miles of underutilized land, probably controlled by the rich. It was completely unlike the Punk territories. I was reminded how little land my people ended up with, and how brown that land seemed to be sometimes.

Samedi couldn't get Aethernet or wireless service in his prehistoric tin can, so after a short bout of conversation there was nothing but the sound of the wind to distract us as we drove into the cloud-shrouded setting sun. It looked like rain. I shut my eyes after a while, giving them a rest from their constant struggle to adapt to the shifting light. Thanks to my heightened senses, I could feel the even, slow expansion of Nora's chest against my side as she breathed, and I lost myself in it. The sensation of it enthralled me even more once my brain made the connection between its steady speed and the fact that she was currently snuggled up between four zombies.

After a while I felt the car make a turn and heard Chas squeal, her voice distorting somewhat, "We're on the ro-ad!" Upon first opening my eyes, I couldn't make out any signs or landmarks—I couldn't even make out what the road was made of. When my vision adjusted I saw we were cruising over a long ribbon of gravel, nothing but grassland to either side, headed toward a line of trees about a mile off.

"The paper said to 'look for the light,'" Tom said. "I see no light. I see no anything."

Chas glanced out the window. Clouds started to gather more thickly, the remaining sunlight abruptly fading away. Suddenly she bounced atop Tom and shouted, "Wait! Ov-er there!" I followed her pointing finger. Sure enough, back toward the tree line I could make out an assortment of carriages and tents thrown into silhouette by electric lights and bonfires.

"Still want to do this?" I asked of the car at large.

"If anyone says no, I will *nip* them so sev-ere-ly, I swear to Goood," Chas grumbled. The last syllable flickered in her newly equipped throat, the sound reverberating, theraminlike.

"Okay, then," Sam said as he put the accelerator to the floor.

A few minutes later he turned off into a field full of carriages, carts, even monowheeled motorcycles. He found a place to park and we all fell out of the car, unfolding ourselves from one another. Nora and Dr. Chase limped as the blood returned to their legs. Music filtered to us from the area where the tents were set up—pounding, commanding even from a distance. A clap of thunder augmented it.

Looking around, I realized not all of the vehicles I saw could possibly belong to the Changed. In fact there were quite a few people about—both living and dead. Some, like us, were just arriving. Others were making their way back to the carriages, laughing, seemingly in high spirits. It wasn't what I expected to see.

Nora opened the trunk, retrieving her cloth-covered basket of offerings before taking my arm. The crew fell in behind us as we moved toward the camp. I could hear Dr. Chase entreating everyone to remain on their guard, and I knew it should be *me* saying that, but—that was before the scene in front of us registered.

"Are you *seeing* this?" Chastity yelled. "Are you *seeing* this, or have I finally made it to heaven? Dying a virgin has totally freaking worked in my favor!"

It wasn't just a camp we were walking in on.

It was a party for the ages.

The tents marked the outer edge of the campsite, which was located partly within the trees. Above it, tangled within the tree branches, hung a weblike mesh of multihued electric lights, their cords snaking over the grass and terminating at large portable generators. In the very middle of the camp sat a double-tiered stage of new wood, on the lower level of which an all-zombie *band* was currently performing. The deafening music was unlike the complicated, frilly, "high-class" compositions I'd come to expect from New Victorian wireless stations, even the ones that played popular ballads and dance songs for the working-class. It was more like desert rag than anything else, heavy with fiddles and banjos and other things that twanged.

On the upper level of the stage, dead girls with their blouses scandalously unbuttoned and their skirts hiked up were dancing with hand- and armfuls of tiny glass spheres, which they induced, by their sinuous movements, to roll across their bodies. As the stormy weather built I could see the spheres were illuminated from within, their colors constantly shifting. Other zombies, male and female, circulated freely through the crowd, performing tricks with parasols and cages of mechanical fleas, advertising trinkets for sale, and offering to tell fortunes. A few of the performers wore masks. Colorful, intricate masks—animal and harlequin, plain leather and pearl-encrusted. As if the field was the site of a massive masquerade. My imagination tore off without me, and I found myself wondering what else we might find in the crowd.

I also wondered what we might find back in the parking lot.

Aside from the stage area, there were no clear distinctions between those on display and those watching them. The crowd was enormous, and comprised not only of zombies—there were plenty of living people, men and women, fine and poor. Some were dancing; others had spread blankets out on the trampled grass. A few had been picnicking and were now hurrying to pack up as the sky darkened and the wind threatened, their picnic baskets flawlessly appointed with real china and crystal and silver, not to mention the odd miniature absinthe fountain.

As I considered my next move, one of the drummers released a haunting, mournful cry, and at once it was answered both by his fellow performers and about half the audience. A second cry went out, and a dead man answered its call, ascending the high stage to thunderous applause. He wore his roughly braided hair twisted into a bun atop his head, and had daubed his face with flaky red paint in the shape of a skull.

"I'm Bruno Allende!" the man yelled. He was easily heard over the music, though he didn't sound like he was wearing a mic. Without wasting another moment, he launched into song. His voice was frenetic and he moved like a caged animal, repeatedly throwing himself at the edge of the stage as if preparing to launch himself into the audience, only to stop just short.

> *"You wanna control me? Wind me up, watch me go,*
> *Do what you want, jump when you say so?*

Not gonna happen! Never again!
The power is ours now, no need to pretend!"

A hand on my arm roused me from my shocked fascination. Nora reached up and tipped my face toward the edge of the crowd. There, a living girl was dancing with not one but two zombie gents in a way that'd make her father pop a vessel. No one else was paying them any mind.

"What *is* this?" Nora said, eyes wide. "Did you know they'd be having a party?"

My sense of responsibility finally kicked in. I looked around for Dr. Chase and found her standing with Renfield off to the side, both stony-faced. Sam was nowhere to be seen. Before I could say anything, Chase shouted, "We should go! This is some sort of . . . I don't know what!"

The music slowed and Bruno sang out, voice roiling with emotion, *"It isn't over till I say it's over! The Reaper already left me behind!"*

As the music took over again, two gray girls clad in little more than their corsets and bloomers oiled their way across the stage, their bodies rolling in time to the beat. I heard Chas shouting, "I want to do that! Oh, Tommy, I waaant to do that!"

Dr. Chase was right. This was the sort of event that would get Nora chained to her closet door for the rest of her life, if Dr. Dearly ever caught wind of it. And it was way too easy to be caught off guard—clearly the Changed weren't the only ones here. Who knew what else these people were into? "Where's Doc Sam?" I yelled.

"He went that way!" Chase pointed toward the area we'd just come from.

"Okay!" I gestured to the others. "C'mon, we're regrouping!"

"Regrouping?" Coalhouse shouted. A female zombie with the

right half of her head of long brown hair shaved clean was standing next to him, and annoyance creased her features as he spoke. She had a tray strapped around her neck that held paper fans and cigarettes for sale; Coalhouse had a few bills in his hands. "We just got here!"

"No!" Chas leaned forward, looking at me across Tom's head. "No way! I'm not going. This is no worse than any party we e-ver threeeew!"

"Yeah, but we know one another. You want to walk home?"

Nora moved ahead of me, but Chas refused to budge. Coalhouse took two seconds to think, his brow furrowing, before tossing his money at the half-bald zombie and shoving Chas and Tom forward. "Listen to the cap. C'mon."

With far more effort than it should have taken, we got everyone out of the heart of the crowd and off to the sidelines, where other concertgoers had gathered to converse via shouts and sign language. I located Samedi a few yards away and managed to convey, through the storm of Chastity's angry shrieks, that we should head for the parking lot.

Samedi unbuttoned his frock coat as he walked over to join us. He wore twin revolvers beneath, in a shoulder holster. "Pickpockets," he told me. "In the crowd. Came back here to keep an eye on the Rolls and keep my head down, saw them hit a few marks. Everybody check."

"Great," I said, patting my pockets. Luckily, it looked like they hadn't hit us yet. "You think the concert's a ruse, then?"

"I've partied from one end of this continent to the other," he said. "I've drunk many questionable things and danced in many questionable ways. But I never thought I'd walk in on something like that this far north."

"I have so much to learn from you," Nora decided.

"And I've got nothing against them, if a party's all it is," I broke in. "But I've got a bad feeling. The masks." Understanding rippled through my crew, their expressions shifting. "I think we should case the parking lot, see if the Model V is here. Even if we don't find it, look through the crowd."

"It's a bit of a leap from pickpocketing to grand theft auto," Ren noted. "You can get masks like that anywhere up here. And most of the carriages must belong to the guests."

"Yeah, but the Changed would have needed transport to get this far outside the city. Maybe it's coincidence, maybe it's not. Won't hurt to look."

"What about the boy?" Nora asked.

"I'll find him," Coalhouse volunteered. I nodded. He was stepping it up tonight, and I appreciated it.

"You came!"

I turned, the others following suit. It was Laura, with Dog close by her side. She wasn't wearing her kerchief, and the electric lights brought out the pale orange shade of her hair and added gloss to the leaves unfurling from her body.

"Hey," I said. Nora's jaw dropped open.

Dog rushed over to me, holding out his arm stump. He screwed up his face and stomped his foot.

"Missing it?" I had to conclude. He nodded. "Well, I've brought the man you need to see." I used a hand to guide him between his shoulders, pointing out Samedi, who recovered himself and beckoned the boy over. I tried to send Sam a look that read *Work fast*.

"I knew you wouldn't forget!" Laura curtsied to Nora and the others, smiling widely. "I sent you a note. I copied it from the broadsides everyone else made."

"This is Laura," I said, before addressing her directly. "That's all well and good, but . . . what is this place?"

"Our new home." She joined her hands together. "I like living in the open. New London kills everything."

"But I thought you guys were a pro-zombie group?"

"We are! Pro-zombie and pro-living!"

"Is that the reason for the party, then?"

"Oh, this is how we're going to make money to help the dead. Though some of our brothers and sisters are still going to the city every day. The trinket hawkers and beggars. They bring people back with them." Laura spun around. "Because now we can hold *big* parties! It's just starting, and look how many people are already here, giving money to the performers. Word's spreading fast. No one has to do anything wrong anymore! No more stealing, no more fighting!"

I tried to pick apart her words, but Beryl beat me to it. "You're a gang? A guild?" Samedi looked up from his inspection of Dog's unbound arm, his eyes filling with alarm.

Laura nodded innocently and moved closer to Dog. "They used to call us the Grave House Gang. But I like the Changed much better."

"I take it back," Renfield said. "Grand theft auto is apparently completely plausible. You'd think I'd learn."

I cursed inwardly. Before anything else, I had to get Nora out of there.

"You."

The drums built up again as I turned around to find the zombie known as Maria Hagens, formerly of Company Z, standing behind us. "Hagens!" I said, smiling slightly in spite of everything. "Haven't seen you in months."

"Hey! Good to see you made it out," Tom offered.

Laura's eyes went wide, and at once her ebullient mood disappeared. "Come on, Dog." Samedi looked at her in confusion as she stepped in to take him, and she added, "I'm sorry, sir."

"Don't talk to him, Laura," Hagens snapped. "He's not one of us!" Laura cowered away from Hagens, working furiously with Dog's bandages.

Shock momentarily managed to convince me I hadn't heard

right. "What do you mean, not one of you? We were all in Z-Comp together!" I indicated my friends with an open hand.

The bony woman's cracked lips curled back in a sneer. "You'll know soon enough. On that note, how're you and that little piece of meat getting along? What was her name? Nora?"

Anger started to sting my lips and cheeks—my skin trying to flush. Another clap of thunder rang out, as if the atmosphere itself sympathized. *"Meat?"*

"I'm right here." Nora stepped forward, her eyes narrowing. I reached out and pulled her back against me by her shawl. "Want a taste? I could put my fist in your mouth."

"Don't tempt me," Hagens said. "I owe Dr. Dearly a debt for finding me and keeping me going, and this is my payment. You better run to ground *now*, you hear me? Actually, that goes for *all* of you. You better watch your backs!"

"You . . ." Nora didn't even have to use a foul insult—her tone said it all. She tossed down her basket and advanced on Hagens again, but I caught her by her elbows, my body going rigid with anger.

"You don't talk to her like that," I said, careful to speak slowly and loudly. "Ever. What the hell's wrong with you, Hagens?"

Hagens turned to me, eyes burning with rage. "What's wrong with *me*? What's wrong with *you*? How dare you show your face here?"

"What are you talking about?"

Hagens's body tightened, her voice rising in a scream. "Don't act as if you don't know! As far as I'm concerned, Griswold, you abandoned us on the docks the night of the Siege. You left half of us to die, and marched the other half off to hell to save that piece of meat's father!"

"Left you to *die*?" My voice was twisted by a growl. "What are you talking about? Colonel Lopez gave you all an out!"

"An *out*?" Hagens took a step toward me. "Is that what you

call it? Is that what you call nearly having to crawl on your hands and knees through the city after the people you've been trying to protect turn on you, praying someone doesn't blow your brains out?"

"I took as many men as I could, and Lopez didn't have to encourage the rest of you to go anywhere. He saved lives that night. He gave Company Z a chance, even if he had to relay the extermination order in the end!"

"His men hunted us down like dogs!" Hagens's voice was always strident and tough, but when she yelled, she sounded like an angry man rather than a woman. "No. I owe you nothing. *I'm* the one protecting my people. It's out of the kindness of my rotting heart that I'm telling you you're not welcome here!"

"Chas and I woke up in a desert strewn with the remains of our *friends* because of Wolfe and the extermination order, and you think I somehow got out of dealing with it?" The words were out before I could stop them, and to no avail. Hagens continued to glare at me; my friends stared at me with pity. Pity I didn't want.

"You tell me," Hagens said. "We were both betrayed. Which one of us is still working alongside them?"

As the first few drops of rain fell, Laura rallied. "Mártira said all Changed are welcome—"

"Not this one!" Hagens shouted, rounding on her. "Never! I have no real scrap with the others, but Bram Griswold is *not* Changed. He's a living man in a corpse. And he plays by living men's rules!"

The first sparks of a deep, blistering anger started popping in my stomach upon hearing those words. My entire unlife was an exercise in control, but Hagens was pushing buttons that ought not be pushed. I felt myself take a step toward her, even as my higher brain processes told me to back down. That it wasn't worth the risk.

"Bram." Samedi moved in front of her, his eyes boring into mine. "Let's go. Come on. We have a lot of things to figure out, but not here."

"Look at him. He won't even fight me," Hagens said scornfully.

"Miss Hagens," Dr. Chase said as she moved to usher Renfield and Chas forward. "Do shut up. And everyone check your pockets again."

"Did a human say something?" Hagens challenged. "Because I thought I heard a *human* say something. Oh well, couldn't have been important."

Dr. Chase's look of hurt caught me before I could do something I'd regret—because I knew precisely how she felt. Forcing myself to confront my impulses, to take the right path, I spread my arms out, capturing Nora's arm and Tom's elbow. Marching them forward, I trained my eyes on the parking lot, my ears on the rustling grass. This was a mistake. The whole damn day'd been a mistake. We just had to get somewhere safe, and get on task. In control. Figure out a new plan for helping Dog.

Resolute as always, Hagens called after us, "Keep away from here! If fortune favors you, I'll never see you again! Because if I do . . . well. We're not on the same side! Not any longer!"

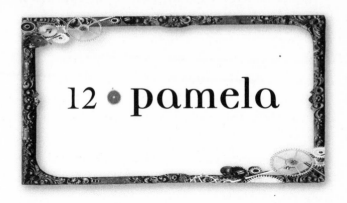

12 • pamela

On the walk home from church, Isambard told jokes. Mom laughed louder and louder at each one, as if Issy were scaling new heights of hilarity the longer he went on. Dad cracked a smile. It was a rare, hoped-for moment.

And I couldn't enjoy it.

Strolling along with my family, I turned my face up to the sun and let my jacket slip slightly off of my shoulders. I didn't care if it looked shameful or stupid. I was tired of being ignored, sidelined. Did I just somehow *look* unimportant? Did something in my eyes, my face say, *She doesn't know what she's talking about. Don't listen to her.*

It wasn't Nora wandering off that truly upset me, although that was part of it. I'd run off myself, many times—to help her, Mr. Coughlin, Vespertine, Jenny—so I had no room to judge her there. I could even admire her for it. And it wasn't that I didn't want to help people, I just . . .

God, when was it going to get easier? I knew I wasn't thinking straight, but it was getting harder to do so. When was someone going to pick *me* as their foremost concern for a change? When was I going to be able to *stop* thinking in terms of saving or guarding the people around me? Not that I'd ever choose to, but when would I again have the *option* to stop?

And how long was she going to keep picking Mr. Griswold over me?

"Pamela." I looked at my mother. "Wear your jacket properly, sweetheart."

Taking a breath, I shrugged it up. "Of course."

Mom wouldn't allow me to help with Sunday dinner. Upon being chased out of the kitchen, I lingered in the hallway, thinking that perhaps I ought to find Dad and tell him about it—but then sounds started to echo from the kitchen that offered me a deep, ineffable sense of comfort. A knife being sharpened, the pop of a jar lid. From the parlor came the sound of Isambard and Jenny playing. Jenny said something, and Dad laughed.

In the interests of preserving the moment, I did nothing.

Instead I chose to distract myself by working on the laundry. There was no guarantee that Lopez would come, after all, and I didn't feel like sitting on my hands. The laundry room was in the cellar, right next door to the bakery kitchen; both had white-tiled walls and floors. The smells of yeast and flaked white soap brought back ten thousand childhood memories—good ones. After a while I found myself humming as I starched and ironed a small glacier of handkerchiefs. We went through so many of them now.

Soon I came upon Lopez's. I had to return it to him somehow, even if he didn't come to call on us. To keep Michael's hankie had seemed romantic and intimate; I didn't want Lopez to think I entertained the same notions about his. Not that he probably would. I'd never gotten a creepy vibe from him. But I wanted to avoid any hint of impropriety—more than that, any reminder of Allister. I'd already burned his.

Something struck me as I unfolded his handkerchief from the

pile, though. After a moment I started cursing myself for not having seen it before. His monogram was embroidered in faint, dignified gray—*E.N.L.*—but a narrow black border lined the edge. He was in mourning. Maybe he'd lost someone during the Siege. Poor man.

Just then I heard the doorbell ring, the squeak of footsteps. As useless as it was, I stopped and looked at the ceiling. "Good afternoon," a deep voice said as the door opened. "Would your parents happen to be in?"

"It *is* you!" Isambard exclaimed. "Come in, Lord Lopez."

This was it.

Hurriedly I ironed and folded Lopez's handkerchief, before turning my eyes to the rows of empty, cocoonlike clothing suspended from the ceiling beams. Among them I found my blue lawn, which at least was good enough to be seen in at St. Cyprian's. For a moment I contemplated changing into it in the middle of the basement. I was currently wearing an old chintz dress with cheap, scratchy lace at the neck and sleeves and a small patch on the back—my work clothes. I'd changed into them after church. And last time I'd felt so out of place, so dowdy, so . . . well, the way Cyprian's had taught me to feel.

Something ultimately stopped me from reaching for the dress, though. It was the memory of my mother forcing me to "read" innocently in the parlor when we knew full well Michael was outside, preparing to call. Forcing herself to embroider in her rocking chair while he was there—my mother, the hard worker, the bootstrap-puller. Just so we'd resemble his idea of "normal," of "respectable."

Bile rose in my throat. I would never do that again. Never let her do that again. Not for a lord, not for anybody.

In the end I just shook out my long braids and pulled my hair back into an impromptu bun, sleeking down the strands behind my ears with water from the washer. Then, taking a breath, I began my climb. "I hope I'm not interrupting anything," Lopez was saying. "I thought Sunday might be the best day to catch all of you at home."

"Not at all! I'm not sure where my daughter's run off to," Dad replied. "But please, let me take your coat and hat, my lord."

"Thank you. And please, Lopez alone will do."

"Are you sure?" My father seemed confused.

"Very sure. Feel free to consider it an eccentricity."

I came up behind them from the basement entrance, Lord Lopez's handkerchief pressed protectively between my hands. *"Lopez!"* I exclaimed, doing my best to sound as if I'd been ignorant of his arrival. "How nice to see you."

The man turned to regard me, his expression thankful. "Miss Roe." He bowed. He was dressed all in black again, but subtle little differences convinced me his current suit was different from the one I'd seen him in before. The lapels were of black velvet, and his cravat was tinseled with silver thread.

"May I officially present my daughter," my father said. "Although I'll refrain from indulging in the three-ring name circus, if you don't mind, seeing as you two already know each other."

After curtsying, I walked forward and offered him his handkerchief. It was the perfect time to do it, with my parents watching. "I was just about to put this someplace safe. Thank you for letting me borrow it."

Lopez accepted it and tucked it away. "My pleasure." My mother smiled at me approvingly.

"Please, join us in the parlor." My father ushered everyone forward. "Is the tea ready, dear?"

"Very nearly." Mom saw herself out.

Dad shut the screen off with the remote control as soon as he entered. Isambard was already inside, holding Jenny by the hand. My father clapped a hand on Issy's shoulder and said to Lopez,

"And this is my son, Isambard. I believe that last time you saw him he was . . . alive."

Issy bowed stiffly to Lopez. "I owe you my thanks, my lord."

"Think nothing of it. I'm glad to see you looking so well, young man." Lopez looked down at Jenny, who was staring up at him, her eyes like two headlights. "And who is this little lady?"

"Jenny Delgado, one of our neighbors."

Lopez inclined his head at her. "Hello, Miss Delgado."

Issy squeezed Jenny's hand, whispering, "Curtsy."

Jenny did no such thing. Instead she pointed at Lopez's face and pronounced, "You're wearing a caterpillar!"

Lopez straightened up, his hand moving to his moustache. After a protracted second, he chuckled. "Is it that bad? I have been away from civilization for quite some time."

Laughing, I moved to pick Jenny up, relieving Isambard of his duties for a while. "Come on, Jenny-bear. Let's find your crayons."

I took her to the corner by the fireplace, where she had a tin pail of crayon stubs and a long roll of butcher paper to draw on. As I tore off a piece for her, Lopez took a seat on our satin sofa, glancing curiously about our poky parlor. I felt another stab of embarrassment, despite the fact that my mother had polished it obsessively upon learning that a *lord* might call on her—but a split second later he caught my eye and smiled kindly, and I found my embarrassment dissolving. Outside, it began to rain.

"We all owe you so much," Dad said as he sat down in his usual chair. Isambard sat in Mother's rocking chair for the time being. "My daughter told us what happened that night, but I'm afraid it still seems rather surreal. I never thought of attempting to locate you, to thank you, and that is a mark against me. Thank goodness you ran into her again."

"Your thanks are happily accepted, but not necessary," Lopez said, addressing my father, his expression growing serious. "If I have performed my duty, that is enough. And I can only apologize for my repeated run-ins with Miss Roe without your knowledge."

Dad shook his head. "No, no, never mention it again." Upon hearing this, Lopez seemed to relax a little.

Mother came in with the best tea service then, and set it down on the table. "My daughter said you're no longer with the army? Forgive my curiosity."

"No. I was relieved at the pleasure of the government, following the death of my elder brother, Lord Atticus Lopez."

"I'm so sorry," Mother said, regret washing across her plump features. "Did he . . . was he infected?"

"No, though he did pass away during the troubles in December." Lopez set his hands in his lap. "It's not a story for little ears, I'm afraid. Nor do I derive much enjoyment from its telling."

"Of course." Mom started pouring. As she did, Isambard sent me a frantic look that told me how badly he wanted to get in on the conversation. Even in death his age prevented him from speaking unless spoken to. Mine did, too. It must have seemed terribly unfair to Issy—he could never actually grow up and reach the stage where he could speak with other men as a man in his own right. The fact that he wasn't arguing against this very thing, fighting for a reevaluation of his social prospects, told me just how much death had changed him. The old Issy would have clawed his way up the social ladder tooth and nail.

I wasn't sure whether to be proud of him or utterly devastated.

"I've been renting in the city since his funeral," Lopez volunteered. Accepting a cup of tea, he joked, his tone dull, "You must correct me, madam, if I make any etiquette mistakes. I'm sure fifteen years in the army have taken their toll. You've obviously raised two wonderful children, and I'm sure I could benefit from your instruction."

Mom smiled at him, and her smile struck me as being from another time, another place. It was a smile born of true sympathy, of pleasure at another's kindness. I only had a few moments to enjoy it before Jenny tugged on my sleeve, calling my attention back to her. I helped her to hold her crayons as she worked.

The adults went on to speak in soft tones of many nontopics—the weather, the prices of things since the Siege, everything but the actual violence and events thereof. I listened compulsively, anxious that Lopez might still give me up, tell them about the real circumstances of our second meeting—but he never did. In fact, there was something calming in his demeanor, something about the way he phrased his statements that made them seem fair and just. It put me at ease. As he and my parents chatted, I could see it was having an effect on them, too. They joked a little. Their postures softened.

It was a priceless gift.

After a while Mother rose to light a few more oil lamps. Premature darkness was settling outside, the rain coming down harder, the blue walls of the parlor turning gray. As she did, Lopez addressed my brother. "Forgive me for being so forward, but may I ask after your health?"

Isambard scratched at his lip. "You mean about being a zombie, my lord?"

Lopez coughed. "Yes. After I left you and your sister behind, I confess, I wondered what fate I was consigning you to."

"Well, after I reanimated and we got back to the house to hide, Dr. Evola went to work on me. He drained all my blood, put in my valves." Isambard offered his wrist to show off his medication valve. "Because my heart doesn't work anymore, you see."

If Lopez was disturbed by this, he didn't show it. "I see. And what are your plans now?"

Isambard thought about it for a moment before saying, "Just to . . . do what I have to. Jenny's my responsibility. I don't know.

I'd help in the bakery, but I can't now." He rotated his paper cup of water in his hands. "I used to never want to, ever. Now I do, and I can't."

"I understand that well." Lopez looked over at me. "And you, Miss Roe?"

Jenny started struggling to her feet, and I helped her stand. "The same. To be with those I love." I had no answer other than that. I couldn't exactly inform him that my highest goal at the moment was to stop dreaming of death and destruction, stop jumping at every noise.

Lopez nodded minutely, before looking to the floor. "Ah, what's this?"

As he'd spoken, Jenny had walked over to him, piece of paper in hand. When she finally neared him she stumbled over a slight hump in the carpet, and Lopez immediately reached down to take one of her hands and help her regain her balance. Once she had her bearings, she shook him off and proudly held up the page. She'd drawn, ostensibly, Lord Lopez. At least the drawing looked vaguely head-shaped, although the head sported a green caterpillar for a moustache, complete with legs and antennae. "You!"

Lopez's lips spasmed, but he didn't laugh. "I am honored, Miss Delgado. A striking resemblance! May I keep it?" She nodded happily. "Will you sign it for me?"

"One last awkward question, if you'll permit me," Dad said, as Jenny ran back to me. "Your surname is Lopez. As in the Lopezes of Marblanco?"

Lopez set down his cup. "I'm afraid so."

This held absolutely no meaning for me, but my mother put the box of matches back on the mantel and slowly lowered her arms, staring at him. "Truly? How sad."

My father attempted to shush her with a look. Issy and I shared a confused glance. Marblanco? What was Marblanco?

"Yes." Lopez's voice was now gruff, and I felt pins and needles in my chest again. I willed my parents to shut up.

"You have no other relatives, then, I take it, aside from your late brother?" Dad asked.

"None with whom I am close." Lopez glanced at the mantel clock just in time to see it strike the half hour. "I'm afraid I mustn't stay much longer."

My father stood up and bowed. "It's my fault. I shouldn't have mentioned it. I apologize for causing you any discomfort."

"No, not at all." Lopez gained his feet as well and extended his hand. "It was a long time ago. Your family is kind in the extreme. It's been an honor to accept your hospitality." Dad shook his hand, obviously relieved. Still, I felt at a loss, anxious about what he'd done. Whatever it was. I didn't understand.

Neither did I understand the explosion that tore through my head the next time I blinked.

·This time I knew it wasn't fireworks, or thunder, or anything outside. The explosion echoed from under my feet. I gripped Jenny to me, her bird-sharp wail cutting through the sudden ringing in my ears. I could have sworn I'd felt the floor shift beneath me, but as my heart started to painfully pound, I wasn't sure if that had actually happened or not. ·

Dad and Lopez flew out into the hall. Mom was screaming. I stood up, seemingly in slow motion, and pushed Jenny into Dad's chair, ordering her to stay there. Issy moved to help with her, and I ran after the men, suddenly keenly aware of the weight of my dress.

Dad was at the open door. There was no panic outside; only a nondescript carriage racing down the dark, rainy street. It was going so fast that when it swerved to avoid another carriage, it teetered terrifyingly to one side. Someone was leaning out of the window, watching our house, and for a moment I thought myself mad—because that person had a beak. Like a giant bird.

Like the people who'd attacked Nora and Mr. Griswold.

Lopez opened the door to the basement and stepped back, yelling, "Down there!"

I turned. Dad grabbed my arm, as if he expected me to run down into the cellar—but I didn't have to. I could see it. The door that led to the bakery was gone, a gaping hole standing in its place. I could make out more damage beyond—cracked flooring, destroyed equipment. Pieces of wall tile crumbled before my eyes, like sugar cubes in water. Dust and smoke billowed upward, small fires kindling in the corners.

Lopez turned back to look at me, his voice forceful. "Gather everyone into the street and call the police. *Now.*"

Without looking back, without even pausing for breath, I ran to the parlor. I was still unsure what I'd just witnessed. All I knew was that the very world was shaking apart around us.

Again.

13 • michael

Parliament was hideous, and its hideousness was a point of New Victorian pride. Not only did it sport hundreds of real marble statues of dubious symbolism and stretches of pretty, but pointless stonemasonry, it was crowned by a holographic lion and unicorn locked in battle, the pair of them half as large as the sprawling building beneath their feet.

As our carriage rattled past, I thrust my upper body out of the window and saluted. "Your obedient son!" The other boys crowed with laughter.

My cohorts for the evening had proven far more capable than the ones I'd been tasked with before—especially the one waiting for our carriage on the corner of George Street, hat off, his signal that the bakery was dark and empty and thus ready to be blown up. There hadn't been anyone waiting there last Saturday. Unwilling to drive by the bakery, we circled around, and I ended up tossing the bomb into a rubbish bin in an alley. It seemed safer than driving all the way to the river with live ordnance in my lap, like we planned. I'd lost my composure.

For all I knew, though, the boys with me *were* the ones who'd accompanied me before. Between the beaked masks and the voice morphers installed in them, I had no idea who any of my "Brothers" actually were, ignorance casting a spell of protection over all of us. It made the other boys rowdy, fearless, and I drank so I could act that way, too.

"I still can't believe the Murder actually got you a *bomb*. *Two* bombs," one of the Brothers said as he pulled me out of the rain and back inside the carriage. I stumbled over the large burlap sack on the floor as I made my way to my seat. The mask obscured my peripheral vision.

"You've got some balls to go after a bunch of living sympathizers that way. Can you imagine? Zombie filth living beside a bakery? It's a public health threat, that's what it is."

I laughed, even as my stomach twisted. I had to keep laughing, had to keep joking, because I wasn't sure what I was feeling—it didn't have a convenient name, like *regret* or *anger*. It was a disconnected feeling, like floating in a bubble of dissipated sensation. Almost euphoric, minus the actual euphoria. Like my mind had somehow disavowed my own body.

The deed was done. Payback had been delivered. Pamela Roe had to pay for what she'd done to me, true enough. She'd run me ragged, put my life in danger, humiliated me—put her *hands* on me. After all I'd done for her. And she was so *low* that I could enact little social revenge. I'd had no choice but to fight back with literal fire.

Now I could focus on the end game. In fact, I could *only* focus on the end game, which lent it solidity in my mind. Made it seem real. The plan hadn't actually seemed *real* before.

The burlap sack lurched to one side, suddenly alive and rolling like a maggot. I kicked it, the reaction purely born of fear, and it stilled with an all-too-human sob.

"I hate it when the entertainment gets uppity," my Brother grumbled.

"Just enjoy the ride, gents," I said, settling back. "Haven't the rotters taught you to treasure every second?"

One of the masked boys cracked up. "Oh, yeah. They're so wise now. So holier-than-thou. Is that why they burn so well, you think? All that holy fire? Or is it because hell so desperately wants them back?"

I kept laughing.

The pub we were meeting in that evening was a dingy little hole in the wall below street level, one step removed from the sewer. Water from the storm drains crept in, beading down the walls. The bartender and his girls kept their faces carefully neutral as they served us, their blaring sound system providing us all with excuses.

As a courtesy to them we all deposited our weapons on a single table, slightly out of the way. The little collection was impressive— guns, bats, even a sword, of all things. We shed our outer coverings, but kept the masks. There were about thirty Brothers in attendance, but I had no idea how many were actually involved overall.

I kept an eye out for a bottle green velvet frock coat, and moved when I saw it. Nobody could say whose face resided beneath that particular mask, but everybody knew him by his jacket. He was #1712, our record keeper, and a one-man dealer of almost everything illegal. Rumor held that he also knew the identity of #0, the shadowy figure who'd supposedly started the whole thing. For all that legend-building, #0, like everyone else, was merely a rich boy in a mask. If he was even involved anymore. The first letter I'd received had included that suggestion: *Even I will not know who you are, or if you are involved, or ever become uninvolved. Neither will you know who I am, or if I ever stand at*

*your side. I may send these letters and walk away, to watch you all
from afar.*

Brother Green Jacket nodded when he saw me approaching.
I'd worn a plain gold oval cravat pin to aid in recognition, as I'd
told him I would in my note. He indicated that I ought to follow
him through an iron-studded doorway, and I did so, drink in
hand.

"Brother," he said once we were alone, his voice computerized. There was little light, but going by the bottles stacked
around us, we were in a storage room. "I take it you were successful this time?"

"You'll see it on the news when you get home."

"Wonderful. I'm glad you wanted to go big. After all, you're
asking quite a lot of me. Of the Murder. A special escort, a special
venue . . . that your Brothers not be there. I respect your vision,
but it's rather complicated to set up."

I knew it was. That's why I'd joined up. My dreams were far
too grand and risky to enact on my own. "Are you sure the police
won't be able to trace the bombs?"

"I trust my supplier." He gestured into the darkness. As I
watched, a large form materialized. Once it neared what little
light filtered in around the edges of the door, I could see that it
was a big man in a grimy coat, a mop of curly hair framing his
wind-burned face. "As well as this fellow. He can find anyone."

"Not just find. Anyone can *find*, I deliver. Alive. Have for over
twenty years." The man gave a shallow nod. "They call me the
Ratcatcher."

"Good, because I know right where the rat is," I said, reaching
into my jacket to grab two more envelopes. I offered one to him.
"Unfortunately, that happens to be with a lot of other people.
And I need him in one piece, in a secure location. It'll do me no
good to attack him on the street."

Ratcatcher took the envelope and turned it over without opening it. Even if he wanted to look at the contents, the lack of light prevented him from doing so. "Couple thou in here, by the weight of it," he commented.

"You get the other half when I've got the bastard's putrid guts on my hands."

"Dead? This is a lot of money for a dead guy."

"Dead, but big. And well trained. Army man. And he's not the only one I want." He lifted his eyes. "There's a girl. Living. I want her, too. Not a hair on her head is to be harmed, do you understand? She's coming along to watch. I doubt she'd come with me, or I'd handle it myself."

The big man mulled this over and spat on the floor. "Delivery date?"

"Twenty-seventh. A week from now."

"Not a lot of time."

"Exactly. I want to get this over with." Brother Green Jacket chuckled. At the sound of it, I felt the sudden urge to lay him out. My skin prickled as I recalled all the ways this could go wrong, all the horrible things that could happen.

I repressed them. All of them.

"You got it, m'lord."

"Good." I handed the other envelope to Brother Green Jacket. "There's your money. Thank you for the delivery."

Nodding at both of the men, I saw myself out, my heart roaring like a zeppelin engine. Behind me, I heard Green Jacket say, "I'll be in touch. I need to arrange someplace quiet to take them. That one wants to do things a little differently. I'm only going along with it because what he suggests is . . . unique. And he brings the money."

It was over. Nothing more to do but drink.

About half an hour later the bar workers went home, leaving the keys by the cash register. Through my gin-fueled haze I heard the upstairs door being kicked in, the laughter of my

Brothers, the scrabbling and screaming of our latest victim. I knew what was coming. I'd seen it before, and I didn't much care to see it again. But something compelled me to stay.

For such an important ritual, there was little ceremony. Brother Green Jacket took a place along the wall. One of the masked lads stood on a rickety wooden chair and yelled, "Our Brother #38999 becomes a full-fledged member of the Murder tonight!" The Brother in question, slight beneath his burgundy brocade jacket, hoisted his glass high as the others bellowed their congratulations. Furniture and feet scraped against the concrete floor as they cleared a space around him. He stood, conveniently enough, above the floor's drainage grating.

The Brothers I'd rode with brought the bag down. We'd snatched the zombie off the street right before hitting the Roes. I had no idea who he was—only that he'd been unlucky enough to shuffle past our carriage in the alleyway where we'd been waiting for darkness to fall. We'd been assigned the responsibility of bringing a "party favor" back with us.

Together they unhooked the belts used to keep the sack closed and pulled it off, revealing a middle-aged man. Over his nondescript, working-class clothing he wore a leather back brace. "No! No! Please!"

The graduating Brother slammed back the last of his drink, holding his mask above his lips to do so, before shoving it back down. He then turned toward the table full of weapons, rocking slightly on his feet.

"Gun! Gun!" someone chanted.

"Fire!" someone else called. "I've a lighter, and we've got plenty of rotgut to use as fuel. Tie him down and watch him roast!"

The young man in the brocade jacket seemed ready to lend an ear to his compatriots, laughing at each of their suggestions, his body bending. But when he finally made his selection, he chose the sword. Sense of tradition, this one. I wondered who he was.

I wondered if he'd pulled the ridiculous-looking thing out of some wall display in his own family manor.

The Brother turned to the zombie, hefting the weapon with two inexperienced hands. The zombie's voice became shrill. "My name is Emanuel! Emanuel Delgado! I have—"

"For my family!" Brother Graduate screamed as he brought the weapon down. There was no hesitation, no consideration.

No strength.

Well. I'd never seen a man attempt to speak with a blade buried in the middle of his face before. Brother Graduate's blow had been true, but lacking force. The zombie's eyes bulged, almost pulsing, his jaw shaking as he tried to scrape the severed bone down the sword's edge. He was trying to open his mouth to talk, to continue his pleading. I recalled losing a hammer in a zombie's head during the failed attempt to save Roe's little slug of a brother. At least that zombie had gone down.

"Get him again! You didn't get the brain fully!" someone yelled.

"No! Toy with him!"

Bored, I headed for the stairs. The screams of the dying dead man followed me, nipping at my heels. Once outside, I removed my mask and breathed out, trying to chase away the stink of alcohol. The air felt cold against my cheeks.

In a week I'd have to do the same thing.

My phone went off, its chime bright in the darkness. I pulled it out and flicked it open, only to find a message from Vespertine.

> I just got a text about an explosion in bakery on George
> St. Isn't that where R lives?

Suddenly sober as a church mouse, I set my phone down on the flagstones and leaned back against the building, trying not to throw up. She'd remembered. Or had she?

My drunken confessions had freaked me out, upon first remembering them. I thought I might've done myself in. Vespertine had been right—I'd found the finger in my pocket the next
day, the ring on my hand, and immediately thrown both into the
fire. Vespertine hadn't said a word until now, though. I'd thought
myself safe.

How could I play this?

Threats sprung first to mind. I grabbed for my phone.

> Your house has security cameras. I have money to hire
> hackers. If it's digital, it can't be erased. The world will see
> you and me together, alone.

There. Maybe I was slapping my ace down far too early, but it
was the only thing I could think of. Hopefully it'd be the only
thing I needed. Hopefully, even if she had no idea what I was
talking about, it'd be a big enough threat to force her to shut her
mouth and never contact me again. Stupid, stupid women . . .

But then, the girl surprised me with an ace of her own.

> I don't want to out you. I want in. I want to see R and D
> hurt. How can I help?

This . . . I could work with.

14 • Noɾɑ

The drive back was noisy, but Bram and I didn't contribute to the conversation. Around me, the others jabbered and swore; beneath me, Bram was withdrawn.

"Are you *sure* you've never heard of these people before, Dr. I Apparently Break Laws Like Other People Skip Out on Tipping?" Renfield demanded.

"No." Beryl shook her head in silent confirmation. "Consider it an unfortunate side effect of keeping our noses clean and our feet down south. *And my head,* before anyone tries to be clever."

"You could ask the Raaatcatcher about them."

"I could. But to what end?" Samedi looked back at Chas. "We didn't find the Model V, did we? Hell, the cops are probably grateful they've left New London."

He was right. Aside from a few pickpockets, what had we *seen* them do that was illegal? The Changed had every right to assemble. The conversation soon turned to Hagens, the others dissecting the weirdness of her words, but I didn't even want to think about them. I couldn't believe she'd been so cruel to Bram. So irrational, uncaring.

It reminded me of Pamela and our fight.

Now contrite, I fished into my purse and pulled out my phone, turning it on. The animated background twinkled as the phone found a signal.

Once it did, it exploded. All messages from Pam.

My heart sinking, without pausing to read anything, I whispered to Bram, "Tell them to drive to George Street."

Somehow, I knew something was up.

The five cop carriages, the ambulance, and the fire engine we found gathered on George didn't scare me. Such sights were all too common now. It wasn't until Samedi found a place to pull over and I was able to crawl out of the back of the Rolls, only to spot the shaken Roe family standing beside a nearby streetlight, that panic started to blur my vision and numb my skin.

I ran to them. Isambard pointed me out, and Pamela turned, her eyes full of tears. I wrapped my arms around her, and she didn't fight me. "I was standing there less than an hour before . . ."

"It's all right. You're safe. Okay?" Truth be told, I was ready to weep at seeing her so. She'd called my switched-off phone frantically, never reaching me, leaving increasingly shrill voice messages. I'd listened to them all in the car, convinced, by the time I got to the end, that she'd stopped calling for a reason I dared not contemplate. "I'm so sorry."

Pam stepped back from me. "I know." She was in an old dress, soaked through from the rain, a rough blanket thrown about her shoulders. Her voice hitched as she added, "We're very lucky."

Jenny approached from Isambard's side, and Pamela wrapped her up in the blanket as if to hide her. "Loooud," the little girl whined, rubbing at her ear with the palm of her mottled hand.

The others joined us. Bram stopped at my side, while Dr.

Chase approached the shell-shocked Mrs. Roe. Mr. Roe was no-where to be seen. "Where's your father?"

"Talking to the police, with Lord Lopez." Pamela nodded in the direction of the basement-level bakery kitchen door, which was accessible from the sidewalk by a flight of stone steps. It looked like a massive shotgun had been taken to it from the in-side, and the small window beside it was smashed. "They said they threw it in through there."

"I'm sorry," Bram said. Pamela looked up at him and nodded almost lifelessly.

"Who could have done something like this?" I said, my voice rising. The flashing lights on the police carriages, the reporters and gawking civilians I could now see gathered at the far end of the street—I wanted them gone. I wanted everything calm, un-disturbed, back to normal. For Pam, not me.

Pamela shook her head. "I saw . . ."

She gave up as her father approached, a man in a black suit at his side. Mr. Roe looked almost as if he'd been completely drained of blood, and all the vitality it contained. The gentleman, obvi-ously Lord Lopez, was deferring to him, walking slowly, keeping his voice low.

Dr. Chase stepped out of the way, and Mrs. Roe ran to her husband, hugging him tightly as she started to cry. He patted her back. "It's all right, Malati."

"Geoffrey, what are we going to do?"

"Right now, the police want you to get out of here. I'll go with them."

"No! I won't leave my home!"

"What if another bomb goes off? In the house?" At this idea, Mrs. Roe shrank back from her husband and stared at him in hor-ror. "The police won't even let us inside."

"With us," I said. "Please come with us." Dr. Chase nodded.

"I'll drive you," Lopez said, gesturing to his carriage, which was parked on the street. Noticing us, he nodded in greeting. "Wherever you wish to go."

"They said we can come back in the morning to get a few things." Mr. Roe stroked his wife's head. "For now, just go."

Sliding my arm around Pam's shoulders, I tried to lead her in the direction of the Rolls. She came along obediently, numbly; Jenny was forced to follow in order to remain inside her blanket.

And I tried to think of what I could *possibly* say.

Once we were back at my house, everyone went into battle mode. Chas and her mother, Silvia, a quiet and industrious wheelchair-bound zombie lady, insisted the female Roes take Aunt Gene's room. When met with polite resistance, Chas looked Mrs. Roe in the eye and argued, "We've got blankets. We gotta get used to the ground somedaaay anyway."

A cot was moved to the guest room for Isambard. Bram and the older lads disappeared with Lopez to some distant part of the house to talk shop. Dr. Chase called Papa and miraculously managed to get through. He asked to speak to me, and although our conversation consisted mainly of platitudes—Are you all right? Do you need anything?—I could hear a note of anxiety in his voice that, oddly enough, offered me some comfort. He told me he'd be home as soon as he could.

When I finally got Pamela alone, it was inside the hinged, open dollhouse in my room. There, scrunched inside with all the fine little bits of furniture, having traded her own home for a minia-ture version, she gave in to her grief. I held her as she cried, un-willing to let go until she gently shrugged my arms away. She told me what happened, her voice never rising above an emotionless murmur. By the time she got to the part where the police showed up, she appeared even more exhausted than when I'd first found her.

"They haven't really done anything so far. They took pictures and evidence and talked to us. You should see the bakery kitchen."

"Do you have any idea who might've done it?"

For the first time, she met my eyes. She looked beat up, emptied out. "That's just it. Dad opened the door, and I saw a carriage racing away. There was someone leaning out of it, looking back."

"Who?"

"He was wearing a bird mask. Like the ones you described after the hijacking."

Stunned, it took me a second to find my voice. "Did you see them do it, or did you just see them leaving?"

"Leaving. But come on, Nora. They had to have done it. It was like the Devil was driving that carriage."

"Was it Aunt Gene's carriage?"

"No. It was black, though."

"Did you tell the police?"

"Of course."

Basics taken care of, I tried to think. "Do you think anyone had it out for your family?"

"No. I mean, we're far from rich, but Dad did an okay trade. I can't imagine him having enemies. The police seemed to think it was someone angry at the fact that he sold food for zombies, or had a zombie son, but Isambard was never even in the bakery." Tears started to bead in the corners of her eyes again. "Why would someone do something like this? We've never hurt anybody!"

"So they think it was some random anti-zombie bigot?"

Pam tried to shrug and gave up halfway. "I can't imagine anything like this being random, but it must have been. Like that bomb that went off before. And the hijacking. They couldn't have known you and Mr. Griswold would be where you were."

I wasn't sure if I ought to feel guilty or not. The idea that the same masked guys would target both my best friend and me was too out there to be a coincidence. Smoothing her hair off her forehead, I said, "We'll find them. If the police can't do anything, we'll track them down ourselves."

Closing her bloodshot eyes, she said, "Nora, I can't do this."

"Do what?" My stomach dropped. Maybe she was finally going to tell me to get lost. Maybe she was finally going to tell me that as a friend, I sucked pretty damn bad. I was half ready to believe her.

"This." Her voice cracked. "Live like this. Every day I feel like I'm going to die—like I got through the worst of it, but it's still going to kill me, one way or another. Like it's a monster that will hunt me forever. My chest hurts, I'm so anxious I can't sit still. I feel like I'm on drugs or something . . ."

"Pamma." I didn't know what else to say.

"I just can't." She leaned forward. "But the problem is, I don't know what *to* do."

At least she was finally talking. "I understand. I swear." I took both of her hands. "But you can't think you're helpless. You've done amazing things."

"I wish I hadn't *had* to. I think of the things I did every day, and I'm still not sure *how* I did them. I *killed* people." She started crying in earnest. "Did you really ever think of me when you were kidnapped? Because I look at all the things you went through, and my first instinct is to shield you from my problems— but sometimes you act like *nothing* happened to you at all. I know that's not true, not fair, but it seems that way. You didn't want to stay with me, when those people came here—you wanted to be with Mr. Griswold. You ran off today, and I couldn't reach you."

"We were . . ." I decided not to tell her. That was another story entirely.

"And it's not really the running away. I'm sorry for yelling in church. I probably didn't make any sense. It's just that—you have all these new people in your life. And I lost you once, and I'll never forget that. Sometimes I feel like I'm still losing you. Like I'm losing everybody."

Hoping I could at least make some amends, I told her, "I thought about you every day when I was on base, Pamma. I knew you'd be freaking out. I begged to be allowed to contact you, to tell you I was okay. I *still* think about you. And I came for you, and I always will."

"And if I had to, I'd come for you. You know that," she said. "But in a way, that's the problem. My parents think I can handle everything now. *You* think I can handle everything." Sliding her hands out of mine, she gathered part of her skirt into her arms. "Do you think I'm a coward, Nora?"

"No. Never."

"Well, I do." She stood up. "And I think if I just accept that I am, I'll be a lot happier. I think I just need to give up. I've been trying to be what I can't, and I just need to give up."

Pulling myself up by the dollhouse roof, I began, "Pam, you can't—"

The door opened and we both instinctively hushed. It was Mrs. Roe. Pam dabbed at her eyes with her skirt, then released her hold on it. "Pamela? I want you to come to bed."

Pam nodded, and turned to look at me before following. "I'm sorry."

"No, *I'm* sorry. I don't even know what you think you're apologizing for."

"I don't either." Pam shrugged, and moved to trail her mother.

I sat down again, my heart hammering. Whoever'd done this, I had to find them.

I had to make them pay.

*   *   *

I meant to talk to Bram that night, but I fell asleep before I could, emotionally drained. When I was awoken the next morning by Dr. Chase, it was with the news that the Roes wanted to return to their house and get their things. I immediately raced downstairs to join them, still in my wrinkled dress from the day before, my hat hanging perilously onto my hair by a single pin.

We took the Rolls to George Street. Alencar drove. Even he appeared worn-out, his leathery skin seemingly more lined than usual. Yellow tape was wound about the metal railings of both Roe buildings, the ends fluttering listlessly in the breeze. We all stood and stared at it for a while, before Isambard stepped forward and removed a pocketknife from his waistcoat, using it to cut his way inside.

The house was untouched, which seemed somehow odd. My imagination had turned the comfortable Roe home into something out of one of my war holos, but the damage seemed to be confined to the basement. We descended into the laundry room to take a look, and I saw what Pamela meant about "standing right there." The washtub was riddled with holes. Tattered clothing festooned the floor, like fallen flags on a field of battle. More yellow tape was slashed across the doorway to the bakery kitchen, though the door itself was missing. I peeked through, only to wish I hadn't. The floor was scorched, the walls scarred, machinery upended. Everything Mr. Roe had worked so hard to build, gone.

We made our way upstairs before Mrs. Roe could stare too long. She disappeared into the room she shared with her husband, and Issy went to his bedroom; I accompanied Pamela to hers. This time I packed for *her*, as she once had for me at St. Cyprian's, gathering her dresses and hats and bow and arrows. She focused on the little things, which were probably enormously important to her in her current state of mind—her archery trophies. Her ribbon collection.

Someone knocked on the door downstairs. I counseled Pam to ignore it, until Issy stuck his head around her door. "Lopez is back."

"So?" Pam asked him.

"So he's talking about all of us going with him."

"Going with him? Where?"

Isambard shook his head, and pointed to the metal heating grate located in the floor of his sister's room. I immediately understood. The heating vent that led to Pam's room was like a pipeline for noise from the kitchen and parlor. We all used to lie there and eavesdrop on parlor conversations, back when they seemed so adult and mysterious—before we learned that, in actuality, they were as dry as dust, and only the "naughtiness" of listening in had lent them any excitement whatsoever.

We all moved into position, lying on our backs with our heads over the grate and our hands on our stomachs, Issy in the middle. I closed my eyes to listen.

"It's an . . . astonishing offer, Lopez." It was Mrs. Roe. "But I think it would take quite a bit of finessing."

"Undoubtedly. I realize it's a bit out of left field, but frankly I would rather extend the offer and have it refused than not offer at all."

"And I thank you for that, I truly do." A pause, and then she said, "If I may . . . what *does* the house look like now?"

"Better than it did." Lopez sounded reluctant to talk about it. "My late brother spent quite a bit of money hunting down all of the machinery that was gutted from it. I confess, I've not spent much time there, aside from his funeral."

"I'm not sure I blame you."

"On the day of the funeral, I did see that the Mermaid's Ballroom is still incomplete. All of the automatons and chandeliers are there, but the tank has yet to be repaired. The Whispering Garden was operational, however, and the Jewelry Box Room completely restored." He laughed humorlessly. "I can't believe I actually remember the names. I was only six when they tore everything apart."

"It's amazing to think any of it has survived. Do you not fear the government? What if they decide to—"

"Every day." He recovered. "Forgive me, madam. You were saying something."

"It's no matter. At any rate, thank you for calling again, Lopez." I knew that cue—that was the end of it. Indeed, their voices faded. We sat up and peered at one another, grief momentarily forgotten. Before any of us could say anything, though, Mrs. Roe called out, "Pamela? Isambard? Miss Dearly?"

We all straightened our clothes, grabbed what we'd packed, and headed downstairs. When we entered the foyer we found Mrs. Roe waiting. She immediately captured her son's hand, her eyes focusing on his face.

"Are you all right, Mother?" Issy asked after a few seconds of scrutiny.

"Yes," Mrs. Roe said, though her eyes were moist. She lifted her head, and I saw her throat move behind her highly knotted fichu. "Come. Let's go."

Once we were back in the Rolls and Alencar was loading the Roes' boxes and bags, Mrs. Roe got right to the point. "Lord Lopez was here. He called at your house, Miss Dearly, and Dr. Chase sent him on."

"That guy is *weird*," Issy said. "A lord, and he does his own shopping? A lord, and he rents a flat in the city? A lord who doesn't want to be called 'Lord'?" The rest of us must have looked at him quite oddly, for he sighed. "I sound like the old Isambard, don't I? It's been a long night."

"No, you sound like someone's who's been eavesdropping."

Issy grimaced, and I turned around on my knees to look at Mrs. Roe. They were all in the backseat, while I was in the front. "Forgive us."

"It's no matter. What he has proposed *is* somewhat odd." She waited until she had our attention. "In case you did not hear it, he has offered to take us in at his family estate. At least until things are back in order here."

"Where is his estate?" Alencar slipped into the car and nodded at me, before starting her up and pulling out into traffic.

"Honduras. A place called Marblanco." Mrs. Roe looked at me. "Do you know anything of him, Miss Dearly? Have you heard any gossip?"

"No, ma'am. Nothing."

"What *is* Marblanco?" Isambard asked. "Yesterday you guys mentioned it, and you looked like you were talking about Chicago, or something. Atlantis."

"Just . . . a house. It was quite something in its day. I never went there, naturally, but there were stories. They say it's still the only great house in New Victoria without holograms. It was . . ." Mrs. Roe trailed off, again staring into space. Before any of us could call her back to earth, she roused herself with a shrug. "There were stories."

"Could we?" Pamela looked up at her mother, her sweet, liquid eyes suddenly filled with longing. For some reason, it pained me to see. "Could we really go away? All of us?"

Mrs. Roe smoothed her hands over her face. "I don't think so," she said, so softly that I had to strain to hear. "But it was an exceedingly kind offer."

"Why not?" Pamela asked. "It might be safer there."

"We have no idea who this gentleman truly is, Pamela," her mother said. "He has presented himself very honorably thus far, but after young Mr. Allister treated you so abominably? I'd rather not owe an aristocrat anything."

Pamela flushed and went silent. I spoke up. "Mr. Allister treated *everyone* abominably, Mrs. Roe. Please don't judge anyone else by his standard."

She didn't hear me. "We shouldn't even be discussing this." Mrs. Roe looked at Issy, a tear finally slipping free of her right eye. "I don't care if the very sky tumbles down around my family, so long as we're together. But if worse comes to worst, we'll send Isambard away. The idea tears me apart, but if it would keep him safe . . ."

Pam sat back against the seat, the word "oh" writing itself across her face without escaping her lips.

Mrs. Roe sniffed and steadied herself. "But to simply live with a complete stranger, a *bachelor,* any of us—it would not do. It'd be far more prudent to stay with your aunt and uncle."

"He's not really a stranger," Isambard said. "I mean, you let Dr. Evola stay with us, and he was a stranger before the night he helped me."

"True." Mrs. Roe smiled at her son, and moved to take him into her arms. "You're such a good boy, do you realize that? You're my little earthbound angel."

Isambard lowered his eyes, clearly mortified. After a moment he said, "Do you think all of this is my fault, though? Because of what I am?"

"Not your *'fault.'* Don't use that word," Pamela said, looking toward the window. Her tone was dull. It worried me.

A few minutes later we entered the Elysian Fields guardhouse and started down the long tunnel that led underground. As we descended, Issy's phone rang. He answered it, before frowning and handing it to his mother. "It's Mrs. Delgado."

"Oh, is she ready to pick up Jenny?"

"Yes, but she also says her husband hasn't been home all night."

Mrs. Roe took the phone. The conversation picked up steam

as we entered the Elysian Fields proper, her eyes filling with worry. "No, we haven't seen Mr. Delgado. When was he supposed to be back?"

Casting my eyes over the vacant, darkened subterranean streets, I realized that Papa was right. The city wasn't safe for anyone. Pamela should go. I thought this even as I understood that no matter how ugly it got, I wasn't leaving just yet.

Not without doing a few things first.

15 • Bram

Upon waking, I wasn't surprised to find that Isambard wasn't in the room. He was a good kid, and that meant he'd be looking after his mother and sister in their hour of need, or helping his father. I quietly made up my cot, letting everyone else catch a few more minutes of shut-eye. As I did, I started mentally racking up jobs for the day. Foremost among them was going after the bastards who'd targeted the Roe family.

Issy and Lopez had mentioned the masks. It wasn't hard to do the math.

I'd hated leaving Nora last night, but I figured Pamela probably wouldn't want me around—and besides, I wanted to talk to Lopez while he was available. Our brief meeting had gone well. He seemed like a stand-up guy, asking, even in the midst of our current crisis, whether any of my men had been able to make it away the night of the Siege. When I told him many had, he seemed relieved. We traded numbers.

Bed made, I opened my trunk and started gathering clothes—and uncovered Jack's old camera and my teddy bear in the process. Well, my little sister Emily's teddy bear. Compelled to pick it up—mostly because I didn't want to think about the fact that the digital camera might've been smuggled south by none other than Samedi—I examined the patch of corduroy my sister Adelaide had sewn on the back, the wood button eyes. It was her parting gift to me. I'd been lurking outside her house, a monster keeping her family imprisoned. A monster her mother had shot in the leg.

Did she somehow know the monster thought he had no one to turn to? Did she think if he had a friend he could find the strength to walk away? I'd never figured that out.

Before I could shut the bear away in the trunk for another day, my phone went off. I found it in the pocket of the trousers I'd worn yesterday and opened it. "Hello?"

"Mr. Griswold, would it be possible for you to meet me outside the house in a few minutes?" It was Dr. Horatio Salvez, Dr. Dearly's assistant.

Standing up, I dropped the bear back into the trunk. "Why?"

"Because . . . they're moving Patient One. And I'm being sent to fetch him. Alone." Salvez's quiet voice betrayed his realistic assessment of himself, and echoed my initial thoughts—he was a taciturn gent, weak in body and gentle of character. And he was supposed to pick up a cannibalistic prisoner all by his lonesome?

And why was the prisoner being moved at all?

I decided not to grill him about the chain of events that must have led to this decision, because I was fairly certain I didn't actually want to hear about it. Instead, I shut the phone and raised my voice. "Guys—we have work to do."

I slammed the trunk shut, hoping the sound would rouse them.

Salvez swung by to pick us up in his food-wrapper-filled, mud-splattered carriage. He was a skinny fellow with gray-sprinkled brown hair and a beard, perhaps a decade younger than Dr.

Dearly. His eyes were red, and enormous bags sagged under them.

On our way to the EF guardhouse, we passed the Rolls headed in the opposite direction. Nora was in the front seat and turned to look at me, all eyes. I saluted and sent her a tight-lipped smile, hoping she'd understand that nothing was immediately wrong and that she shouldn't worry.

Hopefully.

"Where are they moving him?" Tom asked Salvez once we were on the road.

"To the *Erika,*" he told us, eyes trained forward. "I just learned of it half an hour ago. The military's finally taking him into custody. He's been deemed a national security risk. They're not telling many people. Trying to keep it quiet. Hence, me."

"So what, the *Erika*'s a prison now?" I asked.

"That's what I said." At a red light he opened the glove compartment and grabbed a wrapped sandwich. "Apparently, protestors started gathering at the jail after his arrest a few weeks ago. Zombies who wanted him out on bail—like they'd let him walk right out the door? Then the politicians and lords started complaining, saying it was madness to keep him in the city proper. So they moved him to the prison. Drike's Island."

Tom leaned forward from the back. "And the problem is?"

"One of the wardens attempted to kill him last night." Salvez got the sandwich unwrapped and took a nervous, squirrely bite as the rest of us exchanged glances. "And the prisoners know what he is, that he's different. The guards are afraid a riot's brewing. They want Patient One out."

"Great."

"I'm not happy either. But at least we'll be able to study him in person." He sighed. "Thank you for coming, lads. Dr. Dearly is busy. It felt odd going alone, even though they promised guards on the return trip. Safety in numbers and all that."

"Sure. Anytime." I felt for the guy, and had to respect the way he was at least *trying* to keep it together. "You know, as long as I get a few hours of sleep in, enough to keep sane, I can almost function twenty-four hours. You call whenever you need me, okay?"

"That goes for me, too," Coalhouse added. His socket was empty, and I was glad to see him putting himself out there. Capable as he was, he had a tendency to take stuff personally and to seize onto perceived insults like an enraged monitor lizard, refusing to let them go. Sometimes it worried me.

Salvez smiled. "You boys are officers and gentlemen." He exited onto the highway that led north along the eastern Nicaraguan coastline, and fell silent.

Drike's Island hove into view before I saw any signs for it. It loomed in the distance, a dark building divided from the land by a stretch of deep gray water. I'd read in one of Dr. Dearly's books that it was one of the first completely New Victorian buildings anywhere, constructed well after the founding of the nation—fitting that one of the first things they built should be a prison. But its fanciful window casements, intricately carved buttresses, and multiple turreted towers made it look more like a castle than a place where murderers and rapists were housed.

"Any of that holographic?" I asked. "It's beautiful, in a way."

"Oh, no. Not a bit of it. They wouldn't waste holographs on prisoners," Salvez said. "In fact, most of that was carved *by* prisoners. Hard labor meets occupational therapy."

This info stunned me into silence. One of the first real, solidly crafted buildings I'd seen in months was a gigantic monument to backbreaking punishment.

Nora's people were truly messed up.

We turned onto a sandy, tree-lined road leading to an iron drawbridge, and encountered protestors. Evidently moving Patient One to Drike's hadn't taken care of the first problem either.

Zombies shouted at our carriage as we rolled past and hobbled after it long after we were gone, carrying the same sorts of signs I'd seen during the riot a few weeks ago. WE ARE PEOPLE. THERE IS NO DIFFERENCE BETWEEN A LIVING AND A DEAD HUMAN BODY. A skeleton crew of living constables tried to corral them behind wooden barricades set up for their protest, guns and electrified billy clubs on their belts.

I felt the weight of Hagens's words as we turned onto the bridge. *A living man in a corpse.*

Maybe I should have been out there with them. There was no real difference between a living and a dead human body, and there was no difference between me and the thousands of other functioning zombies out there. We were all survivors, and we all had the right to do as much surviving as we possibly could, as much *living* as we possibly could.

But that didn't mean we had the right to dismiss or harm those who still drew breath. No one had the right to hurt *anyone* unnecessarily. I hated to think that these masked bastards, whoever they were, were a sign of things to come. We did *not* need this right now.

"Here we go." Salvez rolled up to an exterior guardhouse and lowered his window. A guard came out to scan his subdermal ID chip, and preliminary information was exchanged. It was all very professional. The guard let us in with little fanfare, and we continued the drive up to the prison itself. After making our way past three more gates in like manner, we parked in a gravel lot enclosed by stone walls and barbed wire, where a final guard came out to speak to us.

"No need to go inside. He's already halfway to the van," he said. "You'll be signing for the prisoner and then accompanying the armored van back to your ship." He signed off on several digital documents on a flat screen. "Officers will make sure the

prisoner is secure, and then he's yours. Good luck and good rid-
dance."

"Very well," Salvez said as the guard handed him the screen
for his own signature. As he signed, the guard sized me up.

I eyed him right back. "Has he been violent since he's been
here?"

"No," the guard said. "But he still creeps me the hell out."

"How many guards do we have coming with us?"

The guard took the screen back from Salvez. "Ten."

"Ten? For one nonviolent zombie?"

The guard cut me off with a grunt. "Look, it's mostly so *the
guards* will feel safe. They're as freaked out as the prisoners.
Things still haven't calmed down in there, even though the dirt-
bags are getting what they want. Hell, I think they put Warden
Tomas up to it." He turned his back to us. The conversation was
apparently over. "Wait here. When you see the white van accompanied by two carriages, that's your cue. You can lead them right
out."

"All right, thank you." Salvez released a breath as the guard
stepped away, then rolled up the window. "My God, this is a
mess."

"Ten guards is insane," Tom pointed out. "I mean, yeah, he's
a threat, but he's also *one* zombie. And we still have Ye Olde
Headshot option. I don't see why they haven't just killed him
already. He's no different than the ones we used to gun down."

"If we went by that logic, Tom, we should have killed you
when you showed up at base." It was all I needed to say; the bald
zombie shut his mouth. He'd actually tasted human flesh—
relished it, in fact. "There's more to it than that."

"Yet, Patient One is both incredibly precious and incredibly
dangerous. We have our safety in numbers, they can have theirs."
Salvez laughed nervously and held up his hand. It was trembling.

"Look. Just for being here. I was never a very confident fellow around authority figures."

"How'd you get into the army, then?" Coalhouse said. "Sounds like the last place you'd want to be."

"Oh, it was a pathway to education. My family was very poor."

"Do you know what he looks like?" I asked, trying to get everyone back on track. "There haven't been any clear pictures of him on the news. Just some grainy riot footage. Why?"

"Yes. I originally came to take tissue samples," Salvez admitted. "He's extremely . . . well, you'll see. Perhaps the press didn't want people attacking other zombies who *look* like him? Perhaps they chose the responsible course of action for once?"

"The press doesn't work that way." The docks had taught me that. "They can't have a good picture of him, or they'd show it. And everyone up here has a camera in their mobile phone— you're telling me no one recorded the riot and put it on the Aethernet? It's just weird. There's security, and then there's *security.*"

"Maybe it's the army." Coalhouse's voice darkened. "Maybe they're not being as honest as they say they are. Like usual."

Before we could delve further into any potential conspiracies, an alarm sounded, shrill and haunting. It faded away after a few seconds, and a heavily fortified iron door opened at the far end of the gravel yard. A white police van idled there, its back doors open. Four officers in full riot gear exited the prison, leading a manacled zombie, guns at the ready. Patient One. I leaned forward to get a better look.

Whatever I was expecting, it wasn't what I ended up seeing.

Patient One was a zombie of indeterminate age and ethnicity— because he was a bloody ugly mess. He was of average height and slight build, his movements painfully slow. His skin hung in rotten black hunks from his flesh, like old banana peels, and his skull, stained by wear, was already showing through the muddy meat on his forehead. He was clothed in a pair of drawstring prison trousers and an open shirt with toggle buttons. A clear plastic muzzle was locked over the lower half of his face, designed to let him talk without allowing him to bite. He didn't look at anyone or struggle, his eyes trained on the ground. For all the horrors he represented, he looked completely helpless. I actually felt bad for him.

"That's him?" Coalhouse sounded almost disappointed.

"I told you." Salvez cleared his throat. "Let's not forget—he could start everything all over again with a bite. He attacked people."

As he spoke, the guards led Patient One to the van, locked it up, and took their positions on board. A few seconds later the van approached us from behind, two police carriages on its tail, their sides and tops alight with rows of blue LEDs. "I guess that's it," I said.

"All right, then." Salvez took the carriage out of park, turned it around and drove slowly back toward the gate. "This is actually going much more efficiently than I expected."

The two guards waiting at the gate opened it for us immediately. The van and the police carriages trailed behind us, evidently content to follow our lead. Once we were past the gates and over the bridge, the carriage in back picked up speed, moving in front of us. When we passed the spot where the protestors had been gathered, I noticed they'd dispersed. The constables weren't there either, and I figured they must have cleared the area in anticipation of Patient One's approaching escort. Still, something didn't feel right. I wasn't quite sure what it was—for once, everything appeared to be going well.

"Would you like to turn on the wireless?" Salvez said. "I don't have in-cab Aethernet, unfortunately. The news is depressing of late, I'll own, but there must be some music, perhaps an audio play. Ever listen to *The Shadow*? Great pre-ice stuff."

As Salvez reached for the wireless controls, I heard shots being fired.

I reached out and stayed his hand. The carriage before us swerved, and Salvez gasped, wrenching his hand back to devote to the steering wheel. Turning in my seat, I saw dark shapes popping up alongside the young trees on either side of us. We were going so fast that their faces seemed to fly by, part of the scenery, but a few interesting colorations and extraneous holes convinced me they were undead.

Cursing, I reached under the seat for my rifle. I should have known. My unconscious internal monster, the part of my being that wanted me to hunt, must've picked up on a sign, a scent, something—but I'd been blind.

"Keep pace with the men ahead of us," I said, cracking my window to better hear. Engines were roaring in the distance, and I figured they didn't belong to anyone on our side. The zombies in the brush had to be a distraction.

The carriage in front of us sped up, and Salvez followed suit. I lowered my seat back and undid my seat belt, my friends doing the same. The dead men in the tree line continued to shoot, and I heard a few shots connect with the exterior of the carriage. They were shouting something, but I only made out a few words—something about "smoke" and "our brother." When a pair of old open-topped carriages raced up onto the dirt road behind us, I knew for certain they were referring to Patient One.

"They're going to try and take the van!" Tom yelled as I joined the others in the back of Salvez's carriage, sandwich wrappers crinkling below me.

"What!" Salvez yelped.

"Just keep her steady, Salvez!" I shouted. "Lower the back windows!"

He did as I said. Cool air rushed in, causing scraps of wax paper to skitter about the rear of the carriage. The two rusty, convertible carriages were now flanking the van, matching its speed. Each carriage was filled with zombies, most shooting at the van windows, targeting the driver and the guard riding shotgun. I recognized a few of them from the protest we'd just passed, and felt my neck tightening in anger. They'd been scouts. God knows what had happened to the constables manning the protest line.

Keeping myself low, half hidden by the door, I let off a few rounds. I managed to tag one zombie in the chest, which at least knocked him off-balance and resulted in him losing his own gun. The other shot went nowhere. Coalhouse, meanwhile, downed two zombies in a row, their bodies slumping over the sides of their carriage. He might only have one eye, but that one eye made him an amazing sniper.

As I lined up another shot, the van's windshield shattered. One of the zombies in the open-topped carriage on the right stood up and leaned into the wind, gripping one of the grated, raised headlamps, and I recognized her as the girl with the half-shaved head I'd seen the night we went to the campsite. Before I could blink, she launched herself at the newly vulnerable van. She managed to snag the exposed windshield mounting, the muscles under her ruined skin bulging as she struggled to pull herself inside. The driver screamed and let go of the wheel, elbowing her in the face. I heard bone crack, and she snarled, snapping at his arm.

With little time to lose, I fired again. I got her right above the ear, and down she dropped, her legs crushed beneath the right front tire as she landed. The van bucked upward, but the driver, to his credit, rapidly recovered.

Just then the rear police escort roared forward and rammed into the carriage on my left. It was enough—both vehicles circled around each other at a nauseating speed, went careening toward the trees, and crashed. Almost immediately two living guards crawled free of the police carriage, only to be descended upon by escapees from the other. Frantic shots were fired; screams echoed through the trees.

"Godspeed," I said for the living guards. That side taken care of, I leaned farther out the open window, targeting the remaining convertible. Tom moved to join me. I managed to get in a couple of shoulder shots, but the driver remained untouched. He saw me, though, and his almost lidless eyes narrowed, his expression full of disgust. Maybe he thought I should be right there alongside him.

Luckily, for me this type of situation was extremely cut-and-dried.

Tom capped him right between his eyebrows, finally getting into his own stride. The rusted-out piece of crud the enemy zombie was driving caught a rut in the soft road and very neatly turned sideways, veering toward the trees. It crashed head-on, smoke erupting from its front end. My eyes rocketed back to the van and I was relieved to see that while the guard on the passenger side had taken a bullet in the arm, the driver appeared unharmed. He waved at me and groped around the dashboard. Next thing I knew his voice was booming at me from an exterior speaker.

"Nice work! Keep going, everyone! Floor it!"

Nodding, I withdrew and secured my weapon before crawling back into the front seat, taking a second to calm my rattled mind. Salvez stared at me, his arms locked on the wheel.

"Keep control of the vehicle," I told him. "We can't go back. We've got to stay with P One." Especially when the zombies targeting him were organized, and we didn't know how many of them there were.

That was the scary thing. Those zombies were *organized*.

"Why the hell would a bunch of zombies target the cops?"

Tom demanded, working on his own gun. "Do they have a final death wish?"

"I think those were the protestors," Coalhouse said. "Maybe they finally decided to take matters into their own hands."

"I saw them, too," I said. "And a girl from last night. The one you were talking to."

"The one with the cigarettes, yeah. I saw her."

"We . . . we . . ." Salvez looked forward and stepped it up, almost edging his bumper against the carriage in front. "We were just . . ."

"Shot at. Almost hijacked. Again. I'm starting to think it's me."

"But . . . but . . . we . . ."

"Have to keep going." I unbuttoned my waistcoat and fumbled within for my phone. I pushed the button Nora'd programmed to instantly dial hers, before lifting it to my ear.

"Where are you?" she asked upon picking up. "What's going on?"

"Safe." I glanced back at the bullet-riddled prison van and informed her, "But we've got problems. On top of everything else, someone just tried to *steal* Patient One."

16 • Noɾɑ

I stayed by Pamela's side all day, but by nine o'clock I'd had it. A quick glance outside told me that all of the carriages were gone, which left only one option. Chas and Ren were about, but I had to go higher. I was doing my absolute best to avoid skipping blithely out the door—causing more worry. Papa could keep his mouth shut.

So I climbed the attic stairs to ask Father Isley if he'd accompany me on the trolley. The priest, Company Z's former chaplain, looked up from his papers when I approached. He was a man who radiated kindness even in death, his features doughy and his eyes warm. A bullet hole marred his cheek. "Of course, child. Where do you need to go?"

"The ships," I said. "I'm sorry to bother you, but I have to. I'll explain on the way." I wasn't about to wait around this time. I'd had it up to my eyeballs with waiting.

Responding to the urgency in my voice, Isley rose and removed his duster and scarf from their nail on the wall. He ran a hand over his thin gray hair before donning both. "At your service."

Chas volunteered to take my place, and I ducked into Aunt Gene's room to let Mrs. Roe and Pam know where I was headed—and that it was with an adult. They looked unhappy at the idea but wished me well.

Once we were seated in the EF special service trolley and headed for the surface, I unloaded everything Bram had told me on Father Isley. The priest responded with a low whistle. "I'm rather glad to be going, then," he said as we neared the gatehouse. "It might prove interesting."

"To say the least."

Isley chuckled. "Well, interesting from the point of research."

"For your book, you mean?" I knew he'd been working on some sort of book about zombie religion.

"Ah, yes. Right now I'm working on a chapter about cognitive dissonance and the phenomenon of postdeath atheism." And with that he launched into his thesis. His facial expressions were often a tad wobbly, due to lack of muscle control. Sad to say, I didn't find the talk very interesting.

For the moment, I was fixated on Patient One.

The city appeared unusually quiet and empty as we traveled through—though that was probably an improvement, all things considered. The streets grew darker as we neared the port, the air heavier with the scent of burning coal and oil. Soon I could see nothing but shacks and warehouses, and the occasional nightbound ship. The recycling trawlers, laden with hunks of salvage hacked off of the semicontinent of plastic that had formed in the Atlantic hundreds of years ago, always came into port at night.

We disembarked near the port authority and walked to the docks. Noticing the reporter-thronged barricade, Father Isley removed his checkered scarf and wound it over my hat and the lower part of my face. I'd been all over the news in December, so it was a good move. He then braved the crowd, allowing me to follow in his wake, my fingers curled into the back of his coat.

As we reached the barricade, Ben Maza caught sight of us. He said nothing, but I could see the recognition in his eyes—and some amusement. He got us through to the other side, and Isley and I hurried on board the *Erika*, passing a few more patches of security along the way. They'd stepped things up.

Inside the ship, technicians and scientists were rushing about like mad. As we passed through, headed for the lower levels, I heard one quizzing a colleague: "Why do you keep personifying the Laz in your hourly reports? It's not *doing* anything other than existing. It's not plotting, it's not attacking, it's not evil. It's not *alive*. Why do you keep treating nonliving things as if they have some agency?"

Isley eyed the man, his head pivoting slowly to follow him as we walked. The tech coughed and said, "Right. Carry on, then."

"Before you do," Isley said, "we could use directions. Miss Dearly here is looking for her father and Mr. Abraham Griswold."

The doctor nodded weakly. "Of course."

He took us down to B Level, where a hospital unit was set up. A few techs waved at us, though their faces looked drawn and worried. From there we went down another level, into the very guts of the ship, passing the engine room and coal bunkers on our way to the makeshift laboratory.

Frankly, I wasn't sure what we'd find. My shoulders started hunching up as we neared the lab, and I felt Father Isley's hand settle down between them. "All is well," he told me as the doctor led us to a heavy door and opened it.

The lab was a large, square room, its walls reinforced with metal shingles. Equipment of the same sort massed in our house, but on a grander scale, was arranged in long, narrow rows that could be traversed by foot or wheeled stool. Large screens had been hung from the ceiling, the walls left empty for the projection of virtual rat cages. At least thirty government scientists were currently at work, all of them living.

Beneath the nearest math-filled screen sat my father's assistant, Dr. Salvez. I ran over when I spied him, my footsteps echoing off of the metal floor. He frowned in mild alarm. "Miss Dearly! What are you doing here?"

"I just want to see the others," I told him. "That's all."

Salvez ran a hand over his beard. "They're in your father's office." He gestured to a nearby interior doorway. Isley urged me on, and Salvez added, "I'll join you shortly."

This was it.

The dead boys, Evola, and my father were gathered in the office we found beyond the sheet metal wall. The room was long and narrow, and home only to some computer equipment and a single desk, no medical or chemical supplies. When he saw me, Bram came over. He wrapped his arms around me, the edge of the valve installed on his wrist digging into the small of my back. "It's okay."

"I know," I said, trying to play it off as I slid out of his arms and approached my father. He embraced me, too. "Before you start lecturing, I had to come."

"It's all right. I'm sorry I haven't been home."

"Where's Patient One?"

"Right behind you." I turned around, focusing my attention down the length of the harshly lit room. Sitting on a stool in a rectangular metal cage about eight yards away was a stooped, sad figure. He appeared conscious of nothing; he didn't even look up when the stony-faced soldiers flanking the cage moved preemptively closer.

Slowly, I moved toward the cage. Isley followed. The guards watched us but made no move to interfere. There was a line of red tape on the floor about three feet in front of the zombie's improvised cell, and I stopped when the hem of my red dress just touched it.

Whatever I'd been expecting, it wasn't this depressed, slimy fellow. His skin looked like rain-soaked clay, and his eyes and exposed teeth were stained yellow. His bones were visibly pressing against his flesh in a few places, as if they were actively attempting to burst free. He looked like a zombie who'd been rotting for years, not someone who was recently turned—the closest I'd seen to his level of rot was news footage of Lord Ayles from last December. It looked so painful I had to remind myself that while zombies could feel many sensations, their ability to feel pain was lessened by the disease that'd made them. Not that I should have cared, in this guy's case.

"Hello?" I tried. He didn't move.

"He won't respond," Bram said, coming up behind us. "To light, noise, anything. I even tried poking him with a stick. The height of scientific research. Nothing."

Confused, I said, "But he bit those people . . . do you think he became like this afterward?"

"No idea. Imagine my joy when we got here after being shot at and almost run off the road, and there he is. As forthcoming as a bloody rock. We're still waiting on the computers. Running some tests. After all this time the police still haven't managed to figure out *who* he is."

"He looks so old. The people he bit didn't look like this, did they?"

"From what I've heard, no. It's impossible for anything to rot that fast."

"Someone wants him, whoever he is." Isley made the sign of the cross. "Poor gent."

I turned fully toward Bram. "Do you really think it was the—"

Bram grabbed my arm and escorted me away from the cage before I could complete my sentence. I held my confusion until we were about halfway across the room. "What?" I whispered.

He cast his eyes back at the cage, where Isley remained, before saying softly, "I haven't told anybody the Changed might be involved. Not specifically."

"Why not? On the phone, you said you guys recognized one of the people from the camp."

"Yeah—*one* of them. We still don't know if the entire group is involved. Laura swore their group is pro-everybody. I don't want to send the authorities after innocent zombies—especially ones that have lashed out in fear before. If something goes wrong they might mow them all down, ask questions later."

My stomach went cold at the idea that I'd almost let everything slip. "Oh God, you're right."

"But it's damn shady. Not just them. We'll talk about it tonight."

As I nodded, Salvez entered the room. "Screen, lower," he said wearily.

"Everything done?" Papa strode away from his desk. Behind him an enormous flat screen dropped down, taking up the entire western wall.

"Yes, and you're not going to like it. Computer, access file P1-2339A." Bram and I moved to join the others. Papa put his hand on my shoulder.

The first slide was a set of images captured from a holographic internal scan. "I went over his internals inch by inch." Salvez moved in front of us, gesturing to the left-hand image. "Several things strike me as very odd. First of all, examine his hips. This is from the rear. Do you see what I see?"

"He's had bone marrow harvested," Evola said, his eyes narrowing. "I can see the aspirations." I looked, and found what he meant—several tiny little holes, where a needle had drilled into his bone.

"Exactly. Postmortem, too. Notice the lack of any sort of healing." He gestured upward. "And yet, his vital systems seem beautifully intact, barely rotted. If I didn't know better, I'd say this shot was of a living man. It's very odd."

"What else?" Papa asked.

Salvez pointed to the next picture, which was of one of Patient One's legs. "Even Miss Dearly should be able to see what's wrong with this."

Before I could fire off a snarky comment, I did notice what was wrong. "He has . . . a . . ." I pointed at his knee. It didn't look right; it was strangely bright on the image.

Papa moved forward, his brows lifting. "An artificial kneecap."

"Yes, and look." Salvez blew up the image until I could easily see that something had been done to the plastic kneecap itself; it appeared the side had been filed or scraped, and then drilled into. "All identifying markings have been destroyed."

"Identifying markings?"

"Yes. Artificial body parts, at least those received by the living, are usually chipped and coded for record keeping and safety purposes."

"Someone didn't want anyone to be able to use that info to identify him," Bram said.

"And that is the story of this man's life!" Salvez started pacing back and forth, images rapidly flickering across the screen. "His teeth? Not his own. Someone yanked out all of this poor man's teeth and replaced them with artificial ones. Thus, no dental records. I ran his DNA again, and scans of his iris and retina; he doesn't match up with any records, anywhere. His fingertips—and thus his fingerprints—have been snipped off. Same goes for the soles of his feet. He has no ID chip, and from the level of rot,

I can't tell if he *ever* did. It's like he's been sealed in a vat and hidden underground until now. Oh." He told the screen to pause on a particular image. "Notice his scalp. Someone attempted to shoot him in the head at some point, and succeeded only in delivering a flesh wound. I think it probably happened a few weeks ago—I'd say a few *months* ago, but that can't be right. If he's been around for months, and if he's given to violence, we would have seen this mutation before now."

"What all has he *been* through?" I asked, looking back at the prisoner.

"God only knows. There's absolutely no way to find out who this poor creature is, unless he recovers his powers of speech and feels chatty." Salvez gripped his head. "I think I'm beginning to lose my mind."

"You're still a bit shaken up," Tom told him. "Buck up. You did great. And insanity isn't all that bad, you know. Nowadays, I tend to think of stark raving madness as just a really flamboyant survival mechanism."

Salvez made a face at Tom, and pulled my father and Evola into a conference. The guys and I retreated a few steps, while Isley returned to the cage. "What are we going to do?" I asked.

"Get back to the house. Pull everyone in," Bram said. "It might seem like we have two different things to worry about, but I'm not convinced they're not one and the same."

I lifted my eyes, peeking up at Bram through my lashes. He wore the same worried expression I figured I must. "Do you really think the Changed might be connected to the masked attacks?"

"Let's get back to the house. Talk."

"Okay." I started back down the room. "Father? Ready to go?"

As I came up behind the priest, I could hear him speaking, his voice low. I soon realized he was either praying or reciting some biblical passage, so I stopped, waiting for a respectful moment to butt in.

"The wolf also shall dwell with the lamb, and the leopard shall lie down with the kid; and the calf and the young lion and the fatling together; and a little child shall lead them," he pronounced, with an accent of finality.

"Father," I began, just as Patient One lifted his head. I stopped dead, watching as the prisoner gazed up into Isley's eyes. His movements were achingly slow, and accompanied by very soft, moist sounds.

"Not lions," he gurgled. He didn't stutter, but dragged out his words to the point where they ticked like a reading off a Geiger counter. "He has no lions. No leopards."

"What?" Isley asked as the guards shakily unslung their rifles and aimed them into the cage. "No, stop!"

"No lions. No leopards," Patient One said. "The Devil keeps tigers."

After enlightening us as to the feline nature of the Devil's menagerie, Patient One clammed up again. We spent upward of an hour cajoling him, without results. The dead man simply laid his chin back on his chest and sank into silence.

Eventually we returned home as a group. It took us all of fifteen minutes to convene our war council and head for the attic. Renfield was already there, messing about with his computers when we stomped our way upstairs.

"I take it class is in session?" he said by way of greeting, as I moved to snag one of Isley's cats. The skinny tabby wriggled in my arms as I sat down on the floor.

"Yep. Pleasantries later," Bram said as he closed the attic door.

"Let's get right to business. First up, bombing. Ladies, spill. Everything."

As the others settled down, I started getting them up to speed. Pamela chimed in a few times. By the time we were done, all eyes were on her.

"Okaaay. Masked dudes do not sound ran-dom to me," Chas said. Her new voice reminded me of the very people she was talking about. It was getting better, her control over the new tech improving, but I willed her to hurry up.

"Isambard," Tom said, "you haven't been out there making a name for yourself, have you? Getting into fights or anything?" The boy shook his head.

Ren piped up. "Zombies have been the target of intolerant attacks since December, though. Mr. Griswold *and* Miss Dearly were in the carriage. This *could* be an extension of that."

"Yeah, but it's hard to believe something this big isn't personal," I said. "And it's too weird that both our families were on the receiving end."

"There's something else." Everyone looked at Bram. "Every time I've been around the Changed, I've heard the words 'brother' and 'sister' bandied about. It was even on that note Laura left. What did one of the masked guys say the night we were attacked, Nora?"

"'Careful, brother.'" My heart jumped into my throat. "Oh my God."

"Yeah." Bram let us in on what he'd seen and heard on the coastal road. When he described the camp briefly for Pam's and Isambard's benefit, Pamela gave me *such* a look.

"Why would anyone want Patient One, though?" Issy asked.

"For ransom? Possibly to use as a biological weapon?" Renfield shook his head. "Shades of Averne. Not a happy thought."

"Seeing that Changed girl on the road," Bram said, "the way

Hagens acted, the way Claudia talked on the boat, the masks at the camp—it kind of all fits together."

"You really think Hagens has it out for us, though?" Tom said to him. "I mean, she was always a hard-ass, but a good soldier. Maybe she just feels she can state her piece now that Company Z no longer exists."

"I could buy that. But this? Zombies attacking the cops?" Bram looked to Chas. "You've gone to a few protests. Did any of the zombies you met talk about attacking the living?"

"If they had, I would-n't have gone back," she said, crossing her arms over her chest. "They just talked about protesting. Marching. Keeping zombies in Parliament."

"Maybe someone's chosen to step it up a notch. Turned anti-living for some reason. But I don't get the feeling Laura's lying, either. That's the problem."

"So *do* you think the masked people are from the Changed?" I asked. "We don't have any hard evidence for that."

"I know it sounds kind of paranoid, but think about Hagens's threats. She told you to go to ground, Nora. She told all of us to watch our backs. That's not evasive language. In fact, she asked how you were right off the bat—like she thought something might've already happened to you."

"But I was standing right there—she might've been mouthing off. And how would she know about the Roes?"

"If they're a gang of criminals, though," said Tom, "someone might know how to make a bomb. This could make sense."

At that, Pamela spoke up. "My father said the police didn't have anything new yet. They're waiting for forensics results on the bomb." Her voice was tired.

Bram sent her a sympathetic look. "While we're waiting on that, I think we should look into things. For starters, I want to learn more about that camp. Hagens. And clearly Nora and I can't go."

"Maybe Samedi could go back," I suggested. "Convince them he wants to help that kid."

"Wait. We're talking about a recon mission to the zombiiie camp?" Chastity raised her hand. "Hello?"

"Yeah, Chas," Bram said. "And I nominate you, Coalhouse, and Tom. No offense, Ren, but if it comes to blows, they'll need to be able to dish it out."

"None taken, I assure you." Renfield saluted the three chosen ones, a smirk playing over his lips.

"Yes. I like this. Back on the horse," Tom said. "So, what's the goal of this little mission? And who's heading it up?"

Bram had clearly slipped back into captain mode, and the others back into a military mind-set. "Coalhouse."

Coalhouse looked at him curiously, only his good eye moving—the other dead, loose one remaining stationary in its exposed socket. "Me? Usually I'm backup."

"You did well today. You deserve a chance."

Tom didn't exactly look thrilled by this turn of events, but he nodded at Bram.

"Got it." Coalhouse smiled broadly. "I'll do right by you, Cap, I swear."

"Good. Head back up, blend, ask around. Be smart. All we need to do is figure out if someone there knows something about the attack on the road, the stuff that's been going on in town. If nothing else, check around for the bird masks." Bram looked at everyone in turn. "Hagens obviously doesn't like me or Nora, whatever her reasoning. If you attract her attention, act like you're growing to hate us, too. Like what she said got you think-ing, and that's why you came back."

"I get to talk about what an imbecile you are, openly and freeely?" Chas punched the air. "Best mission *ev-er!*"

"Be smart," Bram stressed, leaning closer to her. "Meanwhile, Ren—suggestions?"

"I could start a database of all suspected attacks, look for commonalities. I could look for information on any names you bring me."

"Right. Start with background checks on Hagens and a woman named Mártira Cicatriz."

"And Edmund Lopez," I said. When Pamela looked at me, I anticipated her response and told her, "I'm with you. I'll do whatever you need me to do." She actually smiled a bit.

Standing up, Bram added, "I'm going to ask around the boats. See if maybe the Changed have tried to recruit zombies, and if they did, what was said."

Pamela asked, "Shouldn't we also go to the authorities? The press?"

Bram looked down at her for a moment before responding. "It's all speculation at this point, Miss Roe. I think we should see how far we get on our own. Laura, Dog . . . there are zombies up there who I sincerely doubt are in on this. And the last time the army went up against the Changed . . ." His brow furrowed. "The army was ready to kill them. And the press spins things, spreads rumors. You can't control it once it's out."

Pamela glanced at her brother and capitulated with a nod. "All right."

Bram was silent a moment longer, before adding, "No more unnecessary deaths, guys. No more violence, no more lies. We have to handle this. Now."

"Yes, everyone shoo," Ren said, finding his feet. He tapped a few buttons on his round-buttoned metal keyboard, and an email sprang up on his computer screen—a bouncing animated envelope, its virtual wax seal green and stamped with the letters *ACL*. "What in . . . bollocks. Aethernet Chess Live will not stop *emailing* me."

Pamela stepped up behind his chair to watch, Issy joining her. I left them to their distraction, moving to follow Bram. The moment the others got ahead of us, he caught my hand and kissed my fingertips. It was a casual, tender little gesture that made my insides tickle.

And I needed it. Because the idea, as tenuous and unproven as it was, that someone had targeted Pamela and her family because of me? Or Bram? It was too horrible to contemplate—so horrible I found myself actively trying to block the thought. It was enough to make me hope for the first time that it *was* some random madman who'd gone after them.

A random madman would be easier to deal with than that.

17 • Laura

Dog and Abuelo the Treasure Hunter slumbered beside me as I watered my plants with a thick brass syringe. It was another gift from Abuelo, whose sharp eye proved profitable when it came to Dumpster diving. Almost everything I owned had come from him, at one point or another—my books, my plant seeds. He was a husk of a man, ancient and arthritic and legless long before the Laz came.

Elsewhere in the large communal tent cons and beggars stirred at the behest of Claudia, shoving aside their narrow bedrolls and talking wistfully of the days when they might've boiled up a pot of coffee before heading out for their shift. Dead kids were traded off to those who wished to use them in their daily ploys—it always paid to beg with a small herd of children behind you. Drummed up more sympathy. Didn't matter if they were your own or not.

"Christ," I heard Claudia say. "Why are you lazy bums still abed? The carriages are heading to New London in ten minutes!"

I hastened to finish, dropping the syringe into a chipped glass of cloudy stream water. The *tink* it made seemed louder than it ought to.

Abuelo finally opened his eyes and started to sit up. "Morning, Miss Laura," he coughed.

"Good morning, Abuelo." He wasn't really our grandfather, merely the oldest member of the Changed that I knew of. We'd left New London around a hundred strong. Over the last four days or so our number had more than doubled. Zombies had come and just . . . stayed. Like Smoke, once upon a time.

Claudia finally caught sight of us and headed over. I watched her approach with a heavy heart, expecting she would tell me to head into town with Abuelo, to watch him sell his trinkets. And oh, I didn't want to go back there.

Despondency pulled me to my feet. "Please, please, don't make me go back to the city, Claudia. I'll do whatever else you want—"

"Who said I wanted you to go to the city, you useless thing?" she snapped. Claudia's hair always reminded me of a tower of brambles when she got angry—as if she were some horrible Thorn Queen from a fairy tale. "Dog, you get the honors today."

Surprised, I said, "Really?"

Claudia grabbed my hand. "Don't make me repeat myself."

Abuelo pushed himself up into his cart and started fussing with the faded blankets there, swaddling his bandaged leg stumps. I didn't have time to say anything more to him or Dog, for Claudia started pulling me through the tent. The others watched as we passed, lingering over their clothes and packs of cards and trick cups. I knew they disliked that I so often got out of work. They resented the fact that I wasn't expected to bring in any coin— mostly because Mártira knew I was so bad at it. It was hard to ask people to part with their money for a handful of stolen flowers.

"Get out of here! What're you waiting for? Y'all suddenly be- come performers?" Claudia hollered at the others, urging them on their way. "Except for the leaders! We're going to Mártira's tent today!"

Mártira's tent?

As Claudia yanked me roughly outside, I glanced back to see Dog attending to Abuelo, struggling to do so with one hand. Hagens and Claudia *had* to let Mr. Griswold help. Neither of them was in control, and they had no right to chase him and his friends away. If the leaders were meeting, then I could bring this fact up.

And yet I wasn't sure if I dared.

. . Few people were outside, and most of the smaller tents stood empty. It was almost noon, but noon was now like dawn to us—the performers who had danced and sung late into the night slumbering on, the hustlers forced awake and shoved into the convoy to New London to ply their trade. Mártira said they could stop once the parties became big enough, famous enough. I eagerly awaited that day.

"What is everyone meeting about?" I asked as my sister escorted me across the camp.

"You'll see." Claudia's grip tightened on me, and a second later she stopped and pulled me in front of her, tipping her head down so I could better see into her eyes. "Hagens told me to bring you, and I'm not sure why. But you better not mess this up for me. Hagens has plans—big plans. Plans people come *here*, seventy-some miles outside of New London, to talk to her about. If Mártira is smart, she'll start listening to her *today*. So you keep your mouth shut, you hear?"

I had no idea what was going on, but I nodded. I had no choice.

Soon we were at the base of the stage, where we found the others already assembled. Mártira's tent stood perhaps ten yards beyond, in an area all its own. Aside from Hagens, there were seven other zombies waiting—the leaders of their respective crafts. Their impatient voices told me that they'd been there a

while, and I wondered why Claudia had thought to call for strag-
glers. As I did, I tried not to look at Miss Hagens, who appeared,
as always, as if she might happily toss us all into a mass grave.

"You finally ready to get this started?" Bruno Allende asked
Claudia.

"Yeah." Claudia let me go and continued on to the tent, the
others falling in behind her.

Moving to the back, I could hear Mártira interrogating the
first few entrants. I was the last to duck in, and I drifted toward
the low, armless stool I knew awaited me along the eastern sweep
of the wall. The others filed in around me, finding seats.

"What is the meaning of this? I didn't summon any of you."
Mártira stood beside a red velveteen curtain nearly the same
shade as her hair, her eyes narrowed. Her tent was filled with orphaned pieces of furniture, salvaged luxuries, and long swaths of
patchwork fabric created from handkerchiefs that Mr. Invierno's
boys had once pickpocketed but couldn't sell. Just like her room
back in town.

"I'm here to ask for a vote on behalf of Hagens, sister," Claudia said, as she and Hagens remained standing. "That's why I
brought the leaders."

"About time this happened," said Mr. Invierno. He was a little
person, now a little zombie, with a mad thatch of black hair and
swollen features roughened by drink and death. Allende was
seated next to him.

"Indeed." Mother Perfore, formerly the leader of the street-
walkers, leaned forward and flicked a length of ash from her
stubby cigar. She was missing both of her eyes. One of her girls
had used black quilting thread to tether her eyelids open, and the
exposed sockets were black and gaping. "Get talkin'."

Claudia glanced at Hagens, ceding the floor. Hagens hooked
her thumbs into her leather waistcoat—she wore a jacket, waist-

coat, and trousers, like a man—and said, "You never listen, so I chose to talk to the others first. I've come here to convince you that we need to get Smoke back. And I think I know how."

Mártira responded to this strange statement with silence. Hagens apparently viewed that as permission to continue. "I told you that before I came here I served in a company of zombies affiliated with the army." Hagens spared a look at Claudia's face. "The man who formed it was Dr. Victor Dearly. And he has a daughter who's immune to the Laz. The only immune individual discovered so far. She was here last night."

"Immune?" Mártira asked, still puzzled.

"Totally unaffected."

"I still don't see what this has to do with us."

"*Everything,*" Hagens said, pulling her hands free of her clothing. "Have *you* given one thought to Smoke since he was arrested? Especially now that we all know just how important he is? That he's carrying a new form of the illness?"

"Of course I have, but that is none of your concern."

"It *is* my concern. Bombs, guns, none of those things matter anymore—*he* is currently the most dangerous thing on the face of the earth. We can't leave him in human control. Let them use him. You know how these things work—he's a big freaking bargaining chip!"

"Be that as it may—"

"And so is the girl! Nora Dearly!" Hagens's delivery was so forceful that Mártira actually hushed. "If we bring Miss Dearly here, we could exchange her for Smoke. Or, if her people don't want her back, we could use her as bait to reel in a better hostage. Her father, for example? The infamous Dr. Dearly?"

Dearly? Girl? It hit me that they must be discussing the black-haired girl I'd seen the previous evening, and I sat up taller, wondering what this was really about.

"Our brother bit people. He is where he needs to be, at the

moment." Mártira paused. "Are you honestly suggesting we try to get him out of prison? Engage in kidnapping, extortion?"

"Bro . . ." Hagens threw up her hands. "You need to stop talking like this group is some kind of commune! We can't just sit around with our 'brothers' and 'sisters' and sing songs about love and death. Do you not *see* how the living could exploit Smoke? As a nuclear option against the other living tribes? As propaganda, to convince the living of the need to exterminate every last zombie? As an excuse to give the army more power—the very same army that once tried to hunt us all down?"

"I'm not about to participate in your schemes." Mártira pointed to the door. "You know what, Miss Hagens? I don't think you belong here after all. I think you should get your things and leave."

Hagens stared at my sister for the longest time, rage building behind her eyes. "While you've been planning parties, I've been worrying about the fate of zombiekind. This morning, while you were asleep, *I* was coming up with a plan that didn't have to end in bloodshed. And after spending weeks trying to get you to stop acting like some kind of resurrected saint and to move your people somewhere safe! Who doesn't belong here, again? Make it fast, because I won't waste any more time!"

Mártira looked long and hard at Hagens, but in the end said only, "When I took you in, you sang a different song. I don't know what's happened to you, in the space of a month, to make you so angry. But it's unwanted here. *Leave.*"

"Have the men gone out?" Bruno asked suddenly. Without the red makeup he wore onstage, his skin was visible, marked by constellations of acne scars. "Maybe we won't even need the girl."

"Yeah," Claudia said, her voice softening. "They have."

Mártira turned her attention swiftly to Claudia. "Men? What men? What is he talking about?"

I thought for a moment that Claudia looked unsure. "Hopefully Smoke will return today. Late last night . . ." She looked at Hagens, as if for a cue, before recovering. "One of the drunk humans started talking about a plan to move him into the city again, so we sent a bunch of men to stop them. We told them the orders were yours. But it was last minute. A chance we had to take. So if that doesn't work, we *need the girl* as a backup plan."

Mártira reached out and caught the curtain. "What?" She glared at Hagens. "What have you *done*?"

"Zombies could raise money and picket for his release until their flesh started falling off in hunks, but the humans wouldn't turn him over." Hagens shook her head. "We can get him back using a relatively peaceful way, or a violent way, but we have to *get him back*."

"You come to ask for a vote, and you're already ordering my people around? Speaking for me? You forget your place!"

"I don't have a 'place,' " Hagens sneered. "Why do you think I've been hanging out with you guys, in a city I loathe?"

"We have to *vote*," Claudia argued. "We don't *want* to do things behind your back. We want you in on this. But we have to get Smoke back, no matter the cost."

"Absolutely not!" Mártira turned toward her. "Are you insane? What game are you two trying to play?"

"A game that's changing, like she said," Claudia yelled. "You're never going to convince the humans to get along with us. They'll always be afraid of us!"

"The living come here every night! Things have gone badly the last few weeks, yes, but everyone can get back on track. Soon we'll be able to shelter even more zombies—"

Mother Perfore spoke up. " 'Badly'? Were you not at the docks t'other day? I was fine with being an outlaw, bein' hunted for what I done—but I won't be hunted for what I *am*."

"Aye," Invierno agreed. "And it's time to teach 'em that. I say Hagens has the right of it. The humans need to learn a lesson. Get knocked down a peg. We got to avenge our dead, and you won't let us. You won't even let us work. Hagens speaks sense."

"Stop using that word!" Mártira drew herself up majestically. "We are the same species, the human living and the human dead."

"And so Smoke means nothing to you?" Claudia said hatefully, her eyes cutting over Mártira's shoulder, boring into my own. "What about the zombies killed on the docks? What about the rest of us? Do you not hear what we are saying? Do you not see how Smoke could even keep us safe by making the living afraid to mess with us?"

"Is that why you want him?" Mártira asked of Hagens.

"One of ten thousand reasons," Hagens replied. "But the less you know, the better off you'll be."

I looked away. Still, something in me wanted to speak. "The people on the ships helped us," I said softly, hoping only Mártira would hear. "Claudia said they wouldn't, but they did. The living doctor there, he helped Dog. Another living doctor came with Mr. Griswold. They're not all bad."

"Of course they're not, dove." Mártira tilted her head. "But what do you mean, 'came with Mr. Griswold'?"

I could feel the others glaring at me as I answered, "He was here last night. To see Dog. Hagens told him to leave." My fingers started to tremble as I said it, but I knew I had to. "The girl's his doll. I think. The girl they want to . . . kidnap."

"I see." Stiffening, Mártira faced Claudia again. "Of course Smoke means something to me. We will take him back if they free him, just as we will show mercy to any zombie who tastes madness and then repents—but we will not cause more fear, more destruction. We can only change attitudes through *love*. And you need to stop listening to those who would tell you otherwise."

Oh, how I loved to hear Mártira speak. Her words were warm, inspirational, dear as gold buttons plucked from the costume of a rich woman—like the stories she always told.

"Where are you getting this stuff?" Allende said. "When we were the Grave House Gang, we were *feared*. That's why we were so large—everyone wanted in. Because we could offer protection, organization . . . we could *kill*, if we had to. We could defend our turf." For a moment Allende almost looked despairing. "You've changed. The rest of us haven't."

"That was before I died." Mártira looked ashamed, but her voice remained strong.

"Sister, listen." Claudia laid her hand on Mártira's arm, a strange light filling her eyes. "You *have* to help us. This is your one chance. Tell us to get the girl."

Mártira took her arm back. "No. It is I who must help you. Don't you see what you're talking about, Claudia? Don't you see this is madness?" She turned to Hagens. "How dare you come here, to my home, and twist things the way you have? Confuse people? You have no right."

Hagens studied my sister, her expression hardening. "I thought you might say that."

I heard the muffled but oddly sharp sound, even jerked in response to it, long before I realized what it meant. I saw Mártira fall to the floor, almost like a piece of fruit drifting through half-set aspic. I saw the hole in her forehead, a dark and unseeing third eye.

"Mártira?" I said, rising to my feet. Around me I knew the leaders were rising, yelling, but they might've been miles away. I pushed through them and fell to my knees at my fallen sister's side, clutched her ice-cold arms.

She was silenced. Forever.

"No!" Claudia screamed. "We were going to convince her,

vote her out as leader! You goddamn bitch, you didn't say you'd kill her!"

Before I could even look up, before I could think of doing anything, another shot rang out. To my left, inches away, Claudia landed in a heap, something oozing from her temple and her eyes horribly wide.

"Get up." I heard Hagens cock the gun again, felt the shadow of her arm pass over my body. Lifting my eyes with a tearless sob, I found her own, so damningly placid. The leaders hadn't taken her down. Instead they were all standing, watching the scene with a resignation that made me want to scream. "I won't kill someone kneeling."

"No." Bruno stepped forward and got in Hagens's physical space, baring his teeth, forcing her back. "She's just a girl."

"She's a Cicatriz." Hagens aimed her silenced pistol upward and let Bruno have a bit of ground. Still, she was firm. "Isn't this how a regime change is done in your world? How a new leader is chosen? Like a pack of wolves?"

"It is." Mr. Invierno came forward and took Bruno by the pants leg. "Leave it be, Allende. We been talkin' about this before Hagens even showed up. Mártira had to go. Only reason she lasted this long, what with her rule about not bringin' in ill-got money, is 'cause none of us need t'eat now."

Mártira. Claudia. My family. As if nothing was going on around me, as if people weren't calmly debating whether they should let me live or die as I sat between my sisters' bodies, I bent over them, my own body trying to weep. The last time I'd heaved and choked like that had been the night I'd turned her, at her request—turned Mártira, lovely Mártira, my only protector against Claudia's cruelty, into the most beautiful of zombies by letting her sip delicately from my wrist, as one might from a glass of wine. No bite. No fear. Only acceptance.

Let Hagens shoot. Let it happen.

Silence took over. After a moment I dared to look up. I found no shock, no wonder, no fear among the leaders. Instead, *I* was the spectacle.

Hagens relented, clicking her safety on. "Take her back to the tent, then. Make sure she doesn't talk."

Bruno did as she ordered. I tried to struggle as he lifted me, tried vainly to cling to Mártira's cold body, but he pried my fingers free and hefted me over his broad shoulder, hissing into my hair, "I saved your life. Don't make me regret it."

He might as well have said nothing. As he carried me outside, ignoring my wails, I stretched out like an imbecile for the bodies on the ground. As if my arms were long enough to reach them, as if my heart were large enough to fold both of them into and keep.

By nightfall, everyone knew.

When the cloud of fairy lights was aglow and the fires were roaring, Hagens and the leaders took the stage. By then the zombies sent to fetch Smoke had come back to report on their failure. They brought the bodies of the fallen with them.

Hagens told the rank and file that they'd gone to the tent that afternoon, only to find Mártira dead. Shot through the head, cleanly and once, as only a human would think to do. That the sight had caused Claudia to kill herself before anyone could stop her.

"One of the human visitors must have slain her as she slept. Slain two of them—one through grief."

"We can't go to the police," someone said. "They'll arrest half of us just for standing there. Some of us got rap sheets that could wind inside a player piano."

"That's why we take matters into our own hands!" Hagens

shouted. "Starting now. In Mártira and Claudia's memory, we free the zombie known as Smoke. It was Mártira's final wish. He's too precious to leave in human control. We take him north and form our own tribe! We're already dead—what have we got to lose?"

"Mártira! Claudia! Martyrs for the cause!" Mr. Invierno yelled.

Lied.

Even in my benumbed, grief-stricken state, I knew they were all going to tell the same lie. They would make it so no one would believe me, even if I dared to speak. It was like I'd never been in the tent at all. The Changed were apparently content to have Hagens as their leader. So many of them were new, they didn't know any better—they only knew that Mártira had taken them in, loved everyone, and that her kindness had gotten her killed. Hagens could do anything she liked.

God, what were they going to do? What was *I* going to do?

That night the music was angry. That night the living who tried to join in the festivities were turned away, shadowed by the dead until they got back into their carriages and took off. Everyone was bitter, raging, full of fire.

If I felt anything at all, it was fear.

Unable to sleep, unsure where to go, I walked. I knew I ought to keep walking, leave the camp behind, but I also knew I wouldn't get very far on my own. The dead around me danced, and ballooned their collapsed lungs to sing and scream, and played cards and knife games to forget, and I walked, seeing nothing, hearing nothing.

At least, not until I saw the three young zombies from the night before. The ones who'd come with Mr. Griswold. Perhaps it was the girl's metallic voice, the sleekness of the noseless boy's head, or the sturdy size of the short-haired, one-eyed lad that caught my attention, I don't know—but my dead heart contracted as I recalled Hagens's anger at them and those with them.

A forbidding feeling took hold of me. They had to get out of here. It wasn't safe for them. And if Mártira had been alive, she would have told them so. She, who had saved so many.

The girl and the shorter boy were engrossed by the performers on the stage, but the taller boy was actively surveying the crowd. He wore a hearing aid hooked over his left ear and he kept reaching up to scratch at it, as if it bothered him. It was him I decided to approach. "Pardon me?"

He looked down at the sound of my voice. His one good eye was a warm shade of brown, which the glare from the glittering lights turned into gold. "You."

Without thinking, I half bowed my head. "Yes. I was there last night . . . when Hagens . . ." Just saying her name made my voice seize up.

"Yeah, I remember you." He didn't look at his friends, but stepped forward, forcing me to move back. He was quite wide and well muscled. "Laura, right?"

"Yes," I told him as I tripped on my hem. I caught myself before I could stumble and shut my eyes, launching into it. "But that's not important. You have to go. At least, if your friend is here, the girl with the black hair—she has to go. Now."

"Go?" I opened my eyes and saw that the boy was staring at me intently. "Why?"

Picking up my skirt, I lowered my voice and took a risk. "Because Hagens is in charge now. And . . ." How could I put it? "Hagens doesn't like her."

His expression altered, becoming more serious. "What happened?"

"Bad things," was all I could think of to say. In my own voice, I could hear the tears that would never fall. "You should all go. Just go. You're in danger."

The boy held steady for a moment, before leaning very close to me. "Listen," he said, and something in his voice compelled me to. "We're here to figure a few things out. We actually need to talk to Hagens. If you honestly think she'd shoot us on sight, we'll leave, and owe you a big one. But if there's a chance we can meet up with her, we have to take it. Maybe you can help us."

"Coalhouse?" The short boy came to join us. "What's up?"

"Today, she . . ." I clamped my jaw shut. I didn't want to say it. I was afraid it would come back to haunt me.

"Waaarn us about who?" the girl asked, stepping up beside the other male zombie.

"Hagens," Coalhouse said, his eye never leaving my face. The tall girl hushed.

There were too many people. Too many strangers. I didn't want to deal with this—I'd just wanted to whisper my warning and run. "I hate her for all she's done and wants to do," I said, keeping my phrasing vague, like Mártira had taught me to do when being interrogated by the cops. My books and her stories had always helped with that skill. It felt weirdly theatrical; I was filled with the sudden desire to laugh derisively at myself.

Coalhouse nodded slowly. "Okay, then. Good."

"But you can't do anything tonight." I rubbed at my cheek. "Trust me. You should just leave. I greatly fear for your friend . . ."

"She's not here," Coalhouse assured me. "Neither is Griswold. It's just Tom, and Chas, and me."

"What about the road attack?" Tom looked at me, his gaze sharper than Coalhouse's. "We were attacked on the road near Drike's earlier. Your people have anything to do with that?"

They knew. They'd been there. "They're not my people," I said, putting no heat into the words. He seemed to understand, uttering a curse.

"Do you know why they were sent?" Coalhouse asked.

"To get Smoke. Hagens wants him back for some reason."

"Smoke?" Chas wondered.

"The prisoner with the new illness." I decided I had to tell.

"Today she was talking about getting the black-haired girl, too, trading her for him. Or her father. I'm not sure."

"Getting Nora?" Tom asked, his black eyes widening. "Jesus."

Chas looked to the camp, her eyes narrowing. "We can't take them alone." She returned her attention to me. "Come with us. We'll geeett you out of here."

For an instant, I thought of going with them—then I recalled Dog and Abuelo, and all the people Hagens had lied to, and I knew I couldn't leave them. Not without knowing for certain I could come back. And I couldn't tell the entire camp, not without throwing it into chaos, possibly turning it against the three offering me their help. "I can't. Go. Come back with more people. I could help you then."

"Okay." A pause, and Coalhouse added, "Thank you."

"C'mon, man. We can cut through those trees. We gotta get back."

I watched the other zombies as they walked away, their feet heavy on the grass and fallen leaves. After a few seconds I found myself standing alone, feeling hollow.

What had I just done?

Fueled by a sudden fear, I hurried across the field, doing my best to skirt the crowd. I wasn't a strong runner in death; my legs were slow to listen to my brain. Once in the tent, I threw myself onto my pallet and buried my face in my pillow, my heart and mind a mess of turbulent, unconnected feelings and thoughts. Above all, I thought perhaps I'd made a monumental mistake. I didn't know for certain whether those people were potential allies or something else. Not without Mártira to put it in words I could understand, to guide me through it.

She was gone. She was really gone, and I felt like I couldn't move, couldn't think. I just wanted to close my eyes and join her. Even Claudia. I would have given my own pathetic second life to have Claudia back.

Later that night, they fed the bodies to the flames. Mártira's body popped and sputtered—undignified sounds, sounds she never should have made. Even when she drank my diseased blood she was neat and dainty about it. Bruno and several buskers stood at the open tent door to view the pyre, terror or dark anger muting their lips. I could feel Bruno's eyes on me.

I stared beyond them, my own rotting eyes calling magical shapes out of the raging fires, wondering if I would ever see Coalhouse and the others again—and unsure if it even mattered.

I wished desperately that the flames were eating me instead.

18 • Bram

The next day, Patient One still wasn't talking. Not so much as a gurgle. So, crossing over to the *Christine,* I sought out zombies to interview. There were plenty receiving care that day, but none had anything to tell me concerning people in bird masks.

When I got the call around 10:00 P.M. telling me the crew was already back at the house, I was prepared for yet another brush with too little information. It seemed like they'd just left. I borrowed Salvez's carriage for the ride, already disappointed.

Due to the forever rerouted traffic patterns in the city, I had to detour by the Morgue again. It looked even more desolate by night, with lights and oil drum fires few and far between. As I idled at a red light, my attention was caught by a pair of zombie children sitting by the park's wrought-iron fence, which was shingled with ragged protest signs. They were playing with some sort of toy, taking turns aiming it at each other, but I couldn't make out what it was. It didn't look like a toy gun.

"We have to rethink almost every law on the books," the talk show host on the carriage wireless said. "Take marriage, for example. Does living death officially sever a couple, as in, 'till death do us part'? Are the children of dead parents legally orphaned, and does that mean the state should send them to orphanages? What about homicide—can you technically 'kill' someone who's already dead?"

A delivery van passed by, bathing the dead children with light for an instant.

A soldier. They were playing with a toy soldier.

In my current frame of mind, I found this fact more pathetic than enraging. The kids didn't know any better. I couldn't help but be reminded of everything I'd done, though. The fact that just yesterday I'd had to cap a zombie in the head.

When I'd first been ushered into Company Z and taught how and what to shoot, I quickly learned to process the guilt caused by killing people so like myself—for in a way, they weren't like me. We'd always targeted the insane zombies, the hosts, the ones who either embraced or were engulfed by their cannibalistic desires. While I'd argue for their humanity until the day I truly died, they were helpless in the face of their disease. That's what I'd always told myself, so I could sleep at night. That we had no choice. That, in a way, to dispose of them was a mercy.

That justification was hard to extend to my fellow high-functioning zombies, however—especially now that the vaccine was out. Honestly, I could sympathize with Hagens, with the fury she directed at the living. The extermination order had been the last resort of a living populace staring infection and death in the face, and the army wasn't a monolithic evil—I knew that. Dearly proved that, Lopez proved that, Norton's men proved that. Yet, while I didn't condone Hagens's views, I could *understand* them.

The light turned green and I shook myself free of my ruminations. I took my foot off the brake, and the carriage started to inch forward.

That's when a black shape flew in front of the carriage, a brown one shadowing it. I nearly collided with the brown thing, and it stopped with its hands on the carriage hood, glaring at me through the windshield. It was a young dead man in a leather duster, his shoulder-length dishwater hair pinched into a ponytail, his skin yellow and his lips black. A second later he raced away, and I turned to gape after him.

He was chasing a mask.

I was fifth in line at the light, so contributing to the pursuit in the carriage didn't even occur to me. Instead I abandoned the vehicle and ran out on foot. I wasn't sure where I was going, what had gotten into me—I only knew that I had to follow. Maybe seeing the other boy running had triggered some instinct to join the hunt, the chase.

All three of us dodged traffic across two streets, shot down an alley. The other zombie was slowing. He said nothing to me until I caught up with and surpassed him, at which point he yelled, "Get him!"

I was trying. The mask was fast, his long black coat billowing out behind him. Pushing myself on, I felt my body weakening, my muscles loosening, my joints grinding. I was doing horrible damage to my body.

That didn't matter, though. Not when a mask was actually within my grasp.

The mask darted through a narrow archway, and I turned just in time to see him leap down into a recessed area of the street. It wasn't the sewer, but it was close. "See you later, deadmeat!" the mask panted, voice like a robot's.

Launching myself at him, I found myself shut out by the slamming of an iron door. It was locked. I couldn't beat my way in. *Damn it all.*

As I stood there, trying to recover, the other boy caught up to me. "Did he get away?"

"Yeah." He took his turn to indulge in a curse, casting his arms down angrily. "Did you see him hurt a living person?"

"Living?" the boy demanded, turning to me. "Those guys've been kidnapping zombies from the Morgue for weeks! The cops won't believe me—he was my proof!"

The guy's name was David Braca. Former laborer, current hobo, and fountain of information.

I did the only thing I could do. I took him home.

Upon entering the house, we found the younger half of the household, minus Renfield, seated on the wide front staircase. Nora and Pamela were in their dressing gowns and lacy caps, and when they noticed the strange male zombie, they both ducked behind the closest clothed person they could find.

"Hellooo," Chas said, her eyes widening at the sight of David. Tom's expression morphed from curiosity to dislike almost instantly.

"What's going on?" Nora asked. "Who's he?"

"Ladies," David said, voice stilted and expression awkward. Turning to me, he removed his hat and said through gritted teeth, "You didn't mention ladies."

"Sorry?" I kept it simple, introducing the new guy and adding, "The masks aren't only attacking living people. We just chased one."

The group hushed. David glanced at the stairs, then at me. "I did see them target a breather," he said. "Cobbler by the name of Bihari. Been doing shoes for free for the dead—some of 'em walked so far. Last week a bunch of guys in these weird long masks set fire to some trash outside his shop. Had it pushed up against a wooden wall. Never did catch the blighters. That's what started my asking around."

I'd heard this already. "Tell them everything."

David remained standing, looking everyone over uneasily—especially the girls. "I'm still mostly in the dark myself. For a few weeks now there've been rumors about zombies 'taken by the birds.' Zombies come and go from the Morgue every day, so I didn't think much of it till that night at the cobbler's. Then I started asking around in earnest, and I got stories about zombies going out on errands and not coming back, things like that."

"Did you go to the coppers?" Issy asked.

"Yeah." David scowled, rolling up the brim of his hat as he talked. "They told me there was no such thing. That zombie mothers were probably makin' up tales to scare their kids, keep 'em in the park. So I started walking at night, and tonight I finally saw 'em. There were two originally. Hanging out in an alley near the Morgue. I heard 'em saying something about trying to get a woman, because she wouldn't be as strong. For what, I don't know. But for now, I'm assuming every story's true. That these ruffians've been taking people."

I sat on the stairs near Nora, and she sent her tiny fingers into my hair—an act that made me long to plunk my head into her warm lap and fall asleep, and caused David to peer at her as if she were some sort of alien. "And the Changed?"

"Know *of* 'em," he said. "They've been giving things away, taking in homeless. Haven't heard of 'em doing anything else."

"That doesn't fit with what we learned," Coalhouse said.

I gestured at him. "Share."

Coalhouse looked skeptically at David, as if unsure whether he should get to hear. Chas rolled her eyes and picked up the ball. "Tom and I spent the evening scouting the crowd. It was a lot aaangrier this time around." She tugged at the ribbons holding her neck closed. "Geez, these things tickle after a whiiile."

"Yeah, but it is so good to have your voice back, baby doll. That board used to make about as much sense as a bloody Sumerian tablet."

Chas made a face at her boyfriend before continuing. "Anyway, every time a living person showed up? Intimidated. Told to scraaam. Not like the first night we went."

"And we know why." Coalhouse leaned forward, his knees spreading apart. "I talked to this girl, see."

"First time that has *ever* happened, for the record," Tom said. "Shut up!"

"Easy, Tom," I told him. "Girl?"

"The garden girl. Laura. Tried to get her to come with us, but she wouldn't."

"What is *up* with that whole flower thing?" Nora asked.

"It does take funeraaal pre-planning a little far, doesn't it?"

"Guys," Coalhouse said. "Anyway, she came up to me and told me we should beat it. That it wasn't safe for us." He pointed down with two fingers. "She said Hagens is now in charge of the camp."

I sat up. Nora gave me a worried glance. "In charge? How?"

"She wouldn't say. Said 'bad things' happened. So I figure if this girl's going out of her way to warn us, clearly she does not share Hagens's hatred of us, so I start asking questions."

"Um, not just you?" Tom said pointedly.

Coalhouse rolled his eye. "Look, it doesn't matter. What matters is the hijackers at the prison *were* her people, and what's more . . ." He looked at Nora. "Apparently she wants you or your dad, to use for something. She wants Patient One. Laura said his name was Smoke."

In silence, all eyes turned to Nora. Pam moved a little closer to her. "Why us?" Nora asked, voice hushed.

"Trade, probably," I said, my voice throaty. "Did you guys see Mártira at all? She seemed shocked that her people started biting back at the docks, but maybe it was just her blind optimism talking. Maybe Laura gets that from her. Something's not right."

"No."

"And thank goodness they didn't." I looked up to find Renfield quickly trotting down the staircase, an encyclopedia's worth of paper clutched in his hands. He gave David the briefest of glances. "Ran those background checks you asked for."

"And?"

"Can't find much on Hagens, since she's Punk-born. Lopez is a saint, but I can't get to his army records." He handed what must have been Lopez's report to Pamela before sitting down next to Nora and letting the remaining pages fall from his hands. They landed on the step below with an impressive *thunk*. "But *that* is Mártira Cicatriz's rap sheet."

We all stared at it. "Abridged version?" I asked.

"Everything. Mostly theft. Been in and out of the clink all her life." He scooted forward. "If she's currently as you describe her, death has made her drink long and well from the Peace Punch. She has about twenty aliases, most of them variations on the word 'hellcat.'"

I slid my hands over my face. "And the kind of people who'd follow a 'hellcat'?"

"Hellcats in training. The hellcat ascendant," Ren said, echoing my thoughts. "I looked into her gang, too. Looks like she started small, getting people to commit crimes she planned. In exchange they'd get work, food, shelter. Took off from there. Soon minor groups involved in things like prostitution and pickpocketing were allying themselves with her for protection."

"So maybe her people are still acting out?" Nora said.

"I think so," I said, looking to David. "Because as personal as all of this clearly is, you and Miss Roe aren't the only people they've gone after."

"But why would zombies go after zombies?" David asked. "You think they're conscripting them into this group?"

"And why hasn't this been on the news?" asked Nora.

"No idea. Maybe it's gotten lost in all the other violence."

"Laura said members of the Changed were still heading into town, remember?" Tom said.

"Yeah." I leaned back against the stair railings but I didn't relax. "I hate to say it, but we should just report everything to the police before somebody tries something else. Get them to pay attention."

"Seconded," Nora said.

"Aaand you should stay inside," Chas said. "I say that knowing you will veto me in two-point-three seconds."

"No," I said as my girl sat up in preparation for verbal warfare. "We report this, and we take care of it so *no one* has to hide. Because this isn't just about us anymore." Nora flashed me a thankful look.

"Wait, what?" Coalhouse shook his head. "No way. If we rat them out it'll be ages before we learn why they *want* Patient One, or how they managed to find out about the Roes." He glanced momentarily at Pamela. "Besides, like you said . . . what if the cops decide to take them all out? Bad stuff could go down. I can do this, Cap."

"It's not 'ratting them out,'" I said, irritated. "It's reporting people who might've attacked innocents and tried to steal an armored van from the police!"

"Look, what have we got? One visual confirmation, a couple random stories, and the word of a flower girl? Like the coppers are going to believe us? Braca there already got shut down." The crew went quiet at this idea. "Let's investigate more, find out if they're really the ones responsible. If they are, we can go in locked and loaded!" Coalhouse looked to the others for signs of support, and met looks of bewilderment instead. "What's the issue?"

"That is the stupidest idea I've ever heard," Tom said. "And I've heard a few in my time."

"Yeah, well, you think everything I do is stupid, so I'm not going to—"

"No, it's incredibly stupid," Nora said. "This isn't like when we rescued Pam and Issy from the city. Then, there was no one else to help them. But now everything's out in the open. Like Papa said. We can't wage a private war." She blinked. "I can't believe I just said that."

"We're not in the army anymore," Chas pointed out. "We're civiliiians."

"And these zombies aren't like the hosts we faced before, John." I used his real name to get his attention, and it worked. "These are functioning dead folks, like us. If they've done wrong, we have to let them face the authorities, even if it's not the best solution. Besides, thirty-odd Company Z soldiers to hundreds of unarmed, brain-dead zombies worked at Averne's base—five soldiers to at least fifty armed, *smart* zombies would be suicide. My days of never having enough men, of losing people needlessly, are *over*. This is serious."

"I know it is!" Coalhouse stood up, unsteady on the stairs. "Stop ganging up on me. I'm not an idiot, and I'm not a child. You gave me a chance, you can't just yank it away from me before I've even started!"

"Nobody cares about your *'chance'*!" Pamela said, glaring at Coalhouse. He stopped, stunned. "The others are right! We should tell the police, the army—somebody. Turn this over to *someone* who can figure out who wants to ruin my entire *existence*!"

For a moment everyone was quiet. Coalhouse looked like Pamela had just slapped him. "I want to help you, too," he said. "Didn't I help you and Isambard before?"

"You did," Pam said, rising. "I'm just sick of talking about this." She turned and headed up the stairs, her brother scurrying after her. Nora sighed, leaning forward to wrap her arms around her knees.

After they were gone I said, "Coalhouse, you did amazingly tonight. But things are different now." I stood up and helped Nora to her feet. "I'm calling the police. Now. I'm not saying we stop working, I'm just saying we do the smart thing and let the cops in on this, too. Not the army. We'll figure out a new game plan tomorrow."

"I want in on that," David said. I nodded at him.

Coalhouse looked at us all in turn, his single eye pleading for some kind of backup. He didn't find it. His hands curled into fists and he shouted, his voice echoing in the grand hall, "Fine!" Before anyone could say anything else, he picked his way over Chas's body and stomped toward the front door.

"Coalhouse!" Tom called out. "Where are you going?"

"Like I'd tell you. This is your fault to begin with!" Coalhouse pushed past David and slammed the door behind him. Tom swore and hopped over his girlfriend, moving to follow.

I caught his shoulder. "Don't. Just let him cool down."

"My fault? I just want to know how the hell this is *my* fault!"

"The Topic," Chas reminded him. "You bit him. Everything is your fault. Foreeever."

Tom relaxed a touch. That was old ground. "What if he takes the car?"

"Let hiiim. He has to come back. He doesn't have anywhere else to go," Chas said as she pushed herself up. "I'm going to bed."

Tom turned to follow her after bowing to Nora. Ren did the same. David watched them disappear onto the landing before asking me, "Are your friends always so dramatic?"

"Sometimes." I moved to shake his hand. "You want a ride up?"

"I can walk. Ask for me at the Morgue. I'll spread the word, see if I can get more info." He looked down at Nora and cleared his throat. "Miss."

Nora and I saw him out. After he was gone, she said, "You did the right thing. But now I have a recon mission of my own. Want to be my backup?"

"Please tell me it doesn't involve zombies."

"For once, it doesn't. And it can wait until morning. I'll share then."

"You're so beautiful when you're cryptic."

She kissed my nose and whispered, "Good night, Mr. Griswold," before heading up the steps. I watched her go, then finally removed my coat and hat.

I left them in a pile at the end of the stairs, carrying my phone with me. I was too tired to do the civilized thing and hang them up.

At seven the next morning I limped into the kitchen and found Nora already at her porridge and tea, dressed in her Sunday best. She was back in her green dress, her hair freshly washed and made glossy with something that smelled like roses, emerald glass teardrops dangling from her ears, and a creaseless satin ribbon hugging her throat.

"For me?" I asked.

"Always," she informed me. "Get your breakfast. You should eat well before you break bread with your enemies—because you're not going to touch the actual bread, not if you're smart."

"I don't think that warning applies to me anymore," I noted, though I did sit down. "And kindly explain which part of 'with your enemies' shouldn't terrify me to my very core."

Nora uncrossed her legs, the hem of her dress shifting slightly, and I couldn't help but notice that she was wearing lacy stockings and little embroidered slipper-type shoes instead of her usual boots. The sight of a well-turned ankle hadn't meant a thing to me till I entered the Land of Perpetually Long Skirts and found someone with an ankle worth looking at, but I was coming to appreciate it. "Remember when I mentioned talking to Michael Allister?"

And the moment was ruined. "Unfortunately."

Nora hopped to her feet. "Well, today's the day. I messaged a few acquaintances from Cyprian's last night and managed to snag his number. I'm going to text him in a few, and arrange a tea party."

I didn't like the idea, and argued against it by snagging Nora's waist and pulling her onto my knee. She laughed, and didn't attempt to free herself. "Why? Don't you think we have enough on our plates?"

"Jealous? I think I like you when you're jealous. You get all snarly."

I gently butted my forehead against hers, my eyes inches from her own. That got her attention. *"Why?"*

"Not because I want to, believe me," she said. "I'm doing it for Pamma *and* Aunt Gene."

Leaning back, I said, "Miss Roe? Why? You think Allister might know something about the bombing?"

"No. He's nasty, but I don't think he has it in him to do something like that." Nora reached out and adjusted the crocheted place mat in front of me. "Colonel Lopez has offered to take the Roes in at his estate, but they barely know him. It's clear Pamela wants to go, get out of the city. So I'm going to make that happen."

That I could respect—though I knew the idea likely displeased Nora on a number of levels. "Is Allister acquainted with him?"

"Of course. All the rich families know one another—most of them are related by marriage, actually. Ren came up with a clean record for Lopez, but there's got to be more to him."

"Why not ask your dad about him?"

"I will, but honestly? I can probably get to Michael before I can get to Papa. He's been home, what, twice since the hijacking? Besides, once I clue him into the stuff we talked about last night, he's going to clamp down again. So anything outside the house I need to get finished *yesterday*."

"You're right . . . and I'm with you. Up to a point."

Nora sighed. "Ducking under Papa's inevitable crackdown looks stupid, I know. But you'll be with me, we'll be in public. It could be our only shot for a while."

I could allow for that. "Fair enough. But how are we going to set this up? *I'm* supposed to leap through hoops to spend time with you—how are you going to be able to meet up with him? You're going to need to get him alone if you want him to talk." In fact, it irked me, the idea that I tried so hard to balance respecting the rules with breaking the rules, and she was acting like this meet-up would be a walk in the park to plan.

Nora pouted her lips a bit in thought. "*I* can't get him alone—but he's from an aristocratic family. They can get away with things, especially the boys. If *he* wants to see me somewhere, we can probably do it. We can rent a chaperone."

"Wait. You can rent a chaperone up here?"

"Oh yeah. Parents hire them sometimes, especially if they let their children date instead of court. Neutral third party."

Biochemistry was easier than this social stuff. "So basically, you have to ask him to ask you, and then pay for the privilege. Your people are *insane*."

"You're just figuring this out? But yeah, he won't talk if we march in with the whole gang. A hired chaperone is probably the best I can do without encouraging him in ways I'd rather not think about." She leaned her head on my shoulder. "It won't be long. Just half an hour, tops, and we never have to see him again."

Even as I shook my head I said, "Fine. Whatever will help the

Roes." Nora stood up, and I looked her striped bodice over once again. "But if he gets fresh, he's losing flesh. For the record."

She narrowed her eyes and stepped in between my legs, her skirt brushing my knees. "If that slug lays a single finger on any part of me, you have my permission to rip his head off and drink long and well from the blood that will spurt from his neck stump like a fountain. Okay?"

I found myself blinking. "Wow," was all I could say. How the royals managed to produce someone like Nora, I'd never figure out.

"Pardon me."

We both straightened up and glanced at the door. Renfield was there, dressed in trousers and shirtsleeves, expression anxious. He looked like he hadn't slept. "Hey, Ren. You got the kitchen bugged? We were just talking about you."

"Funny choice of words." He backed up a tad, his movements tight and energetic. Experience had taught me that this meant he had an idea in mind, or a project he wanted desperately to pursue. Experience had also taught me that this could be a very good thing, or a very bad thing. "I just thought I'd ask before I start tearing the house apart—does Dr. Dearly have any books on eye surgery or illness?"

"Eye surgery?" Nora asked, confused. "I don't know. He's not a surgeon. Try his study?"

"I will as soon as Dr. Samedi awakens, thank you." His disappointment was almost palpable. "None in his room, then, that I could look at now?"

"No." Nora glanced at me. "I guess there's the basement. He's got some vintage medical books down there, part of his First Victorian collection. Two big gray trunks. I always used to unwrap them by mistake when I was looking for his adventure and military history book—"

Disappointment turned to manic speed—seriously, the guy disappeared beyond the doorway faster than a lightbulb could burn out. I stood up and followed him into the hall, Nora moving after me. "What's up, Ren?"

"Nothing," the scarecrow assured me as he started to try door after door, looking for the one that led to the cellar. "Nothing at all."

"It's the next one." As I said it, he found it and disappeared inside. "Um . . . can we help you?"

"No, no, I have it!"

"You're going to want light. Hitting your head could end badly." Nora ducked under my arm and flicked the light switch near the door, illuminating a set of unpolished stairs and a cluttered room beyond. "The trunks are in the corner near the boiler."

"Thank you!" Ren shouted up. Something crashed. "Blast! Wait. Are the city university libraries open to the public, do you know?"

"I have not the slightest idea. You know, you've got this thing upstairs Papa's paying for called 'the Aethernet.' I think you might be familiar with it. If you wanted pictures of marmalade kittens in corsets, you could find them, so if you haven't found what you're looking for online? I'm pretty sure it doesn't exist."

"Of course, using the Aethernet never occurred to me. Thank you, Miss Dearly."

Nora twisted her neck, looking up and back at me. "He . . . does this occasionally," I said. "God knows what's gotten into him. Cure for eye cancer? The key to finally being able to see through walls and watch ladies in various states of undress—the realization of a lifelong dream?"

"I heard that!"

Nora shook her head. "Does this have anything to do with the actual issues we are all facing, Ren?"

"I'm not sure." I heard a trunk opening. "Carry on!"

"I think he'd say so, if it were." I took her by the waist and urged her away from the door, shutting it behind us. "He's the least of our worries. Look, let me follow up on the calls I made last night and talk to Sam. Then we'll do whatever you want with Michael."

Nora smiled gently, and bounced up to kiss my chin again. "I'll make it up to you."

She just did, but far be it from me to tell her that.

19 • michael

The Brother I'd gone with the night before had taken forever to find his mark. We'd ridden in circles for hours through the middle-class parts of town, a third Brother driving, stalking a bit of nameless prey and drinking.

"There," he eventually said. "That's *him*."

"That's who?" I asked, peeping out through the carriage's venetian blinds, only to find that it wasn't just a him. It was a *them*. The zombie wasn't alone. The dead man was nondescript, but the living girl walking with him was nothing less than an uncanny angel. She had what appeared to be naturally snow-white hair, despite her obvious youth, and was dressed in pale purple, with a bouquet of violets pinned into the upswept shell of her bonnet. Above her head she carried one of those stupid gas lamp parasols, the light within it red. "What's red signify? I know there's a code the girls use."

"Sympathy for the dead," the Brother crouched by the door hissed. "Sympathy for the goddamn dead man who infected my sister."

Vodka started to creep back up my throat. Like me, this Brother had a vendetta. He hadn't been indecisive, he'd been searching. "We'll have to wait until they're separated and grab him."

"I won't hurt her." He looked at me, the eyes of his mask expressionless. "Just him. I'm willing to risk it."

"What? You can't be serious. She'll turn around and report us."

"That's why we have the masks, you dolt!"

The Brother playing chauffeur drove ahead of the perambulating couple and slowed, lowering the partition. "So we're not getting this one?"

"No, we can't," I said. "It's madness to kill a zombie right in front of a witness. The Brothers aren't even here to see it."

That was when the other Brother opened the door and sprang out, despite the fact that the carriage was still moving.

My heart stopped and I whirled around to watch as the driver slammed on the brakes. Within two breaths he'd flown at the zombie and pulled out a revolver, shooting him in the head. The zombie slumped to the pavement, and the girl began to wail, her hands going to her cheeks. The scene was unpoetic, cold. Somehow it seemed crueler than anything I'd ever dreamed of doing.

"Strigoi!" she shrieked, dropping her parasol, taking two steps toward the body.

"Are you sorry for him?" Brother Shooter demanded, grabbing the girl by the arm and yanking her away from the zombie. "What about those he bit? What about my sister, crazy and strapped to a bed until she rots! Are you sorry for them, too?"

The white-haired girl started to thrash. "Let me go! Oh my God! *Strigoi!*"

"Be still!" Brother Shooter ordered. "Be still, necroslut! Listen to me!"

But she wouldn't stop moving, wouldn't stop screaming. After a moment of struggle, Brother Shooter lifted his hand, flicking something out from beneath his gun. To my infinite surprise, he was carrying an Apache revolver—gun, knife, and brass knuckles in a single contraption. As I watched, frozen, he started to slash her beautiful face to ribbons. She sank to her knees, trying to fight him off with increasingly bloody hands. "You want to be one of the dead? Huh?"

Just then I saw something and started to scream, myself.

He hadn't gotten the zombie fully.

The monster grabbed for Brother Shooter's legs and pulled him down like a wolverine toppling larger prey, growling, seeking to bite him, to unmask him. Against my better judgment, but knowing that in defending Brother Shooter I was defending myself, I flew out of the carriage and to the prone masked boy, hauling him to his feet. It was a struggle to both get him away and keep the zombie on the opposite side of his body, a struggle full of limbs and teeth, but in the end I won out by kicking at the zombie's arms. Together we ran back to the carriage as the zombie pushed himself up and gave chase.

"Go!" I shouted to the driver as I got the door shut. The carriage revved forward. "Did he get you?"

"No." Brother Shooter touched his mask, breathing hard. "And he didn't see me."

"You *idiot*." I was white-hot with rage. What the hell was he thinking?

"I know." He looked at his hand, the bloody gun still clutched in it. "I know."

The dead man stopped in the street as we gained speed and roared after us like a lion issuing a challenge. I turned my head. He was not my concern. My concern was the girl—who was hurt, who was going to tell, who was going to ruin everything.

I sat back, catching my breath. I didn't even know what to say.

A few minutes later I sat bolt upright as lights leapt out of the shadows behind us. A carriage, hot on our tail. When we drove through a puddle of lamplight I saw the zombie we'd just threatened behind the steering wheel, wound at his temple, his eyes like fire. A mobile phone was clutched in his hand.

"He's following us!" I yelled. "The zombie! He's calling someone!"

"What do I do?" our driver screamed.

"Drive back to the pickup point!" I turned around and thrust my body through the partition, grabbing the terrified driver by the shoulder. "Where we got the carriage!"

"No!" Brother Shooter said. "The pub! The Murder will be gathered at the pub! We need backup!"

"We don't know how many will be there!" I looked back and saw the zombie practically on our bumper. "Head back to the chop shop. Make sure your masks are on tight!"

I couldn't even begin to describe what happened next, or how I managed to keep my liquor down during it. We raced through the city at full tilt, sights both familiar and unfamiliar whizzing past at a phenomenal pace. No shots were exchanged, no daring stunts engaged in; it was all sheer speed, sheer adrenaline. The zombie in pursuit never let up. A couple of times I felt like he was closer to me than my own skin.

When we reached the seedy part of town south of the port, we finally lost his carriage in a maze of poorly lit side avenues. By then we were only two streets away from where we needed to be, but the driver made the decision to keep going, to lead the undead bloodhound away from our rabbit warren. In retrospect it was a good idea.

It took an hour altogether. Half an hour for the maggot man to stop chasing us, and another half hour of sitting silently in the darkness, almost afraid to breathe lest the zombie somehow hear it and descend upon us again. Hunted men, we crept back to our nightly carriage pickup point with the lights still off—the underworld chop shop Green Jacket had arranged for us to work with. It was located in an old wooden building, one so sloppily built it didn't appear capable of sheltering anything, least of all a gang of criminals.

The minute we climbed out of the carriage, I was sick in the gutter.

Inside we found Belinda and her crew at work on three new carriages for the Murder's exploits. Each was cobbled together from pieces of stolen vehicles, traceable numbers and tracking technology removed. Belinda was a severe, kinky-haired woman, and she eyed us distastefully as we trekked into the oil-stained, tool-littered space. My limbs like jelly, I ignored her, seeking out Brother Green Jacket. I found him watching a pigtailed, betrousered girl climb about a carriage chassis with a welding gun. He was the only Brother still in attendance.

"Brothers," he said, turning to regard us when we approached. His mask, as always, was on. "What's the matter? Why aren't you at the pub?"

"I'll tell you what's the matter." The Brothers I'd gone out with stopped behind me as I tried to find the words. "He just went after his zombie—"

"Congratulations!"

"No! Not *'congratulations'*! The zombie tried to catch us! Nearly unmasked him!"

Green Jacket went still. "What?"

"It's true," Brother Shooter said, his voice shaking. He was losing it. "I did it . . . but the zombie chased me. He saved me . . ." He gestured feebly at me. "But . . . I actually cut her. But I didn't get him . . . oh God . . ."

"Cut her?"

"A girl," I said. "Living. And before that, he shot the dead man right in front of her."

"You did this out in the open?" Green Jacket looked at Brother Driver, who was, for the most part, still calm. "Take him into the basement," he said, and Brother Driver obeyed, leading Shooter away as he began to break down and cry like a frightened child.

"It's over. I'm gone." *I* was an idiot. The protection the Murder had offered me was void. If my father found out about any of this, I'd count myself lucky if I was only *disowned*.

"You can't leave," Green Jacket replied, the anger in his voice discernable even through the morpher. "This is a delicate time. We've been planning for months, and now we're finally acting in earnest. Of course a few things are going to go awry. Eventually the news and the police will pick up on us. We *expect* that."

"Like hell I can't." I tried to slow my breathing. "There are no leaders, and that keeps us safe—but it also leads boys to do things like that!"

"You did brilliantly. You got him out of there. That's precisely how members of the Murder should act. Loyal to all in the mask." Green Jacket approached. Over the scent of burning metal, I could make out his strong cologne. It smelled like something an old man would wear. "Our people, the aristocrats of this nation, have always been loyal to one another. We're simply continuing that tradition."

Collecting my thoughts, I forced myself to recall that I was there to kill, convince, and get out. I could put up with a little danger for that—and to see my deeds drown in a sea of black, never traced back to me.

"Remember: you are a plague doctor now. It's your job to cure this sick world by killing the things infecting it. Have some pride." And so Green Jacket left me, orange sparks showering his shoulders as he walked past the welder.

The carriage the girl was working on looked familiar. It took me a moment to identify it as a black Model V, one of its windows knocked out. The same sort of carriage Nora's aunt drove. The day Nora'd been kidnapped I glimpsed it through the window and pretended I hadn't, invading my mother's parlor just to see her.

I'd done all of this for her.

I had to remember that.

I wasn't very gregarious. I had no one I'd count as a best friend. I had my circle, but I could take or leave them. My mother had always been determined to make me popular, and so she'd made sure I attended the right parties, held a few of my own. Nora might've come to the Christmas party my mother wanted me to hold in December. To see her, I'd been willing to own the planning, to act enthusiastic about it.

It was all for her. Everything I did. Every plan I made. Every word I didn't say.

That night, around 3:00 A.M., I pulled a wooden box down from my closet and opened it. My mask and a bottle of bourbon at my knee, I fingered the mementos I'd been collecting of Nora since first meeting her at Vespertine's twelfth birthday party. The way Vespertine told it, her mother insisted she invite every one of her classmates from St. Cyprian's, even the scholarship and new money girls, in order to punish her for some infraction. That was why Nora and the plain, penniless Miss Roe were there.

It was the first time I'd seen Nora, ever. Her eyes had taken mere seconds to capture mine, to cause something mysterious and then unknown in my body to thrum. Our introduction was brief, but it had been enough to open a whole new world to me, a world filled with yearning.

The other girls were content to gather around the towering white cake like a bunch of clucking hens in training, terrified of getting anything on their clothes. Nora would have none of it, though. And none of me. She ignored everyone except for her anxious-eyed friend. I couldn't get a moment with her, and I was half mad by the time her aunt, Mrs. Ortega, saw her out.

As I'd watched her go, one of the white ribbons fell from her curly hair. I ran forward to catch it, thanking the angels, but before I could return it to her my own mother came to collect me.

My father was in the carriage. He asked me if I'd met anyone interesting. I told him I had. When he heard Nora Dearly's name, he looked at me so hatefully it almost hurt. I hadn't understood it then. I barely understood it now. It was her father he despised.

It was her I loved.

Her hair ribbon, a button from her boot, fringe from her parasol—these were the scraps I had of her. Each one collected at a party or gathering where I'd done my best to impress her, only to get the brush-off. How long I'd stared at them when she was kidnapped, and then when she'd been gone.

Gone because Griswold, a dead man—an *object,* like that pearly button was an object—had taken her from me.

She had to *see.* Had to see the lengths to which I was prepared to go to demonstrate my devotion.

Running the ribbon under my nose, I shut my eyes and pretended it was her hair. I tried to enter again into the violent, operatic fantasies I'd been weaving for months.

The fantasies that were going to come true.

In a few days it would all be over. I just had to keep my cool.

At Allister Genetics the next day, as I walked the mahogany paneled halls of my father's office, all I could think of was ravens. Coco had brought a single note that morning. It said, *Saturday. 11:00 P.M. Sewer under Delreggio's. Leave the money there ahead of time.*

There was a date.

My phone beeped. Figuring it might be Vespertine, I reached for it. I had yet to tell her anything, though I knew she was waiting for me to do so. As I recalled the previous evening, as I briefly entertained the idea of sharing anything about it, I suddenly wished I'd eaten breakfast in order to have something to actually be sick with.

I needed her to ground me.

> Hello. This is Nora Dearly. I was wondering if you might have time to talk?

I stopped in my tracks. I'd never expected her to contact *me*. A bit thrown off, unsure how to respond, I bought time with a simple reply.

> Perhaps. Am I going to be punched this time?

There. Bitter, but open. Willing to forgive, but not forget the past. While I waited, I labeled her number with her name.

> No. Do you like Lapin Innocent?

A coquettish invitation-not-an-invitation? Tea? It was the last thing I expected, but knew I'd be stupid to pass up the chance. Playing along, I asked her to meet me there in a few hours.

> Fine. You did the asking, you bring the eyes.

Directly after Nora confirmed our meeting, Vespertine actually did join the texting party.

> Are we meeting today? You were going to tell me about your plans.

Suddenly nothing in the world seemed more stultifying than gushing to Vesper about my grand designs. I told her no and continued on my way.

> Are you sure? I'm literally bouncing around. I want to hear.
> Please?

Let her bounce.

Outside the interior office doors stood two black-clad Allister Genetics guards, members of my father's extensive private security force. They parted to make way for me, and I continued through the lofty Art Nouveau office building toward the elevators. There I swiped my wrist over a sun-shaped reader on the button panel, freeing up access to every floor save the twelfth—that was the animal growth facility, and perhaps ten people were permitted up there. Saturdays my father devoted entirely to work on the twelfth floor, shutting out all distractions, including his family. He called it "Code 12."

I hit the eleventh button, for the main lab. The elevator opened directly into what was known as "casual" decontamination, which involved a mist of disinfecting spray, a harsh blast of air followed by a powerful suction, and a pair of stupid blue elastic booties and clear gloves. I left my satchel and jacket behind in a locker, subjected myself to the process, and stepped out into the blinding white laboratory, pulling on a lab coat as I went.

The main research floor was almost completely open, and yet segregated from the outside world—few interior walls, no exterior windows. Scores of scientists were at work within, either at one of the many long, stainless steel tables, at one of the vast computer banks, or inside one of the isolated quarantine areas. Most of the walls had holographic projectors aimed at them, the results of supercomputer-created rat and monkey colonies playing out before the scientists' eyes—thousands of virtual reality animal simulations testing new drugs, new therapies, new gene combinations. The fake animals bred, were subjected to variables, and died at an astounding rate—up to fifty generations a minute.

I found my father standing before one of them, his expression drawn. "My lord."

He looked at me and cleared his throat. "Son. What brings you up here?"

"I've just received an interesting invitation. Tea in New London. I thought I'd ask permission to leave for the day, and to take your carriage. I'll put in the hours tomorrow." The main AG building was located in the northwest corner of the preserve. It'd be a bit of a drive to New London and back.

My father waved me off. "Go. And while I appreciate the initiative, next time just text me?"

"Of course," I said with a bow. I lingered as I straightened, wondering if I ought to just unburden myself of everything. It wasn't guilt that made me wonder, merely self-preservation. My father could find this Ratcatcher fellow, call him off. I could still walk away.

"And while you're at it, email your mother." When I looked at him in confusion, he added, eyes and attention elsewhere, "She keeps calling me, asking after you. You need to cut the cord. Even though you've acted like an imbecile of the highest caliber, keeping you close to home forever would do nothing but turn you into a pale, dithering little woman. Tell her you no longer want her hovering. You're finally acting like a young man, like an Allister, and I'm glad for it."

Resolve disappearing, I bowed again. I couldn't think of anything to say. I recalled his earlier entreaties not to make him regret giving me latitude, and instantly berated myself for even *thinking* about opening my mouth. He'd disown me, embarrass me on an even larger scale—and he'd never respect me. Ever.

As I turned away a plump man in a tight white coat hurried up to my father and said, "My lord, the results are ready. This combination is extremely promising. I think I've managed to find a way to suppress several necessary proteins, although some problems remain."

"Let's see, Dr. Elpinoy." My father turned to follow him.

At the mention of his name I glanced back, memorizing the fat man's face. So he was the one my father spoke of earlier—the defector from Team Dearly. Interesting.

Half an hour later I left Allister Genetics, surrounded by four of my father's elite security guards. They escorted me to his carriage and saw me off with a salute.

Lapin Innocent was a popular tearoom located in the rear gardens of the New Victorian Museum of Natural History. It was open to the public, accessible by a series of fanciful brass gates. Small signs warned: BEWARE PICKPOCKETS AND FANCY WOMEN.

I found Nora standing beside a stone fountain designed to look like a circle of dancing fairies, water jetting from their puckered mouths. With both hands, she held a leather lead, and at her feet sat a battle-scarred Doberman pinscher. She appeared to be alone.

As was I.

Before Nora could notice me, I allowed myself to enjoy a moment or two of voyeurism. Although I couldn't help but imagine outfitting her more grandly, I still admired the relative plainness of her current gown and gloves, her small pieces of jewelry—they set her natural features off to perfection. Her hair was her crowning glory, and, I would argue, the only ornament she would ever need if she was in my bed. And what crime was there in wanting her there? She was obviously beneath me, classwise, but I could overlook that. I could forgive her everything, anything.

"A dog? Are you afraid I might try something?" I said when I finally abandoned my reverie and drew nearer.

Her eyes met mine and narrowed deliciously. The dog stood and growled at me, and she reined him in. "No. I'm hoping you do." She looked around and asked, "Didn't you bring a chaperone?"

"No." Looking into her eyes, I almost lost my train of thought. "I need to talk to you alone."

Nora looked uneasy—which I enjoyed, honestly. "About what?"

"What do you need to talk to *me* about?"

"Things that could be said in front of an adult."

"I assure you, I want only privacy. And I'm willing to risk scandal to get it."

Nora thought about it and nodded. Satisfied, I stepped past her and approached the host. Soon he was escorting us through a gauntlet of critical adult glances to a prime seat in a secluded area. Once we were seated I plucked the menu card away from her place setting, preventing her from even looking at it. "I'll order." I savored the annoyed look this offer caused.

"Make it fast," she said after getting the dog to lie at her feet. I repressed the urge to kick the cur's face in. "This isn't a pleasure outing."

"How disappointing. What would you like to talk about, then?" The waiter appeared, and before he could speak I specified, "High tea, your best white. And champagne." He bowed and withdrew.

"Several things." Nora glanced aside at some ferns. "Let's start with my aunt."

I dismissed this with a snort. "I believe my family's been nothing but cooperative in that matter. I have nothing new to add." I held forth my arm. "But if you happen to have a lie detector handy, by all means."

"Don't be cute," she said, leaning forward. "My father will take yours to court, you know."

"Over what? We helped Mrs. Ortega, and she disappeared." A server arrived with a towering silver tray of finger sandwiches and cakes, and I helped myself to a scone. "My father let our driver take her back to town one day. The driver says he dropped her off. What happened after that is none of our concern. If ignorance is a crime, lock me up."

"I wish I could." She made no move to eat. "You might as well drop the act. I was on the ship. I saw what you did to Miss Roe, heard what you said. There can be no pleasantries between us. I'm here for information, and you owe me. We saved your life."

Something changed at the mention of Roe's name, at the insinuation that I was some kind of monster. At its heart was a mixture of anger and giddiness that threatened to crack my facade, and so it was very carefully that I stated, "I heard about the incident at her house. I'm so sorry."

"Yeah, right." Nora couldn't lend breath to both words; her voice fell away somewhere in the middle. My heart ached at the sound of it. "Like you care about her."

"I care about *you*," I protested. She made a sound of disgust or disbelief and glanced aside. "Miss Dearly—I mean it. And we ought to talk about that."

"Talk about *what*?" She looked at me again, expression almost insulted.

"The way you compromise yourself." I softened my voice. "After all, I don't think I owe *you*. Rather, I should say I owe that deadmeat you disgrace yourself with, as much as this idea pains me. Was he not your fearless leader that evening?"

"Don't you *dare* talk about him that way." Nora gripped the arms of her chair, but kept her voice low.

"Oh, if we're to be honest today, I'll talk about him in any way I wish. After all, you want something out of me, not the other way around. And I think that's the word we ought to focus on today. 'Honesty.'"

"What is this, kindergarten vocabulary time? Do I get to finger paint, too?"

"What it is," I said, "is rending the veil. I think your life suffers from a lack of people willing to tell you the truth. I think you are overly indulged."

The sommelier came by with the bottle of champagne then, and she was forced to cork her reply. Once he was gone she stood, ripping the napkin from her lap. "I'm not about to sit through this. This was a mistake."

"Sit down," I said firmly, "or I'll turn over the table, and everyone will look and see us together. You chose this venue—this very *public* venue. You have to play it out to the end now."

She rained hellfire on me with her eyes, but slowly sat. I tried to relax. I couldn't afford to be scattered, emotional. "Now. First of all, I'll again assure you I know nothing of your aunt. I'm very sorry for your loss. I mean that sincerely."

She continued to regard me warily, but said nothing. Behind us someone laughed.

"Second, I shall say that you *do* compromise yourself. You think you aren't gossiped about? But you know, I could protect you. Fight for you." She rolled her eyes. "I'm serious. I have a . . . vested interest in you. You've always fascinated me. But you act so rashly."

"Shut. It," she said, each syllable like a grenade going off in her mouth.

"Hit a sore spot, have I?" I said, unable to contain a smile. "But the offer is still extended."

"I don't want your help."

"What about my perspective?"

"Oh. Please. However have I lived this long without it?"

This was almost *fun*. I was fully enjoying her—her adorably exasperated expressions, her fire. "Well, for instance, you want *so badly* to ascribe cruel reasoning to my actions, when all along I have been a gentleman—when all along I've acted in your best interests. I did truly attempt to protect Miss Roe's reputation in order to defend your honor. I risked my life, leaving behind my parents, to physically defend the Roe family. And look what I've received in return. Insults. Threats. Never thanks."

Her eyes widened. "You tried to *kill* Isambard. You told Miss Roe that the reason you paid attention to her was because she was shaping up to be something shameful from my past that you wanted to clean up. That once you *had* me, she'd never see me again, you disgusting cad. She left her own family to save you!"

"*After* he became the living dead." I ignored her second round of statements, but let them add fuel to the fire. This was what I had to help her with. She didn't see things *properly*. "I acted nobly that night. And yet Griswold assaulted me, knocked me out. Do you think it's cute that he shut me up so dramatically? Because he left me helpless in the face of a growing crisis. He's not the hero you make him out to be."

Nora continued to stare at me as if I were some sort of drooling beast. "Let me ask you something."

"Please do."

"Why didn't you ever *tell* me that you liked me?"

The question was unexpected, but the answer came to me swiftly. Capturing her gaze, I said, "Because my father hates your father, and I would not insult him by going as far as I wished with you. At least, not until I was older. The entirety of his reasoning escapes me, but let's be honest, he's right on one score . . . both your personalities could use some improvement. I mean to help you with that."

If she'd looked homicidal before, my last few words caused her features to twist into something approximating the love child of Jack the Ripper and Satan himself. She hopped to her feet, and I gained mine as well—but before either of us could say anything, I felt a cold hand on my shoulder.

"Leave," I heard Griswold say. "Now."

Turning around, shrugging him off, I growled, "How dare you come here? Lay your hands on me?" Good God, had he been there all along?

"I go where I'm needed." Griswold leaned closer to me, and I tried to hold my ground. "Like when I had to save your hide. Looks like I might have to do it again."

The hatred and embarrassment that filled me at the sight of him was nearly frightening. I could barely form a coherent thought, but I still managed to say, "Afraid that once she was alone with me, she'd see the truth?"

Nora smiled, the motion strained. "No. I figured after you paid and left, we'd have a nice little date."

"We're done here." I had to leave, before I gave in fully to my growing rage. This was *not* how it was supposed to go. This had been my moment to admire her before I started breaking her will. I could feel my face, my entire body, growing hot.

"Nuh-uh," Nora said. "If you have any honor whatsoever, we're still talking. The man you yourself said you owe is here." She had the upper hand now, and her features blossomed into a mockery of pretty pleasantness. "Let's all sit. Shall we?"

"What?" I almost spat. Sucking a deep breath into my lungs, I did my best to calm myself. I didn't actually wish to appear cruel to Nora. Not now.

"Are you sure?" Griswold asked Nora, cutting his eyes at me.

"Yes," she told him, returning her eyes to me. "We have to finish this. *Sit.*"

And so I sat. I sat down at the maddest tea party ever held. I sat next to the bloody zombie, a chunk of dead flesh in a frilly chair, who looked like he wanted to consume me from the inside out. The feeling was mutual.

"Let's get off the topic of *us,*" Nora said.

"For the love of all that is holy, yes," Griswold muttered, leaning his chin on his fingers.

"What do you know about Lord Edmund Lopez?"

This question threw me off my guard, and I was grateful for the arrival of the tea. Once the server had poured and disappeared, I asked, "Why?" It seemed completely random.

"Just tell me."

"Colonel Lopez?" I said. "That disgraced old drunk? What could you want with him?"

"Disgraced? Drunk?" Nora spun her hand in the air, indicating that I should go on.

I didn't know what do with my anger when faced with this. Now it was useless, without direction. So, making no effort to mellow my voice, I informed her, "Yes, that *disgraced old drunk*. He's never been part of the good set, frankly because he's refused to be. His brother tried, I know that much, and did manage to rebuild the family fortune and suppress certain truths, but the way he looked—he could never walk about in society. He was a cripple. A deformed freak." Nora stared at me with troubled eyes, now vulnerable in her wonder. "Not that anything either man could do would *ever* be enough to redeem the sins of their parents."

"What happened?"

Looking at Griswold, I said, "His parents were Punk sympathizers. After the Reed Massacre, Lord and Lady Lopez had everything stripped from them and were routed south with the lot—as they deserved."

Nora looked shocked. Griswold glared at me. "Don't talk about my people."

"It's historical fact. I'll talk about them all I bloody want." I made a mental note to talk about them a *lot* while I tore him apart.

"Fine, then I'll talk about yours. Have you heard of any attacks in the city?" he asked, lowering his hand. "By people wearing bird masks?"

For a second the wall seemed to ripple behind him. "No. Why?"

"They're the ones who bombed the Roes." He bent his head. "I'm not proud that my people've hunted down the dead, but at least they didn't cover their faces like cowards."

"How do you know that?" I heard my voice, though I couldn't have said my lips moved.

"She saw them," Nora said. "And they attacked us, too. Hijacked my aunt's carriage. Had us at gunpoint. And yet, I still count it as a better outing than this."

Oh *God,* that had been her carriage. That had been her bloody carriage in the middle of a New London chop shop. Some Brothers must have been assigned to *get* those carriages . . .

And they'd threatened Nora. Targeted her, not knowing who she was.

The idea nearly made me sick. "I'm very sorry to hear that," I said in a rush, doing my best to hide my emotions within a whirl of words. "I'm glad you're all right. But this is over now." I rose, bowed, and walked away before they could say anything more.

Nora'd been at the end of a gun. Suddenly all I could think of as I shoved my way through the crowd was the white-haired girl's bleeding face.

This was madness. I couldn't have something like that happen to Nora. Nothing physical.

I'd wanted to kill Griswold. I'd compromised myself, put myself in physical danger, terrorized the city, to *kill Griswold.* To imagine, that dead thing sitting there, witness to that spectacle . . . no. I couldn't allow that to go unpunished.

But I also couldn't let the Murder anywhere near her again. The Ratcatcher. *No.*

Change of plans. I had to fix this. I had to separate the act of torturing him from the act of teaching her.

She'd need me once he was gone, after all.

20 • Laura

That night I told myself Mártira's ghost would speak to me. Tell me how to save people. That maybe I'd created a zombie, but Hagens had created a phantom—one that would undo her. I believed in ghosts, for the dead walked now, and ghosts seemed as possible as anything else.

But when faced with the light of day, I knew that wouldn't happen. Mártira and Claudia were gone. The time for stories was over. All that was left was reality.

As I lay abed thinking, almost everyone else still asleep, Dog entered the tent and approached me. He knelt beside my pallet and pointed to his ear, then back to the tent flap, before aiming two fingers downward and walking them about.

He'd heard someone outside, I figured. But who . . .

Quickly rousing myself, I whispered, "Go back to your blankets." Dog obeyed, and I found my shawl and made my way outside as quietly as I could. I didn't know who might be watching me, spying, reporting—only the fact that someone would be. Allende had made that abundantly clear.

It was early morning and mist still swathed the ground. Yet I immediately saw what had gotten Dog's attention—and my throat constricted at the sight. Coalhouse was standing at the edge of the field where the partygoers used to park their carriages, his back to the camp. Beside him was an old, beat-up carriage I didn't recognize. At first I wasn't sure whether I ought to approach him or not. He'd returned, yes, but . . . even together, what could we hope to accomplish?

After a few seconds of indecision I remembered Dog, and knew I had to risk it. I made my way toward Coalhouse. When I was within hearing range I said, "You came back." He was still facing away from me, and didn't respond. Moving a little to the side, I caught his attention. "You—"

"Miss Laura." He bowed. "Sorry to just show up like this."

Shaking my head, I crooked a finger and backed away. He took the hint and followed me. I led him deeper within the tree line, where the undergrowth was so thick the land couldn't be used, at least not for our purposes. It was dark under the canopy of leaves, and colder.

After a few minutes he stopped me by grasping my arm. "Where are we going?"

"Here will work," I said once I recovered from being taken hold of. I raised my voice, noticing that both his bad eye and his hearing aid were gone. "Where are the others?"

He frowned. "I'm alone this time. Will be from now on."

"But we need supporters. A force to go against Hagens. We need—"

Coalhouse held up a hand. "Why don't you tell me what the situation is first. Let's figure out where we stand."

It occurred to me, even as I opened my mouth to speak, that I didn't know this young man, didn't know if he could be trusted. But if he wasn't an ally, at this point—did it even matter? I had nothing to lose save my life, and even that was already gone. The Reaper had already left me behind.

"My eldest sister, Mártira, was the leader of a gang of thieves and bunkos in New London before the undead came. All sorts . . . card sharps, burglars. Anyone who wanted a home, someone to look out for them, they split their take with my sister and became part of the group. Mártira used that money to buy food, weapons, protection." I shut my eyes. "During the Siege many of us were turned into zombies, or killed. Even the children. The house on Ramee Street was overrun. I died there. Under the floorboards."

"Jesus."

"Afterward, Mártira said we had to work together, band together even more tightly. Start doing right. So we began to take in new zombies, those who didn't have homes. Zombies from other gangs. Mártira could always put it so beautifully, I'm afraid I can't, but . . . but I know she didn't mean to *harm* anyone. Not anymore. Just to survive." My shoulders started to quiver. "Hagens killed her. And Claudia. Right in front of me. Hagens killed my sisters and took over."

Before I knew it his huge hand was on my shoulder, steadying me. I looked up into his eye and saw kindness reflected there. At the sight, I couldn't have controlled my mouth even if I had wanted to. "The leaders are on her side. They don't like the living. I don't know what to do. I thought of running away, but I can't. They'll find me."

The young man's face was serious. "If I have to, I'll get you out of here," he told me as he took his hand back.

I didn't dare allow myself to hope. I didn't dare allow his words to take root in my heart. "Why did you come back alone? Did you tell anyone what I told you?"

"Yeah. But I need to talk to Hagens," he said, lifting his head and looking in the direction of the camp. "Some bad stuff's been happening in town. People here might have something to do with it. And I want to know why she wants the prisoner."

"Smoke?" I tried to think of anything more I could share. "We found him in the Morgue about a month ago. He never talked much, but he said his name was Smoke. We didn't know he was special."

"Okay." Coalhouse's head bobbed slightly. "What about the masked people in town? They're targeting the living. You know anything about that?"

"No. But I wouldn't put it past her. She ordered the men to go get Smoke without permission . . . she might've sent some into town. She's like a she-wolf. She can smell weakness, and takes pleasure in stomping it out."

"I've dealt with her before. I was in the army with her." The boy sighed. "Look, I have a plan. But I need your help to work it."

"Alone? Without your friends?"

"No," he said bitterly. "No. It's better alone." I answered this with silence, unsure what to say. "I need to convince her I'm on her side. I need to get into her confidence, figure out what exactly people at this camp are doing, if anything. What they plan to do."

Suddenly I realized what this fellow was to me. He was a connection to the outside world. "Oh, but I could do that, and tell you what I find out!"

"No!" Startled by his outburst, I shut up. "I need to do this on my own. It has to be *me*."

Clutching my shawl more tightly about my shoulders, I argued, "But it will only put you in danger. Why not let me do it? I have no friends, aside from Dog and Abuelo. I have nowhere to go."

Coalhouse rumbled, "'Cause my 'friends' treat me like a loser, and I'm sick of it." He looked down at me again, kindness gone, resolution in its place. "Are you going to help me or not?"

I had no choice but to throw my lot in with him. "Yes."

"Good. Now, I need you to get me in to see Hagens."

The very idea of being anywhere around her made me shiver. "What are you going to do?"

"I've got news for her. I'm going to act like I've abandoned Griswold. Like I'm going rogue."

From the direction of the camp I could hear zombies stirring, and knew he might not be able to. "Okay. Wait here." I swallowed. "And if I don't come back . . . get out of here. Promise you'll go."

"Just hurry," he said as he settled down in the undergrowth.

Mártira's tent had been taken over by the leaders, most of whom were still asleep. Only a few were awake and quietly conversing— Hagens, Allende, and "Duke" Rastino, a dark-skinned zombie dressed in a whirlwind of ochre silk and sepia velvet. Rastino looked after all the card sharps and hustlers.

Allende said something, and the others laughed. As Rastino commented on it, Hagens looked up and saw me lingering in the doorway. "What in the devil's name are you doing here, you little weed?" she said in that tone of voice that always made me want to crawl up inside my own body and wait for her to go away.

"There . . ." I shifted my skirt up, and felt it snag on my roses' thorns. "There's someone outside who wants to see you. A newcomer."

Hagens glanced at Allende and Rastino. "See? I told you. More will come."

"How are they going to find us if we move, though?" asked Allende.

"They'll have to. Because we need to get out of here."

"He asked for you." I didn't know what to say, save the truth. "His name is Coalhouse. He said to tell you he's left Griswold."

Hagens climbed to her feet, instantly angry. "Take me to him. Rastino." The brightly clad zombie looked up. "Give me your gun." He did so, and she tucked the pistol into the waistband of her trousers.

I couldn't walk, seeing that. Was she just going to shoot him? Was I leading the firing squad right to him?

"Go," she said, glaring at me. I couldn't, and she reached out and shoved me in the chest, almost knocking me over. I released a choking sound, unable even to draw in air to scream with. "What are you waiting for?"

Gathering my wits about me, I slowly turned and led her out. The sun was starting to burn off some of the fog; the earth seemed far too bright.

"Where is he?" she demanded.

"In the woods." She shoved me again, this time in the back, and I pointed out where I'd left him.

"Why did he come to you?" She stepped in front of me. "Let's talk about that first, hmm?"

"He didn't." It seemed to take forever to come up with the words. "I was walking, and I found him. I couldn't sleep, because of the fires . . ." The enormity of what they'd done struck me, and I barely choked back a sob. "He said he was waiting for the right time to come to you. That you were right all along."

Hagens ran her cold eyes over my face. "You realize if you try anything cute I'll kill you, right?"

I nodded blindly, because I did.

"This doesn't have to be hard. Your sister was *sick*. Her priorities were beyond messed up. I gave her chance after chance, and I only killed her because I had to—but she deserved what she got. You play your part, you keep your mouth shut, and everything goes easy for you." With that she marched beyond me, determinedly heading toward where I'd shown her.

Terrified, I had no choice but to follow. *Oh, God.* Was she actually going to kill him?

Coalhouse looked up when she went crashing through the brush. Before he could say anything, Hagens cocked the gun in her waistband. She lifted it, aiming at him, and his eye widened.

"Mr. Gates," Hagens hollered, so loudly I thought she'd wake the whole camp. "Apparently you're too dumb to know what's good for you."

"I'm not that deaf," the boy said as he slowly stood up. Showing his hands, he continued to stare at the gun. "Nice to see you, too, Miss Hagens."

"I was not lying the night you came here with your gang. You have ten seconds to leave. For your own safety."

"So you don't want to talk about yesterday? The fact that we were the ones to take down your men?" The young man fixed his remaining eye on her even as her expression blackened further. "'Cause it was the last time I'll take orders from Griswo—"

Lightning fast, Hagens turned her hand just a degree to the left and shot beyond Coalhouse's shoulder. He ducked reflexively and then looked ashamed for doing so. I gripped my fingers into my leaves. "I'm through playing games. What, did you think you'd come here and we'd exchange some witty banter? That then we'd laugh and hug and I'd welcome you into my crew? I know this is a setup. I know Griswold."

Coalhouse recovered, though he looked unnerved. "But it's true. We had an argument last night and I left. Thought maybe you could use me. So I bought a secondhand carriage this morning and headed up here."

"Sure you're not just here for the pretty girls with low standards?" Hagens asked, glancing at me. My skin prickled.

"Look, you don't have to insult me," he said, and I could hear real pain in his voice. "If you can't use me, just tell me, and I'll find somewhere else to go. But maybe you should listen to what I came here to tell you first."

"Entertain me," Hagens drawled.

"You guys have to move your camp. The entire thing. And you can't go back to New London."

Hagens lifted a brow. She disarmed the gun with a click and waited for him to continue.

"When I left Gris, he said he was going to the coppers," Coalhouse said, holding her gaze. "He recognized one of your girls while we were defending Patient One. We *know* it was you. Don't try to pretend."

"Hold up. Who's Patient One?"

"The *prisoner*," Coalhouse said. "The biter they locked up. The one Griswold killed your people to make sure stayed in human control, yeah? And now he's going to lead the cops right to you. Only reason he held off was because he *did* send us back here to spy, and he didn't want any of us taking a bullet. But you guys? He doesn't give a crap what happens to you. If you go back to New London, he'll find you."

Coalhouse was a superb actor. I had no idea how much of his speech was fact and how much fiction, but I found myself impressed. It was even easy to act shocked. Trying to do my part, I blurted out, "It's true. They were here last night. I saw them."

Hagens seemed to expand with rage, her eyes opening wide, her nostrils flaring. "Oh, were they?"

"If I were against you, would I tell you guys to move?" the boy asked. "To put some distance between you and the humans? Look, I'll even help. Then I'll go back and keep an eye on Gris, make sure he doesn't try anything else."

Hagens thought for a moment, her eyes darting between us, before saying, "No."

Coalhouse blinked. "I'm telling the truth!"

Hagens stepped closer to him. "It doesn't matter if you are. It doesn't matter what you saw, and it doesn't matter what Griswold tries. We're moving today anyway. Fat lot of good it'll do, as I know they'll find us again, but it's something."

"Who'll find you? Because I'm talking about the *cops*. Wouldn't you rather scatter and survive the—"

"The cops are the least of my concerns. If the *army* showed up, they would be wasting my time. This is bigger than the army."

Coalhouse didn't move, but he was starting to look genuinely scared. "What are you talking about, Hagens?"

"None of your business. Knowing will just get you in trouble. That's my philosophy for everyone till I get this sorted out. And the last thing I need is Company Z vets hanging around." She jammed the barrel of her gun into her chest. "You know me, Coalhouse. Am I crazy? Evil?"

"No."

"I'd be the first to say Averne was a monster. That Wolfe can never be forgiven for what he did. I'm not like them." And with that she swung the gun around and aimed it at my head. I froze. "But I'll do what I have to do. Right now I'm actually protecting you. *Go*. Or I will kill this one where she stands."

Coalhouse looked at me helplessly. I couldn't say it, so I prayed he would go. Even if he never came back.

A second later he did. He retreated to the field, to his carriage. Hagens didn't let up, even once he was inside his vehicle and tearing toward the road. "Why didn't you tell me you saw them last night?"

"I was confused," I said, watching the carriage leave, wishing I could call out to it. "I swear I was confused. Because . . . of everything . . ."

I couldn't even look in her eyes. It was a solid minute before she relented, putting the gun away. "Stay close to me from now on. I don't trust you. I never want you more than three feet from me, you understand?"

Nodding, I waited for her to move before following her.

There was no hope.

21 • vespertine

"Did Suzanna speak to you the other night?"

Careful not to move my eyes, focusing intently on the beaded Oaxacan-print curtains hung in my mother's favorite carriage, I told the truth. "No."

Lady Elsinore Mink—legally, my mother—regarded me shrewdly through the short veil attached to her hat. Her hands moved in brisk, nervous ways that made her look as if she sought to gather the world in and make it worry with her. "Choose your words carefully, girl. I heard some of the servants talking last night as if Suzanna had, and I *will* find out the truth. I will not be disobeyed."

I didn't need this. I had bigger things to worry about. "Suzanna has never spoken to me. A few nights ago someone entered my room and put my washing away. I hardly remember who comes and goes. They're your servants. You won't let me have my own."

Mother huffed musically and turned to look at her companion, Miss Prescilla Perez. They were both brunettes with high curls and beauty marks, nearly twins. "You see what I have to live with."

"Hush, Ellie." Prescilla regarded my mother with large, tender black eyes. "Hush, darling. It's that house. It gets to you."

"I *hate* Éclatverre," my mother agreed, her voice rising an octave, before turning back to me. "You *know* what will happen if I catch you in a lie."

Finally trusting myself to look her in the eyes, I turned from the window and said, "If Suzanna said anything to me, she will be turned out without a reference. She'll never find another household position in the Territories again. She will be forced to pursue work as a barmaid, or marry a goatherd, or do one of a thousand other shameful things." And because I meant to guard her against that fate, I did the only thing I could do—try to get the dogs off her trail. "As for myself, Mother—"

"Don't call me that," Lady Mink snapped. "Don't you ever call me that!"

One figurative creek forded, the scent weakened, I hushed. I didn't even bother to act as if her words surprised or hurt me. She'd long ago lost the power to hurt me. Now she had only the power to embarrass me in ways that told me she'd never mentally progressed beyond her own time at St. Cyprian's, and was slowly losing even that as I grew closer to accessing my trust fund and a husband and was more often seen in public. The ancient carriage sent for me at school, my attic bedroom, and the vow of silence her servants had to take were the final remnants of it; the NVIC interview she'd forced me to do following Dearly's kidnapping had probably been her last big hurrah. Lord, I hated to think I'd ever shown my face on television, like an *actress*. Only the fact that I'd spent that time humiliating Dearly made up for it.

What was it I'd said that had incurred such a punishment? I believe I called Miss Perez "an opportunistic, money-grubbing cathouse reject."

So, all things considered, it'd been completely worth it.

The carriage rolled on, turning to the east. We were on our

way to spend the afternoon with the de La Moscas. I wasn't much looking forward to it, but at least it would be a distraction from my maddeningly quiet, bejeweled mobile phone. I had to talk to Michael before he did something truly stupid. The gridlines of every calendar I looked at now reminded me of crosshairs.

"Do not embarrass me today," Lady Mink said, whipping out a black lace fan and fluttering it madly before her face. "Or so help me, I shall have the shop shut up, and you won't be permitted to go there anymore."

Hoping to enrage her to the point of confusion, I said, "You do, and Father will come down on you like a ton of bricks."

"Don't speak so to the lady," Prescilla said, leaning in dangerously close. "You forget your place."

Smiling sweetly at her, I went mum. I could think of a thousand things to call her, as usual, but I wasn't willing to go *that* far for a mere maid.

I had standards, after all.

Lord Alberto de La Mosca was Attorney General of the Territories. His country estate, Willowshire, was a Georgian re-creation of yellow stone surrounded by terraformed fields of willow trees and cork oaks.

We were received in the grand drawing room by Lady Louisa de La Mosca. Although middle-aged, she was younger than Lord Alberto by a good twenty years. The portraits of her in the long mirrored hall did not match her feature-for-feature, indicating nipping and tucking, or perhaps something more.

My mother and Miss Perez were entertained by her. I was left to deal with her two girls, Opalina and Yaeba. They were children, and I found myself less than enchanted by their antics.

"Did you hear about Hettie Schloot?" Opalina leaned close to me. She was thirteen, and eager to seem worldly. She already wore her black hair up and her skirts to her ankle, which I found extremely odd.

"No. Who's Hettie Schloot?" I sipped my tea, my mind elsewhere.

"A girl from town. Family has money, but no station. Linen drapers."

"Then *why* would I have heard anything about her, pray?"

"Because of what happened to her face!" Yaeba squealed. She was nine, a creature of freckles and gapped teeth.

"No, I want to tell it!" Opalina said, glaring at her. When Yaeba demonstrated her submission by sipping her cup of hot cocoa, her sister continued, "She was out walking with her dead cousin last night, and the Murder saw them. And whoosh! Out one of them flew, and slashed her face for it. They say she looks like Frankenstein's creation now, with all the stitches."

Only years of practice with arm control kept my saucer from clinking against my cup. Carefully, but quickly, I decided on a course of action. "*Who* did this to her?"

"Oh, don't you know about the Murder?"

"No," I lied. "Who are they?"

Opalina glanced down the room toward the adults. From what I could make out, they were talking about winter fashions. Satisfied, the girl whispered, "They're young men of the aristocracy, reclaiming the streets for the living. Making the dead sorry they ever set one foot outside the grave."

Yaeba found this description hysterical. I, myself, went stiff. "Aren't they afraid they'll get caught?" I wasn't quite sure what I was fishing for. Michael had yet to give me any details; he had only confirmed my suspicions. He'd natter on for hours about the exploits he'd *seen*, but he was now infuriatingly silent when it came to his own plans. Often my texts went completely unanswered—like today. It was starting to drive me mad. I'd had a chance to listen, and now I cursed myself for not taking it.

"They wear masks and change their voices. To look like carrion crows, feasting on the dead. They don't share names. They meet in different locations and communicate via real paper letters that can be burned."

That was more than I'd gotten from Michael. "How do you know all this?"

"My brother tells me." Opalina giggled, officially the creepiest sound I'd ever heard.

I managed a smile for her. "Fascinating."

"Isn't it just?" She launched into a similar piece of gossip. I tuned her out halfway, my imagination spinning. Was their brother one of them?

There was only one way to find out.

"Pardon me," I said, rising. "I'm afraid I must visit the powder room."

"Oh, it's down the hall, on the left," Yaeba said. "Do hurry back. I think Mama means for us to play croquet outside. The field is finally dry."

"I should like nothing more," I assured her as I hurried away.

My guardians turned to look at me as I passed, sending me warning glances. Lady de La Mosca caught sight of me and swallowed her tea, calling out, "Miss Mink, dear girl! You must play! We have the new pianoforte, and oh, you play like an—"

"She does not play for anyone," my mother interjected. "She does not like to show off. The more accomplished the girl, the less you should see of it."

Curtsying to Lady de La Mosca, I mumbled something polite and continued on my way, seeking out the powder room and then locking myself inside. There, I sank to the marble floor in front of a wall-length, gold-edged mirror, my heart pounding.

Maybe I didn't need Michael after all. If he'd ever talked to his fellow Murder members as he talked to me that first night, maybe they would know what he had planned. If Opalina was right, they wouldn't even know I was asking after *him*, just a particular *plan*. Gathering information that way might actually be safer than continuing to hound him, all things considered.

But why was I doing this? Why the urge to chase this particular dragon? I hated zombies, I despised Dearly, and I still had nightmares about the night I'd had to put my faith in Roe. And frankly, now that I knew that every word he'd spoken that night in my house was true, I was terrified of what Michael might do if he figured out my real intentions. Really terrified.

So *why* was I doing this?

Looking into the mirror, I met my own gray eyes. Thirteen years ago, when Lord Mink found me nestled between my parents' dead bodies, my eyes had been blue. Sightless, but deeply, deeply blue. I had a photograph to prove it, a single faded photograph I kept in a safe deposit box registered under a pseudonym, never to touch Lady Mink's hands. It was a little bit of my identity she could never erase, a window onto my past that she could never close. They had taken me from my birthplace, given me a dead girl's name, fortune, and gray eyes, but they couldn't kill the old me completely.

There was my answer.

Moving fast, I arranged myself. I pulled the sheer scarf out of the V-shaped neckline of my blue dotted Swiss visiting dress, revealing a bit more skin. I bit my lip and pinched my cheeks, then climbed onto the sink and removed one of the frosted glass shades from the gas lamp above it, helping myself to a bit of the lampblack gathered within. With this I made my lashes darker, a little bit longer, holding my bangs out of the way.

Then I went in search of Rupert de La Mosca.

Rupert was nineteen, and apparently had nothing better to do with his time than supervise a trio of servants as they set up the croquet course for his mother on one of her visiting days. This told me all I needed to know. I caught sight of him through a set of French doors during my explorations, and stepped outside.

Noticing my approach, he stopped tossing the blue ball from hand to hand and bowed slightly. He was an ugly brute, with a bulbous, squashed nose and piggy blue eyes. "Miss . . . Mink, isn't it?"

"Yes. Forgive me, I didn't know you were out here." I curtsied before drawing closer, hoping my heartbeat wasn't audible. "Is the field ready? Miss de La Mosca mentioned playing a round, and I thought I might check and save everyone the bother."

"I guess so." He looked me up and down. "Fan, are you?"

"I have a mania for games of all sorts."

"I bet you do." He whipped the ball at the court, chuckling lightly when it bounced up and bopped one of the servants in the chest. He returned to the patio and from the back of a white wrought-iron chair picked up a green velvet jacket that had seen better days.

"So, how have you been spending your time since the Apocalypse?" It was simple enough to think of things to say. A lady had to know how to entertain, carry a conversation, collect needed social information. Really, this was no different.

"Is that what you call it?"

"Among other things." I folded my arms behind my back, lifting my chest slightly. "You must be terribly busy. Are you not reading for the law?"

Rupert pulled his jacket on somewhat forcefully. "What makes you think that?"

"Well, your father—"

"Is very busy. As am I." He brushed down his sleeves. "You're a girl. You wouldn't understand."

"I'm sorry if I'm being a pest," I said. "And I do believe you are right—well, when it comes to other girls. I've always found the company of young men to be so much more stimulating than the company of young ladies."

Rupert raised a brow. "Oh?" he asked, every suggestion in the world contained in a single sound.

"Of course! Men lead such interesting lives." I needed something to do with my hands, and went for the rack of mallets, selecting the red one. As I hefted the thing, I decided to go for it. "For instance, your sister was just telling me about a certain group of young men, the marvelous things they're doing."

"Like what?"

I took a practice swing. "Punishing those who deserve it."

That got his attention. He came closer to me, and I could smell some sort of strong, nauseating soap—or ghastly cologne. I wasn't sure which. "What did she tell you?"

Affecting perfect innocence, I looked into his eyes and said, "Only of a girl in town caught with her dead relative, and some zombies overtaken on the streets." I laughed. "The gall of them, wandering about as if they had any right to exist."

The words were easy to say, for on the surface I meant them. Rupert didn't respond right away. I breathed through my mouth until he did. "At least one pretty girl knows the correct way to think."

"You flatter me." Doing my best to act as if the idea had just come to me, I ventured, "Speaking of which . . . no. It'd be silly." Hanging the mallet up again, I indulged in a sigh. "And it's clear you can't tolerate a girl's silliness. I ought to go inside."

"I can tolerate it when it amuses me." Rupert smirked. "What is it?"

"Well, there's this girl I have a long-standing feud with. I have it on good authority that she not only has her eyes on a dead boy, but that she lives with the dead, *eats* with the dead. Why, it's the most disgusting thing I've ever heard of. And I was just wondering—do you think those who've been punished are picked at random?" I let my eyelashes flutter upward. "Or do you think someone might . . . put in a word for them?"

Rupert's smirk melted away. "What would possibly make you think I know anything about that, Miss Mink?"

Flicking a sausage curl over my shoulder, I wracked my brain, trying to figure out how to put it. "I don't *think* anything. I'm just saying, if this group does exist, I could use—"

Rupert interrupted me by invading my personal space and squinting at me as if I were a slide under a microscope. His breath was horrid, and I stopped breathing altogether. "Let me give you a bit of advice before you say one more word. You are a young lady, and you should not concern yourself with such dark matters."

For a moment fear took over, and I thought of fleeing the field, heading for the nearby man-made forest of trees. This was stupid. *Stupid, stupid, stupid.* And yet, I tried to feel my way through. "Are you certain? For I've heard of living girls being . . . singled out."

"That was an accident," he said sharply. He looked at me for a tick, before leaning closer. "What are you really doing here?"

Honestly, I didn't know. And so I called it off with, "Being foolish, obviously."

"Good girl. But I do thank you. I clearly owe my sister a chat."

He didn't step back. Neither did I. My heart was fluttering, my thoughts a blur. I hadn't gotten a thing, and what's more, now I'd lost Opalina and her need to brag. I wasn't as good at this game as I thought.

But then Rupert surprised me. After his fleshy mouth moved in a slow circuit, following the orbit of a thoughtful tongue, he said, "Keep an eye on the news. An ear to the grapevine. Whatever it is you females do."

"When?" It came out far too quickly.

"This weekend." He raised himself up. "Consider it an illustration of what might happen to you if you don't keep your mouth shut."

Despite his rank breath, greasy hair, and thinly veiled threats, Rupert was now my knight in shining armor. He'd at least given me something. I touched his arm as I passed by him, allowing the outward swell of my skirt to brush his thigh. "Thank you."

"The pleasure's all mine," he said, turning to watch me go.

Without looking back, I made my way into the house and re-joined my group. It worked. It actually *worked*.

Twenty minutes later we were back outside, Rupert lingering to watch. I tried to quietly encourage this by manipulating the cant of my body, the fall of my hair. I wanted him to remember me fondly, maybe even to grow interested—it'd cut down on the risk of him overthinking our encounter, wondering if perhaps I had a motive other than bringing a competitor to ruin.

Lady Mink noticed Rupert's attentions. At one point she leaned in and hissed at me, "You're shaming yourself. I forbid you to even consider it. You could do so much better."

I knew I could. I knew I would, as soon as I got back to my computer.

22 • Bram

"I'll kill him."

"No you won't. I will."

Sitting behind the bushes at the tearoom had only been humiliating, at first—but the moment Allister showed up and opened his mouth, it became excruciating. Nora forbade me to make a move unless the situation went thermonuclear, and so I remained seated, an obedient beau and bodyguard, having to listen to that moron prattle on about how he could "protect" her. The longer he'd gone on, the more condescendingly he'd spoken to her, the greater my anger had grown.

Then he insulted her and her father. In a funny way, that offered me some reassurance. I'd heard the words, and they occasioned a wave of nearly debilitating anger, but I hadn't ripped his tongue out. Progress. I'd become a regular New Victorian gentleman.

Wherever Coalhouse had gotten off to, he'd not taken Sam's car. I directed it through the EF. "Telling you how bloody innocent he is, how he never did a wrong thing in his life—do you think he actually believes that? Is he deluded?"

Nora pulled her gloves off and pressed her hands to her face, leaning back in the passenger seat. "I have no idea. We didn't get anywhere, did we? That was stupid."

"Very, very stupid," I concurred. "Because now I'm just going to obsess for the rest of the day over what it'd feel like to pop his head off."

"Don't write checks your conscience won't let you cash."

"Says the girl who came up with the idea in the first place."

"Guilty as charged."

"His tone when he was telling you why *he thinks* he did the horrible things he did, like you should just smile and go, 'Oh, I never thought of it that way, I guess you're a good guy after all, tee hee!'" I pulled into the driveway. "I wanted to lay him out."

"Welcome to my world. Oh, and this is why you've ruined me for all other boys."

Parking, I looked at her. "So, you think he knows anything else?"

Nora sighed. "He sounded like he was telling the truth. It got a little weird at the end. If he cares so much about me, why didn't he sit right back down and quiz me about the hijacking?"

And that was the kicker. "Are you sure you didn't know he felt that way about you?" I hated sounding like a jealous lover— snarly or not—but I wanted to know.

"God, no." Nora stuck out her tongue. "Not before the whole thing on the airship. I mean, today was probably the most expressive I've ever seen him. He ran away before I could verbally eviscerate him. I was trying to get info first."

"He finds you *'fascinating,'*" I mimicked. "But you *'compromise'* yourself." Good God, I wanted to punch him in the face again. Just one good, solid, honest, knuckle-itching punch.

Nora opened her door. "Calm down. He's not the last person

who's going to say stuff like that about us. You said so yourself. Just forget about him."

I had, and I knew she was only reminding me of the truth. But hearing it from *him* had set me off.

Once we were inside, an irritated Renfield intercepted us. He'd changed his clothes, at least, throwing a waistcoat over a clean shirt, though his hair was still rumpled. "Where did you two go?"

"To meet up with Allister," I told him, yanking my jacket off.

"You were with *him*?" Renfield asked, agape. "I didn't know! I would've texted you!"

"Texted? Why? Mind explaining what the hell you're on about?"

Renfield looked uneasily between both of us, his eyes flashing. "Yes. Come with me." And with that, he turned and headed up the stairs.

Nora and I shared an exhausted look before falling in behind our skinny strategist. He led the way up to the attic. Father Isley was nowhere to be seen, and Renfield's multiple computers were humming along industriously, his little steam "holographic" projector hissing away beside them. The largest computer monitor, edged in tooled brass, showed a series of virtual chessboards.

Ren gestured earnestly with both hands. "This is going to sound wild, but stay with me." He glanced at Nora. "Vespertine Mink is contacting me through ACL."

"What?" Nora demanded. "*She* emailed you?"

"No. Not email." He returned his attention to me. "I think she knows something. Something that could get her into trouble."

"Something about Allister?"

"Indeed." Ren took his seat. "A few days ago I started getting a ton of emails warning me my account at Aethernet Chess Live would be deleted if I didn't start logging in again. I haven't had a chance to play since the whole airship debacle. So the night I gave you the background checks, I came back up here and logged in, and almost immediately a new account friended me. AllSeeing12."

"Okay?" I said, not understanding.

Renfield called up another screen, also featuring a number of chessboards—all belonging to "zboy69." He clicked on the first one and the Punk projector hissed all the louder, concentrated jets of air "drawing" a misty 3D version of the board and its pieces within the steam. "So, I decided to play. Said hello. The other player said nothing. They played, though. They played *well.*"

"This is absolutely gripping, Ren."

Ren grinned widely, spontaneously. "I know. Anyway, I won. And the other player finally said something in chat—but it wasn't 'congratulations.' It was a series of words. Intracapsular. Macular. Nystagamus. All terms that according to the *Aethernet,*" he peered at Nora, "have to do with eye surgery or sickness."

Nora peered right back at him. "You're right, Ren. You're completely and utterly insane."

"No. Far from it. It was code. This morning, the player was back. She won. A message flashed up that said, 'TE first edition.'"

"What's that?"

Renfield stood and attacked a pile of old nondigital books sitting on the floor. I would've thought them part of Isley's reference collection. He picked up one called *Ophthalmologist's Desk Reference,* written by Dr. Thaddeus Eckleburg.

"Where did you get that? Is that Papa's?"

"Finally found a copy in the New London Library. Wasn't technically supposed to take it out of the reference stacks, but I'm not above wriggling out bathroom windows." He flipped the book open. "This particular paragraph includes the words intracapsular, macular, nystagmus . . ." He showed us the page. "On page H123."

"I don't get it," I said.

Ren's lips twitched again. He almost looked like a schoolboy showing off his winning science project, all the while trying to be humble about it. "It's Miss Mink. The account she used to play me under was Harpist123. She's an absolute bloody genius."

Nora's mouth dropped open. "What?"

"So I got back on here. And that's when she started chatting in earnest." He whirled around and pressed a button on his keyboard, calling up a chat screen. I leaned over his shoulder to look. It was brief, and to the point.

> zboy69: I think I understand.

> AllSeeing12: Allister has taken leave of his senses. D has to watch her back.

> zboy69: We need specifics.

> AllSeeing12: Trying to get them. Risking a lot.

> AllSeeing12: Have to go. More later.

This wasn't good. "So now we've got *him* to worry about, too?" I said.

Nora ignored me, staring at Ren as if he'd uttered the mother of all blasphemies. "It can't be her. Mink hates my guts. Pamma showed me the interview video online—she's practically told the entire *nation* she hates my guts."

"Miss Dearly, listen—" Ren said.

"No, you listen!" She leaned right up into the skinny zombie's face. He pulled his book away from her, hugging it protectively. "Seriously, Mink wouldn't spit on me if I were on fire. She detests me, just like I detest her. There is *no way* she would do anything to try and help us. Besides, that'd be breaking rank with the aristocrats, and she'd never do that either."

"What do you mean?" I asked.

"He should know," Nora said, pointing fiercely at Ren. "The aristocrats of my tribe might play catty games and gossip, but they look out for each other. They can even vouch to get one another out of jail. There is *nothing* Michael could do that would cause her to go to this much trouble. We all *know* he has issues! Just like her!"

"All right, I get a turn now," Renfield said. Nora glowered at him, but shut up. "I played with very few people when I was still at base. Miss Mink was my favorite partner. And she's the only one who knows my face now, and what I am, and about my connection with you. To anyone else, my screen name is just a screen name."

"But you just admitted you played with other people."

"It's her," he said firmly. "I know it's her."

"But it's so complicated. And how would she get ACL to send you notices?"

"You just said aristocrats don't break rank. This way keeps her safe. Who would scrutinize one account out of *millions* on a public game server? She probably signed up for it anonymously. Throwaway email, proxies, she could even spoof the account emails if she knows a little code—*I know* how she did this."

"It makes sense," I told Nora. "I don't know what it's meant to do, but it makes sense. It's pretty smart, actually."

Nora took an enormous breath and held it until her cheeks went purple. When she released it, it was with a little growl of frustration. "Well then, we should pay her a little visit!"

"No!" Renfield practically shouted. "We can't be seen with her. What if she's going to these enormous lengths because she's frightened? We have to protect her."

"Oh, so we're protecting *her* now? Have you even considered that maybe she's not trying to help us? That maybe she's trying to set up a massive practical joke?"

I laid a hand on Nora's shoulder. "Hold up. Let's just see if she comes back. Maybe now that we've met up with Michael, he'll say something to her, and she'll say something else to *us*. Maybe that's what we accomplished today." Lifting my eyes to Ren's, I said, "Keep at it."

"No." Nora backed away from me, her cheeks reddening. "Listen. You two don't know Mink, so don't try to logic me out of this." She pointed at Ren. "She is *messing* with you. If this is even her. This is the stupidest thing I've ever heard of. Something from a cheap mystery chapbook."

Ren blinked. "Miss Dearly—"

"We have bigger things to worry about right now. Even if it is Mink, I'm not about to listen to her. You use your computer, Ren, and you tell her that if she has something to say to me? She can say it to my face."

Renfield actually narrowed his eyes. "Forgive me, Miss Dearly, but who said she wanted to talk to *you*?"

Ouch. I watched as the two glared at each other for a split second before parting. Ren sat decisively; Nora stomped to the door, her dress rustling. I didn't follow, opting to linger near my friend. "Sorry."

"You have nothing to apologize for." Ren put his book down and turned back to his chess program, his posture stiff. "I might have quite a few physical problems, up to and including *death,* but mentally? I'm king of this little castle. Even Miss Mink knows it. She knew I would get it."

"I know." And I did, because Ren's depth and breadth of

knowledge always amazed me. "Look, keep doing whatever you're doing. See if she speaks up again."

Renfield sighed. "Fine."

Sensing that I should get out of his way, I headed downstairs. I didn't seek out Nora, figuring she needed her usual cool-down period—and kind of annoyed at her myself. Instead I went looking for Samedi. He was in the study, alone, just as I'd found him earlier that day.

"Manage to get in touch with the Ratcatcher, like I asked?"

Hearing me, Sam wrenched his body around in his chair. "Have you gotten into some kind of trouble, Bram?"

This was not the greeting I'd been expecting. Leaning in the doorway, I said, "No. Why?"

"I sent a note to Rats, telling him we wanted to meet up, ask a few questions. He refused." Samedi stood and walked over to join me. "He said the Grave Housers aren't worth talking about. They're about four or five years old. Controlled a couple blocks, had some corrupt coppers on their side. Were doing well till the Siege, now not so much."

"Well, that's fair. What's the problem?"

"He said that *you* should not contact him under any circumstances. Ever. That he would not deal with you, has nothing to say to you, wouldn't even talk to me about you."

"What, did I offend him by standing too close the other day?" What could he have against me?

"I don't know." Samedi seemed to examine every square inch of my face. "I'd help any of his crew, so it's damn insulting. And then he shuts me out? Shows me such disrespect? Took everything in me not to curse him into his mother's arms in Hell."

"I'm clean as a whistle. Mostly." It was weird to think in those terms. "And I don't want any dealings with him or his people aside from information."

Samedi considered this, and moved back toward his chair, taking a seat. The small tables to either side of it were stacked high with equipment. "I'll figure it out. God, I didn't want to get involved with this again."

He didn't sound happy. I didn't know how to fix that, so I turned to go.

He stopped me with, "I don't want you to be like me, Bram."

"I do. You're a good guy, Doc."

"Only recently." He glanced at the boarded-up windows, as if the knots in the plywood might tell him something, like tea leaves in the bottom of a cup. "Belinda's into processing carriages. That's pretty straightforward. But Rats . . ."

"What does he do?"

"He catches people. He takes them wherever he's paid to, and he doesn't ask what's going to happen to them." Sam cracked his neck. "And these were the people I counted as friends. That was the kind of life I lived."

Returning to Sam's side, I patted his shoulder. "You've always done right by me. You've done right for years."

Sam nodded. After a minute of silent solidarity, just as I was preparing to leave again, he said, "I will help you all I can, but it might be slow going. The remembering's enough to kill me sometimes. And I hate that. I hate that I'm getting soft when Beryl needs me to be tougher than ever."

"Thanks for doing everything you have." I meant it. "And we're with you, you know that. No matter what."

After making sure Samedi was settled, I finally headed off. Once I was out of the house, I decided that I had my own people to call on. People I *should* call on.

In a way, Coalhouse was right. We had to take matters into our own hands.

*   *   *

Later that night, I tried to tell him that.

I went to the ships after dinner at Dearly's behest, and ended up bouncing between the two, doing whatever was needed. While on the *Erika,* I caught sight of Coalhouse hanging out in the lab area. He looked dirty and tired, and I tried to approach him—but on seeing me, he quite openly showed himself out. Such a childish display should've angered me, but I was just happy to see he was safe. He must've spent the whole day wandering, brooding. Probably wanted medical care for something.

It wasn't until nearly 4:00 A.M. that I saw him again—going for his ride, just like I was. He'd apparently gotten his hands on a beaten-up, square-bodied carriage somewhere. He wore a satchel over his shoulder.

This was it. We had to talk.

Crossing the parking lot, the ocean in my ears, I caught him as he was unlocking his door. I tried to ease into things by asking, "Hey, where'd you get her? Been thinking about trying to get one of my own. Even the crappy ones are really expensive, though."

"I got paid for my time in the army just like you did," he replied, shoving his satchel inside. He turned, watching me expectantly. "So? Going to scold me like a two-year-old again?"

"No." When he didn't respond I added, "Just wondering where you've been. That's all."

"Did you go the police?"

"Called them earlier."

"Well. Hope that made you feel better."

I held my tongue. I didn't want to go off on him. "What are you doing?" When his eye narrowed, I shook my head. "Just give it to me straight."

"What you wouldn't do." Coalhouse removed his soft cap and stuffed it into his pocket, before scratching at one of his bald spots. He looked shaken, for some reason. "Trying to figure things out on my own."

"What things?"

"You act like we should just report everything to the authorities like a bunch of patsies, and smile while we wait for 'em to puzzle things out," he argued. "We have to do some stuff ourselves."

"I agree with that," I told him. "But I'm also not willing to let people get hurt. I'm not willing to let *you* be hurt."

"I'm just fine!" For some reason, that statement really set him off. "I'm trying to help *you*. So just shut up and let me!"

"What have you figured out, then?" I asked, my patience wearing thin.

"Nothing yet. But I will. I have an idea now. Time."

"Idea? Time?" Sharp fellow that I am, I finally realized his hearing aid was also gone. "Where's your hearing aid? And your other eye?"

"Finally threw them away. Figure I'm just fine the way I am. People can speak up and look at this side of my face, or take a hike."

Surprise only compounded my growing annoyance. "Tell me what's going on, Coalhouse. Come on. You're up to something."

"Gonna get Hagens to talk," he said grumpily. "And her group'll be out of New London soon. There, that enough for you?"

"What?" I said, getting up close to him. "How do you know that?"

"She told me. You know, you trusted me once before." His expression curdled. "You *acted* like you trusted me once before, at least."

"Told you? Coalhouse, whatever you're angry about, I'm *sorry* for it. But you can't go back up there. You're going to get into trouble!"

"You know, you're not really my captain anymore. So just let me work it. Do my own thing." Opening the door fully, he hopped into his carriage.

"Coalhouse, you're *right*! I'm going to—" He didn't listen. He slammed his door shut and peeled away, leaving me alone.

What the hell had gotten into him? I felt like he was being contentious just for the sake of being contentious. What did he expect us to do? Take the Changed on guerrilla style? Waste time playing spy, trying to plumb them for information?

Time was the one thing none of us had.

23 • Laura

Just as our den in New London had once been traded in for the camp, the camp was traded in for the road. Hagens and the other leaders acted as if we were setting out on a massive zombie pilgrimage. They talked about how the Changed would grow even as it moved, until we emerged in the Northern Wastelands an army, a cloud of locusts. How we would give birth to our own world.

Before they took it down, and while everyone was distracted, I snuck into Mártira's tent and took the first thing I saw to remember her by—which happened to be one of her favorite hair combs. The silver one that concealed a razor blade. I hid it in my bodice, using a thorn to pin it to my body, like a butterfly under glass.

It was all I had of her now.

It was foolish to imagine, what with the number of zombies we had with us, that we could outrun anybody, hide from anything—but that wasn't the point. The point was distance. The point was *moving*. And so the leaders decided to drive around the Maria Bosawas-Allister preserve before heading northwest, dragging out old, faded paper maps to figure out a route.

"The big roads will take us into the middle of the richies' territory, though," Bruno said. "It's suicide to cut through there."

"Suicide doesn't mean anything to us anymore." Hagens yanked the map from his hands and tore it in two. "Let *them* move, if they're so disturbed by us."

Hagens kept me close, forcing me to ride with her. She was growing angrier by the hour, and I cursed myself for not leaving with the young zombies that first night. I desperately sought moments during stops when I could sneak away and find Dog or Abuelo, try to comfort them. Once, I did, and when I tried to leave, Dog caught hold of my arm and actually uttered a sound—a little moan of fear.

Kissing him, saying goodbye to him, was one of the hardest things I'd ever had to do.

But I did it. I knew no other way.

Coalhouse showed up at dawn the next day.

I was sleeping with the leaders around the remains of the campfire. The voices of the men who'd been appointed to guard duty woke me. They had Coalhouse, and they pushed him to his knees in the midst of our group. He met my eyes, but I couldn't decide if he was trying to tell me anything. He wore no weapons.

As the others woke, they cursed and went for their guns. Hagens did, too, once her eyes were open. "I *told* you to *get*." Though her voice was low, there was something in it that reminded me of a wildcat's scream. She stood, aiming her pistol at his head.

"He had this," one of the guards said, tossing a cloth satchel at Hagens's feet. She flicked it open with her toe. I half expected a bomb, but there were only a few pieces of paper inside.

"I know you did," Coalhouse said. "I know a lot of things about you. Like the fact that you want Smoke back." He turned his eye on Hagens. "The pages. Look at them."

Keeping her gun locked, she knelt down and pulled out a few

of the documents, or whatever they were. I couldn't see. Skepticism was writ across her face.

"Do you know what those are?" Hagens said nothing, but slowly straightened and started to sift through them with one hand, letting anything she examined flutter to the ground. "Those are copies of his X rays. Models of his version of the Laz. Notes on the people he bit. All classified. You think they'd just release this stuff to me, even to tempt you with?"

"How did you get these?" she asked.

"Last night, I was in the same room as him." He lifted his hands. "I *can* help you. And if you think I'm trying to double-cross you? Just shoot me. I'll die knowing in my heart that I was trying to help my people."

Hagens peered at another page, then at Coalhouse. "You really willing to talk?"

"If you are."

"Not now. Everyone put your guns away." The leaders reluctantly obeyed. She tucked hers in her trousers, though she didn't look less wary. "Okay, then. Stay with us today. If I like how you act, we'll talk tonight."

"I want her in my carriage," he said, looking at me again. My chest tingled. I'd thought so little of him, and he was back. Looking to save me. Like a prince.

"No," Hagens said. "Not doing that."

"Then you don't get my help. Look, if I try to run off with her, you guys'll get us. You seen the piece of crap I'm driving? And I'm sure she can talk, but what can she prove?"

Hagens looked at the papers again, separated a few out with her foot. What she saw there was clearly interesting. "Fine. I'm sure she's told you everything she knows anyway."

They were the most beautiful words I'd ever heard her say.

*   *   *

Coalhouse's carriage was a mess. The upholstery was peeling off of the doors and slashed on the seats; the soft top roof was bowing inward. All of the stereo equipment had been ripped out.

Still, compared to what was outside, it was heaven.

Abuelo and Dog came along and dozed in the back. I had time away from Hagens, and a tin canteen full of water, and someone I felt I could be honest with. Coalhouse had risked his life to get Hagens to talk. I told myself that I just had to be patient. That he was my knight in shining armor, a genius, practically a god.

We passed the time chatting. He had a lot of questions. "Why do you call that kid 'Dog'?"

"Well, he can't talk, can't write, can't read. Can't tell us his name. He took to following me around, so everyone started calling him my dog. It stuck."

"Okay. Where'd you guys get your gang name?" Coalhouse asked. "Grave House, was it?"

"They said the gang that held the house before we did buried the bodies of their enemies under the floorboards. I don't think it's true, though." He didn't respond. "How long have you been dead?" The usual zombie *how-do-you-do*.

Coalhouse rested his elbow on the window ledge, driving with one hand on the wheel. "More than a year."

Nodding, I waited for him to go on. He didn't. Trying again, I asked, "Where are you from?"

"Little Punk town. Only child. My parents own a dry goods store."

"You must miss them."

"All the time."

Something in his tone told me that he wanted to ask questions, not answer them. Turning to the window, I lowered the shoulders of my gown, careful to maintain my modesty even as I offered my plants some light.

"You're literally pushing up daisies," he said. I'd never thought of that, and I giggled. It was the first time I'd laughed in days, and I instantly felt guilty for it. Coalhouse smiled a little, too, before looking at my face—then he sobered and turned his eyes to the road. "Can you feel them inside of you?"

"No. I wish I could. It'd probably tickle. I think maybe the roots are messing with my legs, though. I'm not sure how to fix that. I started the whole thing on a whim."

"Huh."

"I've always had a green thumb, just no land. I used to grow flowers in pots in the den, but whenever Claudia found them . . ." I studied the dirt under my fingernails. "She'd destroy them. But I like giving life to things. Like I did to Mártira."

"What do you mean?"

For whatever reason, I decided to share. "Claudia and I were bitten, but Mártira never was. It wasn't until later that she got the idea to drink my blood, get the Laz that way. Took it into herself one night, so she could stay with us. So we'd go together."

"She drank your blood?" Coalhouse boggled. "Willingly?"

"Yes." I looked at him. "It was the most beautiful thing she ever did. Like something out of an old book. Like a magic spell."

"Come now, child," Abuelo said, groggily speaking up. "Mártira opted t'become one of us 'cause she didn't want t'be chased out of her own gang by the dead. You know she meant t'make us a mob of monsters, at first. Living woman couldn't lead that."

My voice faltered, and I wrenched myself around to look at him. "That's not true," I said, willing myself to believe it. She was gone, and I would not have anything about her altered. "She did it for me!"

Suddenly, Coalhouse slammed on the brakes. Facing backward, I was unprepared for the abrupt stop. My canteen tumbled from my lap and I wrapped my fingers around my seat belt to keep my balance. Abuelo swore. "What's goin' on?"

I looked outside. At least a score of dark, armored, official-looking carriages were outpacing us, flanking us on either side. A few of them were equipped with flashing lights and sirens, and it put me in mind of the times police raids had been conducted on the den. My chest tightened, but not with fear.

This was it. It was going to end.

"I *told* her," Coalhouse grunted, putting the carriage in park.

"Are they going to arrest Hagens?" I asked, a shrill note entering my voice.

"I don't know." He stared at the vehicles, then swore viciously. "Those aren't cops. That's the *army*!"

"What?" I turned back around. "So you didn't tell them?"

Coalhouse gave me a frightened look. "What are you talking about?"

"What's all this talk, then?" Abuelo echoed, confused.

All at once my hopes died. What was Coalhouse *doing*?

Dog awoke, fitful. I retrieved the canteen and poured out a lidful of water for the boy, my hands shaking. As I leaned into the back half of the carriage to give it to him, Abuelo met my eyes and mouthed, *S'all right, child.*

I wanted to say, *No, it's not.* But I only nodded.

We were in the carriage for three hours altogether. I couldn't see what was happening up ahead, but I did see army men outside, patrolling the convoy—making sure nobody ran away, I assumed. After a while Coalhouse began to talk again, his voice newly nervous. He told us how he'd been hunted and killed by the bald monster known as Tom, and how he'd gone on to distinguish himself in Company Z. "Hagens would tell you. She was in the army with us."

I didn't want to talk about her, and tried to change the subject. "How'd you get the name 'Coalhouse'?"

On that point, he paused. "I don't know," he admitted. "My mom just always called me that. I think he may have been an old singer." He looked at me almost shyly. "Laura's a pretty name."

Frustrated, scared, this simple compliment almost caused me to burst into angry sobs. Before I could say anything, though, someone rapped on my window. Twisting around, I saw it was a soldier.

"Let me talk," Coalhouse said as he lowered the window.

"Names?" the soldier barked. At Coalhouse's direction, we gave them.

"Laura Cicatriz?" the soldier verified, squinting at me. "Step out of the carriage, please."

"No!" Coalhouse leaned across me, and I felt my skin crawling, trying to flush. "I mean, she can't speak to a man alone."

The soldier outside put his hand to his holstered gun. "Back away, sir. And leave your window open."

"I'm ex-army, man. I can give you my ID number."

"I don't care if you're the great-great-great-great-great-grandson of Houdini. You're a bloody zombie," the soldier replied, unbuckling the holster of his gun. Coalhouse's eye widened. "Miss, exit the vehicle."

Coalhouse flashed me a worried look but did as he was ordered. I tumbled out of the broken-down carriage and took a few steps away from it, holding up my gown.

"Hands where I can see them, miss?" the soldier said. He was young and dark-haired. "No offense."

I slid my fists to the front of my stomach. "What do you want from me?"

"Just to verify some details." He held up a hand and leaned to the side, listening to a buzzing comm unit in his ear. "Sorry. Can you describe the nature of this group?"

Oh, God. I didn't know what to do. I didn't know which lies I was supposed to parrot. What had Hagens told him? What was I supposed to say?

And why was I thinking of toeing the line instead of telling him the truth? This was my chance. I should already have been screaming it at the top of my lungs, terrifying and unstoppable.

"Miss?"

I snuck a look back at the carriage. Dog was leaning out of the window, his eyes like saucers. Abuelo had him around the waist. What would happen to them if I told, now, with no plan in place? What if a fight broke out, what if the living got hurt or zombies were shot? This world was all I'd ever known. Right now it was a horrible place, but it was still all I'd ever known.

Uncertainty and fear tore like buckshot through what little courage I'd ever had.

"We're a group of peaceful zombies," I heard myself say. "We hold protests to raise awareness and gatherings to raise money."

The soldier nodded. "Why are you on the move? Where are you going?"

"North. To find a safe place to stay."

"Do you know if any among you has committed a crime?" I actually laughed—I couldn't help myself. "Miss?"

Despair robbed me of my ability to be vague. Looking at the soldier I said, "Where do you want me to start? There are whores and cons and peddlers of all sorts of things here. But . . ." It almost pained me to say. "It's not illegal to protest, it's not illegal to beg. It's not illegal to be dead. The only thing I can imagine you'd want to know about is the death of my sister, Mártira. She was shot in the head. And because we're criminals, we didn't report it. I'm sure you know me because someone mentioned it." I wasn't, but I played my card anyway.

The soldier eyed me, but then secured his weapon once more. "I'm sorry for your loss." And thus began the real round of questioning. Had I seen Mártira's body, seen anything suspicious—I had. And I lied. I lied about it all, and hated myself for it.

At the end, the soldier dipped his head at the carriage and said,

"You can go back in." I ran to it. The moment I was safely inside, everyone started questioning me. I gave them no answers. I was too heartsick to try. That'd been my opportunity. I knew I wouldn't get another.

It was Coalhouse now, or nothing.

After another hour, the soldiers left. Coalhouse and I climbed out of the carriage. Zombies started unloading from the other vehicles, stretching their legs, trading stories and angry theories, complaining about how the army had rifled through their belongings. I heard Hagens shouting my name, far off, and knew at least they hadn't taken her. No one else had betrayed her either.

When she got so close she could no longer be ignored, Coalhouse spoke up. "She's over here!" He glanced at me apologetically, and leaned against the front of his carriage.

Hagens came rushing over and took me by the arms. She got right to the point. "Did you tell them anything?"

"No, she didn't," Coalhouse said. I was starting to grow truly confused. He gave me up one moment, then defended me the next. "And I told you people would come."

Hagens pushed me roughly away. "Keep it that way." She nodded at Coalhouse. "I know. We might be able to work together after all."

"Good. Army going to do anything?"

"Oh, they already have. Arrested a couple of people to question about the attempt to fetch Smoke. Which means we now have less time than I thought. We'll talk later."

Coalhouse moved closer to me as Hagens stalked away. Before he could say anything, I hobbled off as fast as my legs would let me, climbing into his carriage again and slamming the door. I wrapped my arms around my head to shut everyone out and leaned against the closed window, the glass warm from the sun.

It was only then that I noticed my shoulders were finally sprouting.

24 • pamela

Two days after receiving Lopez's background info, I decided that I had to speak to my father. He said he'd be back from his latest sojourn to the police station around eleven, and so I left Nora in her room with our textbooks and went to greet him, Isambard joining me. The folded-up pages were in my pocket, and I'd finally worked up the courage to hand them over, to talk to him about the idea of going.

I didn't get the opportunity, though. When Dad arrived, he barely responded to our presence. When I showed him the papers, he smiled, but his smile was all wrong. He waved us off, telling us to go rest, and climbed the stairs to Aunt Gene's room to find my mother.

Instinctively, Issy and I followed. When he shut the door in our faces we remained standing in front of it, alone in the portrait-lined hallway.

Behind the door, our parents started to talk. Then they fought. As we listened, long minutes dragging by, I wrapped my arms around an increasingly miserable Isambard. When Mom started crying and I heard my father shout, "I will not let a strange man swoop in and play white knight for *my* family! I don't want any man's charity!" I found the strength to take my brother by the shoulders and move him in the direction of Nora's room. Upon entering, I found her donning her light spring coat and hat.

I shut the door. She turned to look, at once guilty. "Pamma . . ."

"Whatever we've caught you doing, listen to us first," I said.

She paused, troubled for a new reason. "Are you all right?"

"No." It amazed me how much disgust and anger and pain could be channeled into one almost emotionless word. Everything currently in my heart and my head and my life could be easily summed up with "no."

"What's going on?" In the silence that followed her question, I helped Isambard sit on the floor. Nora didn't quiz us further, moving to join my brother on the pink rug.

Isambard was all eyes. "Mr. Delgado is still missing. He went on a job and didn't come home. And the police aren't *doing* anything, just like they're not doing anything for us—is it because we're not rich, do you think? Because the Delgados are poor? Is that it?"

"Not doing anything?" Nora asked.

"Dad said the police don't know anything more. They said with all the stuff going on in the city, they're swamped. That everything's going slowly."

Nora sighed. "Great."

"That's not all of it." It almost hurt to speak, but I knew it was up to me to do so. Issy shouldn't have to repeat what we'd just heard. Before I could begin my dark recitation, however, Issy opened his mouth again, looking at the floor all the while.

"Mom decided to call our aunt and uncle and ask if we could come and stay with them out in the country, while Dad waits for the insurance stuff to go through," he began. His left eye was starting to blacken, and I wondered what was going on inside him. "They said no."

"Why?" Nora asked.

I took over, my voice hoarse. "Because they have a baby, and they told Mom that they didn't want Issy to *eat* him." Isambard shut his eyes. "And they said they're good Christian people, so they couldn't possibly allow a demon-possessed walking corpse anywhere near their house. They said that the scientists have it wrong, and that Isambard is actually a demon, and that we're all going to Hell for harboring the devil's child. Oh, and they'll pray for us. I find that enormously comforting, don't you? That completely makes up for the fact that they think my brother is a sign of the End Times."

"Oh my God," Nora said. "Why the *hell* would anyone say something like that?"

"Because of me," Isambard said. Then the figurative floodgates opened. "Just like Mom's going insane because of me! Just like Pamela almost got killed during the Siege because of me! Just like I've ruined everything!"

Leaning forward, I caught his hands and forced him to look at me. "It isn't your fault," I told him again. "Never, *ever* think it's your fault."

"But it is!" He coughed noisily. "And I'm trying so hard to be good, *so hard*. And Jenny needs me, she keeps asking for her father, but I don't know where he is, and I'm so scared for him . . ."

Nora reached out to touch his arm. "I'm sorry, Issy."

I tried to figure out how to put things. I felt like I had the night I'd descended into the parlor and marched my family out onto the street. I was above fear, above grief, above regret. "I'm glad you have your coat on," I told Nora. "Because we need to go talk to Lopez. Now."

"That's . . . exactly what I was going to do. Well, *about* Lopez."

For a beat I didn't know what to think. "What?" My mental mode abruptly shifted. I should actually lecture her about not leaving the house. Scold her.

Hug her.

"Yes," she said. "In the car on Monday, it was clear you wanted to go. That's why I asked Ren to look into him. I've been trying to ask around, too. I don't want to see you go, but I want to see you happy." She frowned. "Especially if crazy people are going after you because of me."

I remained lost for two more seconds—then it all clicked. I let go of my brother so I could look at her straight on. "Thank you." It was two words too much; my throat grew thick, and I had to swallow before I could go on. "And then, someone needs to convince my parents that we need to go someplace else, before it all falls apart again. And if I say it, I don't think anyone will listen." And just like that it was out. The failure was admitted. I thought it would bring me some kind of release, but it didn't.

"Why don't you think they'll listen? You did this before," Nora said. "You got them to safety."

"It's Dad. And Mom won't go without him." I shook my head. "He said he's not going to run like a coward. That he's worked too hard. That he doesn't want Lopez's charity. He's so *stubborn*." Truth be told, I could now see something of myself when I looked at him, a reflection in his eyes that spoke of fear. It had frozen him. I knew the feeling well enough to recognize it.

"Okay. We'll do this." Nora looked at the bay window, the little bit of light shining through it highlighting her pale face, her almond-shaped eyes. "If it makes you feel better, I've thought about running, too."

This startled me. "You have?"

Nora didn't respond to my question, but looked at Isambard, who'd gone quiet. "And she's right. It's not your fault."

Issy tried to recover, saying, "You always watched those war holos, you know a lot about military stuff—are you sure you don't know anything about Lopez?"

"No. It's not like I've got every regiment memorized."

"Not just the military," I said. "You have contacts in higher society, even if you don't think you do—think about all the houses your aunt took us to the day you were . . ." I gave up, the memory of her being kidnapped too overwhelming.

"Don't remind me." She stood up, determined. "Look, I want to talk to Papa. Of course he hasn't been home, so I'll have to go to him. Do you want to come?"

"Where?" I asked, my heart clicking.

"We won't go to the boats, he'd just yell at us if we did. But hopefully I can get in touch with him from somewhere in town."

"Alone? Were you actually thinking of leaving *alone*? Again?"

"Yes, because that's precisely what'll get his attention." She took a breath. "Sometimes, Pam, you need to break the rules to get what you need. Not *want*—that just makes you a brat. To get what you *need*. If you don't want to go, just say so."

Nora's eyes were clear, her stance expectant. Still, my heart was torn in two. Part of me did want to work with her—the same part that had screamed at a New Victorian colonel and hacked zombies to bits. The part that had rescued my parents. The part that had once fought and won.

The other part reached out for Isambard's hand again, mostly because *I* needed the cold comfort of his touch. He squeezed my hand in turn.

"Yes," I decided. "From now on, wherever we need to go— I'll go."

Nora did the lying for us. She told my mother we were going for a walk around the EF—an idea to which she readily agreed. In actuality we hopped the trolley and left it, disembarking at the northern end of Dahlia Park.

The sun was out for once, the sky blue. This part of the park was bright and verdant and calm, like an oasis in the midst of the city's chaos—the yin to the southern end's yang. Both dead and living people strolled down the many brick walkways, admired the feats of botany, and sailed boats in the large fountains. Almost everyone avoided the commons, where Wolfe had been executed. I wasn't sure if this was a conscious choice or if something there now felt foreboding. I wasn't about to wander over and see.

Nora stationed us near the duck pond. She bought me a handful of bread crumbs from a brass machine for the harassed birds as "cover." She then got on the phone, and after five attempts managed to reach her father.

"Papa, you haven't been home. Your absence has undone years of parenting. I'm at the duck pond in Dahlia Park unescorted, and there are some *fine*-looking young gentlemen here, let me tell you." She glanced at the nearest crowd of men—all older salarymen getting their lunches from a cart, none of them the least bit attractive. "I don't know if I can control myself. In fact, I think I'm going to elope with Mr. Villa here. His five children are adorable, and we can always get him a replacement tooth. Oh, did I mention I'm a quarter mile from the Morgue?" And with that, she hung up.

I would have laughed if my heart didn't feel like it was currently doing a dizzying waltz inside my chest. "He's going to murder you. *Us.* We are both going to die, you realize that."

"I've tried being patient. Now feed the ducks."

Twenty minutes later Dr. Dearly was there. It'd actually worked.

"What is the meaning of this?" he demanded, upon finding us. He hurried down the nearby walkway as fast as his dead-and-metal legs would carry him, and took Nora by the arm when she was within reach. "I thought you were finally taking things seriously."

"We needed to talk to you, and I know it's kind of useless to invite you out to lunch anymore." Nora kept her face neutral. "I'm sorry for taking you away from your work. I know it's important, but this is, too."

Dr. Dearly studied her closely for a moment, then looked around at the people nearby, as if wondering if he ought to launch himself at any of them. Finally, he let go of her. "What is it?"

"We need to talk to you about a guy named Edmund Lopez."

As she said the name, her father's expression shifted, seeming to stem less from anger and confusion and more from compunction—I didn't know what to make of it. When he next spoke, his tone had softened, become more emotional. "How do you know of him?"

Nora and I shared a look. I lifted my chin, urging her to begin. In soft tones, she explained my predicament, ending her story with, "So we need everything. The man's shoe size, if you have it."

Dr. Dearly continued to frown. "All right." He started walking down the path that circled the pond, and Nora fell in beside him. I threw the last of the feed in the general direction of the water, brushing off my gloves as I hurried to catch up.

"You know all the stories I used to tell you, NoNo, about heroic efforts made by soldiers to retrieve fallen comrades?" She nodded. "Well, Lopez is the source of at least a few of those."

Keenly interested, she said, "Really?"

"Indeed. As far as I've heard, he joined up right out of school. Due to some string-pulling on behalf of his brother, he advanced through the ranks very quickly. He's young for a colonel." Dr. Dearly's artificial leg squeaked slightly with every step. "He also made a bit of a name for himself. Part of it came from the fact that he would never leave a man behind. Even if they were dead, he was determined to bring back their bodies."

"And the other part?"

"From the fact that his family was extremely powerful once." Nora's father drew us to the side as a dead child rushed by in pursuit of a squawking mallard, a living woman giving chase. "And from a few unfortunate drinking incidents. Fights. Keep in mind, I was an infectious disease expert in the army. Medical. I bounced from unit to unit. So all of this is hearsay."

I said, "My parents mentioned a place called Marblanco. Something about his family."

Before her father could speak, Nora said, "I know his family sympathized with the Punks." Dr. Dearly and I looked at her in shock, and she added, "I spoke to Michael Allister yesterday. About this, and Aunt Gene. Didn't get far, but the drinking thing meshes with what he said." I'd known she'd gone out—she'd reassured me before leaving—but she hadn't told me it was to work on my problem. I felt a renewed urge to wrap her up and never let go.

Dr. Dearly sighed. "Yes. They did. Which is why this is so difficult for me."

"Difficult?"

Dr. Dearly shook his head. "The Lopez estate, Marblanco, is where I met your mother, Elizabeth. Where I convinced her to give me a chance. There was a ball, I saw her . . ."

Nora's mouth rounded. At once, she looked so saddened by the thought of her mother that I found myself taking over. "What is Marblanco?"

"A great house built entirely by Punks." Dr. Dearly adjusted his hold on his cane. "After the Reed Massacre, the government came for Lord and Lady Lopez. Their house was a monument to Punk ideals, their money had flowed freely into the coffers of Punk artisans and engineers and craftsmen. The government argued that money was used to fund terrorism. They were sent south with the others, the house torn apart, everything scattered and sold. Lord Lopez and his brother were given to relatives to raise until one of them came of age, their money put into trust. Then the land, the house, and the title were all given back. The government didn't dare punish the children for the sins of their parents, interfere with their rightful inheritance—they would have had every aristocrat on edge. It was an enormous scandal as it was. And yet the public supported the exile of millions of Punks . . . make of that what you will."

Stunned into silence, it was a second before I could say, "I've never heard about any of this. You mean there's . . . a Punk relic in the middle of New Victoria?"

"I doubt you would have heard. Even you, Nora—and I raised you to look at the evidence and think for yourself." Dr. Dearly sighed. "So much of that time has been forgotten, or conveniently expunged, and yet it wasn't that long ago. Many people would rather their children never have to think about it—the Punk backlash, the Massacre, the exile. It was a horrible time. A black period in our nation's history."

"Tell us the rest, then," Nora said.

"I doubt it would help you with your current goal." He pulled out his pocket watch. "And I need to get back to the *Erika*. Go *home,* both of you. I will speak to the Roes when I can. I feel I ought to, before you girls try anything else."

"Will you really?"

"Yes, Miss Roe. As soon as I get a chance. From what I know of the man, I'm sure the offer is a good one." Turning his eyes to me, he added, "I am sorry for everything. I truly am."

"I'm just grateful for you trying, sir." And I was. I felt a little lighter—like maybe my plan would work after all.

Dr. Dearly insisted on retaining his spot until he saw us walking away. Nora looped her arm in mine and headed obediently for the trolley stop, glancing back occasionally to wave at her father. "That actually worked *really* well. Next time I'll pick a more exciting location. Like a racetrack. Or a pool hall."

"So what's our next move?"

"Easy." She stopped by the sign. "We don't wait for Papa. We talk to the man himself."

25 • Bram

By Thursday afternoon everything had been arranged. The only person I hadn't managed to get hold of was Coalhouse—he was off the radar again. If he didn't show up soon, I was going to have to go after him.

But first things first.

When I stepped into the house, Nora came to greet me, as usual. Before she could say a word, I caught her by the shoulder and said, "You go out with Allister, I think it's fair you go out with me. How would you like to end-run your father again, and see if we can do something to help the city? Oh, and that would involve you going to a seedy pub near the Morgue."

Nora said nothing, her brown eyes widening. After a few seconds I had to ask, "Well?"

"Yes. A thousand times yes."

Fighting back a laugh, I turned her around. "Go get a gun. Put on something plainer."

"Plainer. Right."

It took her twenty minutes to rejoin me, now dressed in some blue-and-green-plaid abomination I'd never seen before, a knit cap, and a dusty shawl. Her holster was on. When I asked her where she got the clothes, she said, "Charity box. I told Pamma— she'll cover for me."

"You have her sneaking around? Impressive."

"I think she's starting to get on board again, yes." I escorted her to the car, and together we started off. "What's the plan?"

"Yesterday Coalhouse said the Changed might be out of the city."

"But we don't know for sure."

"Exactly. So we're going to go talk to some zombies and see if anybody knows anything more. Because I want to bring them down. And I figure you and Miss Roe deserve a personal go at them. Before we see them locked up, I mean."

Nora smiled brilliantly. "Can I use my scythe?" she asked, in her breathy little voice.

"The nonpointy bits, sure." God, I loved it when she was cute as a kitten and tough as nails in the same breath. "Not to sound like a parent, but have you apologized to Ren yet? You owe him one."

"Not yet. I know I do. 'Mink's' gone silent."

"Good. Because we all need to work together on this." And with that I concentrated on the road.

The pub Ben recommended for our meeting was one street over from the Morgue, nearly hidden between two larger buildings. The sign said it was called THE FAILING LIVER. Everything about it told me it was the last place Dr. Dearly would want his daughter, but I knew we'd be perfectly safe. And the drinking age in the Territories was sixteen, so they should at least let us in.

The interior was dark and dingy. Dim yellow lanterns hung from the ceiling, boat rigging and lengths of chain tucked up in the rafters alongside them. An ancient screen sat on the western wall, showing highlights from a cricket tournament. The bar itself was in the back, while maybe ten wooden tables occupied the remaining space. The place was busy, and every single patron was a zombie, save for two old folks at the bar.

When Nora entered and saw this, she grinned. She took my sleeve and guided me deeper within. A few pairs of eyes followed us. "Who are we looking for?"

"*Captain Griswold!* Ye found us!"

And there they were, like they said they would be. One of the tables in the back was crowded with the results of my phone calls and emails—a dozen former members of Company Z, including a few who hadn't been helping around the boats. They were all older than me, my squad having consisted of the youngest zombies. Sitting with them were David Braca and a couple of strange undead gents, clearly his friends.

Nora ran over to them like she was a toddler and they'd just waved the biggest lollipop in the world at her. I laughed as she was greeted by Amed Hadrami, a simple but hardworking dead guy. He was in his late twenties, his skin blotchy, his build rotund. "Miss Dearly!"

Nora hugged him. "It's so good to see you!"

Heading over, I exchanged greetings myself. Everyone stood up to shake my hand, and I actually felt a bit of a lump forming in my throat. Chairs were crammed in for us, and Nora was, as before, treated like a queen. All the men wanted to know what we'd been up to, what we'd seen in our corner of the city. A zombie lady with ratty purple hair came over to see if we wanted anything, and Amed ordered, "something really pretty," for Nora. For a second I thought maybe I should have offered—but Amed looked so happy to do it, I couldn't hold it against him.

The zombie lady peered at Nora, though. "Chip?" she asked, drawing a wallet-sized scanner out of her apron pocket. "Ain't no way you're sixteen."

Nora glanced at me in panic. We'd taken her ID chip out when she came to Z Beta, and she hadn't had it replaced yet. Before she could open her mouth, I said, "No, trust me, she is. Rest of the guys here'll tell you the same thing."

Amed nodded furiously. "You think I want to corrupt young'uns, Emmie? I might be dim, but I'm not *that* dim."

The waitress bought this, and disappeared. While we waited for the drink, I said, "This is Mr. Braca." David nodded, and introduced his men in turn. "This is Company Z." I identified my half of the table. "You guys have any trouble finding the place?"

One of the older men, a grizzled grenadier named Aberforth Sengen, shook his head. "Naw, most know this joint. Mostly dead in here now, except fer that old married couple at the bar. Rumor has it they wouldn't even leave the pub during the Siege. I think they're actually *part* of the bar stools. Sentient growths."

"I think we're the only Z-Compers around here, though," Amed said. "Everyone's gone. For now or for good."

I nodded, trying to stay stoic. "I know. It's too bad."

"But it's okay. We just make the best of it. Do a lot of planning here. I'm gonna open a tailor shop, you know!" Amed smiled at me. "Because zombies sometimes need sleeves and things removed? And they sell stain protector for carpets, I could put that on people's clothes. The guy I talked to about it said you shouldn't wear it, but I don't think dead people can get cancer."

"That is an incredible idea," Nora told him. "I say go for it."

I hated to turn the topic to business, but I had to. "Okay, look. We need your help." I described a few of the things that had happened. When the men heard about Nora and Miss Roe their eyes narrowed.

"Aye," Aberforth said. "I been hearin' wild stories about masked kids."

"Kids?"

Aberforth snorted. "Yeah, kids. Has to be. Then again, I'm at that 'get off my lawn' stage of life."

"Were the targets you've heard about living or dead?"

"Both."

Emmie returned with a pink drink in a fluted glass for Nora. "On the house. Don't get many living in here nowadays."

Aberforth continued the conversation around her. "But I haven't *seen* anyone wearing bird masks."

The purple-haired zombie whipped her head around to look at him. "What, you mean those scumbags who're cutting people up?"

Soon Emmie was seated with us. "I heard they cut a live girl to shreds the other day. Lady who handles the washing for my building told me. But the way she told it, they've been attacking zombies, too. In the dead of night."

"There've been so many attacks on zombies, though. This living angle's different." Edgar Kaname was almond-eyed, violet-tinged, and had slashing scars along his cheeks and forehead. "And you mentioned the Grave Housers. I'm from New London, born and raised in the slums. Grave Housers are a relatively new gang."

"Oh yeah," Emmie said. "They're bad news, though."

"Their leader sounded almost Utopian. Renamed the group the Changed, was all sweetness and light. From what I heard, she was trying to run it like some kind of benevolent society."

Edgar burst out laughing. "Benevolent society? We talking about Mártira Cicatriz, the Red Hellcat? She was a harridan!"

"They're supposedly out of the city by now," I shared. "But we still want to get to the bottom of this."

"Wait a sec," Aberforth said. "This wouldn't be the big group of zombies up on the Honduran border, would it? My living brother's still in the army. Said his unit got called from Fort Knife up in San Pedro to sniff around a group of zombies earlier today."

"Army? I told the cops." I froze. "They must have passed the intel along."

"Either-or. My brother said they didn't find anything, took a couple people in hand. Should have arrested the lot, but the army's not meant to concern itself with street criminals. And what with all the troubles, the military's kind of skittish 'bout putting any but the most violent zombies at the end of a gun now. They know how the undead might react."

This should have made me feel better, but it didn't. The idea that the army might've gotten mixed up with the Changed—it didn't just scare me, it angered me. I felt like I'd led my fellow zombies to the firing squad. Risked another encounter that'd rip open a wound that still needed time to heal. "I didn't mean for that to happen."

Aberforth nodded. "Don't doubt you. Oh, and he said . . . Mártira? That her name? She's dead. Living killed her."

The table reacted to this news with silence. David broke it. "I'm still not sure if we're on the right track with this, though."

"The cops done anything in the Morgue?"

"No. Nothing of note. But no one has anything bad to say about the Changed."

Edgar took over. "Yeah, but this wouldn't be the first time Grave Housers hid their faces and acted like bloody monsters. Where I was raised, sometimes you'll get gangs going at it in the streets. I know Grave Housers were involved in that at least once or twice."

"And if Mártira's gone," I said, "Hagens would've had room to take over. Like Laura said." Focusing my thoughts, I ventured, "So what do you think about getting as many Company Z vets together as we can—hell, as many zombies as we can—and going after them?" I tried to accommodate David. "Or at least starting a patrol in the city?"

"You're not talking about going to war, are you? Posse versus posse?" David asked.

"No. Not enough of us for that. But maybe these people need

to see that the undead aren't going to let them get away with this. That we're willing to police and protect our own—and precisely because things are so unstable." I looked at Nora. "Living allies, too. Living have already threatened to do whatever they have to do to defend their dead. Why should this be any different?"

"I'm behind the idea," Aberforth said. "But . . ." He looked into my eyes, and I saw some anger there—I wasn't sure if it was directed at me or not. "Like you said. There are so few of us now."

"I know," I said. "And I'm sorry for that."

"It ain't your fault," Amed said. "All of us woulda put down our lives for Dr. Dearly, after what he did for us. And the living were scared, that's why they tried to kill us. Just don't like to remember."

"I don't blame you," Nora said. "I don't think anyone wants to fight anymore. But if people start things like this, we have to finish them."

"It's a risk for everyone," I said. I wanted to be honest with them—and myself. I had more to lose than I dared think about. That didn't mean I could step aside and let all this happen, though.

Amed nodded slowly. "Yeah." He studied Nora for a tick and then said, "I'll go."

David conversed with his friends and lifted his head. "We're in. I think the patrol idea is a good one, at least."

"We're all in," Kaname decided. Nods punctuated the end of his sentence. "And we'll see who else we can dig up. Start tomorrow night? Meet up here?"

I agreed, and thanked them—a small thing in the face of such an offer, but all I could muster up. It meant a lot to me. I felt like I'd let so many of them down. I should be making amends, not receiving favors.

Plan in place, we began our goodbyes. Amed rose to hug Nora again, and looked at me over her hat, saying, "I didn't think I'd see you again, Cap. I'm gonna make you a suit."

"Absolutely," I told him, overwhelmed. "And I'm going to pay you a hundredweight for it." He grinned.

On the way back to the car, Nora asked, "What's the next step, then?"

"Go back to the house, collect the others. Hit the streets as a group. See if the masks are gone or not. And if not?" I opened the passenger side door for her. "Give them a show."

When we got home, Renfield was waiting for us.

He strode forward from the base of the stairs, something at his side. He dropped it at my feet, and I recognized it as Nora's valise. "Forgive me, Miss Dearly. I had to go through your drawers and pack for you. I tried to handle your bloomers with two fingers only."

"What are you doing?" she said. "Is my underwear that frightening? Oh, and by the way—have you gone *mental*?"

"What's going on?" I asked. "Did she finally get in touch with you again?"

Ren reached into his pocket, drawing out a printed piece of paper.

zboy69: Where have you been? I've been worried sick.

AllSeeing12: Nothing dire. Had Aethernet taken away when I needed it most. My mother is like a child.

zboy69: News?

AllSeeing12: Something's going to happen this weekend. D needs to go somewhere where there are a lot of people. Might not be about her, but I think that's the best way.

AllSeeing12: I'm deleting this account now. Goodbye.

"It could be a joke," Nora reminded him, even though she looked properly creeped out. "She could be trolling, for all we know."

"We have to talk to her," I said, grabbing the printout. "This is a specific threat, an actual time . . ."

"But we can't give her away!" For a moment Ren's eyes softened. "If something's truly afoot, something this serious, she's risking everything in reaching out to us. That's why I'm inclined to believe her."

I shoved the paper angrily back at him. "The boats," I decided. "The *Erika*. We'll take you there."

"No way am I hiding on a *boat*," Nora argued. "I'm safe here in the house. Besides, we have plans. You were just talking about going out into the city!"

"Just until we get more info." Turning and taking her hands, I forced her to look up at me. "Will you do this for *me*? Just to humor me? This is getting weird, and I just want you to be safe."

Nora screwed up her face but gave in. "For you, I'll go to the boats to *discuss* this."

Renfield turned to her, even as he ripped up the paper. "I'm sorry, Miss Dearly. I get the impression that you think I've sided with Miss Mink, but I'm only worried about you."

Picking up the bag, Nora said, "I know. I know you wouldn't lie about something like this. *I'm* sorry for earlier. It's just . . . if you knew Mink, you'd realize why I'm kind of dubious. She's a bully. That's all she is!"

"Right now her motivations don't matter." I thrust my hat back on and grabbed Nora's hand. "Ren, look after the Roes. Let's go."

26 • Laura

That night, the others partied.

The fires went up soon after we stopped. Some of the Changed danced and sang with abandon, their brush with the army making them boisterous. A few, angry about the zombies the army had carted away, talked about rounding up a posse to go get them. Others talked of marching to the base the army had come from and tearing it apart. The undead laughed and swore loudly, drinking whatever they had—even if the drink couldn't affect them.

Coalhouse sat mutely through all of it, glaring into the fire.

After a while I made my way over and sat beside him on a fallen tree. I wasn't sure what was wrong. I wasn't even sure if I ought to care. Things were looking more and more dire with each passing day, and my grief was turning into apathy.

Mártira would have hated me for that.

The full moon above had moved by the time he spoke. "He didn't care that I was a soldier." He looked to his half-empty cup of warm rum. "The guy back on the trail."

"Should he?"

"Yes!" Coalhouse handed me his cup and stood up. "I mean,

I wasn't even a dead recruit. I was in the Punk army. You'd think they'd at least listen to me, talk to me like a freaking equal. Even if we were on different sides!"

Setting the cup down, I moved to follow him. "He didn't know."

"I *told* him!" Coalhouse punched one of his hands into the other. "I told the bastard!"

Looking around at the party, the dead dancing amidst the flames that might've cremated them and the trees that might've fed the blaze, I lowered my voice and said, "Look, is that what you're *really* worried about right now?"

"You don't get it." The boy reached up to finger his thinning hair and then violently cast his arm down. "No one ever notices when I do something good. They only notice when I do something *they* think is wrong. My parents used to do the same thing; that's why I lied about my age and went into the army. Even when I fight with Tom about the fact that he made me this way, that he *killed* me, everyone just rolls their eyes and says, 'Get over it. You're stupid.' I helped Miss Roe, and she doesn't care. They don't respect me, they don't care about me. No one does."

I could sympathize with him, and yet I remained unmoved. "You have to talk to Hagens *tonight*," I tried to tell him. "For all our sakes."

"Oh, am I on a schedule?" He turned around and advanced on me. This time I didn't step back. "You just want to use me, too? Like the others? Like the army?"

"You came here to help!"

Coalhouse lifted his hand again, and just as swiftly dropped it. He looked at it, his expression slack, before muttering, "I don't know why I came here." And with that, he marched back toward the fire. Having no other option, I trotted after him like a beaten but loyal dog.

Only to encounter the very woman I wished not to see.

Hagens was waiting for us—or rather, Coalhouse. At the sound of her voice, nearly vibrating with anger, I shrank back, hoping not to attract her attention. "Last chance for you to come clean. You tell the truth, I let you run before I start shooting."

"Truth about what?" Coalhouse groused.

"The army. Today. Did you bring them? Is this all part of some plot?"

"No. They didn't do anything, did they?" Coalhouse walked closer to her and sat down on the tree again, as casually as anything—though I could hear the tightness in his voice. "Except make fools of us."

Hagens stepped forward and took him by the sleeve, pulling him once more to his feet. "'Didn't do anything'? They took some of our people. They're going to interrogate them, charge them!"

"So? Don't you trust your own people not to talk? They didn't give *you* up."

"I don't trust the humans that'll try to make them." She looked at the dying embers ringing the edge of the fire pit, her face demonic by their light. "We have to act. Now. Before it all comes undone."

"What do you mean?" Coalhouse's tone grew steadier. I remained standing and still.

Hagens released Coalhouse and sat herself. She reached into the pocket of her waistcoat and pulled out a cigarette, leaning into the circle of coals to light it. As she did, I was surprised to see that her hands were shaking. "We have to get Smoke. Within the next few nights. I'd hoped for more time, but there is none. Mártira's death might be investigated. The others might spill."

"Why do you want him?"

Hagens took a draw of her cigarette. "That stuff on Smoke— the royals don't like printed materials. Where'd you get it?"

"They can still print stuff off. Had to hang around the ship for hours. Finally Salvez left his station open. Could only get a few things." Coalhouse made a rolling, tickling sound in his throat and sat. "As usual, no one noticed me. But do you even know where he is? Where they moved him?"

This question gave Hagens pause. She shook her head, the motion sharp. "No."

"He's on the *Erika*." Upon hearing this, she turned her face fully to his. "You know how many guards are on him? When they rotate out? How many docs and techs are around? I do. And I'll tell you whatever you want to know, as long as you do the same."

Hagens stared at Coalhouse, and I thought I must be looking at him the same way—not just wonderingly, but with a terrible, sick sort of fear. He'd just told her where the prisoner was. Surely that was too much to give away, even to get information in return. My inner cagey police dealer greatly disapproved.

But at least he was acting. Maybe this was it.

"We were in the army together, Hagens." He gestured at his chest. "Anyone else here been beside you in battle? Can anyone else here help you like I can?"

"No." Releasing a puff of smoke, Hagens shut her eyes. "Fine. I'll tell you everything."

"Good. Start with why you want him so bad."

Hagens looked at her cigarette and threw it into the fire pit. She answered in a soft tone, one almost submissive—truly scared. I'd never imagined such a sound could exist. "To protect him. And Company Z. And all zombies."

Coalhouse blinked on the one side. "What?"

"I never meant to join up with another group, least of all one like this." She looked at the boy. "Until about a month ago I was going my own way. Didn't even have a room anywhere—spent twelve hours a day in a pub by what would become the Morgue. The Failing Liver. Looking back on it now, I want to kick myself for being so idle, but . . . I didn't want to lift a finger to help the living. Not after what they did. I was just sitting around with my anger."

"What changed?"

"One night I was approached by some very odd toffs. Living." I crept closer, listening in. "They said there was a zombie they wanted to get their hands on. Said they'd pay me good money to bring him to another location. Acted like, I don't know . . . they had a debt they wanted to collect, maybe? And they just didn't want to face a zombie on their own? This was before he bit anyone, mind. No one knew he was carrying a different strain. No one knew who the hell he was."

"What? Someone offered you a bounty for him?"

"*Exactly*. Anyway, I told them the only kindness a human could expect from me was to be left alone. So their tactics changed, and the offer went from money to blood." She scowled. "They brought out one of those digital readers and started showing me pictures of my Company Z brothers and sisters—all *survivors* of the December troubles. They couldn't have been picked at random from a public list of us. Said they'd start killing them one by one unless I did what they wanted. And then I thought they had to be army. Only someone who worked with Company Z would know all the details those guys knew—Griswold's story about his damn teddy bear, Amed being a little touched in the head, Sweet's closet full of clothes. The stuff we used to share around campfires and in the canteen."

"Why didn't you tell anybody?"

She shrugged. "At that point I thought maybe I could just give in and take care of it. Because Smoke was nothing to me, but those pictures were. Griswold's was there. Even him I feared for, was ready to sacrifice a stranger for. And what's the word of one zombie who's been burned by the army before? Who'd believe me?"

Coalhouse frowned. "Go on."

"They had a lot of info on Smoke, too. Whole dossier. He'd joined up with a group of zombies called the Changed. The toffs couldn't go in themselves, and didn't want to risk a firefight in the middle of New London. So I joined up. They were taking in anyone, it wasn't hard. Couple weeks went by before I got an opportunity—the execution. Mártira wanted to protest there because of the exposure. I volunteered, said we should take Smoke, put a sign in his hand. Told the toffs they could pick him up." She laughed roughly, almost crazily. "Do you know what it was like, marching around, protesting at the death of the person who *caused* all this?"

"The exchange went bad?"

"Yeah. Managed to locate them, get him relatively alone. But when he saw them, he *freaked*. I'd never seen him move that much." She gestured angrily. "He bit people trying to get away. Riot happened. Police carted him off. I figured that was the end of it, that the army would get him from the cops. I tried to concentrate on getting the Changed out of New London—I was afraid the army might try to destroy evidence of what they did. Namely, us. Mártira *finally* went along with it after that scene on the docks. But . . . it wasn't over."

"How do you mean?"

"Claudia told me about the new strain, and I realized what the army had in its possession. A new form of the Laz, raring to go. I started to think about doing something, but then . . . the toffs came *here*. To the camp. They knew where I was. They told me there might be another chance to get Smoke—that they had word he was being moved from police custody into army custody. That I wasn't done working for them yet. And that's when I knew." She sighed, the sound shaky. "They aren't army. It's somebody else, outside, that wants him. Someone who's got access to army info. Someone who can follow me miles outside the city. Someone who wants to remain behind the scenes."

Coalhouse was silent, shocked. For lack of anything else to comfort me, I sent my fingers through my leaves and gathered them close to my body.

"And so I knew what I had to do." Hagens looked at Coalhouse. "Free Smoke immediately, no matter what. I gave Mártira one last chance to get on board. The Dearly brat was up here. I told Mártira if we kidnapped her, we could use her to get Smoke back. She didn't agree, so she had to go—because I needed her people. And honestly? All of those people will probably die in getting Smoke back. The living guarding him will die. Members of Z-Comp. But they're no longer important. What's important is protecting Smoke, and having him protect us. He's the ultimate weapon. I can't leave him in human hands. I *won't*. I won't let the living use zombies as pawns anymore."

Hagens stood. I stared at her, almost unthinking. Mártira, Claudia—they'd both been killed for this.

"The antihuman attacks going on in the city—is that you? The people in bird masks?"

Hagens edged her head backward, taken by surprise. "What the hell are you talking about?"

Coalhouse cleared his throat. "Nothing. Piece that doesn't fit." The boy was silent for a second. "What's your idea, then? You still want Nora?"

"No. No time. If he's on the boat, like you say he is?" She turned back. "We go get him. All of us. Then we use him as a shield to get as far north as we can. Make a safe place for the undead."

Coalhouse considered. "If I help—you let me decide what gets told when. Our comrades need to know what's going on. And if somebody in the army's giving out information, somebody who used to be Z-Comp . . . they need to be found."

Hagens capitulated, her head bobbing. "You do this for me, I'll make you second in command." For a moment her tone softened again. "You have no idea how long I've had to keep silent."

"I'll need to go back and ready some things."

"Fine. At this point, even if you tell—that doesn't change what we're going to do. Tomorrow we start for New London."

After an eternal minute Coalhouse nodded, the motion grave. Hagens returned the sign and stalked away into the night without another word. The deal was wordlessly arranged, signed with bare physical motions.

As she left, my fists tightened, the sharp, green scent of crushed leaves entering my nose. He'd done it. His ways had been weird, but he'd done it.

"You need to come with me," Coalhouse said before I could think of speaking. "I swear, someone will come back for the others. But you need to come right now."

I nodded slowly, my mouth still unmoving. Words no longer mattered. I only wanted, in that moment, for him to bring down upon her head a force like a tidal wave, like a crushing wall of water. She'd killed my sisters. She was willing to lie, to kill others.

For the first time, I *wanted* to see somebody die.

"Who are we going to tell first?" I asked, waiting for him to stand.

"No one."

At first I thought I hadn't heard right. "We have to tell someone. You got everything out of her."

"No. We don't. Not yet." His expression was darkly meditative. As I watched, he rose, brushing his hands off on his trousers, adjusting his shirt—like he was preparing to drive to a girl's house to court her. The motions were strange to behold. It was like he wasn't sure what to do and was buying time.

No. No more of this.

"Sit down," I said firmly.

Coalhouse snorted softly. "We don't have time for this—"

I shoved him violently in the chest, sending him sprawling over the tree. He landed so heavily that he couldn't immediately recover, which gave me enough time to get to him, falling to my knees beside his jagged face.

"You will listen to me," I told him, my voice not my own. "You will listen to me, and you will hear what I say—or so help me God, I will scream."

Coalhouse stared at me. "What are you doing?"

"I don't understand you," I said, putting a hand on his chest. "One moment you act like a double agent, the next moment you act like a *fool*. Like you're on their side. I don't know what you're lying about anymore!"

"Laur—"

"Do you even *have* a plan? What are you doing here?"

Coalhouse wriggled a bit. "Laura, *you're* acting like a fool."

"Don't tell me you don't know!" My cry, though hushed, seemed to contain ten thousand souls' worth of anger. I knew one of those souls was Mártira's.

Coalhouse looked into my eyes. "I got what I needed. I'll go back to New London, figure out what to do. And you need to come with me, so you'll be safe!"

I laughed. I actually laughed. "Like I believe you."

"What are you talking about?" Coalhouse gestured in the direction Hagens had gone. "What, you think I'm really siding with her?"

"Then who are you going to tell? What are you going to do?"

"I'm not sure yet, but I'm going to take care of it myself!"

For the first time, I felt my plants. They were negative spaces, places where my body couldn't respond to the rage now trying to burn its way through my dead nervous system. "'Take care of it'?" I asked hoarsely. "She *murdered* my sisters! She's lied to everybody!" I looked back to the camp. "And she's going to get them killed!"

"And I'll take care of that, too! Trust me!"

"How? You just told her where Smoke is! There are innocent

people on those boats!" I argued. "And you're still trying to sneak around?"

Coalhouse grabbed me by the shoulders. "Shut up!" he said, almost helplessly. "I'm on your side. All I want is for everyone to be safe. But I am also going to prove a point."

I looked into his single eye, trying to find compassion there, a shred of humanity, something. "Are you trying to use us for *glory*? Use my dead sisters to prove a *point*?"

After two seconds of staring, Coalhouse yanked me closer and kissed me, his lips cold and somehow sloppy—untrained, untalented, too eager.

Disgust flooded me, made the roots burrowing under my skin feel like they were trying to curl. Pulling away from him, I spat, though I had nothing to spit with. Upon my withdrawal, Coalhouse had looked almost hopeful; now his eye narrowed.

"You're worthless." I touched my mouth and shuddered. "I bet Hagens lied to you, too. I was stupid to trust you!"

The boy stood and roared down at me, "You're not the first!" And with that he was gone, stomping toward his carriage.

I let him go. I'd never had him to begin with.

27 • Nora

When I told Salvez I was being forced to move in, he stared at me wearily for a moment before stepping out from behind his work-station. "I'll go get another gurney from upstairs."

"You see what you have me doing?" I asked Bram as Salvez tottered away. "Sleeping on a gurney. Do I get a toe tag, too?"

"You're here so you don't get one," he said. He'd driven me from the house in sullen silence, his silvery eyes troubled.

"Look," I said, keeping my voice low. "I don't want to act foolishly, but this is distracting us from the bigger picture. I don't know what Mink's gotten into her head, but—"

"We'll ask her. Or Allister." Bram finally looked at me. "Ren's smart, Nora. And I think he's right to be worried."

"I'm not saying he isn't." Curling my fingers into fists, I gave in. "Look. Mink just likes to torment people. When Papa forced me to go to St. Cyprian's, she tried to make me her lackey and got nowhere fast. Pamela offends her by existing, because her family's not rich. She's had it out for us for years. That's why this whole thing seems so outlandish to me."

"I don't disbelieve you." This statement actually caused me to decompress a touch. "I was there when she and Allister went after Isambard. She's obviously not an angel."

"I just refuse to let *her* keep me from the streets. We were finally getting somewhere."

Bram nodded, his brows lowering. "Give me the weekend, Nora. I'll call the others, and I'll stay here with you."

"No," I said, my own disappointment audible—but I knew any other response would be too selfish for words. "If I have to be here, you should head out."

Bram was quiet for a second before confessing, "I'm thinking of going after Coalhouse." I crossed my arms, waiting for him to continue. "It's not even a matter of him doing anything he shouldn't—it's a matter of him getting himself killed. The Changed are obviously a bad crowd."

"We don't even know if he's with them, though." I wasn't attempting to sway him, only relating the truth. "Maybe he's just hiding out somewhere, brooding."

"He's getting worse." Bram noticed I was still holding my valise, and took it from me. "He's getting more impulsive. He's fresher than me, his brain's less rotted, so that's scary."

"Maybe he thinks he's making the right choice."

"I know. I was thinking that yesterday." Still, Bram sounded unconvinced.

Tense as I was, unhappy as I was, my first instinct was to comfort him. Pushing my nose into his waistcoat, I shut my eyes. "I'm sorry for being argumentative."

"I like you argumentative." Bram lowered his arms and held me by the head and the waist, my valise on his wrist. "I even kind of like it when you argue with the others sometimes. Just don't tell them that."

"Huh?"

"If you can argue with us, get angry at us—it means you don't see us dropping dead anytime soon. You treat people you think you're going to lose like fine china." Bram released me. "Let me put your stuff in your dad's office and tell him what's going on. Just that we've gotten some weird text messages. I won't tell him who we think they came from."

Humbled by his first statement, I let him go. "No. I'll come with you. But honestly, we still have no idea what's going on. What if that Braca fellow is right? I just don't see why it has to be *Mink* that makes me hide."

"Then tell yourself you're hiding because of Allister," Bram replied.

"Oh, that's low." I fell in behind him, glaring up at the back of his head. "If you weren't so . . . *you* . . . I'd have to kill you for that one. That is freaking low."

Deciding to come clean, I unloaded everything except the names Mink and Allister. I told Papa about Hagens, the Changed, the masks. He took the news badly, so I found myself engaging in the old "disobey, then be sweetness and light for a few days" trick. He insisted I stay at least overnight, and the gurney was set up in a large supply closet off the main lab—not in his office with Patient One, thankfully. For the first time in my life I was grateful to be shunted to the side.

Despite my protests, Bram stuck around for part of the evening. I ended up puttering about with him on the *Christine,* dressed in a white coat, watching as he, with Evola as his teacher, patched up wounds and administered zombie meds. Still, I found my attention wandering, even when Bram took a moment to smile encouragingly at me or Evola cracked a joke. Everything that was happening to us was so confusing.

I didn't watch the clock. I was holing up on an ironclad based on a bunch of stupid bird costumes and an Aethernet threat, so bedtime be damned. But when I finally grew tired enough to lie down, still fully dressed, Bram made a show of taking me back to the supply closet and tucking me in. Truth be told, I rather liked it when he fussed over me. It felt good to depend on someone else, just the littlest bit. Besides, it wasn't as if he didn't allow me perfect freedom to go along with it.

He then shut off the closet light and took a seat in the doorway, pulling his digidiary out of his pocket and opening it, the screen illuminating his face. He let it rest on his knee momentarily as he rolled the sleeves of his shirt up, revealing the scores of wicked-looking scars covering his muscular arms. "Sleep tight. Don't let any other men bite."

"Har de har har," I murmured, even as my fingers slipped beneath the sleeve of my dress, lingering on my scar.

No. I never would.

Even though I was being kept in the same boat with a literal prisoner, even though the door to the main lab was left wide open and Salvez and my father were constantly going in and out, I actually slept soundly. When I awoke on Friday morning, Bram was gone. He'd left a note telling me he was headed back to the house and then to the streets.

With nothing else to do, I finally turned to my phone. Pam had sent me another barrage of texts. From the sounds of things, Renfield had fed her family something about my paranoid father wanting to keep me close at hand. She didn't mention Mink. I responded, and Pam told me she'd come over when she got the chance. When she did arrive, I was flicking through the television channels, watching them on Papa's giant pull-down screen.

"This city's turning into a prison. The poor're stuck here. If they ever bomb the city, set it on fire, we'll go along with the dead. This is a plot by the aristocrats! I'd like to see numbers—how many aristocrats got bit?"

"I'm telling you, they took phones at the riot two weeks ago! Some men in suits took mine! I thought the government was going to disclose everything?"

"If you're undead, don't trust breathers. That's all I'm saying."

"Nora?"

Looking up, I found Pamela in her double-breasted gray raincoat, her tired face haunted by shadows. I stood up, giving her the chair. "How'd you get here?"

"I came with Dr. Chase. She had some work to do." She bit her lip. "Mr. Merriweather told us that Dr. Dearly demanded you spend the night *here*? What is that all about?"

"It's . . . a long story." I knew I owed her the truth, and so I spilled, trying to remain as unemotional as possible. I even told her about Mink and Allister. Pam tensed as she listened, but for the most part she remained collected.

"Are you telling me you came here of your own free will, then?"

"Of course." Pam gave me her usual "liar" look, and I gave in. "Bram brought me."

"If it actually keeps you safe, then for once I'm glad you're doing what he wants."

"What do you mean?"

"I don't know." Pamela sat, and untied the ribbon holding her best hat on. "You honestly think they're pranking you?"

"That's what it feels like." I shrugged. "Did Papa get to the house?"

"I don't think your father's been back, no, or done what he said he would. My dad still didn't mention anything about leaving this morning."

Deciding that I'd have plenty of time to mull over her Bram comment later, I perched on my father's desk. "Okay. I'll figure out a way for us to talk to Lopez."

"Don't." Pam tightened her hold on her hat ribbons. "Wait until this fresh new hell has passed first."

Confused, I said, "But Pamma, your family . . ."

"Oh, Mr. Griswold, Miss Sweet, and Mr. Todd came in early this morning. I think they were out on the streets looking around last night."

That thought didn't cheer me up. At least they'd gone together.

With that, Pam and I lapsed into a semicomfortable silence, the screen absorbing our attention. It wasn't until NVIC went to commercial that Pam looked down the room and said, "I don't mean to be rude, but . . . don't you find hanging out in here a little creepy? If you have to stay here, couldn't we go walk about the ship?"

Glancing around her, I saw that Patient One was watching us. The two guards were staring straight ahead at nothing, about the only thing they could do. They didn't want to look at the ugly zombie, and they couldn't look at us without being accused of a variety of uncouth ideas. For them, I said, "No, I don't find it creepy. The guards are very respectful. Of me and the patient."

"I meant *him*."

"Patient One? Of course I do, but—honestly? I'm starting to think he likes having people besides the guards in here. I've been awake since six, and in and out of here all morning. Every time I leave, he stands up to watch me go. Like a puppy."

"Charming." Pam looked at him again. "Does he ever say anything?"

"He talked once before. He hasn't said anything since."

"What did he say?"

I shrugged. " 'The Devil keeps tigers.' "

"Tigers?" Pamma frowned. "Weird."

"Tell me about it. I'm starting to think it doesn't mean anything. Poor man's brain is likely half mush. He hasn't had medical care till now."

"I wonder where he saw tigers." Pamma lifted her head. "I mean, they're extinct in the wild, all over the remaining world."

"I don't think he saw a *real* tiger," I told her patiently. "He probably saw a painting or something. A statue. A hologram. A hallucination. *Anything.*"

"Yes, because the only place you can find a real tiger anymore is Allister's nature preserve." The name twisted her voice, even as she returned her attention to the screen. "They always talk in the society pages about the hunting parties that go there."

She went silent, and my skin went very, very cold. It hit me in that instant that Mink had never said the name *Michael*. She'd said *Allister*. And there was more than one Allister in the world.

It was a throwaway comment, and I did my best not to let on. Knowing now just how much everything that happened earlier had traumatized Pam, I didn't want to burden her. But the gears in my head started turning, to the point that I barely heard a word she said afterward. I think she was a bit miffed, but I couldn't help it. It was a long shot, improbable, impossible. What on earth could either Allister have to do with Patient One?

Still, I *had* to get Patient One to talk.

Pam left soon afterward. I offered to go with her, to go after Lopez, but she ordered me to stay put. Willingly, for once, I obeyed. All day long I waited for a chance, a momentary lull in the guards. It never came, as they appeared for their assignments like clockwork, the previous set never departing before their relief arrived. I didn't want them listening in.

At suppertime, just after Bram texted me to let me know he was going to head out with the group from the pub to fish for the masked men again, just as I was about to go feeble with frustration, one of the Allisters actually reached out to me through the aether.

Miss Dearly. If you have recovered, I'd like to invite you
out to dinner. Perhaps we can continue our conversation
like adults. Alone.

Jesus.

I needed air. I saw myself out of Papa's office, the main lab,
and up to the deck of the *Erika*. Salty sea air blew through my
curls, tickled my scalp as I made my way to the bow of the ship
and leaned over the dark water. In the distance the lights of New
London glowed brightly.

Staring at the message on the screen of my phone, I knew what
I had to do.

When and where?

Michael responded almost instantly.

Kintzing's, 8:00 P.M. tomorrow. My driver will pick you up.

No. I'll meet you there.

Very well. But if anyone comes with you this time, the ar-
rangement is off.

Closing my phone and my eyes, I turned to face the clammy
breeze. I knew I was doing something stupid, but I also knew I
had no choice.

I'd ignored Bram's entreaties to be careful. I'd ignored my
best friend's pleas to be careful. I'd ignored my father's *orders* to
be careful. No way was I going to brush all of *them* off and listen
to Vespertine Mink. To a *computer*.

I had to find out the truth for myself.

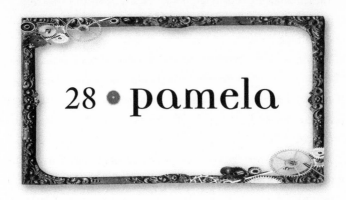

28 • pamela

Nora hadn't asked me how I planned to get home, and I hadn't told her. She'd seemed preoccupied, and for once it worked to my advantage.

Because I didn't want her going after Lopez. I'd already decided to do that myself.

A series of trolleys and omnibuses got me across town, their onboard advertising screens flashing information coded to the publicly accessible information in my ID chip. I pretended to be enthralled by the displays, drawn in by the promises of computer science correspondence courses and ointments formulated to deliver shinier hair. I prayed that no one would talk to me, that no one would single me out as a young lady, unchaperoned. My thoughts seemed scattered, anxious and uncatchable; my foot never stopped moving, tapping nervously under my skirt.

Yet it wasn't until I reached my destination, standing in a puddle on a gusty, obviously moneyed street, that I began to second-guess myself. Renter though he was, the address on Lopez's card was in an upscale part of town. A number of grand inner-city mansions marched down the road where the last bus left me, separated from one another by tall iron fences, their ornate gates locked and monitored by cameras. The carriages that rolled past were luxury models, crafted with gorgeous flourishes along their doors and headlamps.

Despite the fact that I'd never stood on this particular street before in my life, I knew this world. The things I saw made sense; the things I saw had meaning. When I was at school I was allowed to observe this world without ever truly taking part in it. I knew I shouldn't be there now.

Tearing my eyes away from a rich young lady's ostentatious pink electric carriage, I forced myself to press on. I wasn't undertaking this mad exercise for myself.

It wasn't difficult to find the address on the card, which turned out to be a well-landscaped building complex called the Steel Center—a New Victorian architectural maze of blond rock and marble, all of it beautiful, none of it holographic. Somewhat intimidated, I found myself instinctively donning my very best schoolgirl smile as I made my way to the glass doors. The smile froze on my face as a snappily attired doorman appeared to open the door for me, tipping his hat. "Miss."

But when I entered the lobby, I gave up my pretense, my jaw dropping. The first two stories of the building were open, an arcade of leaping iron arches and glass plates that exposed the rooms on the second floor, revealing them to be offices staffed by red-faced men and Gibson-skirted secretaries. The first floor was made up of rows of glittering shops, selling everything from fans to gloves to cigars to heavy household appliances, all of it high end. The exposed iron-and-stone columns supporting everything were decorated with gold-plated sculptures of captains of industry, chased by metallic vines twined with chains of electric lights.

I admired it all for a moment, contemplating just how quickly I ought to run away.

"May I help you?" I whirled around to find a mild-looking gentleman awaiting my response, his pomaded hair buffed to a fine sheen. He was dressed in a black suit, and held a flat screen in his hands.

"Um . . ." I offered him Lopez's pocket-softened calling card. "I've come to call on someone."

"Of course." The concierge, or whatever he was, took the card and looked at it. "Would you happen to have a card of your own I might send to the resident in question?"

"No," I had to admit. I had a few very plain ones, but I wasn't used to carrying them with me. I hadn't thought to rescue them from the house.

"I see. Whom may I say is calling, then?" If the fellow was suspicious or judgmental, he never showed it. I got the feeling his expression never altered, not even should someone cause him bodily harm.

"Miss Pamela Roe. He's a friend of the family."

The man wrote my name down on the screen with a silver stylus kept on his watch chain, tapped a few buttons, and then waited. A small chime sounded perhaps twenty seconds later, and he returned the card to me. "Lord Lopez will come down to meet you, miss. If you'll wait right here." And with that he was gone.

I wondered what had just happened. As I stood there, a group of laughing ladies passed by, dressed in some of the most beautiful gowns I'd ever beheld, their fans whishing and their heavy hats bobbing dangerously on their fine little heads.

It was a few minutes before Lord Lopez joined me. When he did show up, it was via a large elevator bank directly to my right. Although he was dressed all in black, he still cut a fashionable figure, the materials used to make his clothing and accessories almost as rich and detailed as the garments themselves. In his hand, he carried a golden walking stick.

Suddenly I got it. As I stood there, staring dumbly at him, I got it. Lopez wasn't a neighbor offering to help us out. He was so far out of my family's social league that the light from *his* league should take a million years to reach us. No wonder my parents were reluctant to accept his offer. They'd known what Marblanco was; they'd known about Lopez's family. He wasn't just a lord—he was practically a prince. We were paupers.

But I couldn't go back now.

"Miss Roe?" He moved quickly to my side and bowed. When he opened his mouth it became clear it was fear, not politeness, that made him stand so ramrod straight this time. "Has something else happened?"

"No! Yes. I mean . . ." I released a breath. "I need to speak to you. It's about my family. But it's not an emergency."

Looking a smidge relieved, Lopez gestured to one of the arcade hallways. "I see. Well, there's a café over there. I would invite you up to my flat, but I fear tongues will wag as it is."

I knew that. I'd accepted that risk, accepted the risk of traveling through the city, because I'd decided I couldn't let Nora do this for me even if she wanted to. It was my life. My choice. And besides, as much as she had done, what could she do here? I trusted her father's opinion. I didn't intend to interview the man.

I intended to put him to work.

And so I followed him to the warmly decorated café, which cut across both open floors, a brass-chased counter located on each. He directed me to a high-backed wooden booth overseen by its own chandelier and offered to fetch a drink for me. I asked for cocoa. It came topped with foam and powdered chocolate in the shape of a woman's silhouette, the rim encrusted with glittering sugar. The bone china cup was likely more expensive than any dress I'd ever owned.

Lopez sat across from me. "You shouldn't be here without an escort," he said. There was no censure in his voice; it was a simple statement of fact.

"I know. And I'll leave as soon as humanly possible. But please, if you would—listen to what I have to say?"

"Of course. I'll listen to whatever you have to say, whenever you like."

"The thing is, I don't know how to say it." I hadn't even properly thought the idea through since having it. I'd been unable to focus on it, like my brain wanted to disown the very notion it'd come up with. But after encountering my unchanged father that morning, and after learning more about Lopez and the people who might have attacked us—I'd had it. I knew I had to try something.

Like Nora had reminded me—I had to break the rules.

Lopez didn't press me. I took a couple sips of my drink. It went down like liquid velvet and warmed my stomach. "I want you to take me to Marblanco. Alone."

The instant I said it, I knew it was impossible. Lopez stared at me as if I'd just told him I was passionately in love with him. "Excuse me?"

Setting down my cup, I said, "It's been five days since the bombing. My parents don't know what to do. They're scared. And I don't think they're going to take you up on your offer. The thing is—I think it's our only chance. When I think about everything that's happened to us, it's all happened here in New London. I feel like this city is cursed. We're not even safe in our own *house*."

"Miss Roe—"

"If I go with you, if you take me to your estate—my parents will come for me. They'll have to. And they'll have to keep it quiet if they want to maintain my prospects. Maybe once they're there, maybe once they *see* it, they'll listen to reason. I know it's risky, but I can't think of any other way to do it."

And it was out. I snuck a glance into Lopez's eyes. He still appeared somewhat blasted.

"Miss Roe," he tried again. This time, I let him speak. "If we went through with this, your reputation would be ruined. They would think . . . I don't even want to say it."

I felt myself blushing even as I said, "And your reputation, too. Which is why you have every right in the world to refuse me, my lord."

"Don't call me that." Lopez looked down at his hands. "And honestly, I'm not worried about myself. I've been the subject of gossip almost my entire life, and it lost its sting years ago."

"I'm willing to face that shame if it will get my family out of this city. I made that decision before I got here. I was never meant to be a lady anyway. I'm a girl of no station, no fortune—if I fall, the drop won't be very far. And I'd die for my family—a little social drop is nothing."

"Which is quite noble of you." Lopez lifted his head. "But I'm not going to be accused of kidnapping, or worse, Miss Roe. I'm not about to spirit you away in the middle of the night to a broken-down mansion. And I can't believe I'm about to say this, but—for that, I am sorry."

That was the end of it, then. My eyes started to tear up, but not out of anger at him—only because another avenue, crazy as it was, had been closed off. "I had to try. Thank you for listening."

"My eternal pleasure, Miss Roe."

Under the table, my foot started tapping again, the sound audible. I reached out for my cocoa, if only to have something to use to hide part of my face. I wasn't sure what to do now—if I ought to leave, or if politeness dictated that I stay and drink. "I heard your story earlier. Parts of it. I'm so sorry. I should have said that first. You don't deserve to have to deal with my family, too."

That was when I felt Lopez's foot settling down on top of mine, pressing it gently to the floor and stilling it. I looked up in surprise. "I'm sorry you had to hear it. Atticus—my brother—tried very hard to make people ignore it. I myself do not care. But I'd rather not speak about myself, if you don't mind." He let go of my foot. "I'd rather speak about you."

"What about me?" I asked, wondering wildly.

"Have you actually been to a doctor?"

I looked at him in confusion. "No. Why would I? What for?"

"For your anxiety. For your panic attacks. For the pain in your chest? For the—dare I guess—nightmares?"

Staring at him, through him, it was a moment before I could produce a simple question. "How did you know all that?"

"I can see it, Miss Roe. I've commanded men in battle. I've seen it before. They call it posttraumatic stress now, although I prefer some of the old names." He touched his chest, over his heart. "The pain, here, they used to call 'soldier's heart.' Based on what little I know of you, I think that suits you well." ·

I didn't know what to say.

"It's frightening, isn't it? It eats away at you. It won't let you go. It won't even let you sleep. You're constantly waiting, wondering when the other shoe is going to drop. Everything is a threat. What isn't a threat isn't real."

Tears escaped my eyes. I nodded.

"I *want* to help you deal with your family, Miss Roe. I know nothing about them, or you, but I do. You strike me as lovely, troubled people who could do without having to live next to a bombed-out shell of a building—but more than that, you strike me as survivors. And I have a soft spot for survivors. That is why I aided the zombies the night of the Siege."

I had the craziest urge, in that instant, to move to his side of the booth. Like Nora, he had *heard me*.

"You take quite a lot on your shoulders, don't you?"

"Yes," I confessed. "I suppose that's a bad thing."

"No. It'd be a bad thing if you didn't crave any responsibility. But sometimes you must save yourself before you can save others. You will be no good to your family if you ignore your own pain."

I breathed out. "But I can't go to a doctor. I haven't told anyone, because they have so much to deal with. And I've *always* been anxious. I used to worry about whether Miss Dearly was doing her homework. I still do!"

"Perhaps if you told them, they might see that as incentive to get you to a place of calm and rest. Marblanco is miles from anywhere. Sell it that way. It's a seventy thousand square foot fixer-upper luxury resort with an eccentric owner. Bring your entire extended family, for all I care!"

I laughed. "You shouldn't offer that."

"Honestly, I just wish someone would live there. I don't like it empty, and I don't like being there while it is. It was never meant to be."

Lopez smiled. I found myself smiling back. For a blissful second the world was at peace.

He reached forward and hooked a finger around my cup, pulling it across the table. "Now, I think your cocoa is cold. As much as I am enjoying your company, that is probably your cue to leave."

He was right. We rose and exchanged genuflections. With only a brief "Goodbye," I turned and left the café, figuring out my way back to the front entrance by the storefronts we'd passed.

My heart was hammering. But now for a different reason entirely.

I could do this. I could get my family out of here.

Again.

29 • NORA

My boots echoed on the floor as I approached Patient One's cage around seven the next evening. I'd waited and waited for his guard to let up, but it never did. Papa had just stepped out, and I was running out of time.

"Do you mind if I read to him?" I asked one of the guards, once my toes were at the red line. I held up a book, one Renfield had grabbed from my bedside table in his haste to pack for me. I'd found it in the bottom of my valise, one of the first things he threw in. Underwear and books—the fellow clearly had his priorities straight.

The guard on the left nodded. "Do what you like, miss. Can't hurt. I was here when he spoke before. The old dead gent was quoting the good book at him."

"I don't have the Bible memorized," I said as I let my eyes fall on Patient One. He looked up. Encouraged, I went on, holding forth the little red First Victorian volume. "But this book is about a soldier—Brigadier Etienne Gerard. It's written by the same man who created Sherlock Holmes. My father read it over and over to me when I was a little girl. Have you ever heard of it?"

I waited. Nothing.

Opening the book with a sigh, the pages waxy beneath my fingertips, I started reading. I was praying that something I read, something I said, might start Patient One talking again. Even if we were being watched, I'd take what I could get.

But when I got to the part where Gerard consigns himself to death at the hands of the enemy for the sake of his beloved Emperor Napoleon, I started to tear up. " 'It was a beautiful world to be leaving. Very beautiful it was, and very sad to leave; but there are things more beautiful than that. The death that is died for the sake of others, honor, and duty, and loyalty, and love—these are the beauties far brighter than any which the eye can see.' "

I looked up, only to find that Patient One was leaning close to me with his head resting against the metal of the cage. He curled his hand around one of the bars, his eyes full of longing.

"You know that, don't you?" I said gently. The decrepit man nodded.

"Hey, finish the story," one of the guards piped up.

"Hush, Stone." The other guard looked at his pocket watch and sighed. "Relief is ten minutes late."

I hadn't noticed, but my heart picked up. Maybe this was it.

"Let's go see. Maybe they're out in the lab. That one lady scientist is . . ." Stone looked at me and cleared his throat. "Right, then."

And just like that, they left me. I waited until I heard their footsteps land outside the door before beginning my interrogation. "Is your name Smoke? What do you remember?"

Patient One kept quiet. He continued to watch me, though, and with renewed interest.

"Tell me about the tigers." Not a word.

Finally I tried, "Tell me about Allister."

It was as if someone had attached a live wire to the zombie in the metal box. He rocketed to his feet and started bowing his head back and forth, his eyes closing, his hands curling into bony fists. "No, no! Don't put me out! I'm not dead!"

"What do you know?" I asked, surprised by the intensity of his reaction, but unwilling to give up. "Was it Allister's tigers you saw?"

He started to strike his head repeatedly against the sides of the cage, hanging on to a corner joint, and I stepped forward and put my hands on the metal, afraid for him. I didn't want him to bash his brains out, not before I could pick them clean of information. "Sir, please calm down! I need you to talk to me. I'm going to see Michael Allister, I need to know—"

Before I could complete my sentence, he went catatonic again. His pitted face was but inches from my own, and I stepped back, suddenly conscious of the fact that I'd almost touched him.

"Even tigers are afraid of the dead," he ticked. "I didn't know that before they put me out. I walked forever, and the tigers didn't bother me. They were bright in the undergrowth, as bright as I ever made anything burn."

By the devil, he'd really been in the preserve.

Patient One then tipped his head to the side and looked over my shoulder. "You have a visitor."

I whirled around just in time to watch Coalhouse step through the doorway. He looked at me as he slammed the office door shut—and locked it. He was several yards away, but for some reason it felt like he was towering over me. Something in his face, his body, didn't seem right. "Coalhouse? What are you doing here?"

"I'm not here to hurt you, Nora." He removed a pistol from his waistband. "Move away from the prisoner. I just want him."

Something didn't seem right thus turned into the understatement of the century. I couldn't move. I couldn't speak. Nothing made sense. After a second I felt myself backing up to the red line, but I couldn't have said I made myself do it.

"Why?" It seemed like it took me ten years to find the word.

"Because it's the only way." Coalhouse stepped closer, aiming his gun up at the ceiling after a few yards. "He's a danger."

"Danger?" I felt stupid. Like repetition was all I was remotely capable of. "Of course he's a danger."

Coalhouse came ever nearer. "Move, Nora."

I did—backward. My skirt hit the edge of the cage and I stopped. I was far too close to the prisoner, and Coalhouse was closing the distance, his eye narrowing as he apparently realized he could take advantage of my fear. He stepped right up to me, almost touching me, and I instinctively backed up even farther, my hands brushing the metal. Patient One didn't move.

Doing my best to channel my childhood hero, I told him, "You can't be thinking of taking him out of here."

"I'm not." He lowered the gun again, aiming a little beyond me. "I have to kill him."

What? My body acted before my mind could—I curled my hands around the bars. I froze as I heard Patient One shifting closer to me, ducking down. He was close enough to bite me, if he grabbed my hand or my hair. He had his muzzle on, but he could rip it off if he wanted. I was sure of that now. He was obviously intelligent. I'd been wrong.

That was why I had to save him.

"Tell me why," I said to Coalhouse. "Because this is *insane*. Where have you been?"

"No, it's not." Coalhouse stopped, withdrawing his aim again. He didn't seem to want to endanger me, which I naturally took to be a good sign. "Insanity is keeping him alive. I see that now. They have all the samples they could ever want from him. They can keep his body. I don't care."

"But I was just talking to him. He can tell us where he came from! He knows something about—"

"That doesn't matter. I got Hagens to talk." I went still, prepared to listen. "I just never expected to hear what she told me."

"What?"

"He's a danger to *everyone*. The living and the dead. The Changed are going to come after him, under her orders. They know where he is now. I had to tell them."

I felt myself go cold at the idea. Papa. The others. "We can stop that. We can evacuate the boat. Take him somewhere else."

"Where?" Coalhouse shouted. "Because someone else wants him, too! Not the cops, not the army! And he can't stay with the feds—someone's been giving out information on Z-Comp! It was used to blackmail Hagens!"

That was new. New and terrifying. "You think a hacker got in somewhere? How do you even know she's telling the—"

"No, listen. Hagens said they knew more than names and numbers. I think someone who worked with us has been talking." He cocked his gun. "So Hagens can't have him. Whoever's been talking to her can't have him. He's not secure with the army, he's not secure with the living, he's not secure *anywhere*. Tom was right. He has to die. That will end this."

Just then Patient One's arm shot out. He shoved my shoulder. *"Go!"*

My hands were still tight around the cage, and I ended up only bending forward. As I did, Coalhouse took a panicked, frightened shot. Out of the corner of my eye I saw Patient One arch backward and crash into the rear of the cage. My body seemed to burn with empathetic pain, pain so monumental that it caused me to sway and tasted like iron in my mouth.

Coalhouse shouted my name.

The pain didn't stop.

My ears ringing, my vision blurry, I looked to the side, to see that the right shoulder of my dress was swiftly turning into a morass of blood. Slowly, I let go of the cage and reached over, grabbing whatever material my numb fingers could grip and pulling it downward. The soaked fabric of my dress and corset cover smeared red down my upper arm, trickled red onto my corset, the strap of my chemise.

It was just a flesh wound. The bullet had grazed me, leaving a surprisingly short furrow in my skin. It was raw and red and bleeding, the edges of it singed. But more than that . . .

It'd obliterated Bram's bite marks.

It was that realization that caused me to fly at Coalhouse in a sudden seething rage and push him back with a soul-deep scream. Petite as I was, I caught him off guard as he was staring at me in horror. The gun went tumbling from his hand.

As I struck him again and again, ignoring the agony in my shoulder, I could hear someone pounding on the other side of the door, my father's voice. Behind me, I could hear Patient One yelling. He wasn't dead. Logic told me to run for the door, open it, let the showdown begin.

My heart, confused as it was, aggrieved as it was, told me otherwise.

Coalhouse was my friend and they might kill him for this. They wouldn't ask questions if he tried to leave with Patient One, or if he tried to leave both of us behind bloody—they might just kill him.

Bram had to talk to him. To both of them. Something was dreadfully, deeply wrong. This wasn't the Coalhouse I knew. Maybe he'd gotten into trouble, maybe somebody was forcing him to do this.

"Please stop!" I finally heard him begging. "I didn't mean to! I'm so sorry!"

I did stop, my fingers gripping into his clothing. I fought back my tears. "What have you done?"

"What . . . Nora, please, the blood . . . I'm so sorry . . . I never miss . . . I thought he was attacking you . . ."

The smell. I staggered back, looking up at the dead boy. Coalhouse had obviously lost his mind, but he was still apologizing to me. We needed to make the boat safe, sort this out. I couldn't just run away.

"I have to help you surrender," I said shakily, "Or we have to call Bram."

"No. I won't, Nora. Not unless I kill P One first."

He looked to his gun again, and I raced for it, picking it up before he could do anything. I opened it and dumped the bullets into my hand, making sure to get the chambered one. Realizing what I was doing, he shouted and tried to grab me, but I tossed the handful of bullets down the length of the room before he could. I could hear them pinging off the metal shingles, bouncing for what seemed an eternity. I took a quick inventory of the equipment in the room—computers, digital disks—and realized with relief that if there were any pens or long instruments, I didn't know of them.

"Damn it, Nora!" Coalhouse yelled. "If he dies, people will be safe!"

I forced myself to take another step closer, the open gun held in front of me. "Could you really look a sane zombie in the eyes and shoot him?"

"Yes." He sounded despondent. "I knew I couldn't get him off the boat. I was just going to kill him. And I'm sorry for that."

This was better. He was talking. Showing more empathy. I swallowed hard to overcome a wave of pain. "Let me call Bram, a—"

"No!" His expression crumpled. "Not him. I was trying so hard to be him . . ."

That at least made sense. A twisted sort of sense. As I looked back at Patient One to make sure he was okay, I realized that I needed to get Coalhouse off the boat entirely, away from everyone. Maybe then he would open up, tell me more. The only way to get him and Patient One out of the fire, at this point, was to shove them aside and sit in it myself. I'd promised Bram I wouldn't do anything stupid, but Coalhouse, P One—they both needed me.

The idea that came to me for doing this was large and horrible and almost laughable. "I'm your only way out, then."

Coalhouse blinked. "What?"

"Did you think you'd shoot him and they'd arrest you?"

Coalhouse nodded. "Yes. I was prepared to face that. Surrender. Figured I'd get someone to tell the Changed he was dead."

Clapping one hand over my throbbing shoulder to stanch the blood, I pointed with the gun at the door. "Well, I don't think you thought your cunning plan all the way through," I said, using a fatherism. "There's only one way off this ship, and that's the way you came. You locked the guards out, but they'll be closing in behind you. You sealed yourself in your own tomb. You did a crazy thing—the sort of thing a zombie losing his mind does. And now there's blood." I gestured. "My blood is on you."

Coalhouse stared at me. I'd just hit a whole hell of a lot of nails on the head.

"They're trying to arrest zombies, true. But what did Bram say? That last time the army was ready to kill? The scene you're making right now, they might kill you. You hurt me, even just knock me out—I can't help you talk your way out of this. And if you go for those bullets, I will fight you, and you will have no choice but to knock me out."

For a moment he looked almost offended. "I would never hurt you . . ." He gripped his head. "Oh God, what have I done?"

I took a breath and tried it. "But if you take me as a hostage, they won't."

"I can't do that!" he protested.

"You'll have to," I said. "Put the gun to my head and march me out. If you want to live, that is. They won't risk shooting me."

"What?" he barked, voice desperate. "Why?"

"Because you're my friend. *I* want you to live. And you're not thinking straight."

"Stop *saying* that!"

"You're not!" I screamed, thrusting the gun at him. "You want me to lie to you? You either stay here and let me talk you to safety, or you take me with you to get off the boat. Either way, you're not killing P One." Coalhouse swore. "Make your decision!"

He took the gun, his fingers trembling. "Fine." He looked at me. "But I'm not going without him."

"You can't."

"I have to, Nora."

He was huge. I'd disarmed myself. I had nothing to threaten him with. And I'd gotten him this far. Before he could come up with another mad idea for eliminating Patient One, before he could go bullet-hunting, I capitulated and said, "We go together, then."

He nodded, and moved toward Patient One's cage. The zombie within appeared to be fine—he was so physically ruined that I couldn't even tell where he'd been hit. Coalhouse used the gun to smash the lock. Pulling the zombie free, he produced a large handkerchief from his pocket and twisted it into a makeshift rope, using it to bind P One's wrists behind him.

As he did, I steadied myself. It wasn't like I hadn't been in danger before. "Let me take my phone."

"Hell no." He turned around and aimed the empty gun at me. *"Go."*

Blast. Nodding, I moved to the door and unlocked it. Show-time.

Outside was chaos. Guards were flanking the door, their weapons trained on us; several of them aimed upward when they saw me. The scientists were hugging the far wall, and cried out when it became clear to them what was going on.

"There's a hostage! Hold your fire!"

Dad and Salvez rushed forward, and Ben held them back. "NoNo! Oh my God, what happened?"

"I'm okay, Papa," I told him, my voice shaking just when I didn't want it to. "It's okay. We're doing this for a reason."

"What are you doing?" Salvez asked Coalhouse, barely able to utter the words, his voice strangely airy. "What are you . . . you're not . . ."

"I'm okay, Dr. Salvez," I said. "Just let him go." I put my hands up and walked forward, Coalhouse close behind me. He dragged Patient One along by his wrists. "Don't try to stop him. You'll hurt someone."

"No one come any closer!" Coalhouse bellowed, his voice huge in the belly of the ship. "You hear me? I'll let P One go if I have to!"

Looking at my father, I said, "I love you. I'll be all right." I knew they'd come after us the minute we left. I wasn't throwing myself off a cliff, not entirely.

I hoped.

But my little plan worked. Gerard had taught me well. Hell, Wolfe had taught me well. With a lot of yelling, a lot of angry motions, Coalhouse managed to force me ahead of him and off the ship. Once we were on the dock he turned me around, making sure no one would try to take him out from behind. Then it was through the busy barricade, which parted like the Red Sea to let us pass, its members crying out at the sight of us. A lightning storm of flashes went off. Apparently I was going to be on the news again. I should just embrace it. Start an Aethernet site.

A broken-down carriage awaited us at the end of the barricade.

Coalhouse pushed both me and the patient into the backseat, launched himself into the front, and took off down the dock at a terrifying pace. The minute we hit the surface streets I heard sirens, saw flashing lights out of every window, like holographic insects descending on a fallen carcass.

"You make one move, Nora . . ." He trailed off, concentrating on driving. He hadn't secured me. I supposed that's what he was thinking of.

"I won't. I want to help you." I reached out and squeezed Patient One's sticky hand. It was disgusting, but I barely felt it. The man looked at me, and I saw fear in his eyes. I didn't want him to lash out.

But neither could I let him go off, go free.

"The death that is died for others," I reminded him as I slid my fingers away from his and put both hands over my shoulder to show Coalhouse I wasn't going to try anything.

Still, I had to hope that death wouldn't end up being my own.

30 • Bram

"Got everything set?"

"Have I ever let you down?" Ren turned away from his computers and set his hands on his lap, like an obedient schoolboy. "What else would you like to put on the Renny-do list—build a large hadron collider?"

"Cute." I held out my hand. "Info."

"No paper. For once, I will not contribute to the demise of what remains of the rain forest." He picked up a digidiary from his desk. It was connected to one of his computers by a wire, which he pulled out. "Digital is the way to go, my friend."

I knew now was not the time to argue, so I took the thing from him and opened it. I'd been using one as a journal for years, at Dearly's behest. That function'd been fairly easy to get the hang of. "Fine. You've got thirty seconds, Professor Merriweather."

"I've set it all up. All you have to do is press the magical little buttons. On the launch screen you'll see icons for maps, links to his personal information, his school records—"

"You got Allister's school records? Well done."

"C minus in Classical Logic. Suddenly so much makes sense."

Finding the map icon, I thumbed my way in. "Says here his family has *five* houses? Which one is he at, then?"

"Current whereabouts I can't do. Well . . ." He paused, and fiddled with his glasses. "I *could* technically do it. But it'd be difficult. And highly illegal."

"Has that ever stopped you before?"

"*Yes.* I'm not a black hat." I knew Ren was capable of hacking, I just honestly wasn't sure what that "hacking" entailed. I'd known him to get past things called firewalls, into systems protected by passwords. Like, apparently, the grading system at Michael's school. "Granted, at this point my inevitable stint in prison would be exceedingly brief."

"Could you do it?"

"He's New Victorian. He's got an embedded ID chip." I nodded; that's what I'd been thinking. "Most efficient method of tracking him would involve breaking into the government ID database. It's been compromised before. But I'm not going to be able to do that in the next five minutes . . . Honestly, I'd rather not try. Too risky."

"Might not be so simple to find him after all," I said, disappointed. Because I was going after him. Mink's warning had been for the weekend, and I figured as long as Nora remained on the *Erika,* she'd be safe. Which meant this was my best opportunity to corner Michael and figure out what kind of game he was playing.

Alone. It was time.

"Now, I could try security cameras."

"Come again?"

He twirled a finger in the air. "New Victoria is filled with security cameras. I was saying, if I had a general idea where he was, I could infiltrate the camera networks, perform surveillance."

"Ren . . ." I was torn between the desire to hug him and the need to throttle him. "Why didn't you say this before? We could use that to find the masks!"

"No, we couldn't." He lowered his hand. "I physically cannot watch every single camera in New London."

"Yeah, but like you said, if we had some idea . . ."

"Which we won't have until we get more attacks in the database, figure out if there are any patterns. Which is why I'm glad we're canvassing."

"Yeah, but so far we're not having any luck with that. Coalhouse said they might clear out, and maybe they have. Once we have enough bodies on our side, though, we'll make a personal visit to the Changed. At least get Laura and Dog out of there." Giving up, I snapped the diary shut. "Looks like it's going to have to be old-fashioned footwork for now, then."

And footwork it was. Only the Rolls remained at the house, and unwilling to take it, I hopped the trolley to the surface and got off near the Morgue. Opening the digidiary again, I decided my best bet would probably be the richer areas of town. I wasn't expecting to run into Michael on the street, but maybe something I saw or heard would push me in the right direction. I'd have to catch an omnibus there, most likely.

It was then that I heard someone beeping. Glancing up, I saw an old, tatty carriage drawing up beside a wrought-iron parking meter. I wasn't sure if its driver wanted me, not until the window lowered and the pigtailed girl from Ratcatcher's crew leaned out.

"Hey!" she shouted. Her voice was even more girlish than Nora's—she sounded like a five-year-old who'd been nursing a helium tank. "Get in. We need to talk."

A tad weirded out, I took a look around. I couldn't *see* anyone preparing for an ambush. And admittedly, getting to the bottom of the Ratcatcher thing appealed to me. Sliding my fingertips over the pistol at my waist, I decided to go for it, and crossed the sidewalk, hopping into the passenger side. The instant I got the door shut, the girl took off.

"I'm Bai," she said, keeping her eyes on the road but only one hand on the steering wheel. She fished around inside her worn boy's private school jacket—at least, that's what it looked like, with a crest on the pocket—and pulled out three letters with broken black wax seals. "Ronnie's niece."

"Bram."

"I know." She handed me the letters. "Read."

I didn't for a few seconds, watching to see where Bai meant to take us. After a few turns convinced me she was intending to circle the park, I opened the letters.

Five grand now, five later. Nora Dearly, Bram Griswold, 1423 Element Street, Violet Hill, Elysian Fields, New London.

Call off the girl. I will bring her myself, or not, as I see fit. Payment still in full.

Delreggio's, 11:00 P.M., Saturday April 27th. Leave him there alone. Money will be waiting.

The first envelope also contained a wad of cash. I counted it. Five grand.

I was able to count it because I was so angry that I couldn't even *feel* the anger. Like my emotional fuse box had blown in an effort to protect itself. Samedi said the Ratcatcher caught people.

He'd been hired to catch us.

Lifting my eyes to Bai, I said, "Everything."

"I don't know everything. I'm apprenticed to Belinda. She's the Ratcatcher's wife." She turned again. "Couple months back, she started working with these guys. Dressed all in black. First they hid their faces with scarves, then with bird masks. Lot of weird folks in the underworld, so no questions asked—they paid for untraceable carriages, and that's what she gave them. Brought in a few of their own to be chopped."

"But then someone wanted to hire the Ratcatcher?"

"Right. And once he got back from the contact . . . I've never seen him like that before. He did *not* want the job. Didn't know who it was for when he accepted the cash."

"So that's why he shut down on Samedi. Wouldn't talk to me."

"You're good." She grinned a bit. "And can I just say it's *so* awesome that you work with the Undertaker? I had his wanted poster above my bed till Junebug stole it, the little tramp—"

"Later." I had to know. "Did he say why he wanted us? What he wanted to do?"

Bai took a second before responding. "Kill you. The girl was going to watch."

I'd figured as much, but I had to hear her say it. Trying to ride my numbness out to the end, I asked, "Anything else?"

"No. If you want to know who's behind it, we d—"

"I do." It had to be. It made sense. The masks, the warnings, the carriages. This wasn't the Changed. I'd been barking up the wrong tree.

This was *Michael*. Vespertine had told the truth.

"Good. Because the Ratcatcher's on his way out of town." She reached into her jacket again and produced another envelope. "That's for the Undertaker."

"Out of town?"

"If word gets out that he took an assignment and didn't follow through, his reputation will be ruined. Someone might even try to take him out. He's going to lie low for a while." She flashed me a purposeful look. "That's how much he loves the Undertaker. And me. Samedi saved my uncle's life. It was a firefight, the

Undertaker killed for Uncle Ronnie . . . so he needs anything from me, I'm his to command, too."

Sam didn't want anything to do with them anymore, but they were loyal to a fault. Had to give them that. "Got it."

"Belinda said she'd help you go after the masks, but not yet." She slowed. "That's it. Where do you want me to let you off?"

"Actually, if you could drive me to the posh side of town, I'd be obliged." My phone rang—the special ring that told me it was Nora calling. The only one I couldn't ignore.

"Can do. Mostly 'cause it sounds like somebody's going to get his head caved in. Wouldn't like to stand in the way of that."

I opened the phone, managing a gruff, "Yeah?"

"Bram!" It was Dr. Dearly, not Nora. He sounded as if he were crying, or attempting to yell through water. "He took Nora! He took her!"

"Wait, what?" I must have sounded suddenly panicked, for Bai looked at me in alarm. "Who took her?"

"Coalhouse," he said, his voice failing. "He took Patient One, too."

For a few long seconds I actually couldn't understand what I'd just heard. It was as if the words that had just been spoken were noises without symbolism. Gibberish uttered by a fever victim. Random finger-tappings on a table.

When my brain finally constructed meaning out of them, my hand tightened so fiercely my phone's casing cracked.

"Do you know where?" The voice I heard was not my own. It was a level far above death-rattle-scary-zombie, a level far above growling or snarling. It was thunderous and vengeful, and it almost frightened *me*.

"The authorities are giving chase. I don't know. I don't know! He had a gun at her head! He had a gun, and . . ."

I heard crackling, and then Salvez's voice was on the line. "In her phone, she had that she was going to meet a Michael Allister at a place called Kintzing's. He told her to come alone. But nothing about Coalhouse. I still can't understand it, I still keep thinking it didn't happen . . ." The phone crackled again, and Salvez disappeared.

Confusion only whipped me up into even more of a frenzy. I hit the ceiling of Bai's carriage, and she asked, "What happened?"

"Friend of mine has lost his damn mind! He's taken my girl and . . . someone else." I must have been something to behold, because Bai nearly shrank into her own shoulders as I talked, looking at me like a scrawny kid might look at the local playground bully had the bully laced his cereal with creatine and meth that day.

"What are you going to do?" she whispered. "Go after him?"

"God knows where he's headed, that's the problem! The only . . ."

No. Coalhouse wouldn't do something like that.

Would he?

"Let me out here," I told Bai.

She pulled over, and I dropped down. "You need us for anything? I don't have much clout, but I can try."

"I can't use the living. I'll have Sam contact Belinda if I need you."

The girl nodded. I shut the door and she zoomed off. "Salvez!" I shouted into the phone.

"Yes?" he answered, coming back. "Sorry, just trying to—"

"Listen to me. Coalhouse is obsessed with the Changed, and they've talked about wanting both P One and Nora." The words were hard in my throat; it almost hurt to say them. "I hate to even think it, but we have to assume he might head back there. *Might*. Maybe he's got some scheme in mind. He was lurking around the *Erika* the other night."

"Sweet, merciful Science."

"I need you to call me if the people following Coalhouse lose him. Put Dearly on the line."

At first I wasn't sure if he had heard me, but then Dr. Dearly's voice met my ear. "Bram?"

"Listen to me, sir. I need you to pull as many strings as you can. You know that group of zombies in Honduras we told you about? The ones that might've been involved in the road attack?"

"Yes."

"I need their location, and I need the army *away* from them, if possible. We need every minute we can get. Call Lopez, have him help you. I'll send you his number."

"But—"

"The army's already been up there, arrested people. If the army thinks there's even the possibility that P One is there, they'll go in hot. There are innocents in that group!" I said it. "Coalhouse has been determined to get them. He's gone back to the camp at least once. If for some reason he's headed up there now, they're going to gun for him. Nora could be hurt. Do you trust me?"

There was a pause before Dearly said softly, "I trust you."

"I swear, I will get her back to you." I hung up, and pulled out Ren's digidiary, bringing up the map.

The authorities were on Nora, and far ahead of me. I had no idea where the Changed were, and I needed time to assemble what few troops I had. I hated idling, but I told myself it was to emerge better prepared.

Meanwhile, I now knew precisely where Michael was.

Kintzing's was an upscale dining establishment in a good part of town.

Upon entering, I slammed the gold-edged glass doors apart so hard that one of them cracked.

The maître d' ducked behind his little lighted podium. Through two open, garlanded archways to either side I could see well-heeled diners scrambling away from the foyer, while others looked at them as if they'd lost their minds. I showed the maître d' my weaponless hands and growled, "Allister. Waiting on another diner. *Where is he.*"

The maître d' squeaked out something about "our best table" and pointed to another set of closed wooden doors. Without waiting, I strode in that direction and kicked them open. They banged against the walls of the next room, letting out a sound like a cannon and causing several varnished paintings to tremble. There was only one table inside, and Michael was seated at it.

"The devil?" he said, standing up, expression hovering somewhere between disgust and mortal fear.

"You got him," I said as I closed the distance between us. "We need to talk."

"What is the meaning of this?" He stood his ground. "I told her to come alone. You filthy thing, setting foot in a good establishment!"

"Again, you mean?" Finishing the work I'd started back on the airship in December, I decked him. Upward. He flew back and slammed into the wall, but remained conscious. Sinking to his feet with a moan, he cupped his hands around his nose, blood dripping onto his ivory cravat.

I got down into his face. "I know you meant to kill me tonight." His eyes went wide. "You're coming with me. You got any weapons, you better drop them now. Or they're going into my personal collection, and you won't like what I do with them. And give me your phone."

Michael weighed his odds and rose to his feet. He reached into his jacket and produced a pistol, which he dropped on the floor. He did the same with a knife from inside his waistcoat. After finding and handing me his black cell, he turned around and marched forward at an even pace, clearly attempting to hold on to some of his nobility.

"What is going on?" Several employees had gathered in the foyer, including a tuxedoed gent I took to be the owner. "Have you called the police? You can't just let ruffians come in and disturb the customers. Especially the dead! You can't just let . . ."

I met his eyes as I walked in, wordlessly challenging him to continue.

He didn't. "Never mind."

"Call the cops on me. Go ahead," I told him as I removed the cash paid for me from my pants pocket and slapped a few bills on the podium. "That's for your door."

After the glass doors closed behind us, Michael stopped and said, voice infuriatingly pompous, "Let's at least do this in my carriage. I'm not about to argue with a subhuman creature out on the street."

"Sounds grand," I said. "I'm incredibly honored."

He led the way to an enameled blue carriage in the covered parking lot, opened the door, and insisted I enter before he did. We sat opposite each other. The carriage was a fancy little number, with a hand-painted carpet and leather seats. Warily, he called out, "Worth! Open the partition!"

The embroidered partition didn't move. "You sure about that?" I said as I shut the door, then lowered the interior blinds. It was dark outside, but I wasn't a fool.

"I want my driver to watch us," he said. "He has a gun. Worth!"

Slowly, the partition slid down. Tom and Chas turned around in the driver's section, the first waving, the second blowing a kiss. Tom had taken Worth's little cap. I had no idea where they'd stashed the driver. I didn't really care.

Michael's eyes shot back to me. "What did you do?"

"Worth, drive," I said.

"Aye aye, Captain," Tom said. Activating the carriage, he pulled out of the parking lot. Michael was knocked against the side of the cab as Tom turned onto the street, and he reached out to grip one of the handles mounted along the interior.

"I won't string you along, because we have precious little time." I pulled the letters from my jacket pocket and tossed them in his lap.

Michael blinked, though no immediate emotion entered his eyes. It was like his brain spontaneously stopped controlling his face. "I have no idea what those are."

"Yes you do." I leaned even closer, close enough to strike out and bite him if I wanted to. He squeezed himself back against his seat, even as he lifted his chest, attempting to look as if he wasn't afraid. "But I don't care what you meant to do to me. Why did you invite Nora here?"

"That's none of your concern, abomination." He was starting to sound scared.

Quick as a switchblade, I reached out, grabbed his nose and shifted it back and forth, letting him hear the crunching of his own cartilage. He screamed. But he didn't talk.

"What did you *do*?" I snarled, releasing his nose. "Why was Nora coming here? Why did you tell the Ratcatcher not to bring her?"

"You're not worth the air it would take to form the words," he coughed out. "Miss Dearly was coming here to talk. I was going to give her a choice."

I jabbed him in the nose again, more carefully, with two knuckles—like an acupuncturist piercing just the right area. This time I got him to sob. "About what? The whole thing!"

Michael remained defiant. He didn't open his mouth—only glared at me as if he wished he could burn me to ash where I sat. His silence infuriated me more than any insult could. Everything started to weigh on me—Nora being taken, not having an immediate plan, how fast we were racing through the city. Tom swerved sharply to the left, and Michael rocked in his seat. I didn't. I was rigid with rage.

So calmly that it almost disturbed me, I grabbed him by the chin, like a parent might a mouthy child, and rolled his head back, forcing him to look up at me. My voice curled up on itself, condensing and becoming more powerful. In my bones, I knew I had no right to terrorize the living. Faced with Michael's stubborn face, that ideal went out the window.

"Talk. Or I'll get it elsewhere. There are people in the city who have it out for you. Enough to contact us, tell us to be on our guard." Following a gut feeling, I added, "Enough to give us extremely detailed information about you, in addition to those letters. C minus in Logic? You like to waste your father's money?"

Hearing this, Michael stopped struggling. He looked at the letters, and actually reached out and opened one, reading it. For a few long seconds he was absolutely still. Then something seemed to break behind his eyes. He lunged at me, his hands rising to strike me, suddenly incandescent with anger. "I don't know how he found out who I am, but you think I won't destroy the Ratcatcher for this? You think I won't kill *you*? You won't live after tonight, maggot! I'll set off more bombs, I'll burn the entire world down if I have to!"

I had my hands around his throat a nanosecond later. I forced his head back against the wall of the carriage, and he cried out. "Bombs?"

"I bombed the Roe bakery," he choked out when he saw I had absolutely no intention of letting go. "She had to be punished. But no one was hurt. I did it after dark on a weekend for a reason!"

Good God. *"Why was Nora coming here?"*

"A choice!" he gagged. "At first I was going to make her watch me carve you up like a prize stag. But I changed that! I was going to give her the option to rescue you tonight, be mine in exchange for your life. I was still going to kill you, though. I still *will*!"

For the last twenty minutes my body had felt almost supernaturally hot. Now it felt like I was standing inside an arctic Hell. "What else did you masked bastards do?" A deeper level of fear flickered across his face when I mentioned the masks. I cut off just a fraction more air, and that fear compounded. "Remember, you need to breathe. I don't. I can do this all night!"

Michael's fingers clawed at the upholstery. "What masks? The letters prove nothing! And you think you can convince the police to arrest me? I'm speaking to ghosts right now, deadmeat! Nothing will stick!"

The rational, moral part of my brain screamed at me to stop, to let up, but the reptile in me, the caveman—the zombie—wanted to hit him again, wanted to see his blood foam. He'd meant to kill me. Torture Nora. He *had* tortured her best friend.

Just then a sort of chime went off all through the cab. Tom looked at the dash in confusion. "What's that?"

"A call!" Michael said. "My parents. The restaurant probably called them!"

Fantastic. No longer trusting myself, I loosened my grip. "Chas, climb back here and keep little Lord Allister company."

Chastity immediately obeyed, wiggling her way into the back headfirst. Michael screamed when she launched herself toward him, straddling his lap. "Hey, big boy! Like your shirt. Too baaad you ruined it by having, you know, blood."

"You say anything about this," I told him, "my fist meets your face again." I pointed to the dash. "Take the call. Tell whoever it is that you're out joyriding with some friends."

"Connect," he said, after clearing his throat. His troubled, pained voice became a little more controlled. "Who is it?"

"Michael? Sweetie?"

"Mother?" he asked, looking at me to make sure I got it. "Ma'am?"

"Where are you?"

"In town. Hanging out. Why?"

"I want you to come home, all right? Your father's Code 12, and I want you to come home straightaway!"

"What's wrong?"

"There are zombies outside!" Lady Allister sounded hysterical. "Hundreds of them! They're marching toward the Talgua! They're nearly in Lady Madroso's backyard!"

Hang up, I mouthed at Allister.

"Okay. I'm coming, ma'am. Disconnect." Before I could say anything, he asked, his voice still preternaturally calm, "What's going on?"

"That's got to be them." I wasn't wholly relieved, but at least we had something to go on. "The Changed."

"You don't think Coalhouse has bought in, do yooou?" Chas asked, worried. I'd filled them in via phone. "You don't actually think he's taking her there?"

"What else could he be doing?" said Tom. "If they were in danger he would have said, 'Hey, people in danger, let's help them out.' Not march them out with a *gun*." He pointed his finger back at Chas. "I told you this would happen someday."

"The Changed?" Michael asked. "What's that? Who's 'her'?"

Chas slumped against the door, and I said, "Group of angry, violent zombies—but not in the usual sense. And Nora's been taken, along with the biter from the riot. Once she learns what you had in store for her, though, I'm sure she'll look at it as a merry Sunday drive."

"What?" Michael spat, eyes widening. "Why didn't you say something? Why aren't you off rescuing her?"

"Did you call everyone like I asked?"

"Yeah," Tom said. "They're meeting at The Failing Liver."

"Looks like it's time to send my five soldiers against their hundred after all. Get as many under control as we can before the troops descend." And the idea almost made me sick. I didn't have the whole of Company Z behind me anymore. And we didn't know how many Changed there were now—maybe Lady Allister was exaggerating with her "hundreds," maybe she was telling the truth.

"*Five* against . . ." Michael sounded like he wanted to rage again, but he quite literally swallowed it. "Is Miss Dearly there?"

"There's a possibility." When I said it, Tom and Chas's faces fell. It was a heavy thing to say—it felt like I was declaring Coalhouse public enemy number one. Some sort of Outlander. "She has people on her trail."

"But why aren't you going after her, too? What's so important about these people?"

"You're not a zombie. You wouldn't understand." I wasn't about to justify myself to him, but his questions weren't healthy for either of us. Because I hated feeling helpless, hated feeling like I'd made the mistake of waiting too long yet again, and the Laz told me those problems could be partially solved if I ate him.

"Are you . . ." Michael seemed to be acting in fits and spurts, like a malfunctioning automaton. Catching his breath, he said, "Look. I can get us an army. For Miss Dearly's sake."

"What, your bird men?" Anger started welling within me again. "Like I'd let them anywhere near a zombie?"

"*No.*" He sniffed back some blood. "But my father has a private security force. A major one. If he thinks I'm with these 'Changed,' and in danger, he'll send them. I'm his only heir. We'll take care of them, then go after her."

My first thought was a big old *NO.* Like I wanted to owe that worm anything? Like I wanted to give him the satisfaction? More than that—like I wanted to give a group of living people an invitation to open fire into a crowd of zombies? I was trying to *avoid* that. "I'm not about to let your father kill my kind."

"Trust me," Michael said. "If I'm involved, and they don't know where I am, they'll only use nonlethal weapons. They wouldn't risk harming me."

There was probably some truth to that. And Patient One— what if Coalhouse *was* taking him up there? What if he got away? I needed more than a handful of men. More than averting an-other living–zombie showdown, if P One was there, I needed to make sure he ended up in our control.

And of course Nora trumped all other concerns.

I had to figure out a way to play this. The private security force of a lord was far from ideal, but at least they weren't government. He could have a point.

"Only male heir *is* a huge deal up here," Chas said. "I buy what he's saying."

"Okay." I tried to steady myself, find my center. "We've got a few hours, tops. Drive to the meeting point."

The street in front of The Failing Liver was a regular vintage car-riage and gun show by the time we showed up. In addition to Samedi and Dr. Chase, I saw most of the Company Z crew—the few who'd regularly been on patrol. Tom and Chas had done their job well.

The sight was moving, honestly.

Holding Michael by the collar of his shirt like a mother dog might her pup, I stepped out of his carriage and found Samedi and Beryl at the Rolls, the hood up. Beryl was holding Sam's head and a flashlight over part of the engine, while his hands worked elsewhere. He appeared to be connecting wires to a sec-ondary battery.

Coming face-to-chest with Sam's headless but ambulatory

body, Michael cried out and twisted in my grasp. "What are you doing?" I asked Samedi, ignoring the boy like one might a fussy toddler.

"Putting her together," he muttered. Mysterious-looking equipment was assembled at his feet, some of it bundled in twine-tied tarps. "I don't even know if this is going to work."

I looked to the side, and realized what the strange mountings over the front wheels of the car were for. They were newly occupied by steel. "Guns? Is that what was in the trunk?"

"Railguns," he said, withdrawing his body. Beryl tossed him his head, and he put it on as she applied an electric drill to something on her side. "Crash course. Railguns are electromagnetic guns that fire projectiles. You've got five shots each. They're basically missiles, but they're not very large, seeing as this is a car and not a battle cruiser. The controls are under the dash. You can't aim these things, but they're going to rip a nasty hole in anyone they hit and scare the filth out of anyone they don't." He looked at the drill in his own hand. "Word of advice. Never drink anything *green*. Gives you weird ideas."

"You're a wizard, Sam." A bloody insane wizard, but that was part of his gift. Digging into my pocket, I handed him the letter from the Ratcatcher, which he peered at curiously. As he did, I saw Ren approaching. "You're not coming with, are you?"

"No, but do you need anything else?"

"Get in touch with a guy named Havelock Moncure." I looked at Michael. "And watch over the Roes."

"What's the mission, Cap?" Franco called out.

"First leg, we're catching up to the Changed. Tell them your home address." Michael recited it, reluctantly. Keeping hold of him, I then addressed my troops, because I figured they deserved that much. "I appreciate all of you being here. We don't know if Nora is up there, but at the very least, there should be zombies there tonight."

"Aye. We'll fight for our own," Aberforth said. "We're with you."

"Sam, Beryl, you go with Tom and Chas in Michael's carriage. Let me take the car."

"Why don't we go with you?" Samedi asked as he shut the trunk.

"Because Michael's my red flag," I told him. "Go."

As everyone traded weapons, boarded their rides, and set out, I released Michael and brought out his phone. I started looking for his address book.

"No. We can't call anybody." Michael removed a hankie from his jacket and started cleaning himself up. "We have to go to Dad. In a manner of speaking."

"We do not have *time* for this!" Finding his contacts, and a number labeled *Father*, I hit the call button and held the phone to my ear. It rang three times and went to voice.

"Code 12. You will not have the option of leaving a message. I will be home shortly."

The phone hung up on me. I stared at it in confusion. "What's Code 12?"

"Mom already told us that. That means he's . . . he won't answer her calls, he won't answer mine!" Michael turned around. "You have to take me to Allister Genetics."

"Fine! Just as long as you know you're not staying there." His mouth opened, and I leaned in close. "I'm not letting you out of my sight, and I'm not leaving you here. Because I'd have to park you with the Roes, and I'd have to tell them why they shouldn't let you go."

Michael's eyes widened. He shut up.

"Fast learner. Let's drive."

31 • Nora

"Coalhouse, please listen to me!" I shouted above the wail of the sirens.

"Shut up!"

As he tore down a side street, I tried to think. New London was still new to him. He couldn't know it well. He'd get himself caught up in a cul-de-sac or something eventually, unless I helped him. I knew the cops or the army might try to seal off the city, or at least the main roads.

Of course, the Siege proved . . . okay. I couldn't expect anything from them.

Coalhouse swerved sharply to the left, tumbling me against Patient One in the dark. I screamed out of true animal fear and fought my way off him. My wrist had brushed the grill on his muzzle. "Be careful!"

"Yeah, I'll get right on that!" Coalhouse grunted, sending me flying in the opposite direction as he took a curb on the corner. Patient One thrust out his arms and caught himself before he could hit me, his face only inches from my own, the strange geometry of his muzzle brought out by a passing streetlight.

"Thank you." I had to keep him sane. I had to keep acknowledging his heroic efforts, in hopes that he'd keep making them. Raising my voice, I entreated, "You're going to get someone killed!"

"Then tell me where to go!"

Patient One pulled himself back, retreating like a trapdoor spider into its hole, compressing himself into the narrow space of carriage floor at the foot of the rear seat. Once he was safely away from me, I went for the button that'd lower my window, knowing I needed to minimize the smell of my blood. "You're off the boat now. You can stop this. Even if you just pull over and let us out. I'll tell you how to get away! Buy you time!"

"No way!" Coalhouse glanced into the rearview mirror. I could see red and blue lights flashing in it. "I'll let you out, but not him!"

"Then I won't go!" It was becoming harder and harder to say, even though I felt more and more strongly about it with each passing moment.

"Then tell me where to bloody turn!" On the street in front of us a couple dove out of the way of his oncoming carriage.

I looked out the windows but couldn't even begin to fashion a mental map of where we were. The buildings outside were seedy, the streets narrow and dirty. "I don't know," I admitted. "I think we're heading north."

Something brushed my ankle, and I let out a cry. When P One looked up at me and softly said, "Go," guilt like a small sun burned off the remaining fog of my fear.

"I won't leave you," I promised. And with that I found a seat belt and strapped myself in.

Just in time, too. When Coalhouse glanced back at me and understood I would neither help nor hinder him, he set his body resolutely forward and punched down the accelerator. I found myself viewing the ensuing chase like a scene from one of my action-filled holographic movies, not something I was actually *part* of. For a dead guy with no depth perception, Coalhouse was an amazing driver. Some combination of sheer dumb luck and astonishing skill led to him making correct directional choices again and again. Soon the streets were growing emptier, broader, signs that we were headed toward the highway. By the time we started passing small cottages and suburbs full of brick houses with pokey lawns, I knew we were on our way out of the city.

The moment we spun off the final exit ramp and our tires hit the unlighted highway, Coalhouse killed his lights and floored it. My skin prickled as we plunged ahead into the darkness, soon leaving behind the lights of the coppers and their exterior speakers, which had been chanting at us, like a prayer, *"Surrender, pull over! Surrender, pull over!"*

Wrenching my restrained body around, I turned to look fully out of the back window as we lost them. I even placed a hand on the glass, as stupid and invisible as it might've been. I wished fervently for a lighter to signal with, a flare, the screen of my phone, *anything,* but I had nothing.

Soon I could no longer see them, and it didn't matter.

It seemed we drove for days after the lights of the pursuing officers went dead behind us, when likely it was only hours. For the first half hour we were all silent. I think it hit us then—exactly what had happened. What we'd done.

Coalhouse lowered his window. I tore off a section of my petticoat and tried to tie it around my shoulder, pain zinging down my arm. I had to use my teeth to hold one end of the improvised bandage.

Coalhouse must have watched me, because he finally spoke. "I can't believe I did that. I'm so sorry."

I was relieved to hear those words. He was a good guy, a hero, and I didn't want to think that I might have made a mistake trusting him, after all.

"We have to stop," I said. "Find a way to get in touch with someone. Tom, Chas—"

"I can't." He hit the steering wheel, hard. "I can't go back after this!"

He was right. And it was pointless to try to convince him to take us back to the city, at least not now. I knew that. "Get off at any small town. Go to the sheriff. Turn yourself in. Small town, fewer people . . ."

And just like that he was off. He was nearly crying, shaking. "I was just trying to complete the mission. But I don't know what to do now. I don't *want* to kill him, Nora. I don't. And I'm so sorry about your arm . . ."

"The fact that you're sorry is why I want to help you, Coalhouse. Please . . ."

But he wouldn't listen. He just kept driving, changing highways a few times, going down a few back roads. Anytime we caught sight of flashing lights—once a siren whooped, far off, causing the hairs on my neck to rise—he would engage in a dizzying number of turns and eventually follow the smallest, darkest road he could find. We zigzagged everywhere, vaguely northward. I wasn't sure where we were headed. Coalhouse didn't seem to have any idea either.

But then we came upon a field full of bonfires. At first I thought we might find help there—that maybe we were looking at some obscure small-town festival or agricultural setup. "What is that?" I asked.

As I formed the words the answer came to me.

It was the Changed.

They'd packed it in like Aberforth said they had, a long line of their vehicles parked along the side of an empty northern highway, all of them piled high with crates and luggage. They'd set up a temporary camp in a field bordering another set of train tracks, and on the far-off edges of it I could make out tiny shimmering points of light, like landed stars—houses, I figured. We must be in Honduras. Coalhouse must've taken a northern route around the eastern side of Allister's preserve.

He sped up when the camp became visible, the carriage rattling off the shoulder. Fear spiked through me. "What are you doing? Did you drive up here on purpose?" My voice was higher, more panicked than I wanted it to be.

The dead boy didn't answer right away. He pulled over to the side of the road and powered down the carriage, leaving us to sit in silence as well as darkness. "Not originally."

The muzzled zombie said nothing, but his eyes gleamed with panic. Undoing my seat belt, I gripped Coalhouse's arm. "Have you completely lost it? Oh my God, why would you drive us up here?"

"I didn't set out to! But then . . ." He looked to the camp. "Laura. She wouldn't come with me. We can at least save her. I will at *least* do that."

"*No,*" I said, even as Coalhouse opened the door. "Right now we need to be on the other side of the *planet* from here!"

"Quiet," Coalhouse said. He looked newly determined. And that worried me.

I wracked my brain for ways out of this latest mess. At least Papa would have an actual *reason* to ground me this time. "Before, you guys said Hagens wanted me. You're putting me in danger, Coalhouse."

"She doesn't now. She wants Smoke. And you're *both* going to stay right here. I'm going to go get Laura. Don't let anyone see you."

Without saying another word, Coalhouse shut his door and started off toward a gaily-colored carriage with something boxy strapped to its roof. It took me a second, but I soon realized it was part of the double-tiered stage we'd seen the night we visited as a group. Next to the carriage was a striped tent.

I watched him go, my heart pounding, my eyes hot. I knew what I had to do. I hated to leave him behind, Laura, *anyone*, but I might not get another chance. If he'd ingratiated himself with Hagens so successfully, he'd be safe here, at least for a time.

Sliding into the front seat, wincing in pain, I powered the carriage on and took a moment to look at the controls. This couldn't be too difficult. Drive button, steering wheel, accelerator, and brake. That's all I'd need. Right?

"Smoke," I said, deciding to use his "real" name. "I'm going to drive us back to the city. I don't know *how* to drive, so I need you to stay quiet and still, okay?"

"Yes," he gurgled. "Don't like it here. Want to be with people."

"You and me both." Taking a breath, I put my hands at two and ten and hit the button to take the carriage out of park. I reached up to adjust the rearview mirror, as Coalhouse was tall and I was a shrimp.

That's when I saw lights heading for us. From the camp.

No.

My chest going numb, I tried to hit the accelerator. The carriage revved forward far more violently than I expected, causing me to slam on the brake in response with a gasp—a reaction that made me to momentarily question my own sanity.

My idiot reflexes gave the carriages gunning for us just enough time to box us in, fore and aft. I looked into the cab of the one in front of me and saw leering zombies. Guards, probably. I tried to accelerate again, twisting the steering wheel sharply to the left, but all I did was succeed in crashing into the carriage in front of me at a funny angle. One I couldn't recover from without backing up.

I didn't dare scream. I didn't want Smoke to get riled. Our getaway had lasted about two minutes, though, and oh—how I wanted to scream.

The carriages emptied; our doors were opened. We were hauled onto the grass. As the zombies saw Smoke, made out his face by the glow from their headlights, a whoop of triumph went up.

And I was almost sick.

They took us to the striped tent. The only light came from a dented kerosene lantern, and there was nothing inside except two thick wooden support stakes and a few pallets of mismatched bedding.

And Hagens, Coalhouse, and Laura.

Laura was sitting at Hagens's feet like a slave girl out of some dime novel. She saw us first and looked at us in amazement before staring up at Coalhouse. He was apparently attempting to talk Hagens into letting him take her elsewhere.

"They're going to move him again," he was saying. "But I'm not sure where. I think I could get more info out of them if a girl talked to them. Maybe Laura, here? Kinda weird, but this one living guard I know, I think he has a thing for dead girls . . ."

As he went on, Hagens lifted her head and saw us. Her eyes rounded almost cartoonishly. Laura shut her own.

"And I could . . ." Coalhouse finally noticed that neither woman was paying attention to him. He turned, and when he saw both of us, our arms pinioned by the guards, it looked like he wanted to die for real. I'm sure my expression had something to do with it.

"What have you done?" Laura whispered. "Oh God. You got *both* of them for her."

"You did . . . or you didn't." Hagens still looked like a five-year-old who'd been given a pony for her birthday and wasn't quite ready to accept that *that thing* was *hers*.

"Saw a carriage park on the road," my handler said. "Went to go check it out. Look what we found inside?"

"Miss Dearly." I nodded as invisibly as I could, and Laura turned on Coalhouse, asking again, "What have you *done*?"

"Nothing," he argued, his voice weak. "I didn't—"

"Shut up, Laura," Hagens said brusquely. "Coalhouse—"

She didn't finish. Laura rose to her feet and actually threw herself at Coalhouse, raining her fists on him, like I had before. *"You're lying again!"* she screamed. "*Bull!* Bull that you would come back here and just happen to have those two follow you!"

"It wasn't meant to be like this!" Coalhouse yelled, shoving her back.

That was Hagens's cue. As I struggled against my captors she reached behind her waist and drew out a gun. Before Coalhouse could say another word, or even curl his hand into a fist, Hagens shot him. I screamed as he reeled back, one shoulder leading the way. She hadn't gotten him in the head. A couple of the guards behind us tried to back her up, guns emerging and going off around me like fireworks. I ducked my head, trembling, sure I'd be shot again.

That's when I felt Laura grab me.

The world became a blur of limbs and vines as she tried to pull me away, the sickening carnival colors of the tent whirling overhead. Before she could succeed in freeing me, one of the guards stepped forward and clobbered her in the head. She fell at my feet, and my breath stilled. I wasn't sure if she was dead or not.

Hagens finally got Coalhouse to submit and put up his hands, her gun aimed at his skull. "I never would have thought it, but God—Coalhouse Gates. You will go down in the annals of zombie history. You're a hero of legend."

Coalhouse stared at her as if she'd just damned him to Hell

rather than complimented him. "No. This was a mistake. I need to take them back."

"I wish you hadn't said that." Hagens looked almost disappointed. "It's clear you're confused. But that doesn't make you any less of a hero."

"All of this. Please . . . at least give me Nora. You don't need her."

"I *don't* need her. But I'll take her. She'll make a fine insurance policy."

For a moment everything came to a standstill. I had no idea what to do, what I wanted Coalhouse to do. He looked at me, his single eye pleading for something—I don't know what.

"It was a mistake," he whispered. "I swear . . . I'll make it right."

And then, injured and scared, he turned and ran off into the night, the entire tent shuddering with the force of his exit. It was so sudden that even the guards held still for a second before moving to pursue him.

"Coalhouse!" I yelled, slumping down in the strange zombie's arms, surprised and devastated. Maybe he hadn't meant to bring me here, but he was *leaving* me here.

"What was he talking about?" another guard demanded of Hagens.

"I don't know, but tell the camp to get on him. Hunt him down." Her voice was newly vengeful. "This entire thing's been fishy from the beginning, but I'm not about to argue with results."

"What do you want with me?" Being those "results," I figured I'd better just come out with it. Better to know and face my fate than let ignorance drive me insane.

As if finally noticing me, Hagens approached, taking me in hand. She was horribly, painfully strong, her bony fingers digging into my flesh like barbed wire. Struggle as I might, I couldn't get free. "Like you need to know?" I let off a string of ugly words, and she tightened her hold. Beside me, Smoke growled.

"Get some rope," Hagens said to one of her lackeys. He rushed off, and she moved me so I could better see her face. "I just want you as my guest. That's all."

"Don't get fancy on me. Just tell me what you want me for."

"Because you can hurt so many people." Her laughter crackled. "People who have hurt me. Griswold, the army—the living. Alive, you can keep a whole hell of a lot of people off my back. Dead, you can teach them why they never should have messed with me in the first place. Kidnapping you was a stupid idea, and I wasn't even that serious about it, but now? I am very serious indeed." The zombie reappeared with the rope. "Tie them up." Looking down at the ground, at Laura, she said, "Her, too."

"Hagens, if you—"

"Don't even start, or I'll kill you where you stand." Hagens threw me at the zombie who held the rope, and despite my fighting him every inch of the way, he started to bind me. "Not tonight. Not when I'm finally in a good mood!"

32 • Bram

The drive took a while, but the place was well marked. We started passing signs for the Maria Bosawas-Allister Memorial Animal Preserve and Gene Bank about ten miles out, and soon I encountered signs directing drivers farther on, toward Allister Genetics.

Michael said nothing for most of the trip, which was very smart of him. Especially after Salvez called to let me know that the police had lost Coalhouse. At that point I had to admit that the Changed was the best lead we had to go on. At the very least, we had to take care of them so we could concentrate fully on Nora. With Coalhouse gone, the authorities would soon start branching out.

And I prayed that he was *not* involved with the Changed. Although I was terrified for both of them, it was actually Coalhouse I was most worried about—because I knew my girl could handle herself.

"I'm going to get her," I told Salvez before hanging up. "We're almost there. Give me an idea of the lay of the land."

Michael continued to watch me warily, hand curled around his nose, but offered, "The preserve is about three thousand square miles. But we shouldn't have to go anywhere near it. The AG building is pretty straightforward."

"Three thousand square miles of nothing but animals and plants?" I asked, amazed. "And your family owns it?"

"The Last Garden of Eden," Michael said sarcastically, turning his attention to the window. "Dad always says it's the last place in the Territories you can hide anything."

"He have anything worth hiding?"

Michael sniffed messily. "Like I'd tell you anything about my family? You don't deserve to know."

"Fine. Just tell me what we're doing." I knew bickering—hell, even beating the kid up—wasn't going to do any more good at this point. Time to grow up.

"There's a lab on the eleventh floor. We can get on a comlink with him there."

"And a comlink is different from a phone call how?"

"Trust me. It has to be done this way."

"Fine. Then that's where I take you hostage."

"What?" Michael barked.

"Best way to get a rise out of your dad, I figure," I said as I turned off onto another road, one marked for employees. "Besides, you think I'm just going to trail along after you and twiddle my thumbs while you talk to him, tell him some kind of sob story? Double-cross me while you're at it? You're a nasty little git. In fact, I want you visibly in the cross fire. I want to make sure these forces of yours don't switch to live rounds once we get up there."

Michael clenched his fists before yelling, "Why won't you just *die?*"

"Believe me, I have asked myself that question many times since running into you again."

Forcing his hands open, he took a moment to collect himself—he was doing that increasingly. "First guardhouse is coming up." He turned to me. "You're going to have to go in the trunk. They'll let me through without question."

"Little lord, I might be dead, but I'm not stupid."

"It's the only way. I'm serious!"

I took a deep, useless breath and gave him my full attention. "Okay. Explain."

"There *are* guards. I'm not making this up. You think we can just walk into a facility full of equipment and experiments worth millions?" He pointed at himself. "I look like hell right now, but I'm his son. I've been working here, I have clearance. They'll let me in. They will *not* let you pass without a fight."

Suspicious as I was, I had to admit he was probably right. "If I do this, and you play me?"

"Let me guess: you'll make me hurt? You need some new threats." Michael straightened his jacket. "I want to get Miss Dearly back. You don't trust me, I don't trust you, but let's try to trust that we both want the same thing right now."

"Dandy." I pulled the car over and unlocked the doors, removing my handgun from my holster. I didn't want to do it but time was running short. "Let's do this fast."

Michael shifted over into the driver's seat as I left. I moved to the back of the car, eyeing the trunk warily as it opened. It wasn't just having to let Michael take the lead that made me uneasy—there was something about the idea of crawling into an enclosed, tiny space that added an extra aura of doom to the whole thing. But at least I could shoot my way out of my vehicular coffin should the need arise.

I climbed in and pulled the lid down. When everything was closed up, Michael took off. After about five minutes he slowed. As I stared at the lid of the car, I heard muffled voices, one of them belonging to someone other than Allister. A few seconds later we started moving again. This scene was repeated twice, and each time Allister got us through. Hopefully he'd told the truth, and this wasn't some elaborate game.

When the car was finally shut off and the trunk popped, I sat up, my eyes adjusting. We were inside a largely empty parking garage, the few carriages within spaced out due to the lateness of the hour.

Allister got out of the car. "Guards said almost everyone's gone home."

"Good work," I allowed as I hopped out.

"Thank you," Michael said sarcastically before opening one of the rear doors, going for a gun. "If we're both going? I get a weapon, too."

Stepping forward, I shut the door, narrowly missing his hands. "Like hell you do."

He leaned closer. "I deserve to defend myself if you lose it. And if I get the chance? I'll kill whoever has her!"

"Oh, you will?" I was starting to feel hot again, a biological impossibility, and a sign I needed to move. "Then walk so we can get there faster!"

It took him a few infuriating moments, but Michael finally gave up his gun gambit and started moving. I followed him, keeping my handgun out of sight. I didn't know how many cameras might be watching, and I didn't need any guards deciding to attack us prematurely.

At one point he crouched down and said, "Guard station ahead. I'll walk, you sneak."

Buying this, I followed suit. Michael straightened and slowly led the way to a far interior entrance, trying to keep behind cars and to the wall when he could for my benefit. In time we passed the guard station, the guards inside greeting Michael while remaining clueless about me, and made it to a metal door. The chip in Michael's wrist got us inside. From there he took me to an elevator, where his chip allowed him to hit the button for the eleventh floor.

"We're going to the main lab," he said, sounding strangely at peace, as if he'd finally found a thread he could follow through the labyrinth of activity we were currently engaged in. He then slid his filthy fingers through his hair, before grabbing his own nose and cracking it to the side with a cry. Before I could react, I saw fresh blood dripping, smelled it, and realized what he'd done.

"Making yourself look worse?"

He chuckled snottily. "No, actually."

"Then what?" Maybe I'd driven him insane. I was relieved to find that the idea actually troubled me.

"*This* is what will get hold of my dad."

"What?"

"If I can get us through decontamination as we are and into the lab, the presence of blood and dead flesh will set off about a million alarms," he explained. "It's supposed to remain sterile. One of them will get Dad's attention."

Grudgingly impressed, I said, "Does he really pay attention to little things like lab spills? I thought he owned this entire place."

"They're the *only* things he pays attention to," Michael said peevishly.

The elevator opened, revealing a small room. Sensors detected our movements and raised the lights to reveal clear glass walls and an assortment of equipment I couldn't even begin to identify.

"There's a lull between the decontamination announcement and the far door locking," Michael said, pointing to it before cupping his hands under his nose. "You're big, so make yourself useful."

"Got it," I said, holstering my gun for the moment.

"Welcome to Allister Genetics! Please stand by for decontamination!"

The minute the feminine voice faded away, I rushed the door. It gave easily beneath my shoulder, and Michael ran to join me, ducking a sudden burst of gas from the ceiling. We hurried into the lab, the door swinging shut and locking behind us. I ignored it, figuring it'd open on the next cycle.

The lab appeared to be empty. Michael unlaced his fingers and walked toward one of the stainless steel workstations, where he proceeded to smear two exaggerated handprints of blood over the upper surface. The long, sterile white room ran red, warning lights and sirens exploding out of nowhere. Michael cupped his hands over his ears while I drew out my gun.

"Contamination. Contamination," the female voice intoned.

"Where can we talk to him?" I yelled.

Michael moved over to a long wall taken up by virtual cages full of holographic rats, and I followed. As I waited to see what would happen next, a silhouette of a man ghosted over a nearby wall, causing me to turn around and take aim. We weren't alone after all.

"Bram?" Dr. Elpinoy said, the red light from the alarms making his wrinkled face look like a puddle of melted candle wax. I was used to seeing him in a lab coat, but now he wore one with a stylized Allister Genetics logo on the pocket.

"Dick?" I said, unbelieving, as I lowered my weapon. He'd come *here* to work?

"What are you doing here? What are—" He looked at Michael.

Before he could get the wrong idea, I grabbed him by the hand and dragged him over to a workstation. "We've got an emergency!" I said. "Just stay here!"

"Emergency?" he said, even as he backed up to where I indicated. "What do you mean, emergency?"

"Coalhouse took Nora. Patient One, too." At this news, Elpinoy went stock-still, his eyes widening.

The sirens abruptly stopped. Turning toward the wall of rats, I saw they'd been replaced by a video connection with a middle-aged man in a fine suit, his eyes blazing with anger. He was standing in a room that looked similar to the one we were in—the same sort of equipment, the same wall of virtual rats. Several large blue vats stood behind him, strange creatures curled up within.

He was here. He was somewhere in the building. *Damn it.*

"What is the meaning of this?" he demanded. "What's going on, son? What's happened to you?"

"Wrong person to ask," I piped up as I stepped closer to the screen. I raised my gun, training it on Michael's head. "Your only son's a little out of commission right now."

Allister the elder swung his eyes to me—and paused. "My God."

"He wants money, Dad," Michael said impatiently. "A million. Said he'll hold me hostage till he gets it."

Although there'd been no talk of money beforehand, I didn't contradict this—Michael probably knew better than I what would spur his father into action. I merely turned my gun slowly to the side, letting the man see it from all angles.

Lord Allister didn't even look at his son. Instead he met my eyes and said, "I didn't expect to meet you this way, Mr. Griswold. I'm disappointed."

This was a new level of weird. "What? How do you know who I am?"

"Dad?" Michael said, a poignant note in his voice.

Lord Allister actually held up a hand to shush his son, his attention still on me. "And in my building . . . not wise. Not wise at all." The oddest thing was that he didn't sound angry. He sounded almost contemplative.

"How do you know me?" Had Michael told him about me, perhaps?

"You don't need to know that," Allister said. He finally looked at Michael. "Not right now."

Trying to recover the plot, I said, "Then we'll leave. Got a lot of my friends waiting for me. In fact, they're almost at your front door. Did your wife try to call you earlier?" The man blinked quickly, though the rest of his face didn't move. "Maybe I'm smarter than you give me credit for."

That got a reaction out of him. "Dead *trash*," Lord Allister growled. To his son, he said, "Hold on." The feed disappeared, the wall left blank.

I wasn't expecting it to be over so quickly. "Let's move," I told Allister. We'd puzzle out the rest later.

Michael just smiled.

A popping sound captured my attention. I looked to the door we'd come through but saw nothing out of the ordinary. Then another pop, and another. Following the sound, I realized all of the doors were locking, some of them two and three times over. Even Elpinoy looked around in wonder, flinching every time a lock engaged.

"You're an idiot," Michael said. "Not only did you come *in*, you went eleven freaking stories up. Code 12 means my father is on the *twelfth floor* and doesn't wish to be disturbed!"

Grabbing Michael by the collar, I hurried over to one of the far doors. There, I forcibly waved his wrist over the reader, but for naught. They'd already shut off his access remotely. I thrust him off to the side and shot the lock, beat myself at the door, to no avail. Everything was reinforced ten times over.

"How do you think I knew about my father's guards, their tactics? You think planning for things like this hasn't been part of my life since I was an infant?" Michael gloated. "AG's probably the safest place on earth for me, and the deadliest for you. My dad's teams are going to march up here and fill you with so many holes, there won't be a square inch of you left to bury. Then I'm going to head out there, and *I'm* going to save Miss Dearly! You just *handed* me a way to make up for all of this!"

I stared at him in utter horror, realizing what I'd done. I'd dared to half trust the little bugger—dared to think that even though I was going to punish him later, he *did* want to do what was best for Nora. And look where it'd gotten me. Potentially dead. So far away from Nora I might as well have been on Mars.

Just as I was cursing myself, a hand appeared and tapped Michael on the shoulder. Michael turned around, only to be met by the business side of a stainless steel tray.

He spun to the ground, unconscious. Elpinoy stood behind him, blood-splattered tray in hand, his round stomach heaving with exertion and terror. He looked at me and dropped the tray with a clang, before touching his wrist to the pad near the door, which sprang open.

"My clearance is still good," he said. "Pick him up."

I did so, throwing Michael over my shoulder. "Did you tell Allister about me, Dick?"

"No." Elpinoy led the way to the emergency staircase, and together we half flew, half fell to the first floor. "No, I never told him anything about Company Z. Only about Dearly's research, which was all made public anyway."

"This is insane."

"He must know you from the news, or some other source." Elpinoy opened another door, which let out into the parking garage. "Go straight across. It will let out on the same side as the employee entrance, if you know where that is."

"This is where we came in." I turned to look at the man. "Thanks."

"I don't agree with Dr. Dearly's methods, but I do love you all. As foolish as that might sound." Elpinoy waved me on. "Go. Find Miss Dearly. I'll figure out what I can."

"No. Get someplace safe," I told him as I left.

Crossing the parking garage was easy—the guardhouse was empty, and I suspected maybe everybody'd been recalled to deal with the "hostage situation" on the eleventh floor. Just as I finished strapping Michael into the Rolls, though, a new and immediate siren went off, and I looked up to see black-clad soldiers spilling into the garage from all sides and a reinforced door lowering to block off the way we'd come in.

"Brilliant," I muttered as I slammed his door shut and ran to the driver's side. They must have finally started paying attention to the security cameras. I was trapped.

Luckily, again—I could shoot my way out.

By the time I'd gotten into position behind the steering wheel, the soldiers were converging on me, shouting and shooting rubber rounds, the bullets traveling fast enough to shatter the windows of Sam's beloved Rolls. A few slammed into my chest, doing little aside from compounding my anger. I turned on the engine and reached under the ignition, opening the console Sam had told me about. Blindly, as I gunned the engine and started moving, I pushed a few buttons.

The railguns went off, without a hitch. Lightning seemed to leap from them, and a sound like thunder rolled through the car. I swear the entire thing lifted off the asphalt. I hit the button again and again. The projectiles slammed through the lowered door, punching a broad, combined hole in it for which I drove like a madman, swerving to avoid the soldiers in front of me as best I could. I managed to pull off a couple of maneuvers Nora would beg to hear about in detail later and shot out of the building, the ruined door scraping the top of the car.

As far as I could tell, as I peeled out onto the employee road, I hadn't actually hit anybody—but I'd sure as hell scared them. It took a minute for the guards to regroup. By then I was well on my way, and I slowed down just a tad, hoping to lure them out. Sure enough, a few seconds later a couple of massive armored trucks appeared behind me. This time they didn't shoot—though their exterior speakers were on overdrive. *"Pull over!"*

"Let's go, boys," I said as I floored it again. Beside me, Michael shifted in his seat belt, moaning. Okay, this was no longer a "hostage situation." It was now a full-fledged *hostage situation*. Kidnapping, too. And extortion. And assault. And . . . was it only vandalism? Seemed like blowing a hole in somebody's building deserved a bigger word than that.

Maybe I'd wait for the money to hit my account before I gave him back, after all. A million seemed fair.

33 • Laura

I awoke to find myself bound hand and foot, like the living girl next to me.

For some reason, I found it hard to care.

For the longest time, I didn't open my eyes or move. I just listened. I could hear the camp becoming a carnival once more, zombies gossiping as preparations were made. None of them seemed to know what was coming, but they must have thought it would surely be thrilling, since the stage was being assembled. I heard the pieces being unloaded from the carriage next to our tent, dead men laughing as they hauled them past.

In contrast, the living girl never stopped moving or talking. She didn't cry, she didn't scream, but fought the ropes that held her, her body twisting endlessly back and forth across the pallets. She called my name repeatedly, but I never responded. She got the same reaction from Smoke.

"Smoke? Are you all right?" He didn't speak. The girl cursed, and tried me again. "Laura? Listen to me. *Look* at me. Laura!"

"She won't help you." Hagens reentered the tent, and I opened my eyes to find her smirking. "She knows better. She knows she's going to die tonight."

That was it. I did know. And it had frozen me.

"Oh, do shut up," Nora said, turning herself around to glare at the woman.

Hagens seemed to obey her, striding across the tent until she could kneel beside Smoke. His legs weren't bound, but his wrists were connected by rope to the tent pole. She corrected that, using a second length of rope to tie his ankles together. "Sorry about this, but I need to make sure you don't get away again."

"You can't keep him here," Nora said. "If he gets free, if he starts the plague again, there'll be a backlash against the dead. Innocent zombies will be hurt."

Hagens rose and ran the rope to the tent pole, tethering it there. That done, she studied Nora, who glared defiantly up at her. "Innocent zombies are already being hurt, you little fool. Now it's time for payback."

"Payback? How?" Nora tossed her black hair out of her face.

"Fear," Hagens said, smiling sickly. "Just as you said—now that we have him back, we could start the plague again. And fear can paralyze even the strongest person, the strongest tribe." I bent my head.

"You underestimate people," Nora responded. As she spoke she tried to catch my eye.

"Do I?" Hagens knelt down and dug her nails into Nora's wrists, where her struggles had already reddened her skin. The girl twisted anew, this time in pain. "When I made my way out of the Siege, I was scared for my life. I thought I got used to the fact that I'm dead a long time ago, but the living made me feel that terror all over again. I have been frightened for too long."

"I don't blame you for feeling that way!" Nora tried to shake her wrists free. "But this isn't the way to make up for it!"

"How do I make up for it, then?" Hagens's voice was low, al-most friendly, and that frightened me. "How do I make up for it, when humans are still trying to control me? Us? When they sought me out, and had the audacity to act like I should lift a *finger* to help them?"

Nora searched her eyes. "What do you mean? Coalhouse talked about that—is Company Z in danger?"

Hagens made a derisive noise. "Like I'd tell you."

"If you don't tell me, tell the others! Bram fought for you! If you'd told him about this, he would have helped you!"

"We're beyond that now." Hagens shifted closer to Nora and let go of her wrists, causing the girl to try and back up. Her bindings wouldn't let her get far. "I don't want to infect the entire nation. I don't want to wipe humanity off the face of the earth, end civilization as we know it. I'm not that stupid. I will keep Smoke very, very close to me. I just want my people to be safe, him included. I have fought, and screamed, and killed to get to a place where I can protect the dead. I have my own army now. Humans leave us alone? Humans let us live out the rest of our limited days in peace? No one gets hurt."

"What about me, then?" Nora demanded. "You still haven't told me."

"Smoke is my sword." Hagens cast her eyes down at the huddled prisoner. "You can be my shield. I served the New Victorian army with all my heart, and that same army turned around and told its living members that I was to be hunted, destroyed. I followed Griswold loyally, and he left me to die. I came to a new city, tried to build a new life, and still I was chased through the streets. You will make that stop!"

"I'm sorry they did that," Nora said. She was white as a sheet, saucer-eyed, but still she argued. "I'm on your side. Why won't you believe me?"

"Who said I don't believe you?" Hagens shook her head. "We might agree, but we are still fundamentally *different*. That's the point. That's the thing people need to be reminded of, and I can do that through you. Griswold loves you. The army loves your father. At the very least, you can send a message to them. So I'm *not* going to kill you, not unless I have to." She caught Nora's chin and her injured shoulder, squeezing both until Nora was forced to release a cry. "And if I do? It'll be death by a thousand bites. If the army comes after me, or anyone from Z-Comp, I'm going to let every member of the Changed snack on you. Hundreds of shallow little bites, one at a time, while you're still alive. What's left of you will be so ugly even Griswold will be too disgusted to look at it. It will haunt him until he dies—like the faces of the people he left behind should."

Nora's eyes rounded, her chest starting to fall and rise rapidly. She tried to turn her body, writhing uselessly in Hagens's direction. "Notice how you only say this crap when I'm tied up or Bram's there to hold me back? What're *you* afraid of?"

"So *brave*," cooed Hagens. "And so stupid." Music started to play outside, pounding drums accompanied by loud, looping cries of celebration. "It's starting! We're having a little party before we head to one of those mansions out there, take it over, and use the richies' equipment to let the humans of the world know who's got the upper hand now. Because I don't want anyone to get hurt. I don't want anyone to come near us." Nora glowered at her. Hagens laughed, before turning to me. "And you. You I'm just going to get rid of. A lesson for the others. Get ready for the compost heap."

With that, she stomped out of the tent, leaving us alone. The minute she was gone, Nora hissed, "Laura!"

This time I looked at her. Her face was dirty, her eyes bright. "What do you want?"

"The obvious," Nora said. "We have to get out of here. We have to warn people!"

"We can't," I said, turning away from her.

"Yes, we can!" Nora said. "You don't know me, and I don't expect you to feel sorry for me. But there has to be at least one person in this camp you want to help. We can get out of here. There's always a way."

"We can't. No one can." I turned back to her. "I can't believe anyone anymore. Hagens killed my sisters. She's turned the Changed against humanity. I thought Coalhouse was sent to help, but he only made it worse. Mártira was the only person I could believe—I even believed her when I knew she was lying!"

And I had to admit it now. She'd lied to me. About so many things.

Looking deeply into my eyes, the girl said, "Coalhouse didn't kidnap me. I came to protect him." She leaned her head in Smoke's direction. "I swear."

Confused, I said, "Why? Why would you do something like that?"

"Because Hagens is right. Smoke needs someone to look out for him." She swallowed. "After tonight, if Hagens goes through with this, there's no turning back. Your people will be hunted down. The authorities could be on their way here right now. If she goes near any of the houses around here, the cops will come, the army. The very thing that angered her to this point—she's *making* it happen again. Help me get Smoke out of here, and I will help you save whoever you want to save."

Her words struck me as very odd. "You would do that?"

"Of course I would!"

The music picked up outside, and Allende started to sing, female voices providing a haunting backup chorus. I shuddered, for tonight his song sounded like a chant for the great god Moloch, like the start of a human sacrifice. He sang of punishing the humans, of blood for lifeless blood, an eye for a rotting eye.

His song told a story I didn't want to hear.

"What are you waiting for?" Nora asked, and her question hung around me, heavy, suffocating—because I had no answer for it. Hagens had asked me the same thing, and I'd had no answer then. I'd waited and waited for somebody else to rescue me. I'd waited and waited to see how the tale would unfold, never lifting a hand to try and influence it. I'd taken everything at face value, and so eagerly.

At last I made my decision. "How?"

"Turn around. I'll get your knots, you get mine."

I did, and Nora wormed closer to me and got to work. After ten minutes or so I felt the rope go slack, shook off my fetters, and returned the favor. Nora went still, waiting until I'd loosened them just enough to press her fingers together and wriggle her slender wrists free. "Thank you," she said, rubbing them, shaking the blood back into her arms.

"What do we do?" I asked fearfully as I untied the ropes at my feet.

"Tell me who we're going out there to find."

"Dog and Abuelo," I decided. "But if you think the army might come again . . . I don't know how to get everyone else out of here. Some of them think humans killed Mártira." Shame crackled through me. I should have told someone, done something sooner. Now there was no time to figure out who was truly with Hagens and who had merely bought her lies.

"Fire," Smoke said. At the sound of his wet voice, we both turned to look at him. He raised his head, and his eyes were more alert than I'd ever seen them. "Fire makes everyone run. Like little ants."

"He's right." Nora was immediately game. "We could set the tents on fire, the stage. Everyone might scatter. At least Hagens and her lackeys would have to deal with it before setting their sights on the houses. We'd have time to get to one of them, to warn people."

Rushing over to Smoke to undo his ropes, I said, "There are bonfires."

Nora headed for the tent flap and peered out. "They parked Coalhouse's carriage out there. Come on."

*   *   *

After tucking Smoke into the carriage, Nora looked for the keys. She cursed. "They must have taken them. Do you know how to hot-wire a carriage?"

"No. Dog does."

"Great. Wait here, okay, Smoke?" She shut the door. "Lead the way."

Clutching my plants about my body, I tried to think. Dog and Abuelo were probably in the tent I'd shared with them before Hagens had turned me into her abused pet. Careful to keep to the shadows, I led Nora to the west, across the green grass of the field, both of us doing our best to keep our heads down and our eyes open at the same time. The camp had been set up in a horse-shoe shape, with two rows of tents and carriages interspersed with fires. The stage was set up at the point farthest from us, the music going strong. Most of the zombies seemed to be gathered down there, but we picked our way behind the tents nonetheless, ducking under their supporting ropes, on alert for guards.

Finding the tent we needed, I told Nora to wait outside for a second. Inside, I miraculously found Dog and Abuelo sitting to-gether before a kerosene stove—but also someone else. A girl named Ruby, seemingly asleep.

Quietly, I waved Nora in, before tiptoeing across the pallets. "We're leaving," I whispered to Abuelo. "Come on."

"Leaving?" he said, before looking at Nora. Seeing her, it didn't take him long to get on board. "Oh, *leaving*. Well, s'bout bloody time."

Abuelo settled himself into his cart. Dog moved to push him, but I waved him out of the way and took over. We started to make our way stealthily back toward the entrance—but not stealthily enough.

"What's going on?" Ruby sat up, rubbing at her eyes. She was a young woman, her gray-frosted skin formerly the same color as her brown hair.

We all froze. For a minute, we just stared at one another. It wasn't until she stood, her eyes narrowing in Nora's direction, that I blurted out, "Hagens killed Mártira and Claudia."

"What are you talking about?" Ruby said incredulously. "What are you doing?"

Nora stepped forward. "This tent's going to turn into an inferno in two minutes. Come with us, or run away."

Ruby was still for a second longer, before answering with a shocked, "My brother. I have to find him."

"Do it, and get out of here." Nora pulled on my sleeve. "Come on."

As we made our way out of the tent and behind it, taking the ill-lit, long way back to the carriage, I found myself . . . happy. If nothing else, we'd warned one other person. My heart was glad for it.

Upon reaching Coalhouse's carriage, Nora helped load Abuelo into the backseat and put Dog to work. Together we returned to one of the nearby fires, gathering pendulous skirtfuls of the kindling materials stacked beside it. As we loaded up on makeshift ammunition, finally returning bearing sputtering torches, Dog busied himself with a wad of wires ripped from the console. In the end he got it working, the carriage purring to life.

"Can you drive?" Nora asked him, as we lowered all the windows in preparation for takeoff. Dog shook his head, and showed her his missing hand. "Can *anyone* drive?"

No was the general consensus.

Nora took a breath, passed me her torch, and went for the driver's seat. "Better buckle up your seat belts, then."

Abuelo and Smoke remained in the back, with Dog scooting between them. I took the passenger seat. Everyone aside from Dog and Nora bore a torch, which we held outside the open windows. Once we were all secure, Nora started to move the carriage tentatively forward. Jerking only a few times, she was soon driving at a slow pace toward the back line of tents. All of them appeared empty, their residents gathered at the stage.

As she did so, I instructed Abuelo to lean out of his window, take a piece of wood from the floor, and light it before throwing it at any target he deemed fit. His eyes sparkled. "Oh, it's like Christmas in the old days!"

Smoke, meanwhile, needed no instruction. He was already merrily lighting and hurling new torches in every direction, his movements spastic, almost manic. I was reminded of when he used to sit near the fireplace and watch old toys and chestnuts burn, transfixed by the flames.

One by one, working together, we set the tents ablaze. We tried not to target the carriages, aiming instead for fabric and wood—anything that would burn. In a way, it was beautiful. Cathartic. It felt like I was laying to waste everything that had tormented me, everything that had ever hurt me. And it seemed to work. The night air was soon perfumed with the smell of cinders, haunted by the sounds of people running, screaming. In the distance, dark shapes darted between the flames, fleeing for the nearby forest, the road.

"We're doing it!" Nora declared, turning for the stage. She stopped the carriage with a shudder and braced her arms, looking back. "Now. The boss battle."

Looking at the stage, I lifted a new piece of wood from the pile at my feet. "Drive fast, and then loop away. Don't look back."

"Plan to. I apologize in advance if any of you die for good." Nora steadied her arm and threw the carriage back into drive, before flooring it.

The three of us with ammo lit up and leaned as far as we dared out the windows. The wind rippled through my hair, my leaves, littering a trail of petals and torch sparks behind the carriage. As

Nora drove around the eastern side of the crowd, I could see heads turning to look, hear exclamations. From the stage, Hagens's voice rang out. *"The prisoner is a prisoner no longer! He's been reunited with his people!"*

Then our presence registered, and she turned to look—and realized that, no, the prisoner was hurling fire at his people.

As Nora finally got us to the corner of the stage, I took my own shot—only to watch my torch land amidst the crowd. Unfortunately, it wasn't the only one to do so. None of us were managing to hit the stage, and yet the singers and band members jumped ship anyway, running into the swelling, roiling, confused crowd.

"Get them!" I heard Hagens shriek. *"They have Smoke!"*

Nora gasped and made a sharp left-hand U-turn. "The stage butts right against the trees! I can't drive behind it!"

She tried to start back but it was too late. While the literal Hell the camp had become roared in the background, those loyal to Hagens descended upon Coalhouse's carriage. A mass of dead humanity soon surrounded it, preventing it from moving. Abuelo and I fought back with our torches—I even shoved mine directly into a man's face, almost crying when I heard his terrible scream—only to have them ripped away from us. Soon arms were reaching into the cab, clogging it, hard and grabbing.

Dog huddled on the floor as Nora took a piece of wood and whacked viciously at an arm holding her about the shoulders. As she yelled, "Break the windshield!" it cracked, a zombie jumping atop it from outside.

Then, in one quick, blind instant, Nora's weapon was caught. She didn't let go fast enough. Her arm was pulled into the crowd; teeth sank into her flesh. She cried out in pain and managed to wrench her arm away, her eyes going wide as more blood dripped onto her gown. She looked at me in fear, for a single, ageless second—before fury took over. Mashing both feet down onto the accelerator, she caused the carriage to rev, to buck into the crowd. "I!" she screamed, hammering on the pedal in time with her words, even as more arms reached in, surrounded her, "Will! Not! Die! Here!"

Meanwhile, I looked to the roof, reaching within my gown for Mártira's hair comb. With a scream of my own, I hit the little button that released its concealed blade and slashed the thing upward repeatedly, until I managed to cut my way through the material.

"Give me your torch!" I said to Smoke, who'd managed to keep hold of his. He passed it to me without quibble, and I lunged up through the sliced soft top like a shark victim might cut through the water. Pulling my arm up, I hurled the torch at the stage and screamed, every breath I'd ever taken in life behind the words, *"Hagens killed my sisters!"*

My torch arced high and fell to earth just as quickly, landing amidst Allende's equipment. A second later it burst into flames. As I watched it kindle, I kept screaming the same words, over and over. And after a while I thought they were having some effect, the mob surrounding the cab stilling, wondering.

Then I realized it wasn't me they were wondering at.

Behind me, Smoke was howling like an animal. I turned to see the slimy, half-gone zombie clutching at his body furiously, as if he had caught on fire and sought desperately to extinguish the flames. Twisting to the side, he kicked his legs against the carriage door. The door actually shot into the mob, a cannonball-sized dent in it, clearing a path that widened as zombies fled.

Into that path, Smoke staggered. "Leave me," he said, his voice horrible behind his muzzle, turning up to look at me. "Go!"

"What is the meaning of this?" Hagens fought her way into the cleared area. "You little bitch!"

As she spoke, Smoke started to . . . grow.

He didn't gain any height, but his muscles bulged, his torn, ragged skin doing little to hold them back and hiding nothing. His shirt stretched and began to tear, the seams popping, the gaping front revealing his naked ribs, the muscles around them swelling. Through a gap I could see his heart, also growing, beating furiously.

Part of him was *alive.*

With a roar, his size nearly doubled, he launched himself toward Hagens. She pulled out her gun and let off a rapid salvo, to no effect. Smoke didn't even seem to feel the bullets. He leapt at her and grabbed her by the arm, and she tried to pull herself away, doing little but breaking her own body with a final-sounding crack. As he wound his heavy arm back to deliver a blow, Hagens ducked down and spun away, somehow managing to tear her now flopping arm out of his grasp. She ran for the trees bordering the field, never looking back. Smoke howled again and pursued her, leaving the others to scream and stare.

"Hagens!" someone shouted. "We have to go after her!"

The zombies that had been attacking us scattered like a flock of frightened birds. A wind ripped over my head, fanning the flames consuming the stage. I dropped down into the carriage and looked at Nora, who was wrapping her arm up with a scrap torn from the hem of her dress. "Are you all right?"

"I'm fine," she said, shaken. "But what the hell was that? He's like freaking Edward Hyde! He must have snapped his own skin open. Like a sausage!"

"I don't know," I said, leaning forward to help her tie the bandage. "But we have to get out of here."

Nora nodded, gathered herself, and started off again. The vehicle tentatively moved forward, across the grass, and I took Dog onto my lap to keep him from falling out of the open carriage door. As I did, I noticed the lights from the houses in the distance seemed to be joining us, swarming closer. I stared at the road, trying to understand.

"What is that?" Abuelo said, pointing. He saw it, too.

"Yes! Okay. Hopefully that's the cavalry." Nora looked toward the trees again, and jerked the steering wheel in that direction, speeding up. "Which means we've got cover. Let's see if we can find Coalhouse—and Smoke."

34 • Bram

Michael still hadn't awoken by the time I skidded into the final stretch toward the zombie camp, even though the windows were gone and air was rushing through the car with the force of a small tornado. Elpinoy was handy with that tray of his.

Settling forward, I watched for lights. Soon I came upon them—four carriages driving abreast on the two-lane highway at high speed. I beeped, and the carriages flashed their rear lights in greeting. Samedi had made it, along with the others. For a moment I wished I could send them all back.

Turning around, I sized up the chase situation. I figured I had about five armored black trucks on my rear. Maybe ten. Hard to tell in the dark, but it was plenty.

Ahead of me the carriages slowed and parted, sinking onto their respective shoulders, making room for me. I tapped the accelerator and wedged myself right between them.

"Has Dearly been in touch with you?" Samedi shouted as his window lowered.

"No. I have no idea what we're driving into."

"What's the plan?" the driver of the other carriage called out. It was Ben. Behind him I could see Edgar driving the third,

Franco the fourth. Scanning the carriages, I figured altogether we had about fifteen people. *Cripes.*

"Well, I brought a distraction," I said, pointing back. "These guys are probably itching for a fight by this point, so try not to engage them. Concentrate on finding and subduing Hagens. I'll lead the forces back there through the crowd, try to sow some confusion. Ideally, we want the Changed to surrender, talk to us. We want them wrapped up with a bow when the feds come."

"Don't worry about us," Edgar called out. "We'd die for the zombie cause still, you know that!"

I did, and I didn't want it to happen. Still, I nodded, respect almost overwhelming me. "On second thought," I shouted, turning back to Sam's carriage. "Chas, I need you in here! Think you can jump for it, or do we have to stop?"

The girl didn't hesitate. The back door of Michael's carriage opened, and Chas pushed it into the wind with her legs, Tom bracing her from behind. I reached back and unlatched the rear door, before sending an arm through my open window and catching the edge of it, pulling it forward. Sam and I steadied our respective speeds, and Chas gripped the top of Michael's carriage. It was higher than the car, and she was able to swing herself into the Rolls with a bit of effort. "Ten points for the New Victorian Olympic teaaam!" she shouted, lifting her arms.

"I'll flank east!" Ben shouted.

"That means I call west!" Sam said. As he spoke, Tom passed Chas her rifle, blew her a kiss, and got the back door of Michael's carriage shut. "See you on the other side!"

Speeding up between them, I waited until I saw the first carriage turn off behind me before picking a spot to do the same, plowing over the shoulder, a set of train tracks, and right into the heart of the camp—which appeared to already be in a shambles.

It wasn't until I slowed down a bit that I saw just how much.

The Changed had set up camp in a lightly wooded area just off the side of the road. Tents had once stood there, but most of them had collapsed or caught fire, turning into smoking pools of embers. The stage was set up, and also on fire, the flames rising high into the night sky. Zombies everywhere were running aimlessly, shrieking, obviously terrified for their unlives. Many were piled into and on top of carriages, headed for the road.

"Whoa," Chas said. "You might not have needed Allister's goons after all."

Frightened, I drove on. As the crowd flowed around me, I saw what its members were running from.

Ahead of me stood a wide, muscular zombie—not a wall, not even as tall as me, but a sturdy brick of dead flesh. A born bruiser, a raging zombie pit bull roaring and rushing at anything that caught his attention, galloping back and forth across the open space seemingly at random. "Jesus," I breathed.

Then I noticed an old brown carriage circling him. Coalhouse's. The left rear door was missing, and Laura was leaning out of it with a long bit of wood, thrusting it at any zombies who dared to try and take the big guy on. As the carriage turned to cross in front of him, I saw that Nora was driving. She *was* here. I suddenly felt physically heavy with relief, so heavy I found myself marveling at the scene rather than leaping into immediate action.

Marveling, because what they were doing could only be described as "carriage jousting."

I decided to just go with it.

Before I could do anything else, one of the Changed carriages cut me off, forcing me to brake. At first I thought they'd come for me, but they swiftly rocked away, turning sharply a few yards out and zeroing in on the big zombie and Nora's carriage. The windows of the Changed carriage lowered and two dead men leaned out, guns at the ready.

Relief morphed back into rage. I accelerated, aiming the car for the tree line and hitting the button beneath the dash.

Two more projectiles rocketed out of the railguns. They hit a couple of the trees I was facing right in the middle, cutting them off like a lawn mower would blades of grass. The upper portions came crashing down atop and in front of the carriage in pursuit of Nora, forcing it to a halt, collapsing the roof and exploding the windows outward. Dr. Samedi was officially my patron saint.

Chas was likewise dazzled. "Okay, I know what I want for *my* birthdaaay."

One carriage was taken care of, but now I could see more lights swarming, descending. Allister's men. The AG trucks roared onto the field and swerved to cut off the absconding vehicles, a few connecting, external speakers ordering the zombies to hit the deck and lie with their hands behind their heads. None of them obeyed. The AG drones started to launch smoke bombs and flash-bang grenades, only adding to the confusion.

As if sensing that this would be their last chance, members of the Changed started to regroup and converge on the monster, AG forces in pursuit. I had to move. Throwing myself back into the fray, I moved to circle Coalhouse's carriage, to cut it off or slow it down. It worked, in a rather abrupt fashion. Nora saw me and stood on the brake a mere foot from my car, her eyes widening. I did the same. She opened her door and rushed out, and I ran out to meet her, pulling her off the ground and into my arms.

"You came!" she said, raining kisses over my ear.

"I can't believe you're here!" I pushed her back, looking her over. "What's with the bandages? Where's Coalhouse?"

"We can't find him! But Patient One . . ." She looked off, and I turned to follow her line of sight. The rampaging chewing-tobacco-colored zombie had caught another of his kind, and was using her body to beat another dead man into submission, like an angry child smashing toys together.

"That's *Patient One?*" I said with disbelief.

"He swelled up," she said, working her hands as if to demonstrate this. "I swear. He got mad, and he just got . . . big! You should see what he did to the door!"

Laura ran out to join us, casting her stick aside. "I think he's still half alive." When even Nora looked appalled at this, she explained, "I saw his heart beating as it got bigger."

"Salvez said his vitals looked . . . oh my God. Could he still be alive in there?" I asked the question, but I was pretty sure I didn't want to know.

"We were trying to separate him from the rest, but he won't listen to us now," Nora said. "We lost track of Hagens, but some of them still want him back."

Thinking fast, I pulled Nora up to me again and kissed her hot, gorgeous little mouth before setting her down on the ground. "You guys get out of here. Try to meet up with Samedi. I'll take care of this and get the Allister people out of here."

"Allister? Those guys in the trucks are Allister's people? How . . ."

Looking to the Rolls, I said, "I have bait."

Nora glanced inside the car, and actually grinned slightly upon seeing the unconscious Michael. "Okay." Sobering, she said, "He doesn't want to do this. I swear. He tried to protect us. And Coalhouse didn't mean to start this."

"I believe you."

Nora looked into my eyes for a second longer, before taking Laura by the hand and pulling her back to Coalhouse's carriage. I made sure they got off safely before sliding into my car and tearing Michael's cravat off.

Now it was my turn to play. But instead of carriage jousting, my game was more like "car bullfighting."

"Hey!" I yelled, laying on the horn as I drove toward Patient One. He turned to look at me, his face terrible in its rage. "Hey, you smell blood, buddy?" I waved the cravat out of the window, hoping he'd pick up on the scent. He seemed to, bobbing in my direction. "Yeah, c'mon! Fresh meat!"

Directing my car farther off, I drove at a slower pace. Patient One ran after me, even resorting to running on all fours at one point, like an incensed gorilla. The AG guards almost cornered us a few times, showering nonlethal smoke and light grenades in our direction, but thankfully no bullets. Relatively unscathed, together we burst through a clump of undergrowth and out onto what I figured was another field, but soon realized was probably some well-heeled royal lord's enormous backyard.

Spinning to a stop, I grabbed one of the rifles sitting in the back. "Drive," I told Chas. "Go back, get the attention of the AGs, and get them out of here. Convince them Michael's being taken somewhere else!"

"Right!" she said, moving to climb into the front with her gun.

Leaping out of the car with the cravat, I tried to lead Patient One farther away from the campsite. The Rolls veered off, Chas taking control. "P One . . . Smoke . . . it's me. Bram. We met before, remember? We need to talk."

Growling low, pulling himself up to his full height, the bestial zombie stomped toward me. He'd lost his mask somewhere. "Flesh," he rumbled. "Hungry."

"No. We don't do that," I told him, showing him the cravat. I let it flutter from my hand and he jumped forward, capturing it and burying his nose in it. When he found it wasn't flesh, he snarled. "We don't bite the living. That causes fights."

The zombie paused. "Don't like fights."

At least he was more talkative in this form. "I don't either. I like the living. Got a girl who's living—in fact, I heard you stood up for her." He turned his eyes on me. "Nora? Thank you. Thank you for protecting Nora."

"Book girl." I didn't understand this, but he spoke the words with a sort of . . . peace. I figured that was progress. "Like book girl."

"I like her, too. She likes me. So we have that in common, right?"

Smoke took a step nearer, examining me. In the dim light, I could see Laura'd spoken true—his heart was beating madly behind his bare ribs, his lungs fluttering. For a moment I forgot myself and stared at the spectacle, both disgusted and filled with pity.

As I watched, Smoke lifted his head and inhaled deeply, scenting something. Then he took off, resorting to all fours as he rounded my side, running into the night. I cursed, turning around to see where he was headed. I had to chase him. Obviously he could be talked down, if I just had more time.

Something clicked behind me. "Don't move, maggot."

Closing my eyes, I muttered, "Allister."

"Turn around. Slowly." I did so. Michael stood before me, Chas's rifle in his hands. He was even more beaten up than I'd left him—he must have come to and jumped out of the freaking car. Chas must still be driving, AG guards on her tail. He aimed it at my head, narrowing his eyes. "Drop your weapon."

"No way." I aimed my rifle at his chest instead. "Look, we can't do this now. That was Patient One. We can't let him get away!"

"I don't care. If the plague starts again, my father will handle it. Nobody needs Dearly." He released the safety and steadied his finger on the trigger. "You're going to pay for what you've done to me tonight. Assault. Kidnapping. Extortion. Should I go on?"

"I figured I would," I admitted. "They might throw me in jail for everything, deport me, execute me. But Nora's safe, so you know what? I don't care. I'll take whatever comes my way like a man. I'm already dead. You can't do worse to me, you little thug!"

Before I could say another word, Michael screamed and pulled the trigger. I felt myself hit the ground, and figured he must have shot true. Above me, the world went black.

And yet, I could still hear Michael screaming.

I tried to sit up and found I couldn't. There was something in the way. Then the pressure was relieved, the world took shape, and Smoke let me up in order to pin Michael down, bellowing like some sort of prehistoric beast.

Quickly, I sat up and launched myself at them. "No! Let him go!"

"Allister's runt!" Smoke howled. *"You will burn!"*

"Get him off! Get him off!" Michael thrashed, attempting to keep the zombie's mouth away from him. P One was biting at him furiously, catching clothes, hair, everything except the meat he so desperately wanted.

Reaching out, I found Michael's rifle. Turning it around, I let off a shot into Smoke's knee, the one I knew was artificial. He yelped with surprise and rolled to the side, and I jumped on top of him, grabbing his shoulders and shaking him. "No! He likes book girl, too! He likes book girl!" I hated to say it, but I figured it was Allister's only shot.

Smoke went still, breathing harshly. "Does?"

"Yes!" I looked back toward the trees and saw that the fight was still going on. There were no AG forces to be seen, and it looked like my men were gaining control, a few of them standing sentinel over groups of Changed with their hands on their heads. "He brought men here to find her. Look!"

Smoke followed my gaze, and seemed to contemplate what I said. As he did, his form began to shrink. It was as if his muscles were bladders full of air or water that was now being let out, leaving his flesh sagging, broken. He slumped down on the velvety grass, his eyes rolling around.

"It's okay," I told him. "Let me take you back to book girl, okay? To the doctors? Remember Dr. Dearly? Dr. Salvez?"

Smoke said nothing. After a few minutes I stood and helped him to his feet. He was now as weak as a kitten, almost rubbery, barely able to control his own movements. The transformation, if that's what you could call it, had taken everything out of him, shattered what remained of his body.

Michael stood off to the side, weak on his feet, his face like a canvas splashed with red paint. I could have said a lot of things right then. I could have reminded him just how many times I'd saved his sorry life. I could've asked him how it felt to be hunted.

Instead I walked over and punched him one last time, knocking him unconscious again. I told myself it was for his own good.

By the time I found the other carriages parked in a grove of dark, narrow trees just a stone's throw from where the fighting had taken place, Company Z owned the campsite. When I joined them, Nora ran to me again, and I shrugged off Smoke, dropped Michael, and curled her in against my chest, shutting my eyes and squeezing her almost painfully close. I was tired. I hadn't seen so much action in months. I was fairly calm now that she was safe, but I needed to get myself under full control.

I was a hypocrite. A walking contradiction. Both alive and dead, both a leader and nothing like it, both with my friends and occasionally against them, both happy to work with the living and ready to fight them for every scrap of extended time I could get.

Nora was the only thing that made sense. She was the only unchanging thing in my universe. She was my lodestar. No matter which way my emotions and circumstances and the impulses of my dead, dying, *trying* body pulled me, no matter how many mistakes I made, she was always true north. Sometimes I'd side with the dead, sometimes with the living, but always with her.

"I love you," I whispered in her ear.

She kissed my Adam's apple. "God, I love you."

I pulled back, only to see that she was crying. I wiped her tears away with my thumbs, and then scrubbed at her face a bit. "You're a mess. Anyone'd think you'd been through a war, or something." She laughed.

"What did you do with my car?" Samedi said weakly, looking around. "That was my retirement."

"Chas has it. Did most of the AG people follow it?"

"I think they all did," Nora said. "I actually don't think they got many of the Changed. They never left their trucks."

From within Coalhouse's carriage, Laura and Dog emerged. Laura released a sob when she saw what was happening in the field—most of the Changed rounded up, with a few lying dead on the ground. "Oh God. This is my fault."

"What do you mean?" I asked.

She crushed a handful of her own roses. "The zombies here—Hagens lied to them. But I didn't know who believed what, aside from a few, and so I thought I couldn't trust anyone . . ."

Nora moved to put her hands on the flower girl's shoulders. "You did well. I heard what you said. We got some people out, or gave them the chance to get out. That's all we could do."

"Good," I said, relieved. "Where's Hagens?"

"She's not here," Laura said, voice dropping. "She got away."

"So we still have her to worry about. Great."

As I spoke, I heard sirens. Turning to look, I saw a new herd of lights approaching. Army. Soon the advance guard was driving onto the field, speakers activating. *"Show us your hands! Remain calm!"* My men did so.

"Okay. Everyone, we'll get our stories straight later. Right now, we need to move." I gained Laura's attention. "Go out to the field. Tell the soldiers which of those people, if any, are guilty of being truly in league with Hagens. If any committed a crime on her orders. And tell them P One is being taken back to the boats, and that they can call on me if he doesn't make it."

"All right." Laura looked at her hands, then back at me. "Thank you."

"Don't thank me." And then I gave voice to what I'd been thinking since the night at The Failing Liver. "After I finish this, I'll find you. But until then, *you* need to help your people. Anyone who was just caught up in this, anyone who's willing to work with the living—you have to look out for them."

Laura nodded solemnly. Dog edged closer to her, as well as Ben, who offered to escort her. As they headed for the field, Nora turned her eyes up to me. "Going after Coalhouse?"

I squeezed her hand. "Yeah."

"He didn't kidnap me, Bram. I told him to take me. It was the only way he and Smoke were going to get out of the ship alive. He's mixed up, but he was trying to save lives. He said something about Company Z being in danger, and Hagens might've had the Changed attack the ships to get Smoke back."

"Then it's even more important I find him." Leaning down, I kissed her again. She wrapped her slight arms about my neck, pulling me to her just as passionately as I pressed into her embrace. She tasted of a hundred sweet things and just a hint of the blood passing beneath my cold lips, pulsing through the living flesh of hers, a mere membrane away. When she let me go, I said, "I promise I'll come back to you. As long as I have one leg and an eyeball left, I will *always* return to you. Do you believe me?"

"Yes." She stroked my face. "You did it once before."

"Avoid the army. Go home. Take Smoke away yourselves—I don't want him flipping out right now. Get Allister to talk about the Roe bombing and the masks." Her jaw dropped. "I'll be back as soon as I can."

A few minutes later I left in Coalhouse's carriage, alone. After all that had just happened, the vehicle cab, the field, and the night itself seemed far too quiet, far too empty. For a minute I wondered where I should head, what I should look for. Coalhouse might be on foot, and had 360 degrees open to him.

From the dark, something else called out to me. Something old, practically primal, yet extant—it wasn't a memory, or an emotion, or even a thought. It was something real. Something that sang to my very flesh, to every instinct within me.

It was the sound of a train headed down the tracks.

Somehow, I was willing to bet he'd follow them. It's what I would have done. Tracks were a surer bet than roads. They had to lead somewhere, eventually, if you just followed them long enough. There were fewer forks, fewer directions to keep track of.

After a few moments I shut off my lights and turned around, heading away from the camp, keeping a low profile in case the AG guards were still around. I decided to follow the tracks to the north. If I didn't encounter him in a few hours, I'd try heading south.

World ending or not, tired or not, I still had work to do.

35 • Nora

During the drive back to New London, everyone took turns filling the group in. I begged to be told about the Roes, but Dr. Chase insisted I speak first. So I told them about my encounter with Smoke, Coalhouse's flawed reasoning, and Hagens's plans.

Only then did Tom tell me what Michael had done and planned to do. About the Ratcatcher. He had the letters on him. I was so angry it physically hurt. I wanted to murder the boy, unconscious though he was, and Tom had to trap me against his short, muscular body in the backseat to get me under control. After two minutes of struggling I gave in, leaned back against the carriage door and tried not to cry. I didn't speak. I couldn't. It was all too much.

We went to the boats first, and dropped Smoke off. He looked relieved to be back in his cage. I told Papa and a handful of army officials what had happened, what Smoke had said about Allister's preserve—everything but the information I'd newly heard about Michael and the masks. I wanted to get it out, because I could tell, from the tightness with which my father held me and the tremor in his voice, that I would soon be Belize-bound.

"You're leaving," he finally said, as he saw to my wounds. "I love you, but you're leaving."

"I know." And I knew it was pointless to fight him, at least at the moment. Because I also knew what was awaiting me at home. What we still had to deal with.

Interrogation. The whole truth, at last.

It was close to dawn by the time we got everyone assembled in the celestial parlor. I wanted to wait until Bram returned to talk to Michael, but we didn't have time. The Allisters had to be going nuts, wondering where their son was. Of course, if they had been keeping an eye on him, none of this might have happened. Maybe we had all the time in the world.

Lopez stood in the corner. He'd been waiting at the house for hours. Dr. Chase and Dr. Samedi claimed chairs, while the Roes took the couch. Pamela was reluctant to leave my side, and I was reluctant to let her. She kept moving toward her seated family to offer them support, then back to me, sweeping back and forth across the floor like a pendulum. I figured her motions mirrored her mood—happy to see everyone safe, anxious about what was to come.

Michael sat on the piano bench, his hands unbound, his suit crusted with blood and his face swollen. It actually improved his appearance, by my reckoning.

Finally, Tom showed up with Renfield and a living boy—the last people to enter. The boy was lanky, crazy-haired, and seemed to buzz on his feet, all energy and anticipation.

"Who's that?" Michael demanded.

"Havelock Moncure," the boy said. He looked at the Roes, and managed to contain his enthusiasm. "Reporter."

"Who starts?" The situation felt almost informal. My best

friends, my mentors, people whom I admired—they were all congregated in my house, drinking coffee and tea, waiting for the blood sport to commence. The Dearly version of a high-class salon.

"Yes, what's going on?" Mr. Roe asked on behalf of his family.

"I won't talk," Michael said, glaring at Havelock. "This is pointless. If you let me go now, I'll convince my father not to get you all for kidnapping."

"So you don't want to talk about the bombing?" Tom asked. "Remember, I was there."

Pamela slowly stood up. "Bombing?"

Michael rolled his eyes. "Someone shut the baggage up."

Tom made like he was going to start the Pain Olympics, Pamela gunning for his side, but I held up a hand. "No. No more punching." I swept toward Allister. "I'm tired. Tell us what you know. Because you're not getting out of here until you do."

"I won't," he said again, turning his eyes to mine. "In fact, I can't."

"Do you honestly think you're going to get away with this?" I said, my face heating. "You think we're not going to go to the police?"

Michael's eyes widened. "You can't go to the police. They won't believe you anyway." And then they narrowed. "If you do, I'll drag your deadmeat beau down with me. I told him that in the field. I can get him for about ten different charges. You should see what he did to Allister Genetics!"

Fear fluttered in my heart, but I knew Bram could handle anything Michael threw at him. "I'm not talking about just you. I'm talking about all the people you're working with, whoever they are. We don't need the coppers. We're going to bring the masks down, and we'll be sure to tell each one who referred us."

"More than that," Samedi said, almost casually, "think of the info we do have. Who's been snitching on you, Mikey? Who's been selling you out? And who else might he have told?"

Allister looked around at everyone, assessed every avenue of escape. He realized the truth of our words.

And he started spilling.

He told us about the Murder—that the group had been formed months ago and only just become active. He told us about the system that allowed its members to exchange paper notes by numbering and hiding them behind a false stone in a pub fireplace, their attempts at intra-group anonymity. He told us about the zombies he'd seen get killed and all the living sympathizers he'd seen get hurt. About his plans for Bram.

When Lopez heard about the Roes, his fists curled eloquently, and he chose to walk to the very edge of the room. When Michael got to the death of Mr. Delgado, Isambard very nearly tackled him, and Samedi had to step forward and hold the boy back until he got himself under control.

Although I knew it would threaten every scintilla of my own control, I looked at Pam.

She didn't move. Not even when Issy flew past her. She stared at Michael almost blankly, her eyes a maelstrom of unfocused emotion. Behind her, her mother wailed and her father chose to hold her, even as his eyes threatened to reduce Michael to a heap of smoking embers. But Pamela didn't move.

"Why?" she asked. "Just . . . why?"

Michael acted like her question was irrelevant. "If I had any hope that you'd move up in the world, marry a lord, I would have waited. I would've taken you down socially." He frowned slightly. "But I don't. You could remain low and dirt poor for the rest of your life. I had to hit you where it hurt. Because you hurt me, endangered me, disrespected me."

It took every ounce of willpower to remain where I was. "It

was all me, then," Pamela said numbly. "I did this. I brought this on my family."

"*You* didn't do it," I said. "Don't you dare believe him."

"I did do it. By ever liking him." Suddenly, Pamela flew into frenzied action, racing across the floor. She kicked the piano bench out from under Allister and put her boot into his chest when he tried to crawl back across the floor, causing him to cough violently. "But thank you! You hear me? *Thank you!*" she screeched into his face. "Because I know what my life's been leading up to now. Oh, yes. You've given my pathetic little life meaning! Because I am going to use the lady's education I should never have had, and the contacts I never should have made, and I am going to do whatever I must to remain in high society, because I'm going to haunt and torment you for the rest of your miserable life! I don't care what the cops and the courts do to you—you will never atone for this. I will make you fear everything that wears a skirt, including dogs dressed up for Halloween, do you hear me?!"

Mr. Roe ran over and grabbed his daughter by the elbow, urging her back. She didn't fight him, but continued to stare at the prone Michael with a terrifying intensity. I was honestly scared. And impressed.

"Enough of this. Everyone ask their final questions." Lopez finally strode across the room, reaching down and hauling Michael up by his collar. Danger clouded his usually tepid voice like water louching absinthe. "I'm taking him to the police."

"You don't dare!" Michael yelled. "My father will end you if you do!"

Lopez turned Michael around and eyed him steadily, silently. Behind the gentleman's normally kind eyes glittered something unspeakably cold. "You think I fear your father? Oh, young man. You have so much to learn."

"Wait." Tom stepped forward. "The other members of this thing. Make him write a list. His dad's rich, yeah? If he manages to get it covered up, we'll need the other names."

"They cover their faces!" Michael argued. "I don't know any of them!"

"Do you want to be the only one who goes down?" I demanded. "Don't you at least want to give up some details? Because I don't think you're man enough to take all of the responsibility for this."

At this, Michael paused, his eyes agonized. In the end I was right. On my dead mother's stationery, rescued from a seldom-opened writing desk in the corner, he wrote out what he could remember of the letters he'd been sent. He didn't know any names, or how many Brothers were out there—a fact that chilled me.

"What about the 'Green Jacket' you mentioned?" I asked, studying the page.

"I don't know who he is." Suddenly, Michael reached out and grabbed my hand. Disgusted, I cast it off and backed up. "I did it for you, Miss Dearly. Like I do everything for you."

"You're sick in the head," I announced. "You are ill. You need help."

My words seemed to cut him to the quick. Five minutes later, after making a copy of the written information, Lopez escorted him out of the parlor. Even from the back, Michael looked broken, frightened.

Good.

Havelock shut off his recorder, thanking us profusely for "the story of his career" and refusing the money Ren offered to cover the chip Bram still owed him. He took photographs of the pages instead, and agreed not to leak any details about us in exchange for first rights to any other Murder members we caught.

When he was gone, I spoke. "I'm sorry for all of this. What can I do?"

Mr. Roe took a while to respond. "You have nothing to be sorry for, Miss Dearly." He looked at his weeping wife. "And there's nothing you can do. But at least we know."

"What do *we* do now?" Mrs. Roe asked tearfully.

"Go to Marblanco," Pamela said, turning to look at them. "For my sake, as well as yours. I'm sick. I have nightmares. I can't do this anymore. I want to get out of the city, at least for a while— please. Look at what's happened."

Before her father could say anything, I added, "If Lopez will let me, I'll go, too. We could ask him later." I glanced at Dr. Chase, who smiled knowingly. "Papa's going to insist I get out of the city for a while, after all this."

Mr. Roe took a moment but nodded. I moved to hug Pamela, and I could feel the physical relief this small motion caused. She clutched me back, her arms weak.

If we were going anywhere, we were going together.

36 • Bram

For the first time since sniffing out Nora back at base, I hunted another being by using my in-death "gifts." I hated doing it—nothing like scenting someone like a dog, turning your head at every noise like a parrot to make you feel inhuman—but I had no other options.

Driving in the dark with the lights off, practically creeping, I sought Coalhouse. After an hour I came upon a place where the railroad tracks crossed a country road. A series of painted steel signs told me where it led—to a Territorial park including something called the Cave of the Glowing Skulls. Sounded like the sort of place a desperate zombie would head for. Hell, if I'd been in the same condition, I probably would've gone there to get my mope on, too. On a hunch, I decided to go for it.

My hunch served me well. After another half hour I picked up Coalhouse's trail, the faint odor of a passing dead body. I followed it off the main road and onto a series of narrow back roads that eventually turned into hiking trails, necessitating the abandonment of his carriage. My farm boy powers of observation took over, and I noticed places where the ground had been disturbed, branches broken. I took my rifle with me, as well as a first aid kit and a flashlight I found in the glove compartment, and marched into the trees.

Morning was threatening by the time I found the infrastructure leading to the cave. The entire area'd been landscaped for tourists, with informational booths and catwalks everywhere. There were no day-trippers to be seen, but Coalhouse's scent was strong. After drinking from a nearby river and splashing some water over my neck, I followed it to a lee in the rocky terrain. Another sign told me that it, small and insignificant as it appeared to be, was the entrance to the actual cave.

Given my track record with mines, I was reluctant to enter. I took a few seconds to compose myself before making my way inside.

"Coalhouse?" I shouted, flicking on the flashlight. The light bounced off of a series of unremarkable rocks. Tramping farther in, I soon came to a metal walkway with railings, which I followed into a chamber rife with long, slick deposits of calcite. "Anybody home?" I could hear something scuffling, rough, far off. Could be rats, bats—could be my friend. Steadying myself on the catwalk, I kept going.

The first skull I saw startled me, my light calling its shape out of the darkness unexpectedly, making it appear to shine. Then I found another, and another. Soon I was passing one every few feet, as well as an assortment of other human bones. According to the signs outside, the remains of these people were ancient, pre–ice age, more rock now than anything human. The thought crossed my mind that bone really *was* no more than rock to begin with, that we were all built from the inside out like living statues, like animated clay. God, death was starting to make me morbid.

"Bram?"

Turning on the catwalk, the beam from my flashlight fell on

the half-empty face of Coalhouse. "There you are," I said reflexively, before my voice dropped into a well of silence. I wasn't sure what else to say.

Coalhouse was in the same boat. His clothing was torn and dirty, and he appeared to be unarmed. He stood before me, wordless and weary, his right arm slack. In his left hand he held a flickering lighter.

"Are you hurt?" He shook his head. After a beat I tried, "Are you ready to come home?"

I might've rattled off a list of insults at him, he looked so wounded by my question. "I can't."

"Sure you can." I bent down and placed my gun on the catwalk. "You think I'm here to do a citizen's arrest or something? I just came here to find you."

Coalhouse watched me as I straightened up, his lips quivering. "No." His lighter died and he tried to get it started again, eventually cursing and hurling it to the floor of the cave when it wouldn't. Laying his hands over his face, he pleaded, "Please tell me Nora's all right. I'm so sorry . . ."

"I wouldn't be here if she wasn't. It's okay."

"Thank God." Lowering his hands, he glanced aside, one of the skulls catching his attention. "You know how they say skulls grin? They don't."

"Coalhouse . . ."

"They look broody. Don't they? They look like they're stuck thinking forever." He reached out and gripped both metal catwalk railings. "I don't want to think anymore. About anything. I was wandering, trying to figure out how to go back and fix what I did, and it's like my mind froze."

I didn't like where this was going. "You don't have to think right now. You just have to come with me."

"Where?"

"Back to the city. Everything's okay. Nora's safe, Patient One's safe. None of our people got hurt."

At Nora's name Coalhouse stepped forward. "I didn't take her. I swear. And I didn't mean to shoot her. At least believe me when I say that!"

"Shoot her?" This was news to me—news that put my back up. "Tell me what happened."

"I don't know," Coalhouse moaned, pacing away from me again. "I just wanted to prove I was capable. Go big like you have, get the girl, save the day. I was going to make Hagens tell me everything. And then she did, and I had this mad idea that if Smoke was killed, everything would stop. No one would have him to argue over anymore, least of all someone we don't know . . ."

"Explain that to me. Nora started to."

"Hagens said someone tried to get her to hand over Smoke weeks ago. That they were going to take out Company Z if she didn't. That they knew things about Z-Comp they shouldn't." He went on, building his story, layering details upon unbelievable details.

The fact that Nora'd been injured was horrific, but at least she was safe. I concentrated on that for the time being. "We need to move on this. Together."

"Together? You don't need me. No one does." Coalhouse turned back, his eye feverish. "The soldiers caught up to us once, talked to Laura and the others. I told them I was Z-Comp, but they didn't believe me. They didn't want to know anything about me."

That had to sting. I knew there was nothing I could say, right then, to make up for that.

"And the Punks . . . the Punks burn their dead. So I can't go home. No one wants me, I don't belong anywhere. I help people, and they forget about me. Or I fail. I'm completely useless. I can't even shoot straight anymore."

Shutting my eyes for a few seconds, I tried to think of how to phrase it. "Coalhouse, our home is here now. Our family is here."

"*You* say that. You have Nora. Tom has Chas. I don't have anybody."

"You have me. I'm your friend!"

"You didn't believe in me."

"I do now!" He looked up. "You were right, back when I wanted to call the cops and you wanted to keep going after the Changed. You were *right*. And the only reason I've ever been able to do 'big things' is because you guys have been with me!" I looked at him anew. "I won't leave any of you behind."

Coalhouse seemed to hover before me, the beam of my flashlight encircling his torso and face without illuminating his legs. After a long moment of consideration, he said, "Then help me."

"That's what I'm trying to do."

"Kill me."

The first aid kit slipped out from under my arm and bounced across the catwalk. The shock of his words seemed to lock my joints. "What?"

Coalhouse reached up to finger his loosened eye, and remembered it was gone. Slowly, he sank onto the catwalk, the railings shuddering. "I don't want to think anymore. All I think is bad stuff, horrible stuff. Like how I'm going to rot more, become even uglier. How even though I feel like it sometimes, I'm not really alive. And I get angry at Tom, how everyone seems to think I should smile and pick myself up and show the living I'm just peachy . . . when I'm not. And I remember all the bad stuff I've done, and how useless I am, and it just replays over and over. I can't *stop it*. It feels like I'm going crazy, and if I'm going crazy, then I'm dangerous and I have to die."

I moved haltingly forward, limping around the first aid case and my gun. I sat at Coalhouse's side and put an arm around him. "We'll get you some help."

He shook his head and lowered it to his knees. "I keep messing things up. I'm not even worth the powder to blow me to hell. I'd probably even mess up at shooting myself in the head. I just want it to be over."

"You can't think like that." I looked into the sockets of a nearby skull, as if it might have any ideas. "We all have to keep going. All we have is each other."

"I keep failing, though. So if I know I'm going to mess up, why not just . . . accept it? Why can't I give up, if that's what I want?"

All I could think to do was tell him the truth. The same truth that had gotten me to the doorstep of Company Z two years before, tired and devastated and lonely and ready to tear my own dead flesh off my bones, reject it, cast it away like garbage.

"You're right again." He looked up at me. "You always have that option. It's the worst option in the world, but it's the only one that's always there. So there's no reason to do it right this instant." The flashlight started to fade, and I shook it. "What might not be there are the chances you have right now. If you can hold on an-other hour, another day—if you can live one more good, honorable *minute*—those are victories. And they open up the whole world."

"Where'd you hear that?"

"That's what Dr. Dearly said when he found me." The flash-light recovered. "I've never told anyone this, but . . . after leaving the farm, I was ready to kill myself. So I couldn't hurt anyone. I was going to throw myself off a cliff and pray it was enough to break whatever I'd become. I was right on the edge, leaning for-ward, when Dearly and his men came out of the trees."

He didn't respond. I wasn't sure if I should count that as promising or disappointing.

"Coalhouse, you have the chance to come home today.

No one hates you. No one's afraid of you. Nora understands. Everyone else will understand, too."

"They could still kill me, though. Or arrest me and lock me up. Deport me."

"And you just said you wanted to die." The words were hard to say. "So what difference does it make?"

Coalhouse wiped his face off with his sleeve. "All the difference," he concluded. "I'm stupid and helpless in every other way. I at least want to control how I die. I want to go down on my own terms."

"Understandable." I could completely sympathize with that. "But you're *not* stupid or helpless. You did a couple stupid things. And that's on top of all the amazing things I've seen you do."

We both lapsed into silence. The faint rustling I'd heard earlier continued, and I sourced it upward, deciding it must be bats. Water dripped down the walls of the cavern, the drops joining together in a rivulet that ran toward the entrance.

And I considered what it would be like to put one of my friends down. Faced it down, stared at it hard in my mind, prepared my-self for it as much as I *could* prepare myself for a thing like that. Because, if that's what he really wanted—I'd do it. He was my friend, but more than that—I'd want him to do the same thing for me if I went mad, or if I reached a point of despair so pro-found I knew I could never, ever, with my failing mind and body, manage to fight it. Because the fight was everything.

What disturbed me most about this entire exchange was not the ideas being bandied about, but the fact that I fully under-stood them. Accepted them.

"I can't go with you," Coalhouse said, in time. "I need to go off on my own. Get my head right."

All at once the idea of harming Coalhouse in any way flew so far out of mind as to be inconceivable. "Okay," I said, doing my best to keep my voice calm. I scouted my fingers along the metal and came up with the first aid kit. "Here. I don't know what's in it, but it's yours. It's from your carriage. Left it a couple of miles from here. Did you walk here?"

"Yeah. Don't even know how." He accepted the case. After a beat, he raised his voice and said, "Leave me the gun, too."

My first thought was to break the thing, toss it down into the water, run away with it, anything. But I knew in my gut I had to trust him. Whatever he decided, I had to trust him—even if it meant letting him go.

Slowly, I handed the rifle over. I reached into my pockets and pulled out the bullets I'd brought with me, piling them into his palm before standing up.

Coalhouse remained seated, though he lifted his eye to me. I couldn't tell if he was asking for something else or willing me away. "You can always come to me," I said. "I'm here for you."

"I know, Cap." I thought he smiled a little, but it might've been a trick of the light. "Punch Tom for me, will you? I'll be back as soon as I can."

Laughing mirthlessly, I said, "You got it. Good luck."

And with that I turned and made my way out of the cave, leaving the flashlight for him about ten steps from where I'd started. I hiked across the shallow river, my pants slicking to my legs and my boots filling with water.

Upon reaching the other side I found a rock, sat down, and waited.

The sun rose. The day passed. I didn't see Coalhouse, and the wind washed away his scent.

But neither did I hear a gunshot.

When the sun dropped behind the trees, I stood up and marked my way back, finding the hiking trail I'd come in by. I backtracked and found his carriage gone.

Relief compounded my exhaustion. I kept walking, listening both for threats and for the chug and wail of a passing train.

Time to go home.

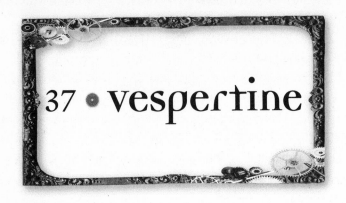

37 • vespertine

"Miss Mink, my apologies for intruding."

Glancing up from my father's bear-headed desk, I found the head manager of the Mink String Emporium awaiting my word. I shut the leather cover of the digital shop ledger I'd been perusing. "Yes, Mr. Sasaki?"

"Everything is secured, per the usual procedures. I know it is early yet, but if I might beg your indulgence, it's my daughter's birthday today. I was hoping to head home in time to wish her well before she is abed."

The heavy silver clock on the desk told me it was nearly nine at night. "Early?"

"It is my custom to leave about eleven, miss."

"Of course." I'd honestly forgotten. It was Monday, and tonight marked my first real visit to the Mink String Emporium since the Siege. I'd been "permitted" to travel into New London accompanied only by a chauffeur in order to attend a card party held by a younger member of Miss Perez's far-flung family, grudgingly bearing her well-wishes and forced to mingle with scads of inferior people. "How old is your daughter, may I ask?"

"She turns eight today, miss."

"The little blue harp downstairs—take it for her, if you think such a gift would please her."

Mr. Sasaki dropped into a deep genuflection. "You are incredibly generous, Miss Mink!"

"Go," I said. The man bowed a second time and backed out of the office.

I opened the ledger again and, with a quill-topped stylus, recorded the loss of the instrument I'd mentioned. When the save screen popped up, I instructed it to send a copy of the report to my father's email address. To the electronic missive, I appended a note.

See you tonight, Daddy.

Once the ledger had run through its backup, I rose and conveyed it to the enormous steel safe in the corner, locking it away.

Then I was alone.

Exiting and locking my father's elaborate, tin-paneled office, I slid the key back onto the shop chatelaine I wore on a chain around my waist and completed my journey to the first floor. The sconces hung on the faux pillars mounted between the shop's long murals were dim, the crystal chandeliers above dark, the rotating display plinths turned off.

It was cold. My frothy ivory party dress was designed to make other girls uncomfortable about their own fashion choices, not to keep me in comfort. Crossing my arms before my chest, I hurried toward the door, where my white angora stole hung from a hook. Curling it about my shoulders and unhooking the chatelaine, I opened the door, preparing to call it a night.

Outside stood Renfield Merriweather, hat in hand.

I screamed, the chatelaine slithering out of my hand and landing on the floor. Backing up, I nearly tripped over it, my fingers clutching into my furry wrapping. Mr. Merriweather himself appeared spooked, and backed up a few feet into the night—into the rain. It'd begun to sprinkle.

For a few seconds I stared at him in dismay. I hadn't thought he'd ever actually approach me. Yet the words "How dare you?" seemed not in my vocabulary; I couldn't even think them. That wasn't my immediate reaction.

Instead, recovering myself, I beckoned him in with a hand. He entered the shop tentatively; I moved to shut the door behind him and bolt it. "Did anyone see you?"

"No," he answered. His glasses were fogging, and he removed them. "Forgive me. I told the others we must never meet with you, that to do so might endanger you, but . . . I couldn't stay away. I've been sitting in the café down the street for the last six hours. It was mostly empty."

"Does anyone know you're here?"

"No."

I could only hope he was right. Turning to look at him, my back to the door, I found myself again at a loss for words. Renfield was the first and last zombie I'd ever stood so close to. I'd thought of him almost every day since the airship ride, his voice and his mannerisms and his looks clouding my brain, following me into my nightmares, and now here he was. He was anxiously regal in his bearing, his wavy hair half matted about his bruised face with its hawkish nose, deep-set eyes, and thin lips.

It was entirely chilling to behold all of his handsome features, functioning together, and know that their owner was dead.

"I had to speak with you," he said, intruding upon my silence. "I beg your pardon. I know we haven't been formally introduced."

"And we probably never will be," I realized. "Least of all because you've been *stalking* me."

He accepted this with a nod. "Perhaps . . . I should just go. Perhaps this was foolishness."

"You're here now." Letting my stole slip from my shoulders, I moved toward him. He went quite still. Slowly, I reached out my hands, silently offering to take his hat. He let me have it. "Sit anywhere you like. The upstairs is already locked."

The dead boy moved toward a white piano, and I turned my back to hang up his hat and gather my things from the floor. When I returned to him, he had the piano open and was trailing his fine, bony fingers over the keys.

"Do you play?" I asked, dreading the answer.

"No." He looked up at me and shut the piano again, taking a seat on the bench. "Who knows? I've a few years to fill, I may take it up. I take it, from your old user name, that you play the harp?"

"Harp, violin, harpsichord, clavichord, pianoforte . . ." When his eyes widened a tad, I added, "I'm told I play very well, but I don't think I do. I'm not passionate about it. Music is simply math, after all. I play by numbers."

Renfield laughed and reached into his jacket, drawing out a handkerchief with which to clear his glasses. "That might be the most beautiful thing I've ever heard a young lady say."

I pulled up another piano bench, sitting kitty-corner to him. The zombie continued to fiddle with his glasses, at times attempting to moisten the lenses by breathing on them—an impossible task, I realized. While he might be able to command his breath still, his body must be dry and cold.

Reaching over, I took his glasses from him. "I'll do it."

He surrendered his hankie. "Thank you," he said, a bit sheepishly. "I hate these stupid things. I keep having to get thicker and thicker lenses. By the time I truly drop, I'll be wearing binoculars."

"I sympathize," I said, polishing away. "I was blind as a child."

"Truly? Gene therapy to correct it, I take it?"

"No." When he gazed at me curiously, I looked up and lifted a finger, tapping my right eyeball with my nail. *Plink, plink.*

"Bionic," he said under his breath, scooting a little closer. "Both of them?"

"Hmm." I handed him his spectacles, and he hurriedly put them on so he could resume staring at my glass eyes. "They tried gene therapy, but it didn't work. So, in they went. I'm rather happy about it, really. Far better to be part machine than to owe anything to Allister Genetics."

Once the name was spoken, our true conversation could begin. "Why did you do it?" he asked. "Why contact us about Allister that way?"

"I couldn't exactly pass you a note in biology class, could I? Before I explain, tell me how everything worked out. I've seen the news. I know he's been exposed."

"Catastrophe was averted. Some things are still up in the air, but everything's holding for now."

"Good." Then, to fulfill my end of the bargain, I told him, "My reasons for doing it are . . . complicated."

Renfield tilted his head. "Mr. Griswold was the main target. Why didn't you mention him? Why only tell Miss Dearly to be on her guard?"

My fingers curling, I told him, "Mr. Griswold is a zombie, and someone I don't care about. I don't *like* zombies, Mr. Merriweather. Your kind frightens me, disgusts me. You shouldn't *be* here. The day the last one of you has 'truly dropped,' as you put it, is the day I will finally breathe easy, along with the rest of the living."

"I see." His utterance was soft. For a moment I thought I had hurt him. It took me a few seconds to remember that I shouldn't *care* if he was hurt.

"That said—I do have a sense of justice, I suppose. In my world, sure, you grind your inferiors beneath your heel. You laugh at them." Twisting one of my rings about my finger, I added, "But you don't kill them. You don't torture them. And the stories I've heard, now—you don't kill people just trying to get their medicine from a clinic. You don't harm blameless living people walking in the streets!"

"Miss Mink . . ." Renfield began. I ignored him and stood up.

"When Michael came to me, he showed me this finger . . ." I studied the floor, my blond curls hanging around my face, heavy with hair spray and rhinestone charms. "He was mad. Ranting about Roe and Dearly. And I thought it was the drink, but then I learned it was the truth—I heard about the Roe bombing. But I couldn't just call on Miss Dearly and warn her. Not that I detest her to the point of wishing her dead, but it would have come back to hurt me in ways you cannot even imagine. So, I did what I could. And now that we're *talking* to each other, we could find some way to make it permanent, some less risky way. I'm a site administrator on Aethernet Chess Live, we could perhaps program some covert means of communication . . ."

Renfield blinked. "Site administrator?"

I admitted, "I own ACL. Well, along with my father. He taught me to play chess when I was a little girl. After he began spending so much time away from home, he looked for an Aethernet version to play with me, but found none to his liking. So he founded it, in my name. We still play every night. That's part of what kept me in this store during the Siege." I looked around. "I was waiting for him to get online. If I was going to die, I was going to die talking to the only person who loves me."

"My word." Renfield stood up as well, and approached me. I stopped moving. "You do wish to continue this exercise, then?" He sounded hopeful.

Did I? Slowly, I forced myself to look up at the young dead man. "Yes. I can go where none of your clan can go now. No one in proper, anti-zombie society will acknowledge any of you. I could even talk to Allister. I don't think he suspects me."

"Good. Because we have many more birds to snare." Mr.

Merriweather stared into my eyes so intently I felt my skin prickling. "Miss Dearly speaks very poorly of you."

"As well she should. But ours is a petty squabble. I say that even though I would never give it up, even though I would happily take it to the grave."

"Why?"

"Because it amuses me. That's all the reason I need."

Renfield considered this. "Then I must ask. How can we trust you to tell us the truth? I should be asking you to go to the police, to back up our claims."

"Didn't I just?" I rubbed my upper lip over my lower one in annoyance. "Isn't that your whole thing now? Don't you trust people *until* they try to bite you?"

Ren smiled slightly. "I suppose. Though it's been a long time since I was in a position to fear being bitten."

It ruffled me, the idea that a *corpse* was debating whether he ought to trust me. "Tell me, sir, what can I do to assure you?" I asked sarcastically.

"I meant no insult. All I mean is . . ." The zombie's smile faded. "What happens when this venture no longer amuses you?"

I tried to find this question offensive. However, in the end I had to acknowledge that it had some merit. "I'm not dedicated to the cause, it's true," I said. "I don't really know what possessed me to do what I did."

Renfield stepped toward the door, as if intending to depart. "Perhaps it would be wise to simply wait and see if such an urge strikes you again, then, and if you can safely act on it. Nothing promised, nothing denied."

"Wait." My cheeks flushed and I felt myself fighting the urge to run after him, to fling myself in front of the door. I found my anger, my mental store of "dares." He was *dead*. How dare he decide the direction our conversation would take?

"I'm afraid I must. It was dangerous to come here, and for that I apologize." Renfield bowed and reached for the lock.

As he unbolted the door, I realized I didn't *want* him to go. And the more I thought about it, the more I saw that I was dealing with an intelligent creature, a subtle one—even more than I'd initially given him credit for. He was, dare I say it, an equal.

I realized something else, too.

"I've missed you," I admitted. The jingling of the ornaments in my hair seemed louder than my own voice.

A beat passed. Ren pulled his hand away from the lock. "And I've missed you, my lady." His words made my chest ache. "When I realized it was you . . . I was supremely honored. I was honored to be remembered." There was no gloating in his tone, nor shyness; he spoke plainly. I found myself admiring that.

"I've missed playing against you," I went on, my pride dissolving. "You're a wonderful opponent. I've even missed the pleasantries we used to type. I used to wait and wait for your name to pop up online, just like my father . . ." My voice hitched. ". . . never knowing there was a monster at the other end."

I fell silent. It wasn't like me to speak about such things, to be so sentimental. Renfield lapsed into thought. Before I could open my mouth again, he beat me to the punch. "I want to take this seriously. I know I can't be as active as some of the other lads, but I want to do my part. And I'm sure you can understand the sense of urgency that now infuses every aspect of my life."

I understood what he was asking. "For you, at least for a time, I could take it seriously."

"Truly?" He came nearer. "Believe me, no matter what happens, I will never ask you to do anything I would not myself be willing to try."

"Truly."

Renfield paused, his eyes roving over the mural on the far wall.

I stood in silence with him, awaiting his verdict. One of the subjects in the painting was a woman with dark hair cradling a blond, pewter-eyed child, and he pointed at it. "Is that a likeness of you?" he asked, seemingly out of nowhere.

"No. That's the real Vespertine."

Renfield blinked. "Pardon me?"

Shrugging, I offered, "I was adopted when I was three. Lady Mink needed a replacement for the child she'd carelessly let drown in a garden pond." Renfield's shocked reaction bolstered me, and I added, "There. Does that suit?"

"Indeed." Renfield held off for a second, before uttering a sort of half laugh and leaning his face closer to mine in such a slow, solicitous way that I felt no urge to retreat. "You're really Vespertine Mink the Second, then."

"Yes, I suppose you could say I am."

"Ha." Renfield took a step back, before bowing low. "Allow me to reciprocate, then. I am Renfield Ichabod Merriweather the *Third*. I'm the third son of a third son, the product of an undistinguished, middle-class family from the far North. And, as I stated many months ago, I am grateful to be dead for the fact that I never would have met you otherwise."

I couldn't help it—I blushed. "You shouldn't say such things. They could be misinterpreted."

Renfield didn't appear the least bit embarrassed; rather, he was now grinning from ear to ear. "I told you, carpe diem."

"While I appreciate the sentiment, I'm going to forget you ever said it," I informed him, doing my best to come off as prim.

"So be it." Renfield slicked his hair back, revealing a widow's peak. "At any rate, I think we're on an even footing now."

I had to give him that. He threw the lock. "Can we play a game before you go?"

Renfield bowed, and put on his hat. "Not just now. But the night is young, Miss Mink. I suppose I await your pleasure."

"Will you be on ACL in a few hours, then?"

"Wild horses and head shots notwithstanding, yes."

I held the door open for him as he stepped out into the night. The rain had abated and all was clear; still, he dodged the street-lights and made his way furtively to the sidewalk across the street. After a few seconds he had hailed a cab and was gone.

Letting the door hang open, I slipped into my angora again and retrieved my keys. I had to go home, but I had something to look forward to, at least.

For the first time in many months, maybe years, I had some-thing to look forward to.

38 • michael

Only a few days later everything had fallen apart.

Lopez took me to the police Sunday morning. Told them everything, though I remained silent. And before the aristocracy protection mechanism could wind up, before my father could even be called, the story leaked onto the news. The written information got onto the Aethernet—uploaded by someone called "zboy69." Someone went to the Silver Bridle and got his hands on the letters waiting there, uncovering the names of a few more zombie targets. The police got a warrant and found my mask in the tire compartment in the trunk of my carriage.

The fallout was almost magnificent to watch. The ensuing scandal was the social equivalent of an explosive device taking out a well-loved monument—so horrible that it couldn't help but scar the landscape of the New Victorian psyche, so enthralling that one couldn't help but watch as the whole thing burned.

Except from where I was sitting. Certain, every second of every hour, that a bird-masked assassin was going to crawl in through my bedroom window. Certain that somehow Green Jacket would find a way to get me. Or the Ratcatcher. In self-imposed exile in my suite, my ignorance mutated into paranoia.

My mother wished to fret over my wounds, to tend them; I shut her out. Coco wished to know her next assignment; I chased her away, half convinced *she* was the one who'd given me up. My father didn't even speak to me.

Nora was right. I went down alone. And it was the hardest thing I'd ever done. Even as the media spun wild theories, even as bird-beleaguered zombies were suddenly taken seriously, their stories sought after and their interviews broadcast multiple times, no other members of the Murder were exposed. I knew that in mansions the nation over high-class parents were probably burning bird masks, taking their sons to task. They'd have a chance to hide—thanks to me. Hopefully that detail would help me later.

God, I'd been an idiot.

It still hurt when my own father confirmed it, though.

When he finally called me to the library, I went with a heavy heart. The room was hologram-free for once, the gold foiling on the furniture the brighter for it, the ostentatious carpet louder. My father told me to close the door and sit in one of his high-backed chairs. He was more of a human black hole than usual, no emotion on his face, his movements reserved. He walked like a robot from the door to his desk. He didn't sit.

"I'm sorry—" I began.

"Don't speak." The voice that came out of him was not my father's. I fell silent.

From his desk, he picked up a digidiary. He began to read. *"Zombies are the Punks of our generation. Like your forefathers, you must rise to exile them. In our case, to the beyond. We shall don the masks of plague doctors, and together cure the world. We shall be a flock of carrion crows, feasting on the dead.'"*

My stomach went numb. "Please, don't read it." They were the letters I'd reconstructed.

"'If you want in,'" he continued, his voice growing expansive, dramatic, *"'place a note addressed to #1712 behind the loose stone in*

the central fireplace at the Silver Bridle pub in La Rosa. The people there are trustworthy.'" His sarcasm nearly rent the air. *"'Assign yourself a number. We shall never know one another. Anonymity will free us. The masks we will come to wear will represent absolute freedom. With one on, you will be one and one hundred at the same time.'"*

"I'm sorry," I whispered again, looking at my lap.

Dad stopped reading. Instead he said, "Really. This seemed like a good idea. You idiotic pantywaist." Before I could even try to come to terms with what he'd just said, he hurled the digidiary onto his desk. "I ought to disown you now, turn you out on the streets. I can't believe that half of my genetic material is riding around in a carcass that is so pathetically *stupid*!"

It felt like the blood was draining from my head. He advanced on me. "Is this your idea of what being an aristocrat entails? Sneaking around at night, performing heinous acts that are sure to get you caught, arrested, tried? Do you know how hard I am having to work to keep you out of prison?"

"Forgive me," I tried. "I thought you'd be proud if I could do what I needed to do and not get caught. Handle it on my own. And after December—"

"Do what you needed to do? Oh, enlighten me. What was this chore? This holy imperative? I'm dying to know."

"Killing Griswold. The zombie who assaulted me. The zombie who took Miss Dearly away from me."

"So it's that little slut's fault, at the end of the day." He looked away. "I can't believe this."

"She's not . . . she's confused." I dug my fingers into my pants leg. "Ever since the Siege, I'd been fantasizing about killing him. When that letter came, I took my chance. I knew I couldn't do it on my own. I knew I'd be caught. I thought—"

"No. You didn't *think*." He stalked away again. "What kind of fools do you take your elders for? This stunt is a mockery of all we do. This is a pauper's bitter mockery of how a mythical 'evil peer' acts, what our clubs are like! This is how the Punks imagine we behave!"

"I thought I could remain anonymous!"

My father was actually *shaking* with rage. "And then that zombie, Griswold, invades my building, takes you hostage, leads my forces on a wild goose chase over half the Territories—why? What was that about?"

"It was to help Miss Dearly. I told him to. He needed the men."

"You sold out my private security force to a dead man? To rescue the daughter of that sick freak?" His eyes flashed. "I forbid you to see or talk about that girl ever again. I knew when you met her that it was a mistake to let you carry on!"

"But she—"

"She is Victor Dearly's daughter! And everything Victor Dearly touches turns to dirt. He has the uncanny ability to corrupt even the most sublime, intelligent people—I've seen it in action. Before she went with him, Elizabeth Soto was—although nameless and penniless—a *diamond* amongst the dross of the earth. I would have made her a queen, and he turned her into a shell of her former self. It was a mercy when she died. And it seems that like her mother during her later days, Miss Dearly will choose to align herself, again and again, with rejects, fools, and scum!"

He was breathing hard. And he'd wanted her mother? I didn't know what to say except, "I can lead you right to Griswold. He has to go down for what he did to me, to us . . ."

"Oh, I need no help finding him. And I'll take care of him."

This tickled a memory. "How did you know who he was?"

Dad ignored my question. "Tell me, did he do *all* of that to you?" he asked, indicating my wounds. I nodded. "Then at this point, I would like to meet him, yes. I would shake his hand and thank him for doing what I should have done long ago. I should have thrashed you every time you acted like an idiot in your youth. Maybe you wouldn't be such a waste of skin today!"

In all my life I never would have said I had the ability to feel as much pain as I did at that moment. My body wanted to curl up, to protect my stomach, my vitals—as if his words were physical threats that could be blocked. Griswold, a monster that didn't deserve to live or love, had taken the love of my life from me, humiliated me, attacked me—and my father'd rather have him for a son.

"I did it because I thought it was how you'd want me to do it," I said. "Without your help. On my own."

"I have worked *so hard* to keep this from collapsing on our heads, and you go and do something like this. Give the police an excuse to waltz right into my house." He walked away again. He couldn't be still. "I planned everything so carefully. I destroyed everything I made with my own hands. And now I have investigators beating down my door . . ."

"Keep what from collapsing on our heads?" Dad didn't answer. His silence swallowed up the whole of my attention just the same as if he had been speaking—but then I felt the need to fill it. "My lord—I was beaten. I was kidnapped. This monster of a zombie nearly bit me, the one with the new strain of the disease . . . I never meant for any of this to happen!"

Rather than calm down or reevaluate his opinion, my father flew at me, his hands gripping the arms of my chair so I was imprisoned. "The biter was there?"

"He nearly got me!"

He pushed himself away and started to pace, turning over this new information, his eyes wild. "We need to stop this. We need to get him."

"Get him?" Was my father going to make *sure* Patient One got a chance to feast on me? "Why?"

Dad managed to collect himself somewhat, his arms almost riveted to his sides. "Because he is my property. And I *will* have him back."

"What?" The word seemed not large enough. It in no way encompassed the amount of wonder, confusion, and fear I felt at that statement.

"And the Lazarus is mine to profit off of. *My* discovery." My father held up a hand, forbidding me to speak. He returned to his desk and sat down, breathing in and out slowly. "You're going to get what you want, son." His voice was returning to normal.

I didn't dare ask. I didn't want to know.

"You want to pretend to play with the men? Then I'll let you play with the men. But you will do precisely what I say." He looked at the floor. "You will have real equipment, not theater masks and winter scarves knit for you by your mommy."

My heart twinged.

"You will have real, world-changing goals. You will actually work to protect your family, instead of casting them into disgrace and shame. In fact, your first goal will be to find these masked idiots and force them to stand beside you in the light."

"What do we need protection from?" I dared to ask.

Lord Allister looked at me, his eyes sharp. "I think it's time you visited the twelfth floor of Allister Genetics." He reached over to hit a button on his desk. "And I think it's time you met E."

39 • Nora

Upon being informed of Smoke's transformation, Papa made him his new favorite project. With everything else going on, it was Monday before I could visit the ships to ask after him. I didn't learn much upon going there.

"He hasn't said a word since Saturday. We're giving him a chance to recuperate before we start running more invasive tests," my father explained. Smoke sat beside us at his desk, clothed and slowly eating a bowl of vegetable soup. "This reaction you've described . . . I'd like to see it for myself. But that might be dangerous."

"So you don't know anything yet? Is he alive or dead?"

"I'm not sure. His internals still look fresh, but I've not seen them in action." Papa sighed. "We'll run more metabolic tests."

Tests aside, it was the potential Allister connection that made me uneasy. "What do you think all of this means?"

Stroking my hair, my father said, "That we need to turn our attention outward. Get to the bottom of this." Withdrawing his hand, he added, "Lopez got in touch with me. Said you called him to talk your way into an invitation to Marblanco."

"I did." Fighting the fatigue this topic caused, I asked, "Can I go? I don't want to go *anywhere,* but if I have to . . ."

"Yes. You should go with Miss Roe. If only to get her settled." With that, he leaned forward to kiss my brow. "My little miracle."

I made a face at that, even if I was relieved—especially at the suggestion that my stay at Marblanco might be brief. Before I could figure out a way to wheedle a timeline out of my father, Dr. Salvez burst in. "Lower the screen. Turn on NVIC."

Reaching across Dad's desk, I grabbed the remote and did both. "This just in." Zombie reporter Marcus Maripose was reading directly from a digidiary. "Again, I apologize for the spottiness of these reports, but this is live. The Punks are abandoning the Border Zone. We have video footage of the Punks simply . . . walking away. No one has contacted the New Victorian government to negotiate terms of surrender, or even said . . . anything." He looked extremely puzzled.

So did the rest of us.

"What?" Papa asked, his face going slack.

"They wouldn't do that," I said. "The Punk extremists hate us." They'd fought their futile battles at the border for decades. It'd been their own homegrown terrorist plots that led my people to banish them to the South originally.

"I'm inclined to agree with you," said Salvez. "But they *must* mean that the extremists are leaving. The army wouldn't up and leave even if they wanted peace. They wouldn't leave the border unprotected."

"Exactly," I said. "The army's just there to keep an eye on things." That was what Bram had told me. That only the extremists cared about attacking the New Victorians; that most Punks were more concerned with building their own civilization.

A second later NVIC started showing footage, and indeed, part of the Punk army was moving away from the border. Their walking tanks and huge war machines—heavy, mechanical, "old-fashioned" and yet terribly dangerous—formed massive columns of retreat. They appeared to be escorting the un-uniformed men marching with them—the mercs and extremists. Behind them the rest of the army watched them go. Apparently they were meant to stay behind.

Just like that, the fight was over?

I slid my hands over my face. It seemed like one thing after another was happening, the entire world collapsing like a row of dominoes. And I had no idea what sort of pattern was being formed yet.

"This is a good thing," Salvez said. There was no joy in his voice. "Isn't it?"

"I don't know." I kept my eyes on the screen. "I don't know anything anymore."

Chas came back that day. She'd led the AG minions on an epic chase up the Honduran coast before losing them near Belize. She had souvenirs for us, trinkets from seaside towns. Pastel pinwheels and taffy. When Samedi asked her about the Rolls, she shoved a piece of candy into his mouth and told him to treasure his ignorance.

That night, with Matilda's help, I packed. As she shoved petticoats and shoes into my trunk, it occurred to me that I ought to take my identity papers along, just in case. I didn't have my chip anymore. So I went to the study and started combing through my father's desk, looking for my birth certificate, anything that seemed useful.

After twenty minutes of fruitless searching I stumbled upon a water-stained folder. I flicked through it out of curiosity—but what I found astounded me. Schematics, budgets, architectural plans. It wasn't until I got to the written pages in the back that I realized my father had been designing a school, or perhaps some sort of institution or asylum. The building designs were High Victorian and beautiful, with gardens, sunny hallways, operating theaters, and . . .

. . . a graveyard. A lovely, sheltered graveyard, for the people who would inevitably die there.

Back in the jungle, he'd said he had something he wanted to keep a surprise. This must be it. It was right after he talked about my education—he must have been dreaming of starting some sort of co-mortal academy or college. Maybe he'd been considering the idea all during his stint with Company Z.

My father *had* looked to the future. Even if only for a few weeks, a few months. He'd wanted to do something great. And New London had trapped him, too.

Closing the folder, I put it on the desk and wiped my eyes.

"Are you all right?"

Dr. Chase was in the doorway. I nodded. "Yes." I wasn't sure if I ought to share my father's secret, so I told her, "I just don't want to leave. Bram. All of you. Especially when we have so much to do."

"It won't be forever." Beryl came forward and wrapped me in her arms. I shut my eyes, taking in the powdery scent of her perfume. "And it's not that far away. You'll just have to commute to the fight."

"It seems a world away." I'd tried hard to avoid thinking about Bram, but now the idea of leaving him seemed immediate, inevitable, and my rib cage felt too small for my heart.

Dr. Chase withdrew and looked into my eyes. "Miss Dearly . . ." She seemed to win some internal debate, and guided me to a chair. She sat by my side. "I don't know why I want to tell you this, but I do. Maybe it's because I see some of myself in you."

"What?"

"As a girl, I had a happy life. I grew up in a sweet New Victorian town in Venezuela. Close to the border. Postcard-pretty. My father was the sheriff." Beryl straightened up. "And when Baldwin showed up at our farm, I ran away with him hours later. I traded everything for him. And then . . . I refused to let him go. I turned him into a zombie. I, too, have made reckless decisions that have brought me both elation and pain."

It wasn't that I didn't know what to say—it was that my brain suddenly wasn't sure how to operate my mouth. "Huh?"

Beryl actually laughed a little, before pressing her hand over the nub of hair at the nape of her neck. "God, it was so long ago. After he gave up smuggling, Baldwin started running these engineering cons. He showed up with this machine he claimed could draw water out of thin air, out of the earth. It was an amazing piece of tech—and a total scam. Dad ran him off, but . . . he had me. You should have seen him when he was alive, and younger. 'Dashing' doesn't begin to do him justice."

"I can believe it," I said.

"I guess you could say I became his assistant. Ran his scams with him. Baldwin was good with machines—his dad was a smuggler before him, and he grew up keeping his getaway carriages in working order. I grew up fixing things around town. We'd build these contraptions that made people think we'd come up with some spectacular new technology—replication of objects, perpetual motion, teleportation. Mom taught me calligraphy in home school, so I used to work up fake patents, fake endorsements. Not under either of our real names, mind." She plucked at her blouse. "I guess now's as good a time as any to admit neither of us has a Ph.D. in anything? Diplomas are exceptionally easy to forge."

That thought had never even crossed my mind. "You're kidding. You're not a doctor?"

"No. I'm an old maid, I'm still Miss Chase. Anyway, people'd invest in the machines, and we'd take the money and run. That's what I have amnesty for. We ran the con on the NV side a few times."

"Wow."

"I know. I regret it. And it wasn't until later I learned how dark his life truly was. That people like the Ratcatcher existed. But by that point I didn't care. He told me I could have adventure, and I could have him, and he never lied to me about either."

"How'd he become a zombie, then?"

Beryl seemed to shrink a bit. "We were running the scam at some Punk's place. She was a dangerous mark—she was also into moving contraband. That's how Baldwin met her. She operated off an aerial platform in the desert. I think one of her men must have come in from a smuggling operation sick." She looked at her hands, which were starting to shake. "Those were the worst three days of my life, with that dead thing on the other side of the door wanting in, and Baldwin dying in my arms from a gunshot another man had fired, and . . . when it looked like I was going to lose him, I let the zombie in. I'd seen another victim reanimate and keep his mind. At least, it seemed that way. So I got it to bite him. I knew I'd lose him forever, otherwise. And I do love him. I *do*." She licked her lips. "After it bit him . . . and I just let it in, and used him as a human shield, it wasn't hard . . . but . . . afterward, the host turned on me, and I killed it with a marble statue. Just hammered, over and over, till its brains leaked out. And then I sat down with the statue in my lap and prayed I wouldn't have to do the same thing to Baldwin."

I didn't dare try to formulate a response to this. She didn't look at me. There was much more behind their relationship than I'd ever guessed. My chest tightened as I realized just how hard she had fought to stay with him, in every sense of the word.

"After he reanimated . . . I still had him, but there's no way I can ever atone for what I did. Especially after it became clear that if we talked, if we went forward with what we'd seen, the Punk government would kill him and lock me up. That's when we crossed the border for the last time. That's when Company Z found us."

At a loss for words, I decided that my only option was to hug her. She returned the gesture gratefully. "My biggest fear is that one day he'll decay enough to tell me the truth—that he hates me for what I did to him. Like I said, I'm filled with regret. But sometimes I think of that day . . . and I realize that I was never braver, never more purposeful than I was when I followed him, and when I killed him so that he would live. And that's what I want you to know, no matter where your life takes you, Nora . . . that you shouldn't be afraid to fight, to break every rule, every law, dare every dare. Not as long as it's for the ones you love."

It was impossible to let her go after she reminded me of that. She indulged me, holding me, even singing to me at one point. I'd forgotten what it was like to be embraced and comforted by a woman. How cool and soft it was. My mother was once like that.

I'd lost so many people. I would fight like hell for the ones I had now. Whatever shape that fight took.

After my packing was finished, I wandered through my house in the dark, as I had a short four months ago. It was different now, crowded with cots and everyone's things. It actually appeared lived-in.

I wanted to remember it this way. Forever.

Just as I was pondering the parlor, a cold hand brushed my arm. I turned around and saw it was Bram, and instantly moved to capture his neck. He hugged me back in the way I loved, the way that very nearly hurt. In one hand, he held a bouquet of wildflowers. "Sorry it took so long. I rode the rails, but had to walk partway. I figured if this is going to become a tradition, I should start bringing gifts."

"What kept you? Did you find Coalhouse?"

Bram carried me to the sofa and set me down, before collapsing beside me and handing me the flowers. He was filthy; he was breathtaking. I set the flowers aside and brushed his windblown hair out of his face, giving him the time he needed to figure out what he wanted to say. "I found him. He wanted to go off on his own for a while."

I felt my shoulders rise. "I'm sorry."

Bram didn't move. "He asked me to kill him."

There was nothing I could say in response to that. The very idea made my blood run cold. I guided Bram's head to my shoulder and let my cheek rest upon his brow.

"I would've done it. Coalhouse decided against it in the end, but I would've done it. I talked a good game when I was there, but now . . ."

"What?"

"I don't even know." I hated to hear Bram sound so lost, so exhausted. "Because I knew it was the right thing to do. That if he wanted to die, and couldn't do it himself, one of his friends should . . ." He gave up.

"You're right," I tried. "I mean, maybe I don't have any say, since I'm alive, but I think you're right."

Bram pulled back and looked into my eyes. "You always have a say." He gestured at nothing. "It's just hard to actually confront it. He was upset because he kept watching himself fail and make bad decisions, but . . . I've failed more than he *ever* has. Three times now I should've gone full-tilt and didn't—and look what's happened. I tried to play it careful when we came to fetch you, and the Laz hit New London. I didn't tell you what Wolfe was doing, and Sam almost got killed. I didn't go after the Changed—"

Shaking my head, I said, "There's nothing wrong with being the voice of reason, Bram. You're always there when we need you."

"I just get so confused sometimes. About what to do, who to side with." He kissed my forehead. "You're the only thing I'm never confused about."

"Believe me, I understand." My free hand flattened on his chest and I studied my fingers, trying to find the words. "Meanwhile . . . the Punks have left the Border Zone."

Bram went stiff. "What?"

"They're abandoning it. Not saying why. Part of the army was left behind." I told him everything—about the Punks, about Michael, about Marblanco. He told me about Allister Genetics, leading me once more to wonder what the hell that man was up to.

"God." Bram shut his eyes. "What if something's going on down there? What if the Punks are reacting to a resurgence of hosts, or something?"

"I don't know," I told him honestly. "It's damn weird."

Bram opened his eyes. "I told Laura I'd find her." When I made a soft *go on* motion with my head, he continued thoughtfully, "I'll admit, the last few months? I haven't quite known what to do with myself. It's like when I first became a zombie. I knew I had to move forward, but I wasn't sure what to *do*. Everything was so new. I've kind of felt that way again lately, but now . . ."

"Idea?"

"Yeah. Both of us—we got used to zombies in a controlled environment. A place where mad zombies were put down, and the rest of us were all on the same page, with people around to guide us. The zombies in this city—they don't have that. They don't have anyone teaching them how to deal with their condition, with the dark thoughts . . . with the hunger. They're in a place where people turn against them at the speed of a newscast. So we've had zombies lashing out, thinking in terms of *us* versus *them*." He lifted a hand to my curls. "In a way, both Hagens and Mártira were right. We need to help each other. Like your dad helped me. I think that part has gotten lost in all the violence, in all the vaccine work, in the move up north. In the loss of Z-Comp. We can't just hand out meds and stitch people up. We have to lead."

"How do we start?"

"I figure by reaching out to as many zombies as possible. Z-Comp vets, the members of the Changed that Hagens lied to. Set it up so we can defend each other. Especially if Company Z is in some kind of danger, and we've still got these masked people to worry about." He looked into my eyes. "But to do that, I have to go find them. And Hagens. I could be on the road for a while."

" 'A while'?" A hefty drive between us I could handle, but I didn't like the sound of that. "How long is a while?"

"I don't know." He lowered his lids. "Depends on where Hagens has gone. I figure she's our best connection to whoever has it out for Z-Comp."

I sat forward. "Then you're not going without me."

"I can't ask you to do that." He captured my tiny hand in both of his and kissed it fervently. "There's no way Dr. Dearly would agree."

"Bram . . ."

"Let me say it." He rubbed his dry cheek on my knuckles, like a cat marking its owner. "I'm dead, Nora. I'm a Punk. I have no money and no station and no name—I have nothing to give you. So I can't ask you to change your life for me, to give up anything for me. It's not fair to you. I'm not going to be here very long. And I can't just while away my days—I have to do *something* with the time I have left. The few extra years I shouldn't've had. And now I don't think that's going to happen in a lab."

"Do you love me?" I whispered.

Bram's eyes softened and he slid the fingers of his right hand into my hair, holding my head still. Slowly, he dipped forward and kissed me, and I leaned into it, my eyes shutting. The kiss lasted for a beautiful instant, before his left hand slid down to my forearm and encountered my bandage. He drew back to look at it, his eyes questioning.

"Proof for your argument. Some of the Changed bit me," I had to confess. I felt strange about it—like I'd cheated on him, even though I knew he'd just been joking before.

His gaze lingered on the bandage, before he uttered a wolfish rumble—a noise so warm, and somehow possessive, that it made my head feel hot. He kissed me again, and his lips tumbled down my cheek, my neck, his hand daring to rise to my chest, his fingers hooking into the bodice of my dress to pull it down, to reveal more flesh for kissing.

And as he did that, he spoke.

"I love you, Nora. I will think you beautiful when I have no eyes left to see. I will remember your voice when my ears go. You can't hold on to me forever, but I will hold on to you until I am nothing but dirt."

I could feel tears flowing down my skin, down my neck. I pushed him back with sudden violence and started to unbutton his shirt as well. He looked both surprised and ecstatic. I kissed his collarbone, and he leaned down again, capturing my mouth. As his lips moved against mine, my fingers slid inside his shirt, and found a hole. Pulling back, I bent my head to look at his ice-white chest. He'd been newly shot. Parting his shirt, I found the wound, dry and small.

"Michael got me," he said, voice throaty. "More work for Evola."

The hole was a tiny new addition to the web of scars on his body, but unlike the others, I hated it. In spite of all I'd just said, the idea that Michael might've gotten his way sent a chill up my spine, and I found myself once more mentally questing after a safe place, somewhere, *anywhere,* we wouldn't have to worry about such things, where we could live together in peace. An idea that was both cold and hot; passionately longed after, yet turned to out of fear, and hated for that reason.

And then understanding hit me.

It wasn't safety that I craved. It was just the idea of Bram and me, against the world. Because he was never meant to be mine; I was never meant to be his. His being a zombie had nothing to do with this, but it actually made it all the sweeter. The relative seconds of time that he could offer me were more precious than any eternity, because we would have so few of them.

That was why I couldn't hide. That was why I couldn't, shouldn't, would *never* let him go, or hesitate a single second longer than I had to. Like Dr. Chase said.

I lifted my head up, closer to his, parting my lips in invitation. He didn't need further encouragement. He made up the distance between us and took the kiss I wanted to give him.

"Marry me," I whispered when his lips left mine. "Tonight."

"What?" he asked, his eyes growing huge.

It took me a moment to process what I'd just said, and I giggled madly when I found that, yes, I'd meant it. "Marry me. I'm proposing! Do you want me to get down on one knee? I'll do it."

Bram just stared at me. "But . . . you threw that book away when I joked about the wedding part, and . . . I held off on telling you I loved you because I was afraid I'd freak you out!"

"Oh, I'm absolutely terrified!" I giggled again, a bit disturbed to find I couldn't control it. "But I don't know how long I have to *be* terrified, so . . . let's just do it!"

"But that's just the point! I won't . . . be here," Bram said. I heard the unspoken words in his sentence: *very long*. I heard them, and I ignored them.

"It's not how *long* you're with me," I promised him. "It's *how* you're with me. You just said you couldn't ask me to give up anything. You don't. You never have. You give me more than you could ever take. So let's just embrace the fact that we are two weird freaking people, and do it."

Bram took my arms in his hands, as he had up near the gun cabinet a week ago, and looked at me, hard. Then he kissed me.

"I want to, at some point," he said, before kissing me again. "I really, really want to. But . . ." Another kiss. "You're seventeen. You can't get married until you're twenty-one."

"Oh, come on! How do you know that?"

"It's in the FAQ section in the back of the Bibles the Cathedral provides," he explained, with another kiss. "Mass is incredibly boring, do you know *that*?"

"Okay, that whole voice of reason thing? I take it back. It's really annoying."

Bram laughed fully, the rich sound that I adored, and pulled me close. "Wow."

I let him have a few minutes of quiet before saying, "Isley could do it. The ceremony, at any rate. We could sneak upstairs and get him. I mean, who cares about the legal part of it? On the news they keep talking like it wouldn't even be legal for a zombie to get married anyway."

"Don't remind me."

"I just want the words. If we are separated, I just want to know you're mine. Besides, married people don't need chaperones, you know." I almost laughed—the only way to solve my freedom issue was to do the most domestic thing allowable by law. My people *were* messed up.

Bram considered this, his nose against my ear. "Do you even own anything white, aside from your nightgowns?" He sounded embarrassed.

"I'll go look," I told him, smiling widely. But before I could pull away, he held me where I was and looked into my eyes.

"Marry me," he said. "You ask me, I ask you."

"Yes," I told him. I liked that.

I'd always heard that girls grew up planning their weddings, but I'd honestly never given mine a single thought. Thus, when I found the perfect thing to wear and it turned out to be a lace-trimmed white satin robe Aunt Gene had given me a few birthdays back, I was fine with it. I had no vision in my head to try and live up to.

For the first time, I truly missed my aunt. I sent up a little prayer for her, apologizing for not caring, for thinking some of the hateful things I had. I was about to do something incredibly rash, something that meant both everything and nothing, and it seemed like a good time to say sorry.

Careful not to wake Beryl, I dressed. I only had dark-colored shoes, so I just went without. I tied a white ribbon in my hair, and didn't bother with any jewelry. Then, after retrieving a cardboard box from under the bed, I went upstairs.

Isley was difficult to wake up. I shook him and whispered fiercely, but it was only when I removed a gray kitten from his chest that he stirred. When I explained what I wanted to do, he sat up and looked at me as if I were talking to him through the bars of an insane asylum. "Are you crazy?"

"Yes. So far it's working in my favor."

"Your father must give his permission!"

"He's not here. Besides, he's dead. Can he even give permission?"

"You . . . you need witnesses . . . we'd need a license . . ."

I picked up two cats. "Blackie and Mimi have eyes, don't they? Can't you write one up? It doesn't have to be *official*."

"And rings!"

"No, we don't," I told him, irritated. "We don't need *anything*. We just need you to say the magic words. I know you understand, Father."

"Yes, I understand all too well!" The priest swung himself off his cot. I'd never heard him raise his voice, and I set his cats down before he could find another reason to snap at me. "This is foolishness!"

"Father Isley—"

"Why do you want to do this?"

"So I can be with him. So that I can have part of him, even if we have to be apart for a while. Doesn't the ceremony say that it makes you one flesh? I don't care if it's legal, I just want the words."

Isley continued to watch me, his expression dark. I wasn't about to back down, but I was lost for options—until he sighed and asked, "Where?"

Relieved, I told him and headed out after receiving his promise that he would bring Bram to meet me there. I took the box to the front door and fetched my bouquet, then climbed the stairs again, heading toward the place I'd chosen for my altar.

Dad's bedroom was unoccupied, naturally. I unfastened the glass doors and stepped out onto the balcony. I'd been close to thinking this entire area unlucky, but now knew that it wasn't. It was practically sacred. It was self-sacred, at least.

It seemed like forever before I heard the others entering the bedroom. I took a breath and almost shut my eyes, half convinced that Bram would try to reason me out of this wild idea again—half ready to allow him. In some ways, he was right. We'd not known each other half a year. We were young. And I didn't want him to go through with it just to please me; as when I'd first ached for him to kiss me, I wanted *him* to want it, too.

When he stepped out of the doors, showered and dressed in his full captain's uniform, I knew he did.

I almost burst into tears, seeing it again. He was dead, but he was so incredibly handsome in it, his smile so warm. His every memory would one day be physically eaten away by the very thing that had preserved him for me to find; his every injury was destined to be a disfigurement.

But until that day, he was mine.

Isley joined us and arranged himself, still looking ill at ease. As he did, I selected a dead rose from the trellis and tucked it into one of Bram's buttonholes.

"Are you sure you want this?" he murmured.

"Yes," I assured him. "Do you want to wake everyone up? I'll do whatever you want." In a way, it felt wrong not to have everyone there, to share it with the people I loved, but at the same time, I knew how horribly unofficial our vows were going to be. It was real, and yet not real. I wasn't sure if I wanted to tell anyone—unsure if they'd bury me alive or celebrate with me. It was insane, it was gloriously *insane*.

Bram shook his head. "No. Just us. Like you said."

Isley waited for us. When Bram turned to him, he must have sensed the priest's reluctance, for he asked, "Are you all right with this?"

The other zombie confessed, "I'm only afraid that . . ." He paused, and then drew himself up. "This will mean something religiously. I just want you to know that. It's not a joke."

I nodded. "Got it." Bram took my hand and lifted his eyebrows, smiling.

I didn't hear most of the words. I didn't need to. I just kept my eyes on Bram. My brain twirled a few numbers around, telling me that four months to the two and a half good years we could expect was about five *years* to any other couple's lifetime. Relatively speaking, we'd been courting forever. After figuring that out, I wasn't afraid. I no longer felt stupid.

When it came time for the vows, Bram recited his half slowly and carefully, as if he was committing every clause to memory. Before saying the final words, though, he paused and turned to me, adding simply, "I know I won't be there for every part of your life, but I'd like you to be there for every part of mine. I do."

I figured if I was going to cry, it might as well be then. I recited my vows tearfully, except for the part about "obedience."

Even Bram choked back a laugh when it came to that. Thinking on the fly, I added only, "I'm here for every bit of your life. The bad parts, the scary parts. And I vow to do all you ask of me that is fair . . . even at the end." I knew I didn't have to elaborate; I could see that he'd gotten it, and that it moved him. "I do."

"By the power vested in me, then, by . . . the dead?" Isley decided. "I pronounce you man and wife. You may kiss your bride, Abraham. And tomorrow we're going to have a nice, loooong talk. Both of you."

Bram laughed and pulled me near, kissing me tenderly. Isley, meanwhile, unfolded a piece of loose paper from the back of his Bible and read it. "I worked up a certificate from memory. You can sign it, but it won't hold up in a court, just so you know. I almost feel like I ought to doodle on it in crayon."

"I know," I said breathlessly when Bram released me. I turned and took the pen from him, using the Bible as a desk to sign my name. Bram did the same, and then the priest. Grudgingly, Isley added Blackie and Mimi's names and the date, before handing the paper to me. I hugged it to my chest, even though the ink was still wet.

"I'm going back to bed," Isley grumbled as he made his way inside. "I think this is an elaborate nightmare."

"Now," I told Bram, "I'm going to show you that I keep my vows, even the ones that don't matter."

"Oh?" he asked, loosening the collar of his uniform. "Is this when the other shoe drops?"

Before he could lower his hand, I grabbed it and dragged him to my room, where I tucked my marriage certificate into my packed valise. From there, I led him outside. "Remember my pinky swear?" I asked him as I knelt down and pulled the box I'd left there close to me.

"About the end of your grounding?"

I untied the twine surrounding the box and opened the lid.

Within it there were a variety of cheap fireworks and a large box of matches. I'd ordered them from a toy shop in town, and they'd come by the trolley. Bram burst out laughing when he realized what I meant to do. "Okay. Fireworks, lawn—where's the underwear?"

Selecting a pair of sparklers and holding them in my right hand, I puffed my cheeks at him a little. "See? We had to get married. You couldn't watch this otherwise."

"Oh, I could watch it."

Handing him the box of matches, I readied myself. "Light up."

Bram's filmy eyes never left me. I felt my cheeks heating, for it was a little embarrassing—and odd to realize that it was suddenly perfectly *fine* for me to do what I was about to do. He was my husband now, at least in spirit. This wasn't daring in the least. Well, aside from the fact that it was on the front lawn in the middle of the night.

I lifted my eyes, looking at the house. Now it *had* seen almost every important event in my life, in truth. The last thing I could do was die within its walls, and that wouldn't be for years and years yet, with any luck.

Shyly, I opened my robe with my left hand. Underneath I had on my usual white Coutil corset, which I'd trimmed with a blue ribbon about the waist. It had frilly garters that held my white stockings up, though a pair of short bloomers covered those for the most part.

Bram stared at me for a long while, until he realized that the lit match he'd been holding was smoldering near his fingertips. Cursing, he threw it away, bringing on a fit of laughter from me. He lit another and held it out, saying only, "You're beautiful."

I joined my sparklers to the flame. Once they caught fire, I backed up onto the lawn, my robe hanging open, and did a twirl. I did promise to dance, after all. Bram's laughter floated after me, and I allowed myself to answer it. By the time my sparklers had grown too short to hold, he was with me, capturing my hands and waltzing with me, the artificial grass cold against my uncovered feet, his flesh deliciously cold beneath my skin, the fake sky above us deep and dark.

"We need music!" I cried as he spun me in the air.

"No we don't!" he laughed, before singing a few lines. I recognized them—it was the song we'd first slow-danced to, back at Z Beta. Before he could get far into the song he stopped moving, though, his hands tightening about my waist. He looked into my eyes and said, "I feel like I should say something more. I don't think I can ever say what I want to say. I don't think the words exist."

"Then don't. Just love me instead." I kissed him again.

And as I did, the dome above us exploded with light, the sky screen buzzing to life with a company logo, followed by a blue loading screen. We both looked up in surprise as clouds and faint stars took their place in the liquid crystal, mirroring the real sky outside. The walls followed, virtual trees glowing into being. It was like watching God create the world for the first time.

"They turned it all back on!" I found this almost as moving as my own wedding.

Bram laughed, keeping me close. "Just for you!"

After composing myself, after enjoying the spectacle for a few minutes, I came up with the idea of feeding one another tofu with sugar sprinkled on it in lieu of wedding cake. Bram bore me inside like a bride. Together we ate in the artificially moonlit kitchen, talking about our plans, figuring out how they could work in reality. We decided to use Michael's bounty to buy rings the next day. He *should* pay for them.

Nothing was usual, for us.

Everything was wonderful, because of it.

ACKNOWLEDGMENTS

Once again I'd like to thank my fantastic agent, Christopher Lotts, and my editor, Jennifer E. Smith. Thanks also to Lauren Buckland, Betsy Mitchell, Joe Scalora, David Moench, and everyone at Random House. You're all amazing people.

Thanks also to my family, Josh, and all my friends for listening to me ramble on and on about *awesome dead this* and *meaningful rotting that* and *ooh sawed-off shotguns*. It's always good to have friends you can discuss the physics of airborne brain matter with.

As for all of the young local writers I've met since *Dearly, Departed* was published—what can I tell you, save that you're all incredible? You deserve every opportunity you get. Never stop dreaming, thinking, writing, or reading, and know that I wish nothing but happiness and success for you all. I know that high school can be hell, but the weird lady in the bustle gown is pulling for you.

I'd also like to thank everyone who took the time to email me to tell me how much they enjoyed the first book. I never in my life dreamed that I would have "fans"—the idea still seems outrageously egotistical to me, like something I should scold myself for even thinking. You are the people who make this entire venture worthwhile. I will never forget your kind words so long as I live. The idea that I was able to entertain and move even one person is an incredible gift.

I'm humbled to have been permitted to go on this journey. Praise is due to everyone but myself. Thank you, thank you, thank you.

ABOUT THE AUTHOR

LIA HABEL is in her twenties and lives in western New York State. She is fascinated by zombie movies and Victoriana, interests that eventually led her to write *Dearly, Departed*. When she first got an agent, she was literally opening envelopes for a living. By the time the auction for *Dearly, Departed* was held, she was considering food stamps—which, thankfully, are no longer a consideration.

liahabel.com